THE KNIGHT'S LORE:

Book 1 of Ancient Lore

Godwin U. Nkere

First published in Great Britain by Pen Press © 2009

Second Edition

ISBN13: 978-1-78003-841-4

All paper used in the printing of this book has been made from wood
grown in managed, sustainable forests.

Printed and bound in the UK

Author Essentials, 4 The Courtyard, Falmer BN1 9PQ

A catalogue record of this book is available from
the British Library

Cover design by Jacqueline Abromeit

Dedicated to Barack Obama and Oprah Winfrey,
For being beacons of light in a black world,
And for leading Our People from the front.

To my family and friends,
(you know who you are)
For all your tender loving care.

And to all those from the IC,
Both Home and Abroad,
Who have stood by me in good times and in hardship.

Love the Life you Live & Live the Life you Love!

Also in loving memory of Chinua Achebe and James Herbert,
Two great Scribes who fell asleep in the same week.
For encouraging me to read and inspiring me to write.

To my aunty, the late Regina Ekpo,
One of the best ever Operatives to have come out of Africa.
For teaching me, for loving me.

And the late, great Nelson Mandela,
Our Pride, our honour, our Dignity,
Aka 'Madiba',
Who showed us what spirituality really means.

You will never be forgotten.

GUN

ABOUT THE AUTHOR

G.U.N. (Lord of Lochaber in Scotland) was actually born in Hackney, East London, back in the day, and has lived in Greater London for most of his adult life. Rather ironically, he left his first degree at Imperial College, London to start writing this book, and then, years later, left his postgraduate degree at Fitzwilliam College, Cambridge to finish writing the very same volume. Fortunately, in the interim, he was awarded an honours degree for the work he had already managed to complete. He also holds a Level 5 Distinction in Physics and is an Associate of the RCS.

His main areas of employment have been as a system's analyst in a very large pharmaceutical firm, as a performance analyst for a well-known world-wide financial company, and as a project worker for the MoD (Ministry of Defence). He has studied both the Bible and the Koran in depth and he is now known as a very capable scribe, seer and visionary by various intelligence and security agencies as well as by other special units from around the globe. The author still practises his religion regularly.

Book One of Ancient Lore: The Knight's Lore is Godwin's first major work of fiction and is the initial story in a series of ten novels. He continues to live in the Greater London area near to his family and friends and divides his time between writing the next instalment in the story, working on new ideas, and by trying to find elegant solutions for many of the key problems society requires us to address. To aid him in his endeavours, he has recently completed a Masters in Business Administration (MBA) with the Edinburgh Business School in Scotland.

On top of this all, he has also managed to write a philosophical, theological, doctrinal and practical accompaniment for the Ancient Lore series, which currently stands at around 82,000 words. This can be found online at one of the addresses listed.

Gee's ambition, through all his endeavours, is to enlighten the hearts of his community, to share his knowledge of the truth with those who are willing to listen, and to change the world around him for the better.

CONTENTS

For further information and a deeper understanding
of the Ancient Lore, please visit:

www.ancientlore.info
www.thezaqen.com

Introduction: The Players

I have written to you, young men,
Because you are strong, and the word of God abides in you,
And you have overcome the wicked one.

1 JOHN 2:14b

They say it could have happened to just about anyone. Well, that's what some say anyway. Others don't reckon it happened at all! Still, there are some who are just not sure – they knew the people involved you see, good guys they were, so they just couldn't be certain, one way or the other.

It all began on a quiet little road named after the patron saint of Scotland, in the north London borough of Enfield. It was a typical, that is to say a slightly cold and windy, Saturday evening, some time in the middle of fall.

The sky was dark and the clouds were broody, casting dun shadows on the ground beneath. And the moon was melancholy blue (although some of the folks said that it had a kind of azure tinge to it). Whatever, it was certainly not your normal bleached-white grain. But all this, it must be said, was indicative of the low ebb of the season, and perhaps even the ill and not-easily forgotten times that lay ahead.

It is worth making the point early on that this narrative could not have been written without at least some reference to the "The Syndicate". Because there was no party in London that was worth the mention without the gang being there. And if you don't believe that we won't get far. Cos these cats were cool, young, trendy, vibrant, intelligent, witty and good-looking – all the kinda stuff, that if found in one person, you'd wanna beat them up through jealously.

In all that they did, they hung out together as a crew. Or else, the truth be known, the thing just couldn't be done! The gang just had to be there that evening too – no two ways about it – they just had to. This definitely rings true when it comes to the telling of this narrative.

In fact if they hadn't been there that night, at that time, partying the way they do, then this book could in no way have been written. So thank you geezers!

As the story goes however it would be the last such day for everyone involved, for a long, long time to come. And all things forever afterwards would never be the same again – at least not in this lifetime.

*

First up in this posse was the Bad Boy Gee, so everyone called him. He was the man with the bashment an' gritty clothing and matching vernacular. Currently nineteen he was the second eldest of the group and the unofficial leader of the pack.

Sash was out next – the eldest, the seeker, the big soft cuddly man with a solid heart of gold. He was a top geezer and got on well with almost everybody. He was stocky and quick-footed but he was half-Indian (a Desi) which meant that he wasn't all that good at football.

Next up was Alisha – she was the strong black woman, vices and virtue to boot, with a long interminable stream of ancestors, mostly Americans. She believed in spooky shit like nobody else, and so, sometimes, the gang just couldn't help ripping her values to shreds.

There was Jema-Jane – a fine natural blond, with Irish blood in her veins, though there was a bit of Jewish in there too, from her mother's side. She was into science in a big way and so she gave off the impression of being quite intelligent. More important was the fact that she was the only one in the group who always had access to a set of wheels, hence the love.

And, of course, one has to mention little Elena, who at fifteen years of age was the much-loved 'child' of the group who couldn't do any wrong. But when she did screw up she screwed up big time, although she probably wouldn't even realise the fact until it was far too late.

Last but not least was Markie – Abi, Charlie and John's bro. Now "The Kid", as his pals often called him, was in fact a Bluefoot (Mbakara) – nothing intrinsically wrong with that I may hasten to add. He was not really part of the Syndicate yet; on paper that is because he was still quite new and everything. Besides, he still had a crew of his own.

Nonetheless, he had spent some time with the Friends and they all seemed to get on like a house on fire – there were no petty rivalries or anything like that – so thus far he was doing just fine. They say that people are on their best behaviour when they're trying to impress, so there you go.

Anyway, The Kid's first encounter with the Syndicate was not in the most awe-inspiring of circumstances, as you are now about to see. What follows is a quick breakdown of how it all occurred...

*

She'd been driving along the Great Cambridge Road doing what normally seemed to be the minimum speed of the car – around 80 kilometres per hour. Fortunately (or unfortunately – depending on your own interpretation of subsequent events) Markie had been on the streets at around about the same time and had decided to cross the road right at that very moment. It was not the same road you understand, but another side street, a few hundred yards from the dual carriageway itself. So he did cross the road – not a major crime in most reasonable cities – as he had needed to get somewhere, and reasonably sharpish too.

So as the story goes, he did cross the road, styling it as you do, even when there is nobody around to see you. *Limp, Drag, Limp, Drag.* While he was crossing however, he could make out the sounds of some lunatic "boy-racer" skidding off the main road and onto one of the quieter side streets nearby.

'Crazy people,' he muttered to no one in particular, 'they should be...'

But as his subconscious was busy stringing together some pretty virulent curses, the white piercing beams of a pale-coloured car came bouncing up and down the road ahead of him. He thought nothing much of it at first, because it happened all the time where they came from. The boy-racer had probably taken a corner a little too quickly and was now racking his suspensions for the sake of style, novelty and effect. He would soon have to be on the verge of recovery though because no one could maintain that speed for much longer and live. Or at least I hope not, Markie thought to himself, resuming the fell thoughts previously directed towards the pedestrian's worst nightmare.

What Mark failed to realise however, was that as he yet harboured his ill-intentions towards the other nocturnal creature, he was still standing there, like a prize melon, smack in the middle of the road; not too different from a stuffed mannequin under the intense scrutiny of the Arsenal floodlights! And these lights (a couple of which were brock) were reflecting off the house to the left of him, casting evil spectres – of himself he presumes – across the entire row of houses. The Kid had then glanced over his right shoulder just in time to see the car hurtling up towards his rear end at some ridiculously unsound speed.

Then for an instant he was frozen solid in fear – Mark that is and not the mannequin. And but by the grace of God, he would have never managed to get it together on time. But he did, and his motor-neurones were reinvigorated just in the nick of time.

He jumped back a little way, which was not much good really, seeing that he was still stood plumb in the middle of the road, which was a rather small road with not too many exits. What's more, he was still in a mild state of shock! (Okay it was severe, but promise not to tell anyone?) The driver just drove on like he hadn't even seen him.

Turns out afterwards that he hadn't.

Partly because *he* was in fact a *she*, and partly because *she* was somewhat more interested in the hulking great houses looming up a little too quickly towards her. It was only then that she had seen the silhouette of somebody at the very last moment and even then she wasn't even sure if that somebody was at all worth stopping for. She was only planning to miss the walls ahead bearing in mind that her car, with its extra body kit, would likely come out on top after any entanglement with flesh and blood. She'd be okay though cooped up there in her vehicle, tucked in tightly behind her airbag. That's what counted init, looking after Number One?

Anyway, so she performed her skid – that manoeuvre which seems to be mandatory for all rude-boys and rude-girls heading out for a night on the town – and managed to spin her car round a full 360°! Headlights glaring in Markie's eyes, her wheels still running off of the purr of the engines, it was not a favourable sight. To make things worse, the motor was still humming, as if seriously considering the human target in front of them.

Permitting Mark's pupils only enough time to regain their natural size, "Evil-eyes" (the name of the car, on account of the vehicle's front-end lights) eventually decided to lurch forwards, again. Evil-eyes clipped his right hip and a bit more besides which sent him spiralling towards the hard, concrete turf.

Bosh!

INTRODUCTION: THE PLAYERS

What a landing!

*

It took a little time for Boyo to get up. (You've got to understand that The Kid was still somewhat shocked at proceedings, because although this was north London and everything, the land of the unexpected, this event was just that little bit too ridiculous. It really did take the piss.) But it might well have been for the fact that the driver had no intention of getting out of her car to help him, just in case her victim really was still alive. Repercussions in north London was not what one got out of the car for!

Anyway, the driver deliberated for a little too long before making up her mind to shift herself out of the area and back towards the A10. (That's the dual carriageway to some of you unenlightened dudes). Besides, she didn't much like the idea of having a corpse on her conscience for the rest of her life.

So what happens then is that Markie makes his way over to the driver's door to lend this injured motorist a hand. And if she wasn't injured, then she was soon enough gonna be, cos Mark's help can get kinda primitive sometimes. I mean The Kid's a nice guy and everything, but get on the wrong side of him and… Anyway, he reaches this psychotically uncool piece of shit just as she's sparking up the ignition to shoot off again.

At first, so the story goes, he said that he'd had it in mind to knock the geezer's jaw out – just a little bit, you understand – promptly followed by a few slaps, a couple of cuffs, and upon opening the door even wider, one or two legs (probably two), which was to be followed by a direct assault with his head upon the bridge of his nose. In short, GBH. Mark had hoped that the person would take it all like a gent, seeing who was doubtless to blame for all this hullabaloo, and that he would not have to use any of the extra implements at his disposal.

Anyhow, a bit of useful vengeance on a boring night always comes in handy, especially when you're a bit stressed-out already… before some fool then tries to run you over. However, when he'd opened his peekers a little further, his whole demeanour had altered. His eyes had become fixed, his hands had begun to quiver, he had put aside his wonderful assortment of tools which included an axe, a claw-hammer, and an eight-inch kitchen knife. Then he had readjusted his body armour. (He'd just come back from Tottenham after a late night deal where, the year previous, he had become embroiled in an argument that wasn't of his own making. One of the brothers had popped a cap in his arse when he had turned around and tried to chip, and ever since then, the flak jacket, courtesy of Vest-Guard at £400, had become a necessity).

Then guess what happened? He only tried to chirpse her believe it or not! This Mbakara had no pride whatsoever. There was nothing physical, not even a verbal assault! A pure chump the crew said afterwards, he acted like a right pansy.

Because behind the wheel of the car, so the saying goes, was a woman. Now that fact in itself would not have necessarily quashed his justifiable rage. What was more important to him was the fact that she looked kind of good (not void of injuries and shit), but like the fit kind of good. In fact, she looked a bit more than that – she looked hungry… For him of course!

The rest then is almost predictable.

He found the forgiveness in his heart, somehow. I mean, her few badly interpreted versions of the "Hail Mary" seemed to go down well with the Old Girl upstairs, because she saw him put away most of his tools, quite quickly too. The carefully adjusted blouse, which revealed the best parts of her cleavage, also seemed to go down a treat (although it was a sight that her Divine Mother might not have been so grateful for!) Even so, just to smooth things over finally, she gave him one of the most buoyant smiles ever seen this side of the African continent. After that, needless to say, it was more or less all plain sailing!

*

Which was the way it went sometimes back there in North London. If you've got the face, shit sticks – unless of course it's pretty enough. Meals on wheels and for those that play the field, if you like. And even deals for squeals, if you're lucky enough, although there weren't too many of them around. These grasses were called "Wrong 'uns" – but that's a different story entirely.

Oh, and kills for thrills and for all who love The Devil, as J-J so obviously didn't? That's a new one init…? You must be kidding matey! There's nothing new under the sun, as the wise man said, save it be outside the realms of our understanding.

*

Anyway, since then Mark and Jema-Jane had actually met up on quite a few occasions; at parties, on the street, and generally wherever they could get an excuse to hook-up. So it was safe to say that they were now, at least, 'good friends'.

Consequently, he was almost like one of the Syndicate now and, getting on especially well with Sash and Gee, who was to say whether or not he might attain to its ranks one day? They were always together anyhow, at all the places to be seen in – like the party on that particular Saturday eventide.

*

Well it's best to get on with the story now, or we might just run out of time. So we'll pick it up at the close of that very boum. On the night when the smoke was thick, the groove was smooth, and all the brothers were hanging off the walls like a bunch of greasy lechers with a taste for something new.

But that was also the night when things really got going, and fate was sealed off once and for all.

Oh, and just one more thing. Do you remember that saying? …
You know, the one that goes:

"The greatest trick that the Devil ever pulled
Was to convince the world that he doesn't exist."

Well it's true isn't it? Except maybe, for just one thing…

"There's no way on Earth he could have pulled it off alone!"

THE CHARACTERS

Black Gee (The Main Player)
*Me Mys*elf I (i.e "Memys"/"Merwys") – the name of Gee's Spirit
Me Mys*elf* I (i.e. "Elf") – the name of Gee's Soul; [Frydor] the Elf
Me Myself *I* (i.e. "Eyes") – the name of Gee's Body

The Syndicate/Friends
Godwyn (Gee) – Nywdog
Sashi (Sash) – Sascha
Mark (Markie) – Marcus
Alisha (Aleasha) – Alicia
Jema-Jane (JJ) – Jemimah
Elena (Helena) – Eleanor

The Guides/Elves
Frydor the Elf/Surp – the friends' chief guide in Krandor (fantasy world)
Flip – Frydor's nephew and No.1 acolyte

The Troop/Company
The Syndicate & The Guides

The Horses/Etheldorians Bold
Pegasus – mount of Frydor and Alicia
Vol – mount of Flip and Sascha
Schatten-Flug – mount of Nywdog and Eleanor
Tapfer – mount of Marcus and Jemimah

The Twelve Lords of the Realm (Krandor)

Fléichïor the Fat – Chief Counsellor to the Prince of Gwr
Drygiöri of the Blackfaces – Regent of the Southern Seas
Pedéyrôr of Meréden – King of all the Lands in the Eastern Seas
Alex de Vitaz from Anbad – Second King of the Realm, slave-trader
Digwïlydd the Ogre – First Prince of the Realm, a giant
Galeg the Gaul – Second Prince of the Realm, cousin to Digwïlydd
Cèrïdyn the Crimson – Prince of the Northern part of Fou-ouls
Badred the Rouge – Lord of the Two Dark Valleys
Princess Malebö – Lord and Governor of Harmswäith
Llöhwryn the Virulent – Third Lord, Sovereign of Krakôuz
Yorath mab Grêyndrwl – Fourth Lord of the Realm, Lord of Hores
Suntribo – Vassal to the Prince of Gwr, Hobgoblin

Miscellaneous

Advance Le Wiser – Apostle, Ranger
Alison Dry-Hen – Chief of all the Bird-men
Beamer Clerk – Apostle, Female Ranger
Benny Zeph (aka 'Boiz') – Apostle, Poet, Performer, Ranger
Byron the Surp – Frydor's cousin
Ceriddenne – descendent of Erynaidd, a black witch
Chrissy Wiles (aka 'Youngblood') – Scribe, Scop, Surp, Ranger
Coleman Lightfoot – bandit, brigand, malefactor
Councillor Maria Air, Queen of Tone & Pabrade, VLNS (aka Vilnus County)
Death – The Angel of Death
Derren Kai – Prophet, Ranger
[The] Devil – Satan, Lucifer
Dionne of the Gap-Teeth – cousin to Wyngod the Bard, songstress
Eraniel Doom (aka 'Doom Rane') – Apostle, Ranger
Fels'noc the Trol(l) – Chief Troll
Geordie Cheryl – Apostle, Songsmith, Female Ranger
Gjagg-son – half-brother to Gjugg-son
Gjugg-son – village troll chief
Hah – God of Mockery, one of Lucifer's chief aides
Hardy (aka 'The Iceman') – Prophet, Ranger
Hearken Wit – Healer, Qi Gong Mistress
Kasey Chan (aka 'The Necromancer') – Prophetess, Female Ranger,
    Physician

Knights and Judges of St Andrew and St George (what The Syndicate hope to become)

Larry Steven Mason – craftsman, wise-man, Ranger

Liz the Tanner – Scribe, Scop, Surp, Female Ranger

Mojo Teens Pendragon – Scribe, Scop, Surp, Warlock

Mongo Slade – the baddest (and blackest!) of all Rangers

Ms Bizi (aka 'Real-Bizi') – Polyglot, Polymath, Ranger

Ms Mewberry Star – snake-charmer

Name-Me-Poet – The Scholar from Mizraim, Prince

Ottoman – part troll, part man, warrior

Prince of Gwr – [evil] Ruler of Krandor

Princess Crystal of the Bushy Hills

Qadesh – the demon-lord of perversion

Queen Natalie of the Cinque Ports

Quicksilver – Doppelganger

Ribtas the Seeker – most cunning of all Rangers

Sandra the Smith – Chief Jeweller to the High King

Saspion – chief mistress to Fels'noc

Shane Fellas – Prophet, Ranger

Shiloh R. Jacobs – step-daughter to Queen Natalie

The Hui-Bee (aka 'The Wise Voyager') – Prophetess, Female Ranger, Healer

Tone Tony 'The Yellow-face' – Prophet, Ranger

Wyngod the Bard – one of the best troubadours in all Krandor

Yah – The One True God, Elohim

Ranks of the Zaqen ("The Ancient Ones")

Soldier – combatant/fighter/mighty-man/warrior (both Knights and Judges)

Scribe – copyist/correspondent/wordsmith/writer (Knight, Master)

Scop – bard/minstrel/musician/troubadour (1st Judge, Disciple)

Surp – boffin/learned/scholar/wise-man (2nd Judge, Disciple)

Sorcerer – magician/warlock/witch/wizard (3rd Judge, Disciple – Dark Zaqen)

The Scribes/Soldiers

Daemon Writer – Dark Zaqen (Evil Zaqen; always travels with 3 judges)

Ready Writer – White Zaqen (Good Zaqen; always travels with 2 judges)

SOME OF THE WHITE ZAQEN

Knights and Judges of St Patrick
Afam with the Thick-thighs – Scribe
Iain the Walker – Scop
Caleb of the Long-storks – Surp

Knights and Judges of St David
Chief Tuo – Scribe
Midu the Physician – Scop
Maul Mine the Money-man – Surp

Knights and Judges of Le Métier
Akine Mark 'Akira' – Scribe
Akene Rake – Scop
The Bristol Ban-Sky – Surp

Knights and Judges of The Dan
Simon "Sah" Sting – Scribe
Tony "Hit-man" Hews – Scop
Bleak "Skills" Events – Surp

Knights and Judges of The Daughters of Eve
Harpo the Black – Scribe
Reseat the Brown – Scop
Nadia the White – Surp

Knights and Judges of The Faithful
Dan Male – Scribe
Marty King – Scop
Great Soul – Surp

Knights and Judges of The Ishmaelites
Salim Mohammed – Scribe
Ali Clay – Scop
Little Mal – Surp

XX

Knights and Judges of The Raggas
Carl Mark – Scribe
The Riddler – Scop
Jon Mall – Surp

Knights and Judges of Modagr
Kenny the Great – Scribe
Harry the Bold – Scop
Andy the Tall – Surp

Knights and Judges of Deliverance
Savanna – Scribe
Tessa – Scop
Bryn – Surp

Knights and Judges of Babylon
DJ Raven Steel – Scribe
Steve Jeffs – Scop
Sven No Jest – Surp

Knights and Judges of Maple Leaf
Gale Le Pen – Scribe
April The Vine – Scop
FT Yankee – Surp

SOME OF THE DARK ZAQEN

Knights and Judges of The Ville
Bill Flynn – Scribe
Paddy O'Sullivan – Scop
Big Ben – Surp
Robbie Wren – Sorcerer

Knights and Judges of NFN (Note Fur Nite)
Keith the Porter – Scribe
Veer Noc Seren – Scop
Stefan the Hunter – Surp
Red Wren Born – Sorcerer

Knights and Judges of Focal Species R-US
Marcus of the Howling-winds – Scribe
Gillian the Wise – Scop
Matthew of the Howling-winds – Surp
Grach of the Gloved-fingers – Sorcerer

Knights and Judges of Legrand
Caisar 'Plonks' Soulzay – Scribe
Bibi Boss – Scop
Brother BHO – Surp
Phraser – Sorcerer

Knights and Judges of The Princes of Tyre
The Lair – Scribe
Ussomo Bin Laitein – Scop
Regal On France – Surp
St Nail – Sorcerer

Knights and Judges of The Faithless
Dear Leader – Scribe
Bum Grab O Tree – Scop
Mad Sad Shine Su – Surp
The Emperor – Sorcerer

Knights and Judges of The Despots
Mast "The Chairman" Tongue – Scribe
Tone "The General" Chip – Scop
Top "The Flop" Lop – Surp
Mi "Big Daddy" India – Sorcerer

Knights and Judges of The Apostacia
The Shah – Scribe
Birty Loan – Scop
Use N Accuse – Surp
Mraz Courts – Sorcerer

Knights and Judges of Young Sages
Deuces Das – Scribe
I See Harps – Scop
Sot Laze – Surp
Dynamo Isiyim – Sorcerer

Knights and Judges of Sheol
The Dragon – Scribe
The Beast – Scop
The False Prophet – Surp
Death & Hades – Sorcerer

THE ÐYSG OF ƆYNDADAU
(WHITE ƵAQEN ONLY)

I.   Thou shalt not kill thy neighbour unlawfully.

II.   Thou shalt not lie carnally with anybody other than thy spouse.

III.   Thou shalt not apprehend thy neighbour contrary to The Law.

IV.   Thou shalt not practise mediumship nor shalt thou suffer a sorcerer to work his dark arts.

V.   Thou shalt not smoke of the Holy Herb unless it is prescribed to thee for remedy.

VI.   Thou shalt not blaspheme the Lord thy God nor shalt thou bow down before any graven image.

VII.   Thou shalt honour and obey always the Ancient Lore and thy elders in the Ancient Lore.

VIII.   Thou shalt not smite thy neighbour without cause.

IX.   Thou shalt not steal nor defraud thy neighbour of his goods.

X.   Thou shalt not slander nor bear false witness.

THE FLIGHT OF AN ELLYLL: ELF'S STORY

For when we were in the flesh, the sinful passions
which were aroused by the law
were at work in our members to bear fruit to death...
For I know that in me (that is, in my flesh) nothing good dwells;
for to will is present with me,
but how to perform what is good I do not find.

Romans 7:5,18

Hello! My name is... Well, never mind what my name is – what's important is that you listen to this story. Oh, and there's no point in trying to figure out who I am because I don't always belong to this realm, seeing how dry it is and everything. But please try and catch hold of this; because the whole thing transpired just as we said it would – it happened just as we're telling it now. And I vouch for these things personally, because I was there for most of it – not all of it mind (cos sometimes a geezer's got to be off doing his own thing) – but for a lot of it nonetheless.

So yeah, Markie, my boy, met J-J, they hit it off, and he's been trying to get his leg over ever since – big deal! Him and that little crew of his, they're small fry. My boys though, they're something special, something to be reckoned with. And Me, I'm the big deal too. Cos I can fight ghosts, conquer demons, speak with angels; I even walk and talk with the gods – no lie! And that's only one of the areas where my boasting doesn't quite match up to the stunning truth. So as you can probably appreciate already, I am set apart a bit from your everyday run-of-the-mill Joey!

Like most ellylls – get a dictionary for that one, Boyo – I do have a reasonable assortment of tools at my disposal; and using some of the more accessible ones, I can sometimes manage to float high above the clouds! There are some occasions where I can even drop right down through The Earth – or Daearawd as some of my boys call it – ending up in a bit of a state, admittedly, with molten lava dripping off my beautiful black exterior. But it doesn't hurt really, unless I think about it a lot.

I can also inhabit bodies too, as I've been doing a lot lately, especially over the past so many years. Moreover, I sometimes lay siege to folks, travelling with my twin to other bodies, to those who are deserving of such noble attention. We perform this act only when times are fierce, when some silly muppet wants to stress out one of our boys; and then it's all in the spirit of goodwill anyway – for "Yours Truly", that is, namely, Me, Myself and I… of course!

Nowadays though with increasing frequency, I cause my man to free his mind from his body. And using one of my many worthy faculties, I allow him to see things that would otherwise remain hidden, and hear things which would otherwise be left unheard. Like on the night of the party when all my crew was messing around something chronic with the Syndicate. I told them that they could kick back for a while and relax, you know, to chill-out a little and loosen up; though I did still remind them to stay vigilant, because one never knows exactly what's around the corner. But hey, who listens to poor old me anyway?

So what did I do then? I let my twin go with my body to the party, because I know that The Flesh gets kind of wanton sometimes, and without Old Memys there to guide him (he's one of the boys belonging to my perthynas), I do believe that he would have truly been lost. Like you are now, I suppose. Confused as hell.

Regardless, I had more important things to take care of than some poxy party – matters of life and death, even if I do say so myself… And I ain't even bragging yet. That was just the magnitude of my importance, so what can I say? It's kind of like I've heard tell before: there's no point in those who are naturally great shielding that glory from the eyes of others; cos it don't do the world any service whatsoever.

Back to the story now, and promptly, because these were hard times. I never wanted my man to indulge in more dark mysteries than he could handle, just enough to set him on the straight and narrow. His life had been tough enough turmoil already, and Me, being the kindhearted chap like they say, did not want to add to his distresses in any way, shape or form. So I set out to do this job alone. I'd bring these matters to his attention another time perhaps, although only when I'd reckon he could handle it. Certainly not before that time though, if I still thought he wasn't really ready for it yet.

If in the meantime any fraggle tried to mess with I an' I, then Myself (being the rather notable fiend I Am), would screw them up big-time; and if anyone only even looked as though they were gonna traipse on him, then I'd get to them first.

But I liked his girl too; so much so that if I even thought My-home-boy was liable to deal with her (in his own iniquitous way, that is), then I'd hastily put a stop to it, there and then. Because I'd jump straight out there, plucking up my spirit as I went, and then I'd turn round and fuck him up, nicely…

*

O wretched man that I am!
Who will deliver me from this body of death?
Romans 7:24

*

Alone, it was always going to be easy, so I won't make such a big hoo-ha about it. I just waited for The Bastard outside Hannah's bed-room.

He was always going to be there – I mean anytime the kids were out, the wife was away out of town, the guys were down the Palmer's Green Taverna playing poker, he would steal away quietly to that lonely old wench in Southgate. It's not that she really was lonely, see-ing that she was married (her husband was the worst gambler of the lot, and remained behind the closed drapes of the café until either his money had run out, or till the beer had gotten the better of him); nor was she that old – more sort of middle age(ish); it's just that I didn't like her one tiny speck.

I mean, having a bit on the side was one thing, but fucking your first cousin – man, that's just downright disgusting if you ask me; which, actually, nobody ever did. That was a shame really too, be-cause I might have been able to add something there.

So I expected company that night, and made sure that I called a couple of the chaps down from the clouds, just in case.

Everyone called the chaps 'Watchers', because that's what they did for the most part. They intervened only at very special times, when the shit was about to hit the fan; and mangle it, before sending it spinning into Outer Space, if you catch the drift! Most of the muck on Daear-awd was left up to us to deal with. Often times though I was left at an ends to decide which of the two spheres I preferred, the golden-gated arches of Heaven or the shit-festooned districts upon the Earth. Difficult one that.

Now don't say I'm complaining or nuffin', cos we might have even stood a chance if we weren't lumbered with these bodies for so much of the time. Oh come on now, square with me – you reckon they're quite pathetic too, don't ya? Always feeding and sleeping, without ever really developing. It makes you think of the geezer that designed them in the first place, like what he had in mind and shit. Maybe he was tripping at the time? Bloody hilarious, I've heard some say; but believe you me, it's not when you've got to put up with them twenty-four seven.

*

So I sees the hick-cunt, Hacosh, pulling up on the kerb, in his late-eighties Beema (his ellyll I remember from another existence – he'd been called Brutus. Because that's exactly what he was, even now – a treacherous brute!).

Anyway, he looked around as he always did, as if he really cared if anyone saw him or not. I mean, all the neighbours knew, his friends knew and even his wife knew (although she didn't seem to mind, so long as he did what he did out of the house). His kids didn't exactly know, but they didn't have to. They saw the way he treated their mother, you see, and that in itself was enough to screw them up no end. The man's role to do jack and give shit; the woman was to lie there and take it. Total bollocks if you ask me, not that anyone ever did. But hey, "C'est la vie" as they say – I ain't complaining.

Up the stairs and through the doors, he was soon standing half-naked in the bedroom. I passed through the windows to get a better view of that fat, blubbery beast (and partly cos I hated reflections, especially when you couldn't see yourself for shit – it made you feel kind of like, I dunno – like you're not really important in the large scale of things). Life could be a bit of a bitch at times, we all well know that, but back to that one later.

I saw the shadows that had come in with him and the forms already there with his cousin, and I signalled coldly towards the small entourage of Watchers I had by my side. Should anything get out of hand and should these Dark-ones arrayed before me become a tad too foolish, more than they usually were that is, then I'd just step aside and let the boys behind me handle it. I could take care of myself, don't get me wrong, it's just that today was an extra special day, and I couldn't risk blowing it.

So there I am, watching Hacosh probing, pummelling, and pushing himself into Hannah, like the world would end tomorrow, funnily enough. Then I watched them switch positions. Now it was her turn to fight her way through his flab, and towards his fanny-driver and accompanying ball bearings. (Okay, okay, so she could be a bit of a stout-hearted whore sometimes, but I still wouldn't brag about it too much!) He squealed like a pig, and she swallowed his swill as though she were one. It was harder to tell who was the more convincing!

At any rate, once the performance had ended, I knew that, if left alone, they would lie there in perfect contentment, until the early hours of the morning when all the fellas at the Taverna would be slaughtered. And that I didn't want.

Lucky they finished then too, because I was getting kind of nervous. Several dark shadows had befallen me, and though I wasn't alone, the awfulness of their presence often made me feel as though I was. If only man knew the truth of the things I'm saying now, he wouldn't be so flippant with his meagrely lot! But be that as it may, most weren't particularly mindful of these things, especially not these two dolts.

I could see all parts of their forms enmeshed in a deceitful web: body, soul and spirit – corff, enaid, and ysbryd: a disgusting tangle if ever I saw one. Anyway, we often jested amongst ourselves that the word coblyn was more suitable than corff for Hacosh, for the undeniable Son of a Bitch that he was. As for The Bitch herself, there are not sufficient words to describe her; either in Webster (whom I used to be acquainted with, to my shame) or in Oxford (who I didn't know at all I'm proud to say!) So I won't even attempt to go there.

Nevertheless, these derisions I soon had to cast aside, as word came through via one of my entourage that proceedings were about to commence down at the party, and that I really needed to be there if I wasn't going to miss out on the journey.

So, swift as Caleb of the Long-storks, whom you haven't actually been introduced to yet, I bundled in there, without warning, quickly overcoming two of the six filthy forms that were lounging about on the bed. The others stepped aside gingerly when they saw that I meant business. Oh, and one or two perhaps, when they saw the fearsome back-up I had at my disposal.

To tell you the truth the smell of them almost overcame my desire for a rumble. Strange recollections took me back to my current abode, to that somewhat dreary life savoured by my corff. But for them that were from the lowest reaches of Uffern (being the place where all the wanton dead go to upon breathing their last), or from the outer reaches of Annwfn (being the last holding place for many of us before either ascending towards Nef, or descending), I desired no such relinquishment. At present.

*

The leader of their brood was an unsightly fellow named Qädesh. He was a notable fiend, with a great many conquests tucked beneath his belt; but he was one whom I have beforetimes conquered. He had tentacles that reached as far as he needed them to, eyes which burnt like glowing coals, and a tongue that formed its saliva with sulphur and its words with venom. All of this made him some mean opponent, I assure you.

But I had to address him kindly (due respect in the higher realms, and all that) loathe him greatly though I did.

'So what, tonight?'

'Sounds good with me!'

'Oh, so when did you ever start to listen?' I gibed, I thought rather glibly. 'Thought you'd lost your sense of hearing when you lost your man, back in the days before Adam – you remember, when you all started settling in swine?'

'Yeah, but I got it back again when the grunts of these two captives became too loud... Before that it was difficult, certainly. Not now though, specially seeing how clamorous they sometimes get, like when their kids join in. But hey...'

He saw me become tense at this and stopped short of a direct insult, he, doubtless, having heard of the short temper that I had in my possession. I brought this one upon myself anyhow, and worse have I seen and heard with shocking regularity. Anyway I'm just about big enough to take care of myself!

'Er-he-he-hem…' (Me grunting my obvious disapproval.)

Then, choking unhappily for their foul odour, I managed to produce the barb that I carried with me at all times. I motioned towards the odious forms to move themselves out of my way, which feat they duly did, shambling as they went, each one seeking to maintain what pride he may. Then I thrust the thorn through the man's foul heart, pinning it through hers also, until the onset of their spluttering had all but soiled my ears.

'Nice to see that you've changed sides,' croaked a voice that was riling to my senses. 'Doing my job now, are you?'

'Didn't know you'd been promoted?' I returned sharply. 'So what, has Death been retired now, like I've heard?'

There, I saw by the look in his eyes that I had stung him with this last remark.

'You are very humorous today, Elf,' (to which I, in turn, cringed). 'Is it because these are your last hours on The Earth… or is it because you're happy to be freed from that great lummox of a form I've seen you with lately – over twenty years since conception I believe now, and still there. Don't worry my friend, your own rise is in the winds – it will come soon my boy!'

I blushed fervently, although thankful was I that I could not see this myself. My company, however, seemed to edge away slightly, as the embarrassment spread all too rapidly through what would have been considered as my veins. Then I turned to face my enemy again, alone.

'You can have these two as far as I'm concerned, cos I know you folks are busy building up such an impressive army of arseholes. But I'll hand them over to you after I've finished dealing with them; be-cause I'm taking them down The Hole, with Me!'

'You can't do that,' my foe objected irritably. 'You can't just…'

'Oh but I can,' I replied, producing the mandate that I clutched in my palms. 'And I will. Now!'

I left him whilst on top – the best way – leaving the splattering, spluttering form of Hacosh and Cousin Hannah to decay where they both lay. It would be something of a shock to Cousin Tony, and his son Philip, when they found them early the next day, but things never worked out perfectly even when you wanted them to. In any case I didn't much like Tony "The Half-wit" (who was her drunken husband), or Phil (their worthless spawn), because they were just weaker forms of the same corrupted vessel.

'In fact, I think I'll take them all with me Qädesh – if you don't mind that is – the entire family!'

'What the whole lot?' (He could observe for himself my rather solemn demeanour). 'Don't be silly now Elf. You know this lot have been our livelihood for a good many years now, so don't be such a tight-fisted wanker.'

(His brusque tones, one may perceive, would get him nowhere).

'Oh come on Elf… I mean Ellyll – whatever you are? I've heard much about you since our last encounter – seems like you're a force to be reckoned with now,' he entreated, all rather mournfully. 'So you don't need to be pulling these sly moves…'

(I proceeded to hum a hymn I had overheard in Heaven one day).

'Don't be so stingy, eh Elf…? Ellyll I mean… And quit that racket, Bitch!'

'Elf? Stingy…?' (Bitch I could understand). 'Since when did Charity become your vanguard?

'…Anyway, not to worry, 'cos this lovely fella behind me has given me something for you,' I rejoined, hinting darkly at the yellow-coloured parchment, whose pink letters, all travelling via the Fifth understood. 'Signed, sealed, and now delivered!'

He snatched it from my grasp before poring through the sheet nervously. Occasionally, he glanced upwards, but noticing that I did not blanch, even for a moment, he continued to read the runes with some considerable interest.

'Everything's in order, I trust?'

(My company had come back to me now, I was pleased to see).

'So looks like I'll see you later, Qädesh. Oh, and before I forget; are trolls okay for these two?'

Without awaiting a reply I jumped out through the lattice-style windows, leaving Qädesh and his greasy brood of ape-men swiftly behind. Presently, I joined the cold nightly zephyr that was gusting its way towards Church Street. Shortly, I found myself transported to the old cemetery which lies hard behind the town's former grammar school, in the heart of Enfield itself. And it was not far from that broody place that we all broke ranks – my small band of Watchers and Yours Truly.

They left me alone in that horrid place; that site which is a haven for demons, a host for devils, a harbour for the foul; a homestead for every repellent creature this side of the Afon Styx (being the river which separates Annwfn from Uffern). And from there, with what courage I might muster, I was to find my own way to the ongoing festivities.

Nevertheless, as we parted company, I did remember them mention this one last thing – that I was not to speak a word of this matter to anyone. Not to my perthynas, not to my friends, and especially not to that large, dim-witted oaf, whom I was cursed enough to be inhabiting.

PART I

THE PERFECT JAM

DROPZONE

Rejoice O young man, in your youth,
And let your heart cheer you in the days of your youth;
Walk in the ways of your heart, and in the sight of your eyes;
But know for all these God will bring you into judgement.

ECCLESIASTES 11:9

The smoke filled out the basement chill-out room and was filtering through to the lounge upstairs. The lights were dim and presently the music was being played at a far easier pace, a less upbeat groove than earlier on in the evening. Only a few people were left at such a late hour, 4:00 a.m. on the Sunday morning, but Gee's boy, Deejay B.J. 'Boogie', had done his job well. What had really sealed off such a safe evening though was one of the last tunes that he'd dropped – the prime time funky sounds of Chosan – "*La Gahto*".

Now 'The Funk' or 'Funk-Daddy Gee' – as Gee was variously known – had made wholly certain that the last couple of tunes were to his (and his lady's) liking. They both liked the fresh and vibrant sounds of *Conner Reeves* as "... the Brudder got soul init?" So the last few songs had been "*Let It Breathe*" and "*I'll Get Over It*" – these were for the guys as they were wicked to funk to. And then of course there had been the mandatory slower songs, which are seemingly played at the end of every evening. Perhaps so that those who have missed all the chances with all the honeys all the way throughout the evening may have one last hope of redemption; perhaps so that "...non-danceable and meaningless... but nice records," may be sold to a forever desperate audience. Nevertheless, "*Ordinary People*" and "*I Owe You So Much*" were both well appreciated, because they definitely had plenty of soul, and so much feeling.

There were a couple of baseheads left around too. They were down in the chill-out zone tripping out on Colombian Spice and Afghan Rice (suitably also known as 'White' and 'Brown'). A few of the *massive* were also still down there in "The Hole", sampling the seedier atmosphere of sex, drugs and whatnots; you understand don't you?

Of course you do.

Cos one of them was Stefan – that was Howls' top boy. Then again there was Julian and Thallia, T.J. and Lora, who were still in fact "*getting it on*". (These were all some of Gee's crew that he'd met at college a long time back; back in the day when the say was on partying, grooving, and making the best

3

of one's moves.) The rest of the spliffers/druggies were unknown to them however, but when Mark had previously checked they had all appeared to be somewhat harmless. A couple of them, Dhruba and Nigel, had been imbued with a gross excess of alcohol, which was not a major crime at such an event like this, but they were cool anyway; or at least they wouldn't be disturbing anyone else for a while!

The sweet smell of the hemp plant reminded The Kid of the olden days, before he had first set foot in London. That must have been about the same time when the aroma from the urban weed had first visited his shires, back in the day when *cats* started moving into the local neighbourhood. Anyway, that was a while ago now and it was a place no longer worth visiting in his memory.

Presently Mark could be found leaving the lower basement floor.

*

Upstairs, only the Syndicate remained along with their chief guest and resident deejay, "The Boogie". The fact that the crew was left there at such a late hour is of some significance, as they were, more often than not, the last into any party and the first bodies to leave, even if the groove was good. Six sweet hours of sweat and body would have been a good enough night's jamming for anyone though, but they spared a thought for Markie who had helped set the whole thing up.

Mel herself had shot off with Paul a couple of hours back, after he'd popped in towards the end of the late-night jam, even though the party was being held in her (mother's!) crib. He couldn't make it for the most part as he was doing his night shift as a security worker – at a graveyard of all places! There'd been a couple of desecrations recently over at the cemetery in Edmonton you see, so he and another one of his co-workers had been posted there over the course of the next few weeks to try and catch whoever was doing it. Not exciting stuff really when you think about it – but it was a job – it kept him busy, and it paid the bills.

But it was always gonna be Mark anyway who was the one left in charge of the clearing out. Fair enough you may say, because he had organised the whole event in the first place. Anyway he was good at that sort of thing wasn't he you're probably asking yourself right now? Getting people together, kicking off a good time, seeing to it that things ended smoothly… yeah, all that kind of bizniz. That's when he put his mind to it.

*

He moved casually through the seeping smoke to where the soul-spinner was caught up cutting his latest "after-hours" track before a dissipated audience.

4

'Bazaar Baz – thanks man – 'cos you kept everyone stepping all night. Smashing job – well done boss.'

His leisurely stroll took him over to the Boogie where, as soon as they were no more than a yard apart, each of the friends leant forwards slightly, extending their right arms of *thanks-giving*, upon which they touched fists deftly with a quick double-tap. The first contact had to be horizontal; the second was vertical after a quick clockwise rotation, with extra sound effects to boot.

"*Tisch! Tisch!*"

'Oh… and tell your boy *Chosan* and all 'is *Silverstreetz* crew that they got a wicked tune there init? Yeah, big-up all them boys, from us to them, and from me to the VIP, seen?'

'Yeah, yeah, straight...' (There was another respectful touch, because the white man's blackness had not gone altogether unnoticed.) 'But I really enjoyed it tonight I'm telling you,' said B.J., while they hauled the last of his gear through to the dimly lit corridor.

'Man, to be honest – and no offence or nuffin' – but I never seen so many White Folks who can dance good in all my days… well, at least not since *back-in-tha-day*…' The deejay looked at The Kid for some signs of approval.

'That's long blud, you're trifling!'

'Come on now, you know I ain't no hater!'

'A'ight, a'ight it's true Bro init,' said Mark, reassured that the deejay was in no way indicting him. He was not to be numbered amongst the failing and flailing massive. 'True say init, the boys up this end can step, even some of us Blue-foot init?'

They cracked up for a few moments.

B.J. resumed, 'Just be telling my man *Gee* for me that I'll be in touch, seen? Oh… and by the way Boyo… J-J's a nice girl man, kinda fine lines all over her, seen blood. She's tic… So w'happen say? Wha'gwan? You know you want to.'

There was a momentary pause.

'Shit man, only kiddin' ya. All I'm sayin' is that she's quite fit man and you're a soulja.'

The deejay turned away promptly, which helped to cover somewhat Mark's blushes.

'Nah, she's… she's just a friend man,' Mark countered timidly. 'I only met her a couple of months back when...' He faltered again as B. "Boogie" J. made his way through and exited the front door.

'Laters people!' blasted the deejay past Mark's right ear-hole. He took the last of his speakers from his demurring white comrade. 'I'm okay from here, cheers... and C'ya! … And give J-J my love – all of it dread.'

Mark watched the cackling black fool saunter off to his souped-up Volkswagen, a deep black figure adorned in a huge yellow puffa (a snowman

5

jacket), which was at least two sizes too big for the man. The swaggering figure walked as though he was the first black man on the moon, and more importantly, like he was being promenaded in front of an audience of billions, comprised mostly of his horny black brothers and sisters.

The jacket was his ardent protection against the bitter chills of the starry skies; his black ski-goggles was there to prevent the dusty litter of the walk-ways from polluting his precious peekers. The walk on his tippy-toes made it look as though gravity was not presently in operation anywhere around him, and, even if it were to have been, it would probably have had just as scant effect; because he was just *too* bad! And the V.W. finished off the deejay's im-age nicely, because that was the man's cruise control; it was the man's space-ship…

Right now though Mark was far more concerned about other things.

Fuck me, it can't be that obvious, can it? he thought to himself, some-what worried about the last flippant remark that had come from the over-casual sound-spinner. *Or at least I hope it's not!*

He clicked the front door shut only to be greeted by a smog-lit room. The cold winds buffeted against the wooden panelling of the outside doorframe reminding him that the journey home for whoever wanted to leave at this time of night would be somewhat of a rough adventure. He turned away from the battered door.

It made him feel all sweet and secure when he could hear stormy winds outside and he was all nice and snug inside. It reminded him of some of the days back in his youth when he was growing up on his folks' farmland in the midst of the beautiful Welsh vales. Some of the weather they had near the Brecons was enough to kill the best of them.

He peered out through the door's only available peephole one last time, to catch the wheel-spinning vehicle of deejay B.J. Boogie zooming off down the empty street.

'I really hope he didn't mean it!'

'Don't worry,' Elena said, grabbing him a bear hug from behind. 'I won't tell a soul.'

*

Meanwhile, Sash the Desi was kicking back with J-J and Gee at the rear end of the reception room. The windows were left slightly ajar not only to allow some of the fumes to escape, but also, some of the unchecked banter which needed to be carried out and into the neighbouring darkness. The evening's progress needed to be followed by all.

'That's one thing I really don't like!' Gee said, complaining in his most caustic tone.

'What's that then, Gee?' queried Sash obligingly, for no other reason than that he knew his boy was gonna continue anyway, so that he may as well give him the benefit of the doubt and look all the better for it. 'What riles *ma-brother* so this time?'

'It's the smoke init – always gets in your baddest clothing when the air gets zapped Bro! My most baddest clothes too…My bashment an' lickdem style outfit… Tchp! …

'Yo! Mark, Elena…' Bellowed the Black-man, looking up suddenly. 'In 'ere dread!'

With the utmost style the two summoned approached the rest of the crew. Mark took the sofa by J-J and Elena relaxed in a spot next to Gee's armrest, squelching herself in the towering torso of her big black bro.

'So where's Alisha then guys?' she queried, casting her eye around at the gang.

'I think she's in the toilet babe!'

'What, really? Is she getting laid?'

'No, no, no! No booty. She's alone. I think she's on number ones.'

*

Alisha was Christian and she took it seriously. But that was alright though, everyone to their own. She'd been brought up that way anyway, hardcore, so there was little she could do about it now. Anyway, all the rest of her family; Auntie Claris, Uncle Clive, Brothers Clifford and Carl, and her 'cool cousin' Clinton, and even many more of her vast American lineage, all seemed to be that way inclined. But that was cool, that was cool. Even for the many hundreds of them!

What was most important for the crew however was the fact that she was pretty. She was also quite tall, though a little large in some seasons (and this happened to be one of those seasons). Nonetheless, she had the most wonderful dark features and beautiful full lips to be found on any A-Class Negro. She was bubbly at the best of times and cheerful at the worst, and added to that the fact that she was a capable actor, singer and dancer (in increasing order of preference), it was inevitably her destiny to become part of the setting at some stage.

One of her acting roles had been to play the quintessential English rose (albeit a black one) skilled in the art of fencing, kind of like Madonna in the James Bond movie. She had taken to this well, and even after the performance had ended, she continued on with this very European of pursuits. Something about the sword of the spirit being the Word of God had inspired her onto greater heights, more daring, and countless hours studying this art of foils, epees and sabres.

At first though she had definitely taken a bit of getting used to; and not solely because of her solid convictions on *just* about everything. Her repulsion towards too much drink; her loathing of drugs; and worst of all, her illiberalism towards all current values, the *zeitgeist*, popularly aired on some of T.V.'s diurnal chat shows like Ricki Lake and Jerry Springer. These things had given her friends more than a little to contend with, although it was this last matter that had arguably been the hardest of all to deal with.) Presently nonetheless, they had grown somewhat accustomed to having her around, and she turned out to be not too bad after all. In fact, sometimes (just sometimes mind), she could actually be a bit of a laugh.

It must also be said however that her deep-seated beliefs had rubbed off on everyone to some degree. Some perhaps a little more than others, but all nevertheless had sampled at least a few of her staunch dogmas.

Sash in fact was a regular at "The Jubilee Dominion", which was her church down in Wood Green; albeit for Sash that wasn't exactly saying much. He'd go everywhere and try and learn everything if it pleased people, so this wasn't too much hassle. Mark had also been there a couple of times and the rest of the gang too had been at least once. (They were all kinda compelled to go last Christmas, while Gee was having his thing about Alisha. He had quite liked the girl at the time, so what she asked, they all delivered – more or less.) Anyway, most of them had been brought up with a little bit of religion and so this much was almost mild in comparison.

*

The truth is though that Gee had been brought up with a bit more religion than the rest of them because he had attended some of the local Catholic schools run by the Jesuits. He'd also gone to church quite a bit up until the age of around thirteen at which point he'd had a radical conversion to '*common sense*', as he so often liked to put it. Thereafter, he'd stopped going to church and avoided anything religious altogether – for safety's sake you understand. Religion was no longer the safest thing to discuss around the boy now, because in truth, he was totally sick and tired of the whole mélange. One has got to understand that it had really messed with his psyche.

Anyway, that's beside the point now because most people born into religion do away with such bondage at some time or another. Either later on in their teens (unless they were unfortunate enough to have a drunken Paddy for a daddy) or somewhat later on in life. But this definitely weren't the case for our man Gee. Because you see, Gee was an intelligent brother (he was black), and none dared to say otherwise.

More importantly at present however was that Gee was actually quite hard, and street-wise coming to think of it, as he had been born in Hackney and had lived around those sides for the greatest part of his formative years. Neverthe-less, he was a bit different from your everyday, run-of-the-mill type ragga, although he was always trying to cover up the fact by using his puff lingo and *down* street-vernacular: except, of course, when he was trying to impress some of the more up-market ladies. Nah ya see, then intelligence was okay – it could even be considered an *admirable* quality. Sometimes. In fact, the boy often professed to having read the whole Bible by the time he was only fifteen, which again, no one dared contest; lest he should quote to them every single proverb from the Old Testament, as well as a couple of his own devising!

He was also fairly well renowned for doing the sports thing quite well. (He had in fact been in the borough and county squads for athletics where he had run round the track like a slave for his freedom, and thrown the shot-putt like Hercules.) But all of that was back in the day now, alongside the basketball and other shit, because nowadays his friends knew him as a capable fighter – not because he did at any time, or anything like that – but because he could. He didn't go round looking for trouble though, that just wasn't him.

Anyway, he was a licensed martial artist and he took it seriously. He had studied karate for almost half of his life and had also recently taken up kung fu. If push came to shove though and he was forced to name what he favoured most, he would say that it was a toss up between the jo (short staff) or the bo (long staff). He had already won a few competitions thanks to his fancy foot-work and flailing arms and this only helped spur him on to learning even more about weapons.

It has still got to be said, however, that to Gee's heightened wisdom, Catholic schools were run by a sorry bunch of devils (and they didn't have to exist for it to be run by them). And trying to argue with him on this matter was pretty fu-tile. He had been to two of their schools and that was enough for him to make his overall assessment. Anyway, everyone knew inside out the type of things they got up to at schools like those, boarding or non-boarding; and everyone knew of the stress that some of the teachers had put him through whilst he'd been there.

'You're doing this today for us aren't you... You're doing that...'

He had felt used and abused. But they were a bunch of sorry sods anyway, especially some of those sports teachers. Gee had seen that earlier on in his time there but it didn't bother him too much now. Besides, he was The Man now, and he wasn't about to let a few ugly people get him down. He had a good life in front of him and he could someday leave the nasty old one behind. So they could sit, spin, and suck on it.

What was a bit ironic though, when you think about it, was the way that he sometimes cheered up thinking about it all. (And Gee cheered up anyone else that happened to be present too!) Because he knew that they would always be lowly teachers, or "… base degenerates"; in truth, bad, sad and lonely people with no end to their ceaseless drudgery – that was the good part. He would be different though, he had to be (cos it was harder not to be, he often said). Far better than those *eejits*. He was not quite sure how he was going to do it, but he would be all the same, even if it almost killed him. It was blatantly obvious to the Friends that he had lost his way, but what was not so clear was whether or not one day he might find his way back again.

*

Having said all that every single one of Alisha's acquaintances appeared to be somewhat different. They were, in fact, far closer to the normal everyday man on the street. That much at least Gee could appreciate, which was perhaps why he seemed to have taken to some of 'The Family', particularly to her brother Clive. Moreover, all of them appeared to be genuine; in fact, they could all rather be a little *too* nice sometimes.

Nonetheless, it would never do to let someone else's unequivocal holiness and that of all her folks stand in the way of an awfully good dig-in, or the crew might think you'd gone soft! Nah mate, don't be *stupid*. You should never do anything malicious though, nothing uncalled for, because that's just bad – they were all still friends at the end of the day, weren't they? But taking it out of her a bit, you know, a little bit of ribbing, a rise, and a few cusses, nothing too serious – what harm could that possibly do?

Besides, it was never personal because it could have been any of them init – they all knew that. And they knew that she knew that. Because the cusses and put-downs never went too far. Well, almost never.

*

The wind blew strongly over the tops of the scattered houses and the rustle of leaves could be made out on the bare streets outside, scrambling over one another in a frenzied action of uncoordinated movement. Some drizzle hovered aloof amidst the blackened skies high above but the wind looked more than ready to oblige in one of its more prolific duties. Hidden moisture was carried across the large open forecourts which marked St Andrew's Street till it arrived on the battered woodwork of the large, old house.

Inside, the incessant pitter-patter of tiny raindrops knocked against the glazed windows, driving hard against the finely reformed silicates of the shatterproof glass. Invisible fingernails rapped lightly upon each of the dual panes of protection before departing, leaving the rain with the choice of another house to enter.

Mark was promptly upon his feet and he shut the window tightly.

'Looks like it's gonna be another evil one tonight boys and girls,' he said, looking sullenly towards the gloomy skies. He paused for a second longer before turning his head towards the pattering sound on the nearby stairwell. 'Here she comes – the soul-survivor herself! It's Alisha...'

'We've been missing you girl; have you had a good time already?'

'Yeah, yeah. I love you too baby,' she retorted to Mark's obvious insinuation. 'Thank you my people, thank you all, but I think I'll save myself for someone worthwhile, even if that makes me as old as yo' mama. That excludes all y'all I'm not afraid to say... but I thank yous all anyways.'

Undeterred, Mark continued the advance; 'We were just saying,' (they weren't really), 'that at slumber parties in the States, they'd probably be getting out them *Oui-ja Boards* now and some and them tarot cards too maybe. Perhaps a little D&D in some places. But we can't do that with you here can we now?'

'Tchp! As if you'd do any of those things anyway, chi-e-e-e-f.'

The embarrassment of Alisha's retort spread all too rapidly across his face, quickly reaching the green-veined protrusions that straddled his feet, hastily reasserting his unique position as the bluest of all Bluefoots. From head to toe the man was finished. Mark skulked back into the corner.

Now Gee couldn't stand such a sight, an abhorrent abomination occurring in his own midst – one of his top boys, cussed, and out on a string – a g-string no less, and with no reply seemingly forthcoming! Nah mate, this was a really bad situ. So aptly, though with rather an unskilled sleight of hand, he began to gently apply the rope.

'Yeah, but Mark didn't mean that now did he!' Gee blurted out the words before his brain had finished checking them. 'Nah... he didn't mean that at all.'

Alisha came down the remaining stairs and turned to face the big black hulkster at the bottom.

'What he meant was that... Well look... We're not being bad or nuffin', cos you're our girl and everything. But your church is kinda like – I mean the people are safe, I ain't denying that – '

Presently, the rest of the crew lounged back, with huge smiles on their faces. They knew what was coming, and they were going to be the hyenas.

'... But some of them *tongue-talkers* at your church girl, you gotta say it – rasclart! They're nuts. And some of that praying and deliverance stuff – '

'Yeah, it's true – '

'I mean... come on girl! It's all fucked up init?'

'Deliver me cos I'm Damien out of the Omen.'

'That's a long t'ing.'

Gee's pleading was false; in truth, he hoped to secure the approval of the fickle, and he knew as much himself. A few laughs from the crew nonetheless, he could always appreciate, because it showed that he was still on top form. It was what he lived for.

He stiffened a little as he felt a cold, lifeless sensation brush lightly across his right shoulder. Nevertheless, he was quick to shrug off the feeling as a belated case of flu, which was, in truth, setting in all over the shop. Whatever former inhibitions may have been lingering from his days as a Catholic was readily enough quelled tonight.

'We've been through all this before Gee, so why are you kickin' this off now!' Alisha turned away from him, a deliberate diss to a cruel fool, in the light of his overt reluctance to quit.

*

When it came down to it, Gee was a basically a stand-up kinda guy, except for those sometimes when he could be a teeny-weeny bit petty. Because often (all too often in fact) he would have to be the first one to show his intelligence, even if that meant him getting into a long-winded argument because of it. And whether or not he violated a couple of sacred friendships along the way, just for the sake of winning, that was neither here nor there, just so long as he won the day. But get into a fist fight with anyone outside the Syndicate or his immediate circle of friends and he'd be the first one in there as back up. That's why he was nicknamed "King of the Bro's".

Nevertheless, even though all the crew were aware of his faults and failings, they enjoyed his *stylee* all the same. It was fun hearing his put-downs – unless, of course, you were the one currently on the receiving end. Cos Brothers always ended up pulling the same old same old. Now that be right ain't it J-D?

*

Shortly, he spat out the remaining strands of sun-dried beef before taking to scrutinise Alisha more closely.

'But it is true though Alisha,' agreed Elena, piping up somewhat beyond her years. 'How do you explain all that stuff, and what is it there for?'

The question really did take everyone by surprise. Not so much the question perhaps, but the one who had posed it. Because Elena would normally be the quiet one, except for the rare occasions when somebody really did rub her up the wrong way. However, this didn't actually seem to be one of those occasions. This had come at the end of a long and arduous party, where Qat and Sensi and many a delicacy were on the menu. Enough to keep everybody well chilled. But who could tell what was going on behind the scenes?

'The tongues I mean,' Elena clarified. 'What are they there for?'

Quizzically, they all looked around towards The Girl.

'I mean… everyone's got one haven't they?'

'Er… Beau… I don't quite think that we're on the same planet!'

The painful sigh that emanated from the rest of the youngster's friends was most definitely audible.

*

Believe it or not Elena was in fact no fool. Of late it must said she had been somewhat affected by the changes she had witnessed in Sash and Mark but that was mostly for the better. She looked up to the girls like they were her older sisters (Alisha in particular) and she would always listen to what they'd have to say, no matter how daft it all often seemed to everybody else! All too often though she kept herself to herself, which was a bit of a shame, because when she did open up it was generally worth the wait. The present intercourse however came at the end of a long night of agreeable ruff & strenuous exertion (partying).

The schoolgirl was half Greek and half English. Her father was a Greek Cypriot, her mother was loosely connected to English aristocracy. Although money was not an issue for the family, they did, on the surface of things, conduct themselves as normal folk do. Anna, her mother, could, from time to time, be a little too soft – *stupidly* so in fact, but she did enjoy feeding the troops. This, amongst a bunch of uncouth savages, was a very significant thing to do. There was absolutely nothing wrong with that as far as the gang was concerned.

However, some of the guys suspected that there was more behind the scenes of her household. Much more. The way Elena was, at times, gave them the impression that not everything was kosher in her life. There were some dark truths which needed to come to the light, shit like incest and abuse which are never easy to talk about. But the gang as a whole didn't know about these things, only Gee, who was the first in the Syndicate to have become close to Elena. Albeit all credit to the man because he had managed to keep these matters to himself and would continue to do so until such time that she, herself, was willing to speak on the subject.

There was also her little brother who had also suffered such perfidious acts though not to the same degree. Despite all of this, he was still a good kid. Whenever the gang went round though, they were usually obliged to have a turn or two on the PlayStation4, and a couple of distressing chats with some of his younger female friends, namely Kathy and Katy, who were the twins from next-door. But they rarely got together these days at Elena's and Ant's gaff because of the divorce and everything. Meeting the head honcho was not the wisest move in these times of crisis!

These things aside, Elena was nobody's patsy. Her acumen, although subtle and habitually misleading, could occasionally be very persuasive and useful.

That was only on occasion though. Now and then she even managed to confound her friends by the powers of lateral thinking, which the rest of the guys, with their more *advanced* learning, could not do. Anyway, some of the geezers (no names mentioned) quite liked her petit figure – especially that overly cute backside!

*

Alisha was the only one to pay genuine heed to Elena's innocent enquiry, as she knew that her younger scion was being wholly sincere. Indeed, presently this was in fact the case but neither her nor her friends were perceptive enough to notice the subtle changes occurring around them.

'Okay girl,' Alisha replied, 'I think I understand what you're saying. Well, it's a bit like I said last time really. Do you all remember how I said that we believe God's Spirit comes into you when you're *born-again*? Well – '

'Born-again?' It was Jema who cut in this time. 'Wassat mean beau, born again?'

For a bunch of uninterested morons, they sure got a lot of questions, Alisha thought to herself.

'Yeah born-again...' She kept the sarcastic, serrated edge to herself. 'You remember last time when I said that you're born again when you accept and confess the basis of the Christian doctrine... Ya know, how Jesus came and died for us and our sins and – '

'*Belieeeeeve!* We remember last time, and we ain't ever gonna forget are we? Cos you be mumbling about such fuckeries since time past, baby.' As Gee spoke he ignored her stern look. 'And cos... now you be speaking like yo mama!'

The crew commenced to crack up in snide snorts of hysteria, which emanated from one of the gang of fools and quickly spread throughout the congregation. Its pace was as quick as Boredom when she extends her umbrage to cover the masses during a service in the Town's main church.

Outside, the stormy winds laid siege to the old building, keeping its open framework under a constant barrage of cold nightly chills. The day seemed to be as frigid as they come and even for such an early hour of the day the silent white frosts that appeared to be spreading were forever grim. Again he felt the iciness fall upon his shoulders, like the snowflakes of a dull and brooding Christmastime. They were cold reminders of a distant boon, forever recurrent in the season's deepest gloom.

Then, Gee rubbed his bleary eyes. For a moment, he thought he had seen something. Not the frozen soft icicles of childish pleasure but something less pallid, something altogether more irksome to the sight and irritable to the grinders, if one were in fact able to taste it. He considered the matter no further after his eyes were cleared of their grit and their grime.

A weenie bit of a frost has started to get at my senses, cos they're going numb. I can't really think straight. Shit!

He tried nevertheless to recall the thread of Alisha's last argument.

Er...

'Yeah... that's right,' rejoined Gee, his faculties now restored. 'You said that the Spirit comes and lives in you when you do all that jazz, and that he won't ever leave you – '

'Nor forsake you – '

'Yeah, whatever girl. So what's with this new turbo-boost spirit jazz? What? You mean to say man and man say a few more prayers and 'im get recharged or suttin'? Oh baby please!' If not obviously scornful Gee's tone was downright condescending. 'Beautiful black sister, you must be kidding me or someshit?'

He spoke to her as though she was one of his nieces, except for the fact that he would have at least shown them a little less disrespect. But after knowing Gee for so long Alisha was now more than used to it. What's more she did still quite like him, which was somewhat of a help at times like these – warts, mouth, warts in the mouth; and all.

Elena however was not content that her question should have been usurped so. She gave Gee a rueful look before continuing; 'Who made God then?' She enquired innocently before opening her mouth more candidly. 'And if there is really a God, why is the world so bad? And Alisha, why are people so wicked?'

'*A wicked an' da bad, a wicked an' da bad! A-woo! Alisha! A-woo! Alisha! Boo! Boo! Boo! Boo!*'

The juvenile delinquents' coarse imitation of the African Mountain Gorilla left little to the imagination. They continued cracking up for some time to come, fists pummelling the air like the pistons on a steam-barge. Alisha craned her head back slowly to the shy, unobtrusive Elena.

'Well...'

But what was that?

Her words fell silent but her palpitating heart sounded loud enough for all to hear as her eyes regarded the strange yellow mist that had just evaporated from beside Gee.

Two yellow eyes and a...

She looked readily to the rest of the gang for their own impressions, but each of them was somewhat too far removed from her present concerns. The laughing subsided shortly as they saw the bitter look of trouble upon her face. They regarded her quizzically.

'What's up girl?' queried Sash.

'*You're getting seriously tired girl. Perhaps it was time you were going home.*'

Yeah, she thought to herself, as one of the Watchers tried to communicate wisdom with the dead weights. *And this conversation isn't helping any.* 'Nothing Sash, I think I'm just getting a tiny bit weary, that's all,' said Elena, voicing her thoughts out loud.

'But...'

'To be honest Elena sweet, you can't always answer things like that,' rejoined Alisha, 'and even if you could, this is neither the time nor the place to be chatting about such things. Plus, I don't reckon any of you would take it in properly, and that's not fair on me...'

*

As we discovered before, Jema-Jane was basically the driver. Basically, because that was the extent of her motoring ability. I mean, the car was her own (well, in truth, it belonged to her parents); the licence was her own (fourth time lucky); and she was the one that did most of the driving (although that didn't actually preclude anyone else from having a go, whether licensed or not). Nonetheless, she was still a student (albeit at one of the greatest institutions in the world, Imperial College). So this sometimes could be used to excuse much of her real-life failings.

Her forte lay somewhere between maths and physics, both of which she was proficient at. But her genius was in the science of mirrors and lenses, the stuff which she had opted to specialise in at university. Apparently, she already knew the set of equations and the laws behind the physics which enabled rays of light to be bent around objects, thus rendering them invisible to the naked eye; all the shit to do with nanowires and metamaterials. She wouldn't ever let on about them though, because, she said, if others got there before she did, it could cost her a mint.

In truth, she would rather have done something else – like being rich and famous like her parents without all the effort – but she was a realist. Nothing worthwhile came without hard work, unless you were born with a silver spoon in your mouth. So physics would have to do for the moment. But she had plans, great designs for both her life and that of the farm boy; ideas that would last a lifetime, possibly even longer; although she wasn't yet letting on about any of them.

However, this rarely stopped her from at times being reckless. It was partly because she was young and abrasive but partly also because she had that faint bit of tomboy in her, evidenced by the catapult which she had become accustomed to using against her brothers since their childhood days. But it was also highly likely because the girl just didn't give a fuck – you just needed to ask Markie boy there. He was still gagging for it after all this time!

To the Welsh Wop however, she had no tomboy in her whatsoever. He hadn't thought so from the very first moment he had seen her – that first night when she'd nigh on mown him down like a stray country chicken lost out on a Christmas stroll. No, he didn't think so one bit. It didn't worry him too much about what the others thought, even though it was usually quite crass. Because to him Jema-Jane was one hundred percent woman – purely bred, especially for him.

J-J however probably got much of that excessive tenacity from her folks: her papa was an Original English Bulldog – uncouth in his youth, proud in the crowd, but as meek as a sullen mule when with the crew. Her mama though was an Irish-Jew (neither of which is intended to be a cuss). Anyway, her mum was fine. Her folks again were really quite well off, and a lot better off than anyone else's parents; part of the nouveau rich as some would say. Moreover, they now had little pretence to keep up because, in the eyes of the world, they had made it, and from little more than tuppence and a dearth of brains between them!

It must be said though that they had both grown to like the Syndicate, including Mark, especially since finding out that no legal action was to be taken against their daughter after the road accident. Indeed, their present reflections about the young band of ragamuffins varied from " … rather nice and pleasant young people" to the more infamous "… very… funny guys". These false perceptions were not unique faults of J-J's guardians, however, for many ignorant parents were shrouded under the selfsame delusions, and frequently so, which only really came about because Mark, Gee and the others were on their best behaviour each time it was expected of them.

All these things aside however, another vitriolic habit of our J-J was her beloved sunglasses, which she had designed and made herself. These she wore always; and when I say always, I mean always! It still didn't stop any of the more prurient from flocking around her elegant curves though. Indeed, it rather seemed to heighten their misplaced arousal.

Some say it was probably all down to that mystique-about-the-woman jazz or someshit. Her parents however were not so adamant. They thought it probable that the only folks she attracted (or privately, ever would glean if she didn't start getting her act together) were vampires, lechers, or, indeed, disgruntled Welsh farm boys in need of much loving. Anyway, whether the sun was up or whether or not it was the shittiest day of the year thus far, she always made sure that her shades were within arm's reach, much like her catapult.

To be truthful, though, none of these things had any detrimental effects on her motoring skills anyway. She was a most shocking driver at the best of times. She was probably the only person in England, so Gee said one day, who could (with or without her glasses) career wildly off the road she was on and hit an elderly geezer, close to his grave, even if the same poor sod was tucked up tidy in bed. She would still find her mark even if he was couched in a distant part of a neighbouring town! Wisely therefore, J-J never once spoke of her near-stacks – except, obviously, for the time she had first met Mark.

*

The next deafening thunderclap erased part of Jema's questions. Albeit, she did soon manage to carry on where Elena had left off.

'… he make the Devil in the first place?' J-J probed further. '… And who on earth was Cain's wife? Get it? Who on earth…?'

'Yeah right *Janey*, nice one.' They sniggered at her futile attempts of jesting.

Between them all the Syndicate had found some of the most problematic questions that can be posed to any zealous individual (in parlance which is not politically correct, a religious freak), which is what Alisha obviously was. The Christian however, was left undeterred. They were friends, she was confident in what she believed, and she was right and they were all wrong. Such blatant assumptions always helped at times like these – made you feel like you're something special.

'So you gonna answer then or what?' murmured Sash. 'Cos you gotta admit it though, some of that stuff *is* pretty whack?'

The heat was back on.

*

Precipitous, sometimes even two-faced and quizzical, Sash, who was near enough twenty, was the oldest member in the young bunch of renegades. However, it didn't always seem like it. He did actually like going to church with Alisha but it wasn't really the done thing to say that in front of the Syndicate, not unless they had uttered the same thing first. That was just foolish as it broke the number one cardinal rule of survival – never be first or last but stay tucked tightly in the middle.

He could be bold though, sometimes, and on account of his age he was somewhat more confident than J-J, and therefore he could at times seem commanding. Moreover, he was also more mature than Janey, or at least the gang thought so on most occasions. This false notion was unhealthily compounded to some extent by the fact that he was quite well read (they had forced books upon him at the local C. of E. school).

Truly though, India was this young man's heartfelt desire. Like blackness was to Gee, brownness was to Sash. Since his earliest memories his talk had always been on their plight, their sufferings, their positive worthiness, and then later on when he had 'come of age', he was adamant that he was one day going to help "…redeem their souls" from the tyranny of the White-man (Mbakara). In practice that meant he wanted to go to India and undertake some kind of charitable crusade for a while – you know, to do something useful in life before being forced into the standardised rat race, held so dear by so many of the faithful.

But a mortgage-slave he never wanted to be, lest it should detract from the young man's humane heart. For few people were as willing as he was to put up with things they ought not to have done, solely out of the selfless consideration of others. But he frequently got himself into the grossest predicaments because of this. As was the time when he'd attempted to bestow his own brand of charity and benevolence/condescension on some down-and-out living rough somewhere between London's Leicester Square and Covent Garden. Those first faltering steps were almost met by a brick in the face. Again, however, that was in no way a vilification on his person because his heart was in the right place. That's why Alisha (and the crew) called him Salem Hasleg or Sashi "King of Peace" because the scriptures say, 'How beautiful are the feet of those who preach the gospel of peace, who bring glad tidings of good things!'

Nevertheless, he had to get the money in and stand on his own two feet somehow, so Sash made full use of his build. He was a labourer and worked most of his jobs around the capital. His favourite tool was the sledgehammer and this he wielded with the skill of Thor himself, breaking down walls that blocked him in as though his life depended on it.

Such a friendship as Sash had with Gee could only have been forged over many years, which indeed it was, even from the times when they had run together for the London Borough of Enfield. Even though they had both matured somewhat their brotherhood was still left in tact – which was nice to see as all too often that's not the case in such a highly-pressurised society. They were also an encouragement to one another in their search for the finer things in life. True brethren, if one ignored the constant cussing.

So what was really needed at present was common sense coupled with some of that maturity-with-age shit, to prevent their continuing downslide into the confused world of chaos. Yeah, go on Gee, act your age, not your shoe size…

*

'Look Alisha,' Gee retorted again, 'we're just trying to find out why – '

'Why do you always wanna catch me out everyone? I'm not God am I? How do you expect me to know everything about life, the universe, and everything, and all the rest of that sh – anyway, why don't you all just give it a break eh? …' She managed to check her voice at the height of its ascent. 'You almost made me swear,' she whimpered to herself, turning around to face away. 'You good for nothing low-lifes!'

Alisha turned to face the main protagonist.

'Look, I'm not sure on many things, but why don't you ask God yourself, you sad bunch of miscreants?' She grimaced inwardly, 'You know that I love you all but next time you fu– Well, let's just say don't hassle me any more people, cos this girl's not for the grieving. Besides, it's a late evening and by the looks of y'all, you could do with the extra beauty sleep.'

'*OOOOOOOhhhhhhhhhh!*' the sound resonated amidst the massive. 'That was cold Alisha,' Gee said, ' – I bet you yo mama taught you that one… Face to face!'

'*OOOOOOOhhhhhhhhhh! That's n'ang blud!*'

Then Mark said in lightened tones, once the laughter had died down, 'Tell us about the Fall again girl and what you say happened at Jesus' death…' And then to Gee; 'I don't know where all you guys get all your cusses from but you've got to teach me some of them, man…'

That's because Mark was always interested in knowing things. Quite a curious chap he was too, sometimes. And genuinely so. He was almost like Elena in that respect, maybe because they were both still so young. For a while now, he had been kind of quiet, lost, perhaps, in the comfort of his idealised sofa. But with the freshness of the new vibe resonating in his eardrum he was once again fully alerted to the action. And what is more, no amount of smoke was going to put him off this time.

'... And I remember last time when you said something about when your man – '

'Jesus?' Alisha offered.

'Yeah, Jesus,' Mark confirmed. 'About what devil-worshipers believe happened to him when he died? Go on now 'Leash hit us with it!' *And vie for your freedom bitch.* 'Tell us everything you know… '

He paused for a second.

'…Maybe not – just stick with the best of them cos I know you can go on a bit sometimes.'

With the accompanying laughter brought by The Kid's request, Alisha tried to recall which avenues would indeed yield her best lines of vindication.

A MARKED MAN

For we do not wrestle against flesh and blood,
But against principalities, against powers,
Against the rulers of the darkness of this age,
Against spiritual hosts of wickedness in the heavenly places.

EPHESIANS 6:12

If ever there could have been a man for all seasons, Mark would have been him. He was no less a man for every party, a man for all the jams, the man with the friends, as well as being the man to quell ninety-nine percent of all arguments, no matter who they were between. Even when this boy was bullshitting it still sounded good. Damn good.

One minute he was riling off for this one with all his heart, advocating his [direst] policies with that harmonious voice of reason of his, but the next minute he would be firing on all cylinders for his very adversary; and all very genuinely done too! Now he wasn't really like Sash – two-faced or nothing base like that – he was more sort of the professional negotiator; a peaceful type; the man somebody wants around when things are about to go wrong. But he was never without a contingency plan. And that was his brutal side.

Mess with him once and he'd put it down to blatant ignorance. Take liberties with him a twice and he'd be sure to be having words with you. But fuck with him a third time and he would fuck you up like a motherfucker. He had to, because that's how he made his money, dealing in drugs and someshit in the Haringey and Hackney sides. Like he always said, "It's better to be caught with a tool when you don't need it than to be caught without a tool when you do."

His philosophy was from The Street, from The University of Life. Carve somebody up once and you warn one hundred; but slice up two people and you will earn the respect of a thousand. Should you chop up three raggas, however, and jook them to make them look like Swiss cheese, then there's none who would stress you out after that, not even 5-0. That's where Markie stood at the present and all the gang knew it. That's why everybody knew him as "The King of the Road".

Anyway, at this particular event, he'd at last perceived that a smart question was the only way out for all parties embroiled in this argument. Never discuss politics or religion not even after a late night slumber party. Mark's idea though would be a nice way out for all sides involved – enough to satiate the appetites of the hungry and sceptical, but with just about enough grace to leave Alisha feeling somewhat vindicated with her apology.

Therefore, motioning with his head over towards the Dark Girl, he parted his gilt-edged lips:

'Alisha dear? Er... Satanists?' queried Mark, the theory of politics and religion turning to bunkum once again. 'What about Satanists girl – that's quite interesting?'

It would have been good if it wasn't for the fact that Alisha had already told them everything to do with anything even touching Satanists, more than once! So she looked more than a little flummoxed when they kept on asking her. In fact she looked positively upset. Well, at least The Kid had tried his best!

*

The Fall: Why and how it had happened in the first place? Jesus' death and descent into Hell: In one opinion captured and chained to a giant rock in the middle of Hades somewhere; in another's surmise, victorious at the cross, busting up many hordes of fallen angels when he'd descended (as Alisha so often loved to put it for the *Crew*), before, of course, he'd ascended again, into glory. But then there was all that stuff about the Last Days and the Mark of the Beast, which she loved going on about from dusk till dawn; the stuff that the two 'Originals' (Sash and Gee) didn't mind hearing about; because it was to do with eschatology and the numbers 666.

Both of the guys had heard of some of these things independent of Alisha because, as we discovered earlier, Sash and Gee were somewhat more enlightened than the average teenagers. (The fact that they were nearing the end of their teenage years was neither here nor there most of the time, because they spent half of their days acting like kids!) However, they found "The Prophetic" to be the most interesting parts of the Bible, as many frequently did. And that's without the vainglorious delusion that Gee often held, which was that *he* would be the first one to interpret much of its wisdom. This, even though he didn't actually believe in the God behind it all!!

Gee had this vanity thing about him that belies a man's understanding. Even Sash, who had read all of the predications himself – the ones in Revelation and Daniel pertaining to the End-of-Days prophecies – fared little better. The Daft Muppet privately thought that he could bring 'The Light' too.

"They were the most relevant bits in the Bible though, init?" Gee frequently said, rationalising these profound anomalies. "And if any of these things are shown and proved then I'll believe." That, believe it or not, was the only real guarantee he would ever give Alisha on the subject. These boys were proud that they were humble.

'What's the time gang?'

Alisha was hoping that the gloom lingering outside would subdue all further talk of the dark days ahead.

'Anyway, how long do you people have? Ain't we gotta be having our snooze already?'

'Fer real blud, back in yard!' said Gee. 'Cheese and bread… I feel mash-up dread.'

'It's just gone four,' replied Elena, trying, as usual, to ignore Gee's vernacular. 'We've got plenty of time. Go on, girl, step up to the plate'

'Okay, okay, I'll talk,' Alisha moaned. 'But I won't stretch it out too long because I'm sure you'll all start to remember…'

'You done know!'

Promptly, she delved straight into the deepest, darkest mysteries of her faith, whilst disregarding the evil clutches of weariness that so desperately wanted to put an end to her speech. The natural defences of scepticism and scorn dived for cover as she continued to unfurl testimonies from men long since dead, about things not yet seen.

She spoke of a time, aeons past, when Lucifer had risen up in pride against God in his foolhardy attempt to usurp His throne, and how Michael, one of the '…chief princes', and Israel's Guardian, fought with millions of angels to quell the widespread rebellion that followed. She told them of the demons' defeat, being outnumbered two-to-one at her reckoning, but was also quick to add a disclaimer as to why the world was still in such a bad state.

It was mostly down to the Devil, of course, and the fellow cohorts he'd gleaned in The Uprising, or so she said, although humans inevitably had to take more than their fair share of the blame. Though when pressed further by Elena she was not able to elucidate any more quantitatively on the matter. Suffice to say that according to the Black Girl, they were all in cahoots, either knowingly or unknowingly: that is; devils and demons; the profane and the perverse; or people indeed, in general.

Then came the Devil's subsequent humiliation at the hands of a most powerful adversary (which raised stalwart objections, particularly from Gee), and other fell admonitions, which she blasted with all the power of her lungs…

Thus she went on to hail
The end that awaits those who pale,
And all of them there, should they not fear
Even as they were presently loth to hear
Her precious words and that silent call
Of a groaning heart and a dire fall.

23

The Friends sat there frozen still in silence. Even if her narratives weren't altogether true (which, naturally, most of them were not), the way that she told them made up for it. For her it was a personal delight, as wonderful as munching three legs of jerk-fried chicken in front of a half-starved brother who had just tried to grope her.

Anyway, they had asked for it, that's to say, up until the time when the story took a downward and more sinister twist, which was when she started to hark on about the "… Flames of Destruction". They hadn't asked for this much; and even if they had, surely there was no need for all the embellishments!

*

The wind outside abated for a while, receding as if by command of an unseen acquaintance. It was as if all those roundabout needed to hear these words, and that if anything would attempt to scupper this occasion, it would have to be quashed. Soon, the prolonged threat of rain also faltered, leaving open the channels for communication. The sounds of morning birds were dulled, the distant police siren was fizzled, the ambulance behind it resounded with little more vigour than a plane in faraway skies.

Not long afterwards Fear entered again, utilising this, its greatest opportunity so far amid the still, stony silence. It was benumbing and chilling. And it produced a sound which seemed to manifest itself as a slightly muffled wheeze.

What was that?

Sash's eyes darted around first.

'Yo! Quiet for a second…'

He thought that he'd seen a pair of red eyes accompanying the rasping noise; although when he'd looked again, towards the walled mirror, he could see nothing – not even his own reflection. He closed his eyes and opened them again. There was still nothing there before him, which shortly began to cause him some alarm. Before too long however, he saw that he was sitting down well below the level of the looking glass, and this incisive realisation helped allay his fears to some extent. The Desi slumped back into his seat, somewhat gratified to still be in existence.

'Listen up gang, how about some Lauryn Hill?' He sprung up from his seat without awaiting a reply and looked over towards Gee.

'Yeah, heavy blud, cos her tunes are tic.'

'Kick off with "Every Ghetto, Every City" would you, cos that's a sweet tune for the ending of a Ghetto Jam in the middle of The City, eh Bros? – Choose the rest yourself if you want.'

'A'ight fellas.' But he seemed barely able to grasp the concept of a CD-controller. The firm press of his fingertips upon his temples wasn't doing too much good either.

24

'Sash mate, do you know how to work the thing?'

'Shut yer face Boyo cos I'm a little bit tired. You know how it is, like when you've just finished jooking the innocent… or like when you've just become bored chasing an Irish-Jew, of the female persuasion, all round the gaff?'

Mark got the picture. The Kid remained stum, at least for the moment. Soon though, he was relaxed back again in his place next to J-J, just before Sash himself rejoined them all, having at last figured which way was up for the controller.

'Well done boss, Mr Record-Selector, Sash. The Man has finally solved the puzzle!' Trust Gee to break a moment's silence. 'So what blud, was that a bit of divine inspiration there too?'

'Come on guys, sort it out – what's wrong with you all?' It was Elena's turn now to feel irritated. 'You all look like you wanna kill each other – don't you all ever stop cussing?'

'Meow! Keep your paws to yourself girl.'

She was certain she'd heard someone snigger, as the stares of all those around reproved her for her youthful wisdom.

'You're really beginning to scare me now!'

'Yeah,' Sash affirmed, 'leave the child alone. I bet you all wouldn't like it if you were her age!'

While the others giggled, he let his eyes rest on the dark corner of the room.

'Well lookie here, now who's crying?'

'What do you mean 'Leash?'

'Well, Elena, dear, first y'all want the stories; and then you don't; now you don't know what all y'all want, because you can't handle it, ain't that right sweetie?'

Predictably perhaps, there was no response.

'…So then you try worming your way out of it by putting on some music – since when did you like Lauryn Hill, Sash? Make up your mind people because it's getting *bore-ing*.'

Having had her little say however, none had failed to notice the distinct distortion in the morning's miasma; and that included Alisha herself. A laugh was a laugh and everything and they had discussions like this all the time. But this time things seemed a teeny-weeny bit different – like there was a touch of spite in the air. Or something.

*

After some time the smoke sifted through the air like an all-encompassing gaseous envelope, emanating darkly from the lower basement. It disappeared into the thin strands of their clothing. It was not long before the ugly mist settled to a barely tolerable level of impartial symmetry; enough to keep everyone ever so slightly relaxed, but there was just a little too much for the irritating smell to be ignored completely.

Outside the house the weather seemed to undergo its own brand of temperamental designs. The rain came back in continual droves, choosing targets towards the rear end of the house and above the porch where the loft was aching against the pressure of the rallying onslaught. New waters filled with midnight gunge sought out fresh entry points by which to gain access. Streaks of lightning flashed across the vast open skies, dissecting the sodden atmosphere with its brilliant blue hue. And the rolling thunder of a low depression could be heard rumbling its deep displeasure some way off in the distance, as though a sleeping giant was about to be awakened.

Close to the gathering, a solitary milk float drove through a dirty puddle, which lay only a few yards off the front lobby area, as moonlit shadows compelled the darkness towards further dominance. The icy waters continued the relentless assault on the building as slime from the filthy pool splayed itself across the basement windows.

Nevertheless, the impromptu splashing was triumphant in reviving the drowsy occupants in the back room, even while the miry liquid drooled down the windows with a suitable delectation of its own. The abruptness of the stirring, however, led to a brief moment of uncontrollable panic. Within the Friends' hearts Fear seemed to want to grapple on further; hence, because of their partial submission, they offered a slightly greater leverage for the oncoming darkness to intrude.

Alisha was the first one to stir, and it was to the muted sounds of "Lost Ones". Her mind was adrift, aloof somewhat of her previous tirade. The reams of smoke that were fanning out from beneath her soon became an irritant, which was raw and readily distressing. It was so much the more so as she had never herself sampled the untold "delights" of the herbal weed. The Yank didn't let this faze her unduly though as she moved down to the basement with Gee.

'Turn on the lights would you Honey-buns?'

'Okay sweetie-pie – anything to please a babe, beau!'

The lights came on, quickly revealing the object of her chafing.

'It's not good is it Alisha?' Gee said, trying hard to conceal the dirty big smirk on his face. 'It's a pity init? A great shame! The woman who hates smoking skunk, being forced to smoke other folks' skunk and someshit – it's the way of the world girl, you just gotta learn to roll with it.'

'Oh don't you worry about me Gee; I learnt a long time ago you see, soon after I first met you.' She continued on through the basement, as Gee stood aside, amazed at her turn of tongue. 'I tell you what though, I feel like putting out somebody's lights once and for all. I mean, a little blow I'm used to, but this… this is pure fuckeries!'

26

They passed on through the scene of no vibe and no beat (save for the dull throbbing, coming from up above), and completely no movement. There were no sounds, no recording studio background humdrum, not even the dark gabbling of fools high on ganja-smoke. There was nothing. Except for the thick haze trapped within the four hidden walls.

'Come on Gee let's go – there's no one left alive down here.'

As they turned towards the stairs;

'Er, Alisha?'

'Yes Babe?'

'W-w-wh-what…?'

'What's "what" Babe?'

Now, as the story goes, it actually turns out that Gee was genuinely thinking of some form of an apology, something that he wasn't quite used to – hence the stammering and spluttering. Alright, he could be sensitive one minute, crude and abrasive the next, but he had a heart in him somewhere.

'Alisha?'

'Gee, I don't want anymore of your cusses today you hear? Okay…?'

'A'ight then, if you really feel that way…'

'Well… well fine then!'

Alas, it was not to be! Because Alisha, either not being aware of his designs, or indeed, noticing them but choosing not to respond, continued on up the stairs, undaunted at his latest challenge. By the time they were again in their friends' company, Gee's heart was gone, and his good intentions were lost forever.

*

There was no new setting for Alisha as her foot left the last stair. There were no new friends, no rewinding of the clock, only a new tune which seemed to be chilling out frayed nerves a little. She could see that Elena, in particular, appeared to be more shaken than the others, as the gravity of her stories began to take their toll.

'Nice to see you where you belong, Mark.'

(He was over by the mirror, which was nothing extraordinarily new, some say.)

'Init girl, look at him there, pampering and preening himself. Check him out beau!'

With his other hand, however, Mark did his best to fondle his structured cheekbones, just like a mama would the bottom of her baby son. His actions were bordering on the usual; there was nothing particularly strange in Mark loving himself in this way.

Elena leant forwards slightly, whispering; 'Go on J-J just tell him something or else he'll stay there forever!'

'Butters or buff?'

'Buff, definitely!'

'What, you think so?'

'Unless you're blind, girl-friend.'

The two girls giggled. Mark carried on though, in the dire hope that perhaps, on this very night, J-J might recognise him for what he truly was. A god, and not a mere finely chiselled, hand-crafted caricature of one. Her noticing his other dark features, on top of that, would just be an added bonus.

'Oh leave him be then J-J, maybe I was wrong… Look at him there, kissing his own reflection.'

'It's true ain't it?'

J-J's ribs were hurting at seeing him. Because she was no more impressed with his pursuits than with a bare-buttocked goat in a farmyard. So after a minute or so, vainly spent in trying to attract her attention, his mind soon turned to less narcissistic things.

'You know,' Mark began, addressing nobody in particular, 'I've heard it mentioned somewhere that if you say the "Our Father" backwards in a mirror, demons will come out to get you! You know like straight from the pits of Hell.

'So, er, what do you reckon guys?'

Very nonchalantly, to the first couple of rifts of "Everything Is Everything", the Friends lounged back in their seats.

'Yeah, we've all heard that bollocks Markie,' replied Sash. 'So?'

'You mean to tell me you take that bogusness seriously?'

The crew wanted to laugh, but this just didn't seem quite so funny, it being late and everything.

'So what you saying Kid?'

Mark ignored them all.

'Yeah, right Markie,' Gee slammed, bugged somewhat that Markie didn't quite seem to care about the anxiety he had just helped to spread. 'And you know what? I've heard that yo' mama would be the first one out too!'

The narcissist glared round sharply, only to be greeted by heads that were bobbing up and down to the funky beat.

'Oh... and if you're unlucky enough mate, on the night of a full moon, I hear you might be transformed into a werewolf or something equally daft – again, like yo' mama I hear!'

'OOOOOOOhhhhhhhhh-dear, that was another cold one from the stables of Gee.'

'Blitz in fact, Sash. Blitz like the Arctic.'

But the victim glared up angrily at Jema-Jane, stubbornness growing within his bosom.

'So you don't reckon it's true then do ya?'

'Innit boss!'

There was more crude laughter from the illin' band of hyenas.

'Sorry Markie-baby, dear.'

You see, everyone knew that Mark was speaking crap – because you had to sometimes to be a top negotiator – except that right now, no one was absolutely certain, that's all.

'I think we all need some kip guys, and Gee, maybe you'd like to rest that swelling head of yours too, because to be honest mate, it looks like it could do with it.'

One-all – The Equaliser! Gee was out for the count.

But then he saw something again, something a little out of the ordinary. It bounded around the room like a firework that had been let loose indoors. His head followed it around instinctively, as far as it could go, up until the point when the thing just disappeared.

'Guys, no joking around now, but I thought I saw some-thing… And that wouldn't be for the first time tonight!' said Mark in even tones.

'And not for the first time in your life neither.'

'Shut the heck up Gee,' Sash roared indignantly, turning on Gee suddenly. 'What do you mean Kid?'

'Oh, come on, he's been smoking too much sh–'

'What do you think you saw Mark?' Elena cut in, boldly. 'I keep thinking that I've seen something too – a pair of eyes or something. But this time though I thought I saw – '

'I think I had that too, Elena!' It was Alisha's turn now. 'I told you not to invite those basehead friends of yours, Gee… Mark… cos it's the smoke that's affecting our brains – or yours more like it.'

The Dark Girl receded into denial quickly: 'Don't forget how long it took for you to come off that stuff, guys! Now see what it's doing – it's driving us all mad…I mean its making me real tired.'

Bold words aside, even Alisha couldn't shrug this one off. That cold, clammy feel that the room seemed to hold, especially for her, seemed to be getting worse. Nonetheless, she carried on with her brave oration defiantly, unfortunately, without the full complement of brain-cells to match.

*

Details of the European Union were expounded in depth, with apt guidance from Alisha for anyone wishing to discover its soon-to-be chieftain, the so-called Antichrist, also known as the "Man of Perdition". She made mention of his main man, whom she called "the False Prophet", and the Mark of the Beast which she was adamant was about to sweep the currencies of the world.

Forget any story about some demon-possessed kid called Damien with some whacking great stamp on his head, who walks around looking like an *eejit*, this was the real deal man, totally exclusive, courtesy of Alisha.

In the short time available she also managed to rustle up other meaningful tit-bits, so that the fear of God could be instilled somewhat more rigorously into her overly-flippant cronies. She moved deeper, as the rhythmic pulsation of beats increased, and she stripped away the remaining layers of confusion, lest anyone should still be in doubt; lest anyone should not yet dread as they ought. She then delved into the hellish realms of death, drawing on the vivid imagery laid down by both Dante and Baxter, the latter of whose writings seemed far more convincing to her friends, judging by the comprehensive silence of the Syndicate.

There was no let up either as her brusque speech took them onto future wars, future famines, future pestilence, future... fuckeries – she'd forgotten who the other horseman was but it was all good anyhow! The gang listened on, terrified witless by what they were hearing. Her ingenious method of blending hocus-pocus with prophecy was absolutely tantalising to the ear, even if there and then, they didn't wholly appreciate either.

'...I tell ya guys, he's gonna head up the European Community in a few years time and he's gonna run it as a despot... I mean,' she clarified, whispering more guardedly this time, 'they've already got your individual details on a big, powerful computer in Brussels, called "The Beast" funnily enough, and that means everyone being born around these parts, in these days...'

No words are sufficient to describe the horrible feeling of insecurity that promptly swept over the crew. There was no movement amongst the ranks.

'...And I ain't lying either,' The Versifier reaffirmed. 'You know that much too don't ya Gee?'

'All this, on some big fuck-off computer... in Belgium?'

Somewhat predictably, there was no favoured response.

'Listen to yourself girl,' chided Mark, 'at least if you're gonna tell a story, let it make sense!'

The Kid cracked up at his own lyrics, and Sash and J-J also thought that it had been quite well done.

'Then he's gonna confirm the peace treaty with Israel,' Alisha rallied, undeterred. 'A seven year thing – but that's not gonna last too long. It's going to be very short in fact, and very, very tragic, believe you me. All the signs you're now seeing are birth pains, as it were, like all the troubles you hear about in the Middle East...'

'Oh shut yer mama up, Alisha; you don't even know where the Middle East is!'

'Yeah, right J-J. She'd think it was the middle end of Deptford or something.'

'All very funny I'm sure, but it does get worse after this.'

Silence.

'Why?'

'Shut the hell up, Elena!'

'No Sash, I want to know!' She rounded on Alisha. 'Why 'Leash? Why does it get worse after this?'

'For two reasons girl:

'Firstly, because what was the Soviet Union, together with all her Arabian allies of Northern Africa and the Middle East is gonna attack Israel.'

'So?' Elena asked, rather simplistically. 'Shit happens there all the time.'

'Well this time dear, the Good Ol' Ruskies are gonna be wiped out by the hand of...' Thunder erased the last part of her chilling discourse.

'Secondly, leaving aside Global Recession, Earthquakes and Pestilence for a second, (and about another million things cleverly concealed behind A Thousand Points Of Light) – cos there's no end to all of your woes people – the Antichrist is gonna make everyone have a chip on their right hands or upon their foreheads; because everyone who's left is gonna be made to swear allegiance to the Beast and submit their entire will to him, as though he was God.

'And it's even gonna carry very important financial, medical and other personal details – all that kind of stuff – so that no one will be able to buy or sell anything without those chips... That means that everyone, more or less, has to have the chip – that's if you're gonna wanna live, that is. Even though most people at that time probably wont want to be alive.'

'So what does that mean then exactly?'

The fact that Alisha's head swayed gently as a daisy on the wind to the easy groove of "Superstar" made little difference to the naiveté of the youngster. But then that was the girl for you; Baby-E was often the least wise at times like these, and therefore, the least inclined to panic in any given situation...

'Is that going to be like a brilliant advance in technology or something?'

Alisha responded in patent disbelief; 'My dear child, you haven't really been listening have you? You haven't really been following the thread of my argument!' Everyone laughed coarsely. 'An advance in modern technology it may be, girl, and well you say it, but what it really means,' she stated solemnly, brushing the dust off of her blazer, 'is that there shall be no such thing as liberty anymore!'

All eyes were set intently upon Alisha.

'You mean like "Enemy of the State"?'

'Worse!'

'Big Brother?'

'Worse!'

'How much worse?'

'There shall be no freedom left whatsoever. None!' Alisha pronounced gleefully. 'Furthermore my dears, whoever takes His Number – as the Books call it – will have sworn their devotion to him… So – and here it comes now – you… sorry, they… They shall each have sworn to his or her own private portion amongst the Eternally Damned.'

'Simply put then?'

'That means curtains already. Kinda like, "See ya, and I wouldn't wanna be ya".'

After a short pause, in which the music again seemed to cut out, it was Elena again who piped up enough courage to get a most important point clarified.

'Well… er… what do you mean Big, Cuddly Sis? "Curtains"?'

'Curtains means that all y'all will burn in Hell forever! But that's okay, cos this girl is not gonna be around to see it!

'So how about we all get some sleep now?…'

*

> *"For those who do not believe these things*
> *Shall receive these things*
> *But their cries shall not be heard.*
> *And all of those who despise the truth*
> *Shall be kept in lieu*
> *Not to be bereft… of the Second Death!"*

*

He decided that it was not yet time for a full-scale confrontation. Instead, he travelled southwards at the speed of thought, arriving quickly at the tunnel in only a matter of seconds.

There was one over in South London. It had been in operation a long time. Situated in Blackheath for reason of the plagues that had swept Western Europe over half a millennium ago, it is required nowadays for the huge number of souls expected to descend to the gaols below. In former times, the funnels already in place had proved insufficient for the increasing volume of human traffic; hence, this latest one had been added.

Pirates, countrymen, highwaymen, and other notorious vagabonds, and indeed those who had roamed the streets in confidence, without deference to custom or the law, had been requested by the Gods of Daearawd to visit the holds buried deep within the earth's mantle. So the command for an extra passageway was made soon after the Black Scourge of those days, lest the rush to the gaols should erupt once again, and its Keepers be caught unawares. Now it was the turn for Old Red Eyes to traverse those gates, as he had before him a most important date.

In size, the entrance was comparable to a whirlwind perhaps even that of a tornado. The different layers spun around and around constantly, resembling a child's top in precession. But they were much larger and seemingly more abrasive. It was there that Red Eyes passed into the interior blanket of gloom, as he moved his lissom form back into real-time, until his soul energy was conjoined to his surroundings.

Inside, the tunnel walls were thick, and they housed living forms of all kinds. Within the bubbling mortar there were ugly creatures of many foul designs. Some vacillated to and fro as lone organs with tentacles that stretched far beyond their structure; others gave birth to spores, it seemed, which quickly grew to become sprites with no set contours. Beneath the dusk-coloured ether there were hives of putrid activity, and this was at the place where the conscious met briefly with the non-venial, the spot where the vilest rancour was spewed out in continuos reams, too awful to describe. But the messenger appeared to welcome it all. Indeed, the sodden passages of filth and grime and the broken hands of those who were dead to their natural body seemed to have little effect on him. Nor did the shrieks of dire pain, which seemed to faze him little.

He ventured through the smell of rotting flesh, an ache too difficult to describe by those not in the midst of a pestilence or by those who have not yet tasted the scourge of war. But nothing could bring him revulsion. Even the fragrance of the fallen dead, which rose through the scattered bones and filled layer upon layer of compacted soils, up until the gates of the Highwayman's Lodge near to the green vales of the Common, did not trouble him. Nor indeed the icy grip of the tentacles which spread outwards upon the surface above. None could prevent those reins from gathering in all those who should have been attendant at the Feasting of the Dead. So all those without the Mark of Fidelity upon their scalps, or without the protection of a Man from the North, lay within its reaches.

Back below the surface, the nauseating reek of rotting garbage mingled readily with the harsh stink of excrement to produce a noxious smell, not easily recapitulated in earthly terms, save at the bottom of the Dead Sea. Decay was also present, coming in the form of damp humus, sodden leaves and animal corpses, all severely blighted; as too was destruction. The tunnel soon opened out into a conduit composed of rows of higher life forms, but all this was evident only as the screams for clemency became more zealous, the denizens of the caves yowled, the heat of the mortar intensified.

With each new step a more unsavoury scene was unfurled. All of these, however, are wisely concealed from the eyes of men, lest their hearts should faint before time. There was an abundance of grey, dusty matter, few of which still had the semblance of life left within their cloisters. They dropped past the voyager with increasing rapidity, just as he sought to find the correct egress out of those accursed plains. The cries were ugly, the torments were foul, the victims were twofold; there were those there who had never known what it is to love; others, more noble in *gradd*, were there for some minor infraction of The Master's rules.

Whoever they were, neither was ever likely again to see the light of day; not unless by the end of their torments someone from above, that is to say from the lands beneath the *Seren*, with boldness and a befitting mandate, had called them forth to occupy; and even then chances were slim and fraught with uncertainties. But rare was it for any of The Embodied Ones from the World Above to disturb Death's final encampment, even as those below preferred not to trouble the resting-place of the Oreads. Instead, most opted to walk the paths of the dead for themselves, that is until it was yet their time to come to this perpetually dark haunting ground.

*

Now it was Alisha's turn to the feel the wrath of the mocked. The impression of a cold, callous hand passed over her broad-bowed shoulders. Its lifeless animations sent quagmires towards her reason, and presently it stopped her monologue dead in its tracks.

'What's wrong baby?'

Gee wiped his hand over his forehead, removing some of the excess sheen that had collected above of his Vaseline-intensive lips.

'Don't stop like that girl, cos you're scaring the kid and the rest of the gang. Man, you even got me a bit worried too now. Seriously though Alisha – baby girl – what's going down with all of this beef? Is there something the matter, or are you just playing?'

The rest of the gang too was passionate in their nods of acquiescence, but to no avail.

Sash, however, panicked: 'Gee, the fool, was only messing with you before. He weren't really cussing you out or nothing. And you know that init 'Leash? Because you know we all love you, cos we're the crew Alisha?'

'Yeah, the Kings and the Queens.'

Again, the rest of the gang nodded vehemently. Her words had stopped as they had wished, her breath was laboured, as they had been praying for, but it was the way she just sat there and tottered which marked the gang out for anxiety.

'So why did you stop all of a sudden? I mean, we didn't do nothing bad. And why are you swaying like that for… What's wrong with – '

'I've just had the strangest feeling!' Alisha replied, cutting in deeply.

The background hum of the freezer compartment was evident.

'So, are you gonna tell us then or what?' J-J queried, reaching for the remote control, hitting the pause button. 'Or do we – '

'…Just sit here and brick it?'

'Mark, I've just had the feeling of a strong sense of evil present. I can almost feel it hovering somewhere. It's like a heavy curtain on stage, waiting to close at the end of a most extraordinary performance.' There was a subtle glint in her eye as her earlier chills were distanced, somewhat alarmingly, from her present recollections. 'It's seems – you know – oppressive and malevolent like… like something bad is in the air… something horrid in fact. J-J – can't you feel it too?'

'*Male*-what?'

'What are you going on 'bout bitch? What did she say?' cried Gee, full of exasperation. Quickly, he turned on his friends; 'Male-what, Sash?' But the blank expressions said it all.

'Malevolence,' said Alisha, back on top.

'So what? Shall we call it quits for the evening then? I mean, only if you really want to…'

*

He moved on through the dim passageways through where arms reached out from lifeless forms to seize travellers as they passed by their way. All hoped that somebody, someday, would dislodge them from their sticky abode and from the interminable worms.

Deep in the chamber of horrors were macabre monstrosities, pleading for mercy, and the dark denizens were there to torment them. Many of the forms were torn from top to bottom; all were ravished by disease and many were afflicted by the misery of their captors. Over time, Red Eyes was finding that many more now were dysfunctional with grief, more than in the Olden Days. Perhaps it was for the huge increase in numbers, or was it for the fact that time offers no remedy for these prisons, as the curses within its abhorrent bounds are renewed everyday?

He gave little thought to the flesh writhing amid the pitiful cries of sorrow. Even he, if he were constrained to the walls within the depths of the fire-holds for every hour of every day of every year, though he would be loth to admit it, might turn a shade paler. Nevertheless, the grim yelps continued, the soundings were made worse, the messenger continued on in his walk.

Darkness enveloped the fleeting form like the waters which cover a diver when he casts himself off from a great height. He saw the subdued – those that had been there since a time out of mind; and he saw those smitten to the last, those who passed their seasons by counting time. But these were The

Foolhardy. For it is known wisdom not to be able to bring infinity down to a mere zero in a finite space, or otherwise, by which time it was hoped that all numbering would be finished, all tortures ended, all bitter crimes committed in the past life, forgotten. And what is more: most of the newer inmates clung on to this hope for up to one hundred years or more. After that spell however, having been cocooned in shells fixed by mucus-type membranes, they too tended to succumb to the inevitability of unending evil.

The moans were unrelenting, young voices were hoarse, the aged were cowered. Widows plucked lecherous creatures from their withered flesh. There was much shrieking in those parts of the dungeons, as it was the sole medium for unleashing any personal anguish. And this was one of the few things that would not be denied them, until the day they had run out of breath, that same day when they could issue their last forlorn sigh no longer. Then would a new day dawn, in the pitch-blackness of the gaols.

Many a soul would be driven insane by the prolonged nature of events. Fell tortures repeated over and over again, without recourse for remedy. That is a bad situation to be in. The worst. Red Eyes had just passed through the gateways which lead to the place called "Unmöglich Zu Verstehen" which in other tongues mean "The Impossibility of Reason".

*

Saliva dribbled down the corners of Gee's mouth, reaching his chin long before either one of his hands could. He looked past Alisha and saw the little ornaments in the half-opened wall-cabinets, and then the remaining forage of chicken wings, dry-roasted peanuts, crisps and all the other shit, all of which he presently hated, most of which lay strewn by the side of the washing basin. Then he saw the flat, lifeless cola, and in his present mindset it seemed to resemble a small foetus which has been carved up alive and placed into a black wastepaper bag, dead, to be housed amongst all the other discarded slime. Kind of like how he was now feeling, knowing that he'd been had by Alisha of all people. The thought of it was enough to make him feel sick.

'I think this is a good time to end this nice chat,' suggested Elena. 'Don't you think guys?'

'Yeah!' J-J's reply was instant. 'I reckon that's about enough for me tonight. Time to turn in. Thanks for nothing gang, but I think we all need some rest, so I'm heading off to bed. No offence or nothing, Alisha, but I hope you don't feel offended me not thanking you for your contribution. Good night!' With that she stormed off through to the kitchen.

Mark, stole a glance towards J-J, then cast his eyes upon Gee. He didn't in the least bit like the whimpering wreck he saw in front of him – I mean a nigga tall and mean and built like a brick shithouse whipped like a chief. It was not a good night for the brothers. Besides, J-J was a far more seductive sight anyway.

'Right, that's it for me too because I'm leaving. I've had enough of all this! And take it from me, Alisha, it *is* personal. You're born, you live, and then you die, and sooner rather than later if you're lucky – and if you get really lucky, you don't get to meet any *friends* like you guys in the first place!' He sprung up from his seat.

'I'm off to get some sleep now because I – and that's me, personally – have had enough.' He passed along the corridor muttering strange curses into the early morning ether.

'Gee,' Elena said, 'I think that J-J might have something there. So how about we all chill out a little while, and get some rest?'

The look on Gee's face, though, was tinted with uncertainty: give in like his pale-skinned, yellow-bellied, blue-footed companions?

Although the Syndicate as a whole were undoubtedly sceptical about the very idea of good and evil powers, or the notion of ghouls and ghosts or goblins and Little Green Men from Outer Space, something grave had definitely altered in the air – of that there was no doubt. Whatever it was though, now was definitely not the time to be enquiring.

'A'ight beau, let's kick back a while then yeah?'

So they all soon followed suit, Sash, Elena, Gee and even Alisha as they accompanied their friends to their early morning bunkers. But not without that extra organ of tissue which they held by their sides always – just in case things did take a drastic turn for the worse. Then their mobiles would become their last port of call with the outside world!

*

Over the course of the worlds there were a few who had been granted visiting rights to some of the prison's less repellent districts. Afterwards, they were compelled to return again to the lands of their birth. These ones were seldom brought under the compulsion to stay, as their forewarning was more useful to those without the gaols than those, lost, within. However, these things were a rarity, an almost nil-occurrence; because for most of those arriving, it was for keeps. Their stay was completed only when the sands of time had run dry, the lands had become flooded, the skies were tinged by that demon-draig Death; when Beelzebub is bound to an heavy boulder and cast deep into the Bottomless Pit. In the unlikely event that all was to be achieved in the selfsame moment.

Sometimes though there were other degrees of suffering which the captives could endure; from the abominable, which roughly equate to the foulest tortures that one might receive whilst upon Daearawd or any of the Other-

worlds (though over an infinite period), to the downright indescribably heinous. All the ones mentioned within these records, however, are those which
lie at the fairer end of the spectrum, as words cannot adequately describe the
damnation that awaits those who, whilst they made their journey upon either
of the Higher-plains, went out of their way to do wickedness. But to mark this
occasion was a judiciously secluded place known as the "Fun Arena".

*

The landscape was bland with rocky ridges, sharp incisions, and huge boulders carved from the mountainside. Seas of fiery blood scooped up much of
the loose topsoil giving the scenery the appearance of a dusty, accursed land-
fill, which had been set to the flame and torched, leaving behind a reek so foul
that even many of its demons reckoned it toil not to spew.

Many also resided beyond the murky shadows of The Hill, which is an
infamous site for torments, torture, and degradation, and many were the years
spent sampling the darker enigmas of this space. Some had been born in the
Early Days before any of the deeper mysteries were ever made known, but of
these, most had failed to recognise the wisdom of life, even though it had been
fully laid down as touching the dispensation of that day. Instead, they received
only the foolishness which they were born into and shunned the recognised
predilection of the hour.

Then the predictable followed: dark desires, grave misdeeds, Grievous
Death. Thus, many were eventually killed, cold, so that they came directly to
this warm place; not of grace or indeed of healthy abiding, it must herein be
added, but Fate's penultimate gate. Red Eyes however was interested in none
of this, for he now had an important date to keep; and that most precious of
commodities, time, was gradually slipping away.

*

The Prince of Darkness himself had entered in from above the Main Descent.
There, several of his servants were awaiting their master's passing. They
bowed their stooped haunches lower still as the footsteps of the darkened figure pattered past them. Others, not so mighty in stature, recoiled from the
scene in terror. Even the walls themselves seemed alive, like a dreaded accumulation of vices strung together for a fitting judgement. They too soon
receded at the ominous presence of evil.

Gloomy lights filtered through to the barren precinct and reflected off the
chains binding some of the latest prisoners. Hundreds of moth-eaten forms
were being dragged deeper into the foulest segment of The Heart, which was
the epicentre of evil, through murky shadows and the ungodly avenues that

lay some way beyond the Carnivores' Caverns. Shortly, the first of these souls was to undergo his initiation. And the hospitality that was to be rendered him would be to the same degree as that which he administered when he had dwelt Above; save for that its magnitude, as one would reasonably expect, would be amplified to an untold degree.

Nevertheless, his misery would also be to the very last, as would be his pains also. But it was the same for all those who passed through the walls bordering The Heart, until the Times of Destruction. It was then that its inhabitants were granted temporary reprieve for Judgement Day, before being found guilty and cast for eternity into the Lake of Fire.

Alas, for their condemnation was already set! And the latter state would be far worse than their former. At that time therefore, anyone not called of Nef would perish alongside their gaolers in the engulfing acrimony of flames. But not even then were their torments ended, but they shall then alter, taking on the similitude of a differing, though much darker kind.

*

Nearby, there was another form belonging to that of a woman. She was now in the process of reaping her rewards for the walk she had made whilst traversing the plains of Daearawd. Even as second by second, minute by minute, hour by hour, day by day, week by week, month by month, and year by year, had conspired, so cruelly, to pass her by, she had also given scant credence to the charge that had been maintained so delicately within her bosom.

So after such a long time it was this thing, more than anything else, which had sealed her present fate; although it was not aided by the fact that she had helped to secure the same ill passage for a great many others, including her cousin, her son, his woman. Now was time for her to register before the Dark Lord of the Six Armies, who is also called "Conqueror of the Fallow Lands", and to lay all of her assets before her new, permanent masters. Now was the time to swear to his allegiance, so that what she had truly been struggling for, so hard, for up until the very closure of her being, which occurred at the beginning of her fifth decade, might come to pass.

Nevertheless, when she had realised that Death was finally upon her, she had striven with fearsome resolve to reject the merciless advances of the Grim Reaper, that harbinger of ill tidings. Her eyes had been opened at that very instant and she had seen four fit men dressed in black scales. They had skin so hard and thoughts so callous that she understood them to be from Annwfn. Then came a fifth, squat-faced, twice as hideous, with a scythe in his hand and bulbous-blue eyes, who was called by Qädesh, the sixth; then she knew that they had come from Uffern.

So out came the chains they had borne in anticipation for a long time, which then caused her to stir from her vain imaginations, and from her kinsman. But it had all been just that little bit too late. For she was captured and taken away, passing briefly through scenes of The Earth, and haunting some alongside her captors, as ghostly apparitions of some talent. However, after another short spell a second bell was struck, she was summoned, the chains were yanked. Then she came through the Hole to her present environment.

After this space she shall be relocated, to a place where neither age, sex, nor any other fickle emotion bear well with her tormentors. There, they would restrict neither the quantity nor the quality of her misfortunes. Notwithstanding, she was one of the negligible few who might one-day be removed to Annwfn, to re-clothe her form, and equip her for additional torments in the Other-world, or so was the word across the Aetherbelt. Therefore, before her final years of drudgery in these dungeons and prior to being cast into the Lake of Fire, she might one-day, again, see the setting sun…

*

Her eyes glazed over so that she failed to notice the foul beings that had once again come in to surround her. Not that she could do anything to prevent them anyway. Even her heart, which had long since stopped, seeing that she was dead, continued to breed horror into the rest of her corrupted form. Meanwhile the dying embers of The Lost, who were rotted but not yet withered away, continued to rise all about her in time for their subsequent humiliations.

She could feel the worms crawling through her flesh, as though she had not really parted from her previous existence at all; the one that she now bitterly realised had been based on so many transient sensations. It was an uncanny feeling of despair, and it was one which she hoped she would never have to come to terms with. Moreover, because she had left her former life with that ailing heart, which had been so crippling for the last few years of her life, she now found herself in custody with the very same ailments. The power to heal her was now lacking, as was mercy, and even the mention of the word "love" within the darkness of these fell confines brought about swift retribution with pitchforks, stones, fires, and spells, the like of which can only be alluded to in person.

Her hunch-backed assailants drew closer to her near-pensioned skeleton. Without ever sensing the hurt they would undoubtedly cause her and oblivious to the pain she had already been forced to endure, they approached her with selfish intentions in mind. She remained where she was, her hands folded in penitence, her heart beating vigorously, and trapped, which made it easier for the first blows to find their mark.

Presently also, a squat-faced creature laid aside his scythe for the moment, before his duties were scheduled to resume upon the surface of the World

Above. He climbed on top of her, moving his bulbous-blue-eyed head closer to her withered visage. Then he, too, bit *lovingly* through her tight, scrawny neck…

The Prince passed them by, though not without making some cursory notes of his own. In the darkness of his evil mind he sealed away the times and dates when he would afterwards return to that place, to exact retribution upon the soul who was just beginning her first few days in Torments. And he would not forget, especially her, whom he hated much, just as he never forgot; and never ever would. Even as now The Bitch was all but completely forgotten.

*

They awoke with a start a little while before dawn.

'What's the time peeps?'

'It's a quarter to five,' Elena said in response to J-J's question. 'At least, that's what I think it says!'

'Oh come on guys!' Alisha moaned, allowing her eyelids to flutter open. She was still hungry, although not for the culinary delicacies of the Thai Pot, or for the excellent meats offered at the Mongolian Barbecue (which were their favourite downtown restaurants). At present, she had a different craving.

'If y'all don't mind, I'm going back to sleep. Is that all right people?'

Although she found it difficult to forget all the previous times when Gee and the gang had riled on against what she held dear, she couldn't bring herself to wake up properly. Because she was mashed, he was finished, and the rest gang just didn't seem to give a damn. Why not just lie there and soak it all up? This, she was willing to do; that is up until the moment when Gee opened his big trap, for one last time.

'A-Yo 'Leash, so are you finished?'

'Yeah, I do feel kinda tired to be honest.'

'I mean like your man, Gee-suss,' hooted Gee, as his entourage cracked up at the cruel jest.

'Oh Gee man, that's just too much man, that's like blasphemy and shit!'

'But it was funny weren't it?'

'Oh my man, I didn't know you had it in you.'

'I'll take that as a complement Sash, thank you.'

'Not a problem ma-black-hombre, not a problem. Just check Alisha's face. Her juice has gone blud!'

'There's enough of that…'

'Too true boss.'

'Shut up Gee, leave her alone. You're such a dog you know that?'

All faces peered round to observe Elena.

'It's okay, girl, I can handle this one myself,' Alisha scowled.

The eyes were promptly back onto the preacher. Then an outward smile of an inward grace scrawled itself upon her face; because she looked a cross between Jack Nicholson as "The Joker" and The Black Mother Mary herself. Sucker was gonna get it this time.

'So Gee, and all y'all; yeah, you are right, he did die. But do y'all remember last time when I told you that it was probably a night much like this when he died, you know, when people actually came out of their graves and went into King David's City…'

Another summery glint was quickened to her eye.

'Yeah but – '

'Anyway – sorry to cut you J-J – but we believe that he died and descended into Hell for three days and three nights, the same amount of time Jonah was in the whale – all in the spirit of the season, you know… And in the spirit of the millennium too, if you ask me. Though if you remember what I said last time, it didn't end there now did it?'

The puzzled faces peered back blankly at her.

'Because he conquered the Devil and all of his demons whilst he was down there,' Alisha resumed, 'for you and for me.' Judging by the sardonic hue upon each of the faces about her, perhaps what was needed was a little more elaboration.

'You know guys, those big, massive, ugly beasts, and those small impy things; those evil ghosts that no one really wants to talk about, especially not on a night like this. Demons – y'all have heard of them haven't you? Well…'

The resurgent gale blew stronger than at the fore, bringing the walled cutlery hanging up inside the kitchen to an unsettling rattle. Spoons clinked against forks and forks clattered against knives, and the knives, which had been readied for earlier use, tumbled haphazardly onto the floor. They carved gory swathes in the dank atmosphere as they fell.

From upstairs, the creaking sound of the roof rafters was heard to descend, whilst further forces continued to rise against the buckled wood, causing it to give way slightly for the fury of the oncoming winds. The old oaken timber frames arched inwards, the inanimate neurosis of nested guardians bending forwards to hear their every uttered word. Then, perhaps, power might be gleaned from each one's fear and from every act of folly and futility.

Theirs, however, was a fruitless existence, as corrupt as decayed wood that was fit only for the pyre. It always had been, since the days of The Fall, and from there on in it always would be.

A sudden twinge struck the storyteller sharply, hitting her sides, while the unleashed roaring of the elements doubled backwards into the wind-strewn streets beyond. She grabbed instinctively for her exposed ribcage to soothe the motion of the scalpel, and she tugged up the jacket covering her well-protected sides. All too quickly the feeling was gone, leaving hardly enough time for consideration.

The coloured thespian straightened her posture, the psychosomatic occurrence not weakening her stance in the least bit.

'As I was saying, Jesus set all of his believers free…'

'Alisha – I don't know how to say this without offending you too much – but enough *already*! Do you at least understand that much or are you *completely* fucked-up in the head?'

She blanked Jema-Jane one-hundred percent.

'All those who looked forward to him coming like Abraham, David, and The Patriarchs, were expecting a place in his kingdom,' she explained further, 'because afterwards, when he'd finally cleared out Paradise from next to The Pits – '

'What Pits?'

'Shut up Elena, I don't wanna know.'

'But…?'

'Nope! Don't encourage her,' Gee stated firmly, turning on Alisha. 'Because we're not listening to this shit! You're just trying to wind us up – can I get an "AMEN" to this fellas?'

Silence, again.

'Guys?'

The silence this time though was more stoical than anything.

'Chaps at least? My fellow k-kings?'

'As I was saying,' Alisha resumed, 'he rescued them from Paradise, which used to be situated next to The Pits themselves, believe it or not. Can you imagine that; all those screams of torment and torture with fires sweeping past twenty-four-seven, all year-round…? Man, kinda like forever! Makes your mind boggle don't it?' They looked at her in blatant disbelief. 'All y'all feel free now to speak what's on your heart.'

'Look, Alisha, you're speaking as though these places are real,' Sash offered, somewhat half-heartedly. 'Now we know what you're trying to do – and it didn't work last time so it's not gonna work this time either. But now enough's enough girl, so give it a break would you!'

'It's true Alisha, nice try but – '

'Yeah, we'll admit it, you had us going there for a minute.' The clamouring came from Gee. 'Well-done girl! But I's not gonna be fooled by a foolish man's fuckeries – '

'Bollocks Gee!' exclaimed Sash suddenly. 'You're not half full of it sometimes Gee; why don't you just admit it – she had you well and truly man. I mean, I saw how you began sweating a while back, so give it up won't you Gee?'

'Shut up ya *eejit-Indian*.'

'Shut up yourself you big, black mama,' exclaimed Sash. 'I'm only a half-Desi. And what has that got to do with anything anyway?'

Although it was sometimes something of an effort for her to maintain her charades, Alisha did so for the sake of him who had seriously insulted her. Deep, deep down, she was made of much sterner stuff; sure she was – and she had only just started. There was plenty of time for her to be getting her own back.

'Now the Satanists,' rejoined Alisha, above the noisy fidgeting coming from Elena's direction, as if to say:

> *"Drive carefully, entering children's area.*
> *Please spare the kids.*
> *I'm actually begging you now…"*

'*Some* Satanists, I should say, reckon that it was the Devil himself that captured Jesus, when he went down to Hell for those three days, and that, even till this day, The Lord remains chained to some big rock, frying near the Belly of Hades somewhere. Ever since the Armies of Heaven tried to overrun their master in a take-over coup of The Underworld, they think that he…' Again she remembered Elena. Unfortunately though, the memory faded fast.

'…has held dominion over The Earth, and over all the Universe. Almost makes sense when you see all the evil that's in the world, don't you think Gee…?'

At length she did conclude, although not without reducing her young female companion to the verge of tears.

'But that didn't happen now did it?'

No one was prepared to answer her. Indeed, no one dared utter even a syllable.

At length Alisha spoke again. 'People, are you going to answer me then or what…?' Still all remained quiet. 'Well say something at least, or you'll make me want to explain it all over again!'

Alisha waited a while in the utmost silence, observing their solemn faces and their rather frayed nerves, until she knew that she had them. Then she waited until they knew that she knew that she had them. She waited again, until she knew that they knew that she knew that she had them. Then she waited a little longer still, just in case.

'Other worlds Alisha!' Mark burst in, after waiting a tiny bit longer than the rest of them. He rejoined the rest of his companions.

'What about other worlds? Do you believe in other planets and shit like that?'

Alisha looked almost exasperated.

'It's gotta be said Markie – and all credit to yourself – cos you've got a knack of employing your gilt-edged mouth in getting *your* friends out of trouble.'

'No, really, I am interested,' he persisted. 'Besides, they're your friends too, aren't they?'

'Sometimes you have to wonder.'

'Anyway, like I was saying, what do think about Area 51 and someshit, an' all those sightings of aliens in New Mexico; at least I think it was New Mexico. And what about Atlantis, Black Magic Practitioners, Crop Circles, David Blaine, Derren Brown, Dynamo, Psychic Surgery, Psychic Travel, Telepathy – and my man Uri "The Spoon-bender" (or Mindbender)?' His query brought on a few nervous laughs from the guys.

'And *Vampyres*, Zombies and all the rest of that jazz. What do you folks believe about all of that stuff, hey Sash...? Oh yeah, and what about that other thing – you know, when somebody (or some *poor*-body I should say), explodes, just like that?'

There were a few icy grimaces, but nothing Alisha couldn't handle.

'Good point! – Spontaneous Human Combustion that's called,' Sash cited. 'And do we believe in aliens by the way?'

The new speaker was quick to recalculate what he should have said.

'I meant, er... do *you* er, believe in that sort of thing?'

Everyone looked intently at the tan-brown face of Mr Duplicitous. He corrected himself once again, shifting agitatedly towards his cushions.

'What I meant to say was that, do you, as in Christians I mean, believe in aliens from other planets... Or any of that kind of thing... Y'know?'

'Well Sash,' Gee retorted emphatically, 'you'd better go now and start asking all of them, hadn't you Bro?'

'Shut up Gee or I'll slap the black off o' you.'

'I'd love to see you try, Desi. You couldn't even bitch-slap a baby!'

'What I mean is that can't you be serious for a change?'

'No!' said Gee Funk scornfully.

Anyway, he managed to receive a couple of surreptitious giggles, which is what he lived for; one from Elena and the other actually came from Alisha herself.

'Come on boys sort it out. Why don't we at least try to act like adults?'

'Yeah, 'Leash, as if you know.'

'May the Lord help us!'

'Again, nice thought Alisha, girl. But judging by the things you've just said, even if he did we still wouldn't stand a chance...'

$\boxed{S}$ PIEGEL $\boxed{S}$ PIEL

Not everyone who says to me, 'Lord, Lord,' shall enter the
kingdom of heaven,
But he who does the will of my father in heaven.

MATTHEW 7:21

Now the saying "Occupy till I come" applies only to those who still have breath in their bodies, blood in their veins, to those whose eyes may still see the glorious colours of day. It does not apply to those who, through their wilful rebellion, have the Mark of the Lost upon their scalps. Nor does it apply to The Damned or the servants thereof or the demons who spend their time castigating man in his fallen state.

'My Lord! I have come to report, just as you have commanded me.'

'Yes, Mystery, report!'

'Master. I am under the Regent of London and have brought news of the group of heirs – the ones of whom you spoke, lord, even at the birth of these fools.'

'Ah... yes?' He peered deeper into his associate's blood-brilliant eyes.

'Master, we shall soon make them speak presumptuous words, of which you shall doubtless be pleased; words that shall render them *game* according to the guidelines laid down by The Ones Above,' drawled the black form. 'Indeed, I have some of my choicest servants up there now to ensure that all is completed in accordance with the Law, just as you have previously ordained of me, master!'

The voice soon faded into a low servile hiss.

'All as you have required, Master!'

'Good!' the other replied. 'Use the boy, the curious one, to ensure that all things go well, and I will reward you greatly. But also remember the proud one – not the black one, lest his innate wisdom override his present dearth of fear – but first use the other one, the one who does not believe in any of these things. Use the girl, the scientist, for I have marked her also for my attention...' The terrible rumble of burning masonry ate up his remaining words as more hapless bodies dropped in not even a few hundred yards from where they were standing.

'Of course master, I shall do exactly as you desire. For you alone are wise.'

46

The Master nodded his approval:

'Know for certain, however, that if you should fail me, Mystery…' The Other raised his arms abruptly; and from a short distance behind him the perfect mould of a human body appeared. He puffed his breath again, and the framework seemed to be given life. Animation was soon coming from her arms, legs, and torso, as The Master commanded the foul contrivance to dance alluringly before them.

'Observe, my slave, and watch closely…'

The messenger's eyes were allowed to settle upon her beautiful countenance, and he found himself observing her tantalising movements. A deep craving for wantonness soon swept over his repulsive frame. It was then that the Lord of Darkness dropped his arms again, in one fell motion.

'See, my slave…'

In a few moments a searing heat passed by the two evil forms, ripping ferociously into the flesh of the one beyond. The patsy shrivelled in a matter of seconds – a complete bodily meltdown, ultimately disappearing into fusty ash tracks, in this gross act of needless insanity. The rashness of the process delayed her anguished screams for the best part of a second, but they ceased altogether when the charred remains of that which could not be dissolved slumped forwards upon her ledge. Albeit, two clammy hands, with evil talons where fingers ought to have been, had been waiting for this barbaric act to be accomplished. They restrained the pulpy part of her flesh from falling away any further.

The empty carcass was quickly returned and she was thrust back into her gloomy cell for rejuvenation, and the remainder of a long and very painful night. The same death that she had just experienced would occur again in only a few hours time, in lieu of her wonderful services in an earlier life – she had once been a merchant peddling what The Ones Above called *Religious* Whoredom or Idolatry. Presently however, her services were no longer required, could no longer be employed, as her allocated time upon the Plains of Life had now come to an end. Her maggot-laced purple robe was placed back upon the nape of her neck; and for the present came the agonising feat to rest.

'Slave?'

'Yes master, I understand perfectly well. I understand you very well indeed.'

Mystery's heart… no his inner soul, pounded frantically inside his throbbing chest. But he did not manage to quench its storm before a company of worms had savaged all the remaining cinder. And this he did by subjugating the sprits within him.

'All shall certainly be as you wish O Great One.'

He bowed again, leaving the venue promptly by the way he had, not long before, entered. Now, however, he parted with the strictest sense of duty within his bosom. He was in no need for any more *subtle* demonstrations, particularly ones of this kind. Had he not been in his lord's service for long enough to know all the torments reserved wholeheartedly for those that opted to fail? He had no desire to see his spiritual form dismembered and the different parts of his body concealed in divers parts of The Arena. A colleague of his had been racked thus in times past and he had been forced to be a witness to it. Even now, if one listens carefully enough, one could hear the screams of this brutal-ised incubus above the ever-rising tumult of the gaols.

Before the next twenty souls had enlisted he was up upon Daearawd and moving swiftly towards the house that was currently under observation. He hastened quickly with his steps, as though each one might be his last, although he took time to consider the fraught breath that trickled away from his mouth. He moved lightly through the all-encompassing gloom, through the tunnels, and towards the sombre gloaming of doom.

*

The crazy vibes of "Doo Wop" were playing in the background; Alisha's face was paled (as much as it could anyway!); and now it was her turn to feel anx-ious. Because the tides had turned and now she was the one in the running. So, there was nothing left for it. Off came the breaches and out came the strained accent of the professional thespian.

'Now if there really was something *out-there*,' she rounded finely, donning her most prized voice, 'then I'm sure the Bible would have told us as much, don't you think, Mark?'

'So what, have you checked the Codes then?' queried J-J, cutting in.

Jema-Jane hated superstition, especially nonsense that bound people up in their foolhardy ways. Besides, she was as was supposed, a scientist, or at least a student scientist, and so there was no room for such mumbo-jumbo. She had checked out the paper on the Bible Codes (at Alisha's insistence) and her lecturers, somewhat grumpily, agreed that there might *not* be anything wrong with them after all. They didn't understand it, and after she had wasted ten minutes of their time, they hadn't wanted to; but it had been "…all rather interesting" all the same.

At that precise moment J-J woke up with a start, as if something had just inspired her.

'…That's if the Code is really there!'

'Safe blud, it's true!' added Gee. 'Wha'gwan with that shit?'

'What do you mean J-J?' asked Sash in rather more meaningful English. 'I thought that one of your boffins checked it out – '

'Hold on, Sash, wait a minute – think of it like this. *If* God really does exist, what makes you think that he would tell us anything anyway? I mean, come-on people! Don't you think that it's just a bit soft… all right, primitive if you like – or arrogant? I mean…' (The Syndicate always said that J-J never thought before she spoke, or that when she did think, it was just not worth the mentioning). 'Don't you think the whole thing is a bit of a cultural spook. You know – ' she hinted darkly, motioning towards Gee. 'Kind of like – well – you get me don't you…?'

Gee was flabbergasted.

'Yeah, so I'm black, but what gives. You saying that all of us are primates or what? Just stupid? Go on J-J, say what's on your mind or someshit!'

But without the slightest hint of alarm in her voice, J-J turned to Alisha:

'So what do you think girl? Don't you think that a lot of this stuff is for down and out people… and everything?'

Sure of herself as always, J-J didn't bother to await for some fastidious reply. Instead, she went over to the looking glass, above the richly dressed commode, which was panelled with fine cedar strips and lined with swathes of polished pine. She fixed her blouse somewhat more securely before examining the bags beneath her eyes.

'This is not good,' she said to herself, 'not good at all! Guys, I'm really tired.'

None of the boys were interested though. Mark looked at Gee, who was already sending coded signals straight to Sash. J-J's rump looked fine from where they were sat; she didn't need any sleep. So "The Old Boy" really did exist after all, *Thank you, Lord!*

'So…' Jema-Jane continued in a few moments, plucking an eyelash out from its root, which subsequently caused her bum to ripple, 'what do you think then? Is it all down to cultural spooks or not?'

Elena nudged hard at the leering fool Gee, almost breaking his ribs in the process.

'Sure J-J, cultural bogusness, primitive manners, pure arrogance; whatever you want baby. Whatever it is that you want!'

Of the other two boys it was Mark who had his tongue further out like a thirsty dog in search of nourishment. Cos he hadn't had a good fuck in time.

*

The dark smudges belonging to the skies evaporated gently, leaving the grey-auburn stratosphere behind it to sidle nature's first major conquest. It was these dregs of primordial light which sought to peer across the vast eastward oceans. Though some of the clouds had already departed some way laterally to disperse the longing gloom, a narrow path was formed in its midst, perhaps for the coming of an inbound voyager, as it sometimes happened. The stars albeit would not yet beat a hasty retreat, until the appearance of the imminent Sun God, who daily consumes all lingering shadows and all things that are formed in darkness.

Cold blasts of air ran concurrent to the emerging twilight. It played out its fanfare, like a tornado pounding down an old tin alley. Simultaneously, however, it thundered its rage against the shed door towards the rear end of the premises in question; but not before time had this come.

It was an old wooden shack of little value or consequence save for the polished metal hinges which were crafted in India on the estates of Mel's forefathers, the Saunders. But they now seemed cast in crumbling iron, which sometimes looked brown though at others, grey-white, for their great age. They had been in the family for each successive generation since they were first forged, and were similar to an amulet worn by the credulous. Nonetheless, these metal hooks were there to keep property and not preserve humans.

In a moment of time, the wooden portal swung open on its hinges. A slow, sullen creaking sound was released. Then came the clack-clacking sound, as of a woman's heels when she taps upon a church dance floor as she awaits the approach of her good-looking mate on a cold winter's eve. But the door, as the brooding minx, moved no further than arm's length in his direction; lest any of the darkness encased within should be made known to the forces outside. Instead, the frigid wooden encumbrance pondered a while where the flurry had taken it to rest. There it paused for a time so that, perhaps, before the ether came back again to seduce it and fling it onwards toward a new, grander world, it might flash another star-studded jewel in his direction. However, it was not the decrepit band of wood that was the main interest at present, nor was it the contents that was kept behind her flayed beams. Nor was it the amulet he had so generously bequeathed, generations ago, to Old Palmer Saunders.

Congeries of discarded litter were scattered thickly along the garden path, from the foot of the shed all the way along to the small rockery which housed the garden's gnomes, elves, and goblins. What an evil-looking patch it was too! It consisted mostly of rubbish thrown down from the bin in an earlier blustery rage, and as such, the space would make suitably for a foetid meal, fit only for stray hounds. Nevertheless, what soon manifested the cold, chilling sound creeping intentionally through the morning's dull echoes, was anyone's guess.

For hidden amid the trash were spent aluminium cans, useful only for recycling; the remnants of cheap soda water, which simply means that they were crass plastic bottles of no art or description. There were some to several pages of scattered newspaper, containing the information of a decaying and fucked-up world (which is there to make the reader feel better about his meagre lot in life); green-glassed bottles in which eyes ever peaked and about which heads ever swirled; plus a whole host of other things, although few more were worthy of a citation. Just the general rubbish that comes with any dark territory. Except, perhaps, for the scraping sound which provided accompaniment to his steps, as he danced his pattern along the littered path. He picked his way through strewn fish heads and gnawed chicken bones, and soft silver trays of emptied Indian takeaways.

The dance was nearing an end, the night was nearly spent, and the inviolate still needed to be corrupted. But what had started the music in the first place? Was it the branch of an elm tree that had keeled over to examine more intimately one of the lattice windows above? The wind playing kindly across her wooden hair? Or else what? Presently, however, the wind stopped. Without making any further utterance of its own, it left the restless can to stay peacefully where it lay – by the side of his buckled feet.

*

Inside, the foolish chatter resumed.

'So what was that again Mark, the thing you said earlier? Markie?'

'What do you mean?' he replied yawning widely, taking a few moments to reply.

'You know, about praying in the mirror backwards and stuff – was that a joke, yeah?'

He let loose another loud, smelly yawn, the foul stench of which was more than Sash could bear. It goes to show you that not even the gods were perfect!

'Close your gob, Farmer-boy.'

'Oh, sorry about that, Desi.'

'Mark? Did *you* hear me?'

'Yeah, sorry about that Elena,' he grunted. 'Yeah, I remember now. You see, when I was younger, I knew some geezer at school who was part of this really superstitious family. I mean, his brother used to come round sometimes and tell me some right fab stories, but then again he used to tell us some downright freaky ones too. Some of the things he would talk about though were just plain whack!' He looked over towards Alisha. 'Even by her standards.'

'Yeah, very funny *ma-bratha*!'

'Now though, some of the nonsense he talked about – and I'm not afraid to admit it,' Mark pronounced, squaring up audaciously towards Gee, 'some of it scared the shit out of me – and it would scare you too Gee before you start going on about it!'

'Tell us some of it then. Go on Markie, tell us one of those stories,' pleaded Elena. 'But don't try to frighten us! Because I wouldn't like that,' she added, as she snuggled up closer to her big, fluffy cushion. '...And Gee may start to cry!' she giggled.

Before Black could respond, Mark's fatigue was conquered, and his thoughts were reassembled.

'Well it goes something like this: my mate's brother came round one day, around Halloween time. This all happened quite a few years ago now. So he's speaking of where the holiday (holy-day, get it?) came from, and all the stuff they used to do; like kidnap virgins, and then slot them, before sacrificing them to their gods. To tell you the truth, some of the gory stuff he spoke about made me have nightmares for weeks on end afterwards, and I ain't too proud to say so.'

The Friends lounged back in their seats. This time, because the beef was coming from Mark and not Alisha, they took the story somewhat more seriously.

Thanks for the virgin...
Demons abroad!
Kinfolk back from the dead!
Have a Great Samhain!
Yours, Myrddin,
"The Druids' Head."

'Then they used to leave a pumpkin behind as payment.'

'You serious, Mark?'

'Dead straight, Gee!'

'Oh man! That's fuckeries!'

'But I won't even go there...

'Anyway, we move onto talking about spells, incantations and hexes. And Voksey – that's my mate's br'er – begins to tell me of things people can do themselves to gain more power. One of them was making a pact with the Devil; but he knew somebody who had done this, half-seriously, and he died at the age of twenty-four, just as he knew he would. He told me a whole heap of other stuff about this guy as well, but I didn't really wanna listen at that point because it was getting kind of late, and I needed to go out trick-or-treating. Oh yeah, and I had already pissed myself something silly!'

The girls began laughing at this. 'You're trifling,' one said.

'No, 'fraid not ladies...

'So he moves on next to this thing about mirrors. He said that if you say the "Our Father" backwards in a mirror then God would give you over to Satan and demons would come out and get you. "The Mirror Game" I think he called it; or "Playing with Mirrors" – one or the other.'

'You know anyone who's ever tried it then?'

'Have you, more to the point? You know, Mark, have you given it a go yourself?' Sash inquired.

But it was the naïve youngster who cut in again. 'I mean, really tried it Markie?'

'No guys. To tell you the truth, I've never had the bottle, and I don't care what people say!'

There was silence, and no obvious retort coming from either Sash or Gee.

'Well, go on then Markie, show us what you're made of. You're a little bit older now.'

Everyone looked around at J-J.

'Go on Baby, if you've really got as much *balls* as they say you have!' J-J said provocatively.

'Come on Jema-Jane, guys, don't be stupid!' Alisha was perturbed at the glazed look that had come quite suddenly over Mark's face. 'We may as well mess around with some silly little tarot cards or something, for the effect you're saying it would cause… or even those Oui-ja boards or something.

'And how many of you would really do that?'

'Well nothing's going to happen is it?' Mark chided. 'I think you'll find, my friend, that superstition died out a little while ago – with the dinosaurs... except maybe in Africa!'

It was spiteful shit from The Kid, but when it comes down to it, there was no way that a bloke was gonna risk looking bad twice in one day, especially not in front of the crew.

'Aw come on girl,' Mark resumed. 'At least this way we find out if God is real or not. Or if not God, then the Devil?'

'You guys just don't get it do you? You don't know the powers you're messing with. So why do you wanna test them? Have y'all gone mad or something?' Alisha made it over to the windows, through which she peered out into the gloomy skies.

'Gosh, if my family were here, they'd give you what for – they can tell you all sorts of stories – real too – about folk who've messed around with things they ought not to have.'

Nonetheless, her words were drowned out by the next angry deluge which was scheduled to arrive from the heavens at that precise moment. Alas, wise though the counsel was, it was cut short in mid-sentence.

Again she felt that cold chill within. Her body reeled involuntarily in an attempt to ride the implacable current besetting it, but the spasm was short-lived. It was momentary this time, although no less foreboding to her senses than the last. She scrunched her haunches as much as she was able, leaving her pre-natal instincts, birthed in Eve at the beginning, to carry her forwards from that point on in.

'Alisha baby, are you okay, cos the chaps don't reckon you look that great?'

'Oh thanks for that Sash… No, seriously, I think I'll be okay, I'm just lacking on the sleep front, you know how it is.' But for some strange reason, Sash didn't altogether believe her.

'So, has anyone else got anymore good stories?'

Sash carried on after a second or two; 'Then it looks like you've given the most compelling one yet Mark, matey.'

'So what?' crowed J-J. 'Has anyone got enough *cojones to* try it out then?' She looked around dubiously at her company. 'I believe then, that it's got to be me, init? I'll do it!' She gave Elena a sly wink.

'So what is it to be then, guys?'

It was not entirely her own fault that she failed to notice the heightened look of dismay that came from her two closest friends, because she, unlike the others, had already set her face like flint towards the mirror in her determination to disprove Markie's earlier challenge. Her friends just didn't seem energetic enough to respond.

She walked over towards the wall in question. Her stern face, pretty though it appeared, was now an aberration and her perfume was like the twisted scent of a skunk. Even so, once in front of the looking glass she began to recite, word by word and sentence by sentence, all that she could remember from a badly faded memory.

'*Amen…*'

*

He who digs a pit will fall into it,
And whoever breaks through a wall will be bitten by a serpent.

ECCLESIASTES 10:8

*

Whether or not he should actually visit The Gates was one thing, but laying down the gauntlet for the Chief of his foemen was an altogether more eminent affair. Such a bold act could not possibly fail to provoke a full-scale war.

His hairless face peered through the steamed windows, while his ears became attuned with the easy throbbing rifts of "Tell Him" – a song which he very much despised. Nonetheless, as any other *Black Man*, he couldn't help but bob his head to the pleasing melody of the drumbeat.

'He had better give me an audience this time,' the dark form rasped, turning away from the looming wall. 'Anyone with any foresight must see that this one's coming. These dolts are provoking the both of us to wroth, and not even *he*, with his softly countenance and gracious nature, takes too kindly to this brand of foolishness!'

For the last time he returned his gaze towards the window to ensure that *she* could remember the remaining words which she yet had to utter. As he did so he became even more enchanted to see another one of his own, standing besides the other fool, the marked man whom he would soon use. Together, their consciences were being stroked, and their senses, particularly the boy's, were being made into a palpable, harmless slush. As he observed the thin tentacles that reached into the sconce of his first victim, he instantly came to this conclusion: that the whole event would be unashamedly trivial.

'Good, good, keep up the bad work,' the Dark Man insisted.

And then, suddenly as he had come, he was off.

*

He was quickly above the ground in another one of the heavenly spheres. Before long, he allowed his eyes to roll back below, and he once again viewed the principal house of interest. It floated away effortlessly beneath him, as though the ground on which it was stood was a contrived landscape, and the scene that compassed it about was but a fantasy. Content that all things progressed as they should, he quickly refocused his mind to where his flight was taking him. His gaze returned upwards, towards his vast numbers of labourers coming and going amid the two heavenly planes.

Three mighty strangers were carrying three hampers dressed in whitened pearls. The baskets were filled with the vapours of young ones who had been sacrificed before their times. No more than three months from a seed to their present journey, which had been set towards the glittering array of stars. Even so, there would be no more sorrow for them, and they would not have to witness the toils and troubles of the passing world.

The Adversary saw many of his own men hauling great, heavy burdens. With these they were descending towards the small circle above Daearawd. Others quarried stones, thousands by the number, which were sufficient in size to fence in nations. But all were there to serve him, to consolidate the Dark Realm, to ensure that all goodness will one day be finally quashed. And as he watched his traffic moving towards the Four Corners of the Earth, he turned again towards his rear side, and he saw something else.

A flying beast hovered eastward, between the centre of the lands and *Rome*. Frequently, he was summoned by the name "King of Albion". But great though his title was, he was made of ghastly stuff, both awesome and terrible to behold.

His shoulders were dressed in the greys and blacks of sin and his chest was stiffened in the putrid starch of disdain. His neck was laced twice around with the skin of men's hides, and they were bolstered even further with an aura of pride. Upon his dark face was a proud and ugly nose, and this defiance reminded The Master of his hideous role. Then The Adversary looked again, hoping to view by this one's side, his heinous lackey from across the Eastern Skies.

Again, The Adversary lifted up his eyes, but this time he cast a glance over towards the Northern Lights, and there was Perversion coming in from the Eastern Winds; and Apollumi was with him. They greeted their lord from the distance, before setting about their previously assigned tasks with diligence. Then he peeled off towards the byways, towards the darkened streets beyond, and his sight quickly fell upon another unsuspecting victim.

A man was wandering aimlessly through the dimly lit passageways when The Adversary saw Apollumi filter in behind him. Others, too, lurked nearby, as close to him as his own shadow. Again The Adversary looked and again he saw, this time another offering. His servants had been following Charlie for quite some time, since the same seasonal sacrifices the year before. The ghosts traipsed after the tracker who himself was trailing after the wanderer, and they all headed deeper into the street's diminishing darkness. Charlie kept himself well, however, and he remained hard-pressed to the shadows, even as they stayed close to him. He moved silently like warm vapour, flitting breathlessly through the early morning breeze.

From the midst of the sullen skies the Voyager soon discerned another outline. It was the faint contour of a cutter, reflecting its evil malice in the city's dim streetlights. Then, even as he was looking, many things happened at once:

The foul creature named Apollumi disappeared in a sudden puff of smoke, and he temporarily fell out of The Master's eyeshot. Soon however, The Master saw him again, as it reappeared in a different form, mingling with Charlie's own spirit. Then, quick as you like, a pack of rats was up from the pithiest regions of Hell; these were the other phantoms emerging from the surrounding darkness.

On hearing of the sacrifice, The Rats drew nearer alongside Qädesh's silky black form. They remained a small distance off for a short time, until all things were as they should be and the signal was revealed. The Adversary's reflections returned to The Natural where the silvery blade was raised aloft. One pair of hands, guided by six strong arms from The Spiritual. But any last glint of hope was shattered when the dark forms had completely surrounded the both of them.

He called out through the darkness of the ether:

'Yes, my sweet Son of Carnage; do thou your worst!'

To which the next few movements became all as one. And the first blow severed the main artery to Philip's neck.

'Go on now, finish him...'

As he looked on, he saw a wallet drop longingly to the ground. It reached the moistened turf before its owner did. All was confused, all was a mess, all was tangled with the Dark Hosts of Nef. Then came the coagulating red gore, a blasphemy to the layman's law. It was not this however, nor was it the repeated strikes from the cold, inimical steel, which caused Philip to begin choking. This responsibility belonged to the dark ghouls that crept stealthily atop of his inanimate form. This they did so as to gain a crank upon his soul, so that they might take him to where they desired to go, so that he might visit his mother, and her cousin, whom he had years ago begun to know.

But as suddenly as the dark forms had come, they were gone, vanquished from their current passage into a far more iniquitous world. And as a very good work had been rendered, The Master also moved on, shortly after he let Charlie go. The robber clutched the money from the purse, leaving behind the blood-splattered photographs where they lay; because they were no good to anyone anymore. The Dark Man was gladdened at this darkest of briefs, for he could hear the gloated rumblings of The Dead Man Beneath.

*

Watching his lackeys doing what they did best was no problem for him, and he could do so all day. But for now he had to be on his way as time was pressing. He shifted above the deep-sea clouds, from which point he was able to view the wide-open circle of the Earth. In so doing his path crossed with more from his own ranks, some of the Mighty Ones of old who were currently in battle preparations.

As always, they maintained a fast pace, quick as was their will, which was to accomplish the foul bidding of their master. The pickings were too hot at present and the season was as ripe as summer fruits; only a fool would do otherwise. Presently, from across the dimming globe came a plethora of dark entities, led by the princes who commanded them in their deeds. All were tall, around eight feet or so, each one was valiant, and there was none without muscles so bold that women everywhere would fail to faint. None had either blemish or fault to carry reproach; all were dour, all were cruel, all carried battle-axes together with swords and shields. In fact the only variance in their physical appearances was the minor deviations of skin tones. For some were hued in the most profound ebony covering whilst others, slightly smaller in stature, were cast white as the searing heat.

Even so, for all of their noted grandeur, one would still be hard-pressed to find such a one as Satan himself. For who was as beautiful, who was as intelligent, who had there ever been created who was as perfect as he? Lucifer he was made, the Light-bearer for all seasons.

Nonetheless, the lucid glory of the Aurora Borealis was thwarted by the presence of the dark phantoms. Soon, the dozen or so members at the head of the procession stopped, and each one took it in turn to dip his head in recognition of their liege. He, himself, drew closer, and presently he was to be found deep in conversation with the head of the procession. He was a magnificent man, dressed accordingly in traditional battle fatigues.

'My Lord, how pleasing it is to be in your presence!'

(At which The Other nodded.)

'But to what do we owe this great honour, Lord?'

'Thank you Abaddon and The Lord welcomes your humble courtesy,' replied Satan pensively. 'I have come to make it known that shortly I will require an escort of warriors, for I pass through the heavens to visit the Central Celestial Temple, and to challenge for our supremacy upon the ground.'

'Yes, master…?'

'Emm… There are some that I have had my eye on for quite some time now, in the docile habitat of Albion – '

'Albion, my lord?'

Some amongst the company raised their weary eyes in suspicion, if not surprise.

Albion indeed? What good can come out of Albion? This perhaps may be worth listening to.

He lifted his eyes: 'The insignificant little backwater that was once grand, which is now governed rather effectively by the King thereof, that stiff-necked Ruler of the Northern Waves?'

'Yes, my prince,' The Adversary confirmed. 'And I have come to challenge mere children at that, yea, and slight whelps they are too! Teenagers. But they are not without protection.'

Upon the mentioning he perceived tension rise in his prince's torso.

'Protection? From whom, lord? What should trouble you so that you should pay heed to some flimsy covering?'

'My prince, my prince, valiant till the last,' Satan mused. 'But know for certain that they are guarded, both day and night, by a small but virulent band of Watchers. Nevertheless…' And in the twinkling of an eye all minds present were opened.

There before them they saw a troop of noble warriors belonging to their enemy, who were standing between the Earth and the Heavens to oppose them. They maintained their guard at all times and worked in shifts, so that there was always at least one soldier per head with each one of The Friends. Their appearance was also mighty, dour as the ones to whom the sight was granted, and their forms were radiant as the midday sun. Moreover, the swords, so Abaddon saw, were bold, and more accustomed to blood than his own.

'I see!' rejoined Abaddon. 'The Black Watch!'

'Precisely.'

'But who are these ones that such a noble guard should be provided them?'

'They are children who have been marked from their very birth, as touching the forewarnings of Joel.'

'The Son of Pethuel?'

'Yes.'

'Emm… I'm beginning to understand now.'

'…But they are foolish and witless and therefore I may put them down with ease. And now – lest in days to come they become a stumbling-block to me!'

'Well-said, master, well said. For now is always the best time – a thing the enemy is still yet to learn. And we shall soon triumph, as is our destiny. But now, pray tell, what is your counsel for my retinue?'

They eyed each other bitterly before the flickering glow of lights. To those with a reasonable degree of discernment, the scene was a vivid reminder of why his Dark Kingdom was subject to uncertainty and losses. Moreover, it helped to indicate why Daearawd was not entirely his. Abaddon loathed being in the company of anyone who was his senior whereas The Adversary (that is to say "Satan") despised being in the need of any 'lowly assistance' to help him accomplish his means. Most of the time however it made for a truly terrible coalition.

'Continue with your assignment and do not alter,' ordered The Adversary, 'either to the left or to the right.'

'Yes, master.'

'Only, make your evil as foul as can be.' He stared closer at his servant. 'As for these fools,' he resumed, not for an instant breaking his glance, '– they are simple and arrogant – and much more besides. Therefore, I have sent one of our Mysterious Ones to handle the case. His travail is both night and day, under the auspices of the Regent of London, and he shall not fail me. Because I have also tasked him to follow after them wherever they go, for the better or for the worse, to the higher plains or even the lower worlds.'

'Of course, Master.'

'Anyway, these babes are about to corrupt the hedge of protection that has been surrounding them since their miserable beginnings. So this is why I forge onwards, to ensure that the ensuing stratagem is fulfilled according to our play. I will charge The Master of Nef of unfaithfulness – for not applying the same law to one and to all; contempt for justice – for not permitting me likewise; and cowardice – for his refusal to condemn those fools, who are wilfully violating his guidelines.

'It is likely that he shan't refuse me!'

'Never, my lord, for you alone are wise!'

With that The Adversary waved them on and he watched them filter off in pairs towards the lands, which on Daearawd are called Persia and Sidon. Their main aim now was to reinforce the resident evil in the areas most afflicted by the coming tides of darkness (their own) and to hasten in The Seven Year Covenant that would provide them with a stronger foothold in forthcoming days.

As he looked on, he knew that none of his hierarchy lacked understanding in any of these things. According to the Infernal Books all knew that he would shortly be compelled to take on the form of a man, no one less than the Antichrist himself! News had been circulating in the Celestial rumour-mill since the plundering of his deepest holds on the day when the skies were blackened, the veil was torn, the graves were rent asunder, and he had recently been hearing such sayings coming from across The Aetherbelt. Such salacious hearsay was seldom inaccurate.

However, he was not alone in his thoughts. Abaddon could also sense the warm glow of their foes' steel following their every movement and tracking their every deranged path. But at present The Shining Ones had not been granted authority to intervene, in order to squash the rebellion, should they at all be able, but only to disrupt, hassle, harry and protect, as stipulated by their current mandate, till such a time as Adam's lease for Daearawd had run its course.

Meantime, the troop headed off behind Abaddon with ill cheer, their dirge loud and their voices exuberant. For these were maligned beings of the foulest accord, corrupted spirits far beyond redemption. They were darkened entities oblivious to the ways of The Lore since the Age Before Men. In truth that is how they would remain, even till the ending of all time.

*

Nothing happened. But in all honesty, both Jema-Jane and Mark were quietly relieved to see this.

There were no hobgoblins hatching out from underneath the woodwork, there were no malformed sprites bounding about the place, there were no black spumes reeking of smells worse than the smelliest stink-bombs. Disregarding the man Gee, that is to say.

Anyway, J-J coolly concealed this pleasure behind the easy façade of a girl-racer. Mark, though, looked as guilty as a black elf caught shoplifting – always kind of distinguishable in the shopping mall. Their friends breathed deep sighs of relief also, almost as though they believed that something *might* actually have happened. The harsh winds outside soon abated, enough to allow the warmer murmuring to continue on its present, easier, course.

'All I'm gonna say is this, Markie; you're lucky.'

'Damn right, Gee.'

'You best believe bro…'

*

Satan picked up his pace once again, arriving quickly on the edge of the present solar system. It fell away behind him, the streaked darkness a varying mélange of spotlights set on blackness. Then he was hard by the very edge of the galaxy itself. This too seemed to recede at a phenomenal rate, much faster than light itself could transit. But he paid little regard to the disorientating shapes and sounds, for he knew that, one day, he would have all the time in the world to delve into its deepest, darkest mysteries.

'One day, I shall be ruler of you all,' The Adversary bellowed aloud, 'and I shall govern you all according to my own volition. Because I it is who shall reign as King, even as now I am The Master. And forever I Shall Be!'

He looked forwards again, before concerning himself with other, more pressing, details. In his vision, he could now see the approach towards the edge of the universe. Indeed, for the beginning and the end of all things was at hand. The emptiness was still expanding, somewhat more cagily than when the word was first spoken, and the void all round appeared less dense as the ages passed. But there was still much to see.

The vastness of the established realms was great enough already for a full administration to handle, so there was little need for him to be concerning himself with the added dominion he would obtain when he conquered his foe, plundered his wealth, put him to spoliation and reduced him to grave shame. But Word had it that there was a mystical set of keys in existence which the Governor of the Celestial kept concealed at all times. The saying again was that they unlocked the doors to other, unknown dimensions, at any point along the space-time continuum. It is for each one now to believe what he or she will, but Satan himself had garnered proof of these matters a long time since.

Whilst he passed through, the vast expanse of blackness continued to unravel towards the east and the west. Moreover, it seemed to disregard the evil intentions of the foul guest who was flying through its midst. Left to its own, and if the ether had been weary of his presence, it would have surely rescinded of its valiant efforts at existence, took flight, and quashed all planets, stars, and systems within all known plains, globules, and galaxies. But what forms the black inky fluid that comprises the Dark Unknown?

'So shall you all be mine, one day!'

A *wurm* passed him confidently by, an emerging pinprick of light within the comprehensive spread of darkness.

'And even now I see the greatness of the glory that is before me...'

Not long afterwards he followed the creature through the hidden rent. And, shortly afterwards, The Hole closed behind them both.

*

'Never again guys, I tell ya, never again! I can't believe it, how comes we've sunk so low? This is so unbelievably stupid!'

'I couldn't agree with you more Sash,' Alisha whined. 'And y'all have a go at me for telling you *true* stories?' She breathed another extraneous sigh. 'At least mine didn't almost kill us!'

'Well neither did this Alisha, so let it go yeah?'

'But…?'

'Come on, girl, get a grip,' Gee rejoined, giving her a shallow wink. 'They're a bunch of idiots: we know that and they know that; so everything's cool yeah?'

'Yeah, alright, maybe… This time. But don't go around doing such foolishness again!' She eyed Mark and Jema-Jane with anger in her eyes but there was yet a little more that needed to be said. So Sash said it.

'All these cats are crazy man, straight up crazy!' whispered Sash to himself.

'What d'ya say Sash?'

The oldest in the group looked ruefully at Elena. 'It was nothing! Don't worry 'bout it.'

'Not too pleased then are we?'

At this, the large Indian chap slumped back into his seat.

'Sometimes Elena, I can't tell whether you're just plain dumb, or extremely funny. Maybe, and this is me being generous, you're a bit of both.'

'I think, my friend,' Mark stated, 'that she's a little bit of both…'

*

They went back a long way, back to their first days of service together, which were before the long dark trials of Yesteryear. He had ranked just above Chrionious with regards to the Divine Hierarchy, or *Graddnef*, but he still regarded him as one of the greatest warriors ever to have been created.

An affinity had been borne because of the unique functions granted to the both of them: they had been two of only a few messengers given the dual purposes of warring (or protecting and reinforcing as it was formerly called) and worshipping. Satan's major accomplishment meant that he was cast more towards the worship side of things, a nobler calling than the other, Chrionious, who had sooner been appointed for war.

Therefore, even now, many of The Adversary's own ranks coveted Chrionious' mastery; for with the battle-axe he was skilled, with the sword he was proficient, with arms of burnished bronze there were few stronger. There were few able to pound the skies of heaven as he could, or cause the rolls of thunder to sound at a mere heartbeat, or the lightening to brighten up the night sky.

SPIEGEL SPIEL

*

Chrionious had sided with the Celestial Governor during the Era of the First Sedition. He had chosen to remain loyal, wisely some say, rather than trade in his rank for some pipe-dream of a position in any future kingdom, which may or may not one day be established by Satan, Leader of the Insurrection. It was then that they had parted company, each one going his own separate way, and now it seemed as though the decision would last for an eternity as Chrionious had resisted all of The Adversary's advances ever since. Moreover, The Brawler still paid homage, tribute, and daily showed fealty before the illustrious Hilasterion and the Great White Throne.

Therefore, Chrionious was, without doubt, loth to shift his allegiance. Why should the same fate that had befallen Satan come upon him also? Indeed, he was even more mindful now! For after such a long time in his master's service, any show of fealty towards their enemy would be dealt with immediately. His friend and Commander-in-chief, The Watcher of the Holy Lands, would be sent to bind him (which few could) and would cast him forthwith into the deepest, darkest dungeons beneath. Even this brave warrior did not at all doubt his companion's ability to do so. Such seditious treachery was rarely reckoned with more kindly! Yea, and 'tis a grand and noble truth well worth noting! So it was not a difficult decision to make. Chrionious loved his master well.

*

'You are to wait here until your escort arrives!' he proclaimed shortly, appearing from beneath the golden-gated bridge. 'A guard will come out shortly to lead you in.'

It was a mere second that passed before he broke off from staring at the visitor.

'Stand there!' he resumed, pointing to a place near his side. 'You shall wait for The Lord's Emissary before we take you inside.'

Chrionious promptly swivelled around his heels, and sited himself a few dozen yards in front of the two Gate-guards. Each of these guardians bore aloft a flaming sword, and each one looked as though he was made of the toughest, grimmest steel for the harsh demeanour they presented. Their stares were bleak as any found in the Celestial Courts but they were also filled with love. Few chose to examine them any more intimately, unless directed to do so by the Governor himself, and then only in brief encounters, not the draining exchanges designed to put enemies on the defensive.

'I will wait,' The Adversary called back, deciding wisely to avoid their scrupulous glare. 'I will not challenge these two great goons, worthy though their forms may appear. There are many of you and only one of me...

'Yet I wonder how I still have dominion… over all that I choose?'

The watcher turned his back on his grim guest and he passed quickly by the cherubim. They overlooked his spiteful jest, as the joker had never been more than one of them anyway.

As if reading their thoughts he continued, 'I'd far rather be a ruler in Hell than a lackey in Heaven any day. What do you think?'

Chrionious, ignoring him, hastened over towards a small congregation of workers who were assembled around the main entry to the forecourt. After exchanging a few pleasantries with some of their chiefs he passed them by also. Presently, he gave issue to a swift flurry of commands as Satan waited on in silence.

*

They sounded like a scurry of rats, parting from an ignited barn, but the pitter-patter of footsteps ascending the stairwell belonged to Stefan, Lora, and Julian. Now Julian's old dear had just recently won the National Lottery and so he thought it wise to save himself at this stage, lest he fail to utilise the guerdon that would one day befall him. So he was first out of the door. The rest of them followed tight on his heels, abandoning the ailing residence without so much as a "Goodbye!". No explanation was given, and none was sought. It was safest that way. Anyway, the party was well and truly over now, and though it *had* been great, they wouldn't be returning to Mel's yard in a hurry. Because something had seriously freaked them out, big time.

Some of the gang overheard the mention of demons, and Sash swore blind that Stefan was mumbling on about goblins and even The Devil himself. Lora didn't say much though, and neither did Julian, who had long decided to chip after he'd seen his first pair of eyes. Nevertheless, he'd only summoned the courage when he'd seen Stefan drop his spliff and split.

After that there was silence.

'So what was that all about people?'

Alisha caught the startled look on Sash's face, but opted to stay quiet.

'I don't know, boss, but I don't reckon it was 'cos of the food!'

From there on in no one dared utter even a single syllable, as Gee and his friends witnessed the next hasty exodus.

George the Greek was next, and then came Ryan (another Blue-foot) – both of these guys were skilled fighters – that's when they weren't stoned. They weren't meant to be scared.

'John…?'

Psycho John stumbled outside quickly afterwards. This was another mate of Gee's from Wing Chun who had earned his name not only for his abilities to mangle folk with his big-up knuckles, but also for his tendency to brawl against unseen antagonists, especially when he was in a somewhat inebriated state. And he, supposedly, had no fear.

'Come on guys, wassup?' pleaded Gee, upon seeing the few folk that might have given him a hard time in a brawl, vacate the premises with rather swift promptitude. Then, turning to Sash he said; 'Listen up Sash, jokes over for a sec, what's going on here man, what's come over everyone?'

'Now you're asking Gee. But you're asking the wrong person mate, cos I haven't got a clue!... Mark?'

'Don't look at me, Sash. Not the foggiest. Anyway, I've had enough of this lark already!'

As he whirled his way through the remaining strands of smoke, John prattled on incessantly about the plight that he and his friends had just had to endure.

'Gee mate, I would stay a little longer, 'cos the jam started off a well-wicked...' The Psycho paused for a second and appeared to consider the atmosphere about him. '... But I can't fight 'em off Gee, I really can't fight 'em all. They're too many of 'em mate, so I'm leaving.

'Anyone, at any time, Gee, and that includes Lennox Lewis – fair enough game for me – but ghosts and demons, they don't count for shit. They never counted Gee! Laters!'

When these dark words had etched themselves onto his brain, Gee was almost tempted to do the same thing himself, and D-D. Only the gang's presence had prevented him, lest word got out that the Black-man had lost his cool and bugged-out.

So the basement was emptied as all of its inhabitants rushed out headlong into the street beyond, again, without so much as a coherent word being uttered. It was there, on the concourse, that some chose to remain to puke up their excesses, whilst the remaining cloud of darkness stayed tight on the heels of their comrades.

*

Three illustrious forms accompanied Chrionious on his return, and their combined aura, which some say was as glorious as many suns shining all at once, caused the dark visitor to quail, tremendously.

'The Mighty Lord is ready to see you now,' boomed a loud voice.

Satan looked up promptly.

'You're fully aware of our observances by now and so I shan't bore you with all of the finer details. Nonetheless, you have been commanded to follow me. So please remain in position, if that's not too difficult for once?'

'Get on with it Chrionious.'

The Envy of Many took his position to the front of the guest gaoler and traveller a little way across from his off side. Dorian also remained attentive, but stayed ahead of him. And upon seeing Chrionious take up his position to the side, he took a pace of his own, which brought him directly to his opposite flank. There, they both waited, until a second, more familiar countenance, appeared to enter their vision.

Nonetheless, this one was an altogether more foreboding figure than that of Dorian, more dreadful even than that of the Great Chrionious. Because in all the Celestial hierarchy there was not found any who was higher than himself; save for the one sat on his throne, and his flaxen-haired, golden-chested messenger.

'Ah- ha! So it's greetings, Old Friend...?'

*

Gee looked ruefully at the wide-open door.

'Seems like the smoke must have been bad down there,' he jested, 'cos I haven't seen folk split like that since the time when...' He looked over to Sash.

'Go on Gee!'

'Well, so I heard anyway... Since the time when all them Eejits at Enfield Grammar split, when word was out that the I.C.F. were heading down to their school. I heard that one geezer said that they were coming up from South of the River and East of the Manor, ready for a rumble with the ragamuffins. There and then in the lessons, about an hundred chicken-style base-heads jumped out the classroom windows and *chipped*.'

'You're kiddin' me? In front of the teachers you mean!'

'Yeah blud, fer real!'

'Serious?'

'Straight up man – no lie. All crazy Black Folk, Indians, Greeks and shit – even the coconuts! You know how a brother never thinks before he acts...'

'Now ain't that right.'

'What was that Alisha?' Gee craned his head as he got up from his seat. He looked around at his friends, and decided after seeing them all, that he too was tired, and not ready for another protracted engagement. 'Did you say something girl?'

'Sit down, Gee, you're making me weary.' The Elder had spoken.

'Well, Sash, you always look tired mate, so don't you worry about it "Nohow" the Indian!'

'Don't talk to me Gee. Something isn't quite right, and you can still joke the way you do?' Sash forced himself into a more comfortable position on the armchair. 'Come on Gee wake up!'

'Oh shut your trap Chief Running-Mouth.'

Dipping his head slightly to alleviate the sudden rush of blood to his temples, the Indian, shortly, did so. Then he toppled over sideways into an untidy mound.

'Bollocks!' he mumbled. 'I don't need any of this, I really don't.'

'J-J,' piped Elena, 'I think I really need to be getting home.'

'It's true init El, I reckon it's time you were off home; and funnily enough I don't mind running you.' (Mock confidence Gee was invariably good at, because he could style it out on eggshells without cracking them if need be. But this was blatantly ridiculous, as the Boogie would have sworn himself if he were still mad enough to have been hanging around.) 'I don't mind at all.'

He managed the Bad-Man's Mosey over to Jema-Jane, who, after indicating that the wheels, all of a sudden, belonged to her folks, expressed her strongest reservations at letting Gee (a far more accomplished driver anyway) have the keys. After a short exchange of words, she handed them over, albeit begrudgingly.

'Thanks babe,' Gee whispered, blowing her a totally unsuitable kiss. 'I'll bring it back in one piece, without any blood tarnishing your inside mirrors – and that's a promise. If I don't make it you can always sue me.'

'Don't even go there Gee, I'm serious. Don't even go there.'

As the door slammed shut behind them, the two absconders ran out first onto the slippery veranda, and then into the cheerless night beyond.

'Good riddance to the two of you then,' Sash mumbled. 'See if I care!'

'Y'know!'

'Tchp!'

*

'No greetings for your old comrade, Michael?'

For a second the chill found in their stares was enough to paralyse even the most vibrant beings within the city's vast frontier. The great warrior glared intently at the sunken figure, peering deep into those malignantly dark eyes. However, he was yet cautious, as all must be when scrutinising such a vast hive of evil, lest he too should be drawn deep into that abyss.

'None sir!' came the staunch reply. 'There is no greeting for one so foul… And may the Lord rebuke thee, you Fiend of Ages!'

'Ah, it *is* nice to see you isn't it, Michael? Still the same, still noble and bold until the very last. Yea my friend, it encourages me to see you no end – that you are *still serving* so well… and it's also pleasing to know that you've lost none of your respect, especially for those who are naturally greater than you.'

Chivalrous till the last, Michael replied, 'Till the times of the end, sir, till the times of the end; which are not far off now, so it would seem.'

Satan tensed, ever so slightly, but it was perceptible all the same.

'So cherish your rank for your this season, O Dark One, because it may well be your last!'

But the visitor was left undeterred.

'We shall see then, Comrade,' he replied. 'We shall see.'

'Indeed we shall, shortly. But first it remains for you to keep your position. Wait here please whilst I look into your escort.'

*

Highly tanned and beautiful, Michael was the taller of the two men. As well as having the strength of seven great warriors within his veins he had also been blessed with one of the most wizened minds of any messenger. Satan, however, was an exquisite seven-footer and was truly without the need for any boasting – his splendour had always been evident, indisputable. Notwithstanding, he had no hair upon his chest to warm his soul, nor lashes upon his brow to conceal his most pretentious eyes; for the beauty revealed by his handsome countenance easily transcended description. Michael, nevertheless, had the most beautiful, flowing locks and kept his hair tied back with an Alice-band.

The Devil's skin was tough and resilient, without hair, without blemish, like a leathery coracle which had hardened for its age. His face indeed was much the same, save for the two blackened orbs that were set in its midst, which were his eyes. He was, without doubt, immaculate, and when he chose to appear in the fair light of his bygone splendour, that is to say, as Lucifer, he was marvellous. These things aside, his manners now were no more than surface deep, as all who knew him knew too well.

Folk frequently claimed that his skin, ebullient though it often appeared, was as shallow as the vanity that first cast him into his current abode with Men. And that his coating, brought on by the pride of his previous exaltation, was nothing more than a snake's skin.

*

A warming glow shone from the farthest sides of the north, upon the head of the escort, and it brought the guest to a standstill. He was ill at ease, for not often was the Son's light cast upon his furrowed brow. Nevertheless, The Adversary forced himself to relax, still somewhat nervous to be in such prestigious company once again. From the direction of this beacon came the light of another form. He was not as stout as Michael, but he was more powerful, in a different sort of way; and he was no less fearsome.

'Michael, The Governor has much to do at this time and he is awaiting your company! But do not worry about This Reproach: he shall be dealt with shortly, and you know this promise will never fail! And you, My Prince, shall be highly instrumental, from the times of his deconstruction to the times of his annihilation.'

'And to you, Keruv,' Gabriel declared, after finishing addressing Michael, 'you will hold your words for now – that is if you wish to seek access past The Tunnel.'

'My Lord Gabriel, you too are still in *his* service I perceive?'

The Messenger ignored the question.

'Prepare yourself for another audience with my Lord, O Rejected Keruv.'

Presently, the guest was unceremoniously shuffled into position. Issuing a curt nod towards the two towering figures, the leader of the procession ensured that all was in order behind him.

'Prepare for us a portal.' The Messenger of the Gods gestured towards the two mighty cherubim who promptly turned their swords towards his direction in tribute. 'Thank you Darach.'

'Move into position, Keruv, and quickly!'

Immediately, The Adversary took his position behind Gabriel, though in front of Michael, who was ready at a moment's notice to deal him some swift retribution should he even consider stepping out of line. Dorian and Chrionious made up the foursome, staying wide on the flanks, as much to protect their wily visitor as to help restrain him. From their standpoints, they soon moved in closer.

'Keruv?'

'Yes Gabriel, I am ready... But are you O Prince?'

The Chief Messenger cocked his head around ninety degrees to his left. It was enough to send shivers through the entire procession. But it hit the fallen beast hardest, with a fell report.

'Keep your peace O Blackest One and hold fast your words for sympathetic ears!'

Satan cowered slightly. 'Oh get on with it, Gabriel. You no longer have any authority over me, so let us move on, and swiftly.'

'No, but do you at least have control over yourself?'

'I have control over Daearawd, dominion over Dreams, and understanding over all the divers realms in the universe, which shall, one day, all be mine!'

'But what of the savagery of Men? Is it not for their father, or is it because of themselves?'

The guest pondered awhile for the implication of these words. If it was for their father, a position that he often laid claim to, then they were an ill reflection of him. If, on the other hand, their savagery was of their own, then what dominion did he have, or indeed, what lordship could he ever hope to attain?

The Messenger waited until he had silence in the ranks.

'Now you will follow me, O Vile Guest, quickly, and in an orderly fashion. Dorian and Chrionious, you know your charge well. Michael, you will keep him boxed-in and others out... for now. I will head this procession, for we have much to say and very little time in which to say it.'

'We have,' The Ill-favoured One responded. 'It's been a long time Old Friend.'

'It has. And you look none the better for it!'

Shortly, Gabriel commenced his final approach. He headed towards that place where unclean men cringe, where desperate men plead mercy, to the place where even angels were fearful to tread. Yet The Adversary followed hard behind him, into that deeper and most blinding of lights.

OUT OF S-PACE

They draw near who follow after wickedness; they are far from your law.
You are near, O Lord, and all of your commandments are truth.
Concerning your testimonies,
I have known of old that you have founded them forever.

PSALM 119:150-152

Behind the large dark frame covering the doorway lay the small, timid form of a ginger cat. Snivelling pitifully from the depths of its core (kind of like a crooning old hag whose tonsils and teeth were both missing) this was currently its only way of vocalising the abject terror it felt due to the loud noises being made by that hulking black monstrosity.

She had seen him striking the door repeatedly, as often but even more vehemently than her owners used to strike her! Then, as she had previously anticipated, shortly afterwards, he had piled in there using his arms and legs as a battering ram, again, much like her own proprietors. Such abuse is called 'The Moroccan'. Therefore, even after considering some of the sickest punishments that she'd often had to suffer, this sorry episode was far more macabre. *Does the door have any feelings? Is it really worth it??*

Earlier that same evening she had received some rather bad tidings. Her closest feline companion, who was a male, a protector of the species called O'reh (an Irish Moggy), had drowned out back in an exceptionally freakish accident. Fatty (now that's another one of her brood), had said that the local canine terrorist, Rabies, who was a crossbreed, had been heavily involved. The word out in the feline community was that the mongrel had become unusually moonstruck late on the previous eve. Incoherent mumbling, rabid salivating, eyes glazed over like he'd been cast into a werewolf; the scene made for ill recounting.

These things are not as dubious as they may first appear. For Rabies had indeed been muttering in dog-speech, about wolves, goblins and the like, as well as other fiendish elements, which form no part of the visible world. It was only after such dark sayings that he had set about ravishing the local population of cats. However, what was perhaps the most alarming thing to the feline community was that there had not been any obvious precursor to the frenzied onslaught that followed.

71

There were none of the standard dog-cat chases, which to men, are doubtless fun to observe, although to the stranded moggy out on the street, more often than not it is not so. There was none of that incessant barking as such, nor even the high pitch drones that only dogs will recognise. There was nothing, not even the other two felons, Butch and Bruno, to back him up. It was queer by any creature's standards. Highly curious indeed for a dog…

Therefore, the result now was that six of her friends lay injured, another four lay stone cold dead, and Fatty – she's the one who had taken the trouble to narrate this part of the story to her – well, she was in a somewhat sickly state in between. So Laxative – that was the unfortunate name given to our cat – thought. (It wasn't exactly true because, Fatty, just under a half-hour back, had passed onto that Great Sofa-chair in the sky; but Laxative was not to know that at present.) 'The Litter' was now well and truly vanquished.

With deep discontentment raging across her bosom, she curled up into a round fluffy ball, thoughts full of plump mice (belly empty though), which she hoped would help send her off to a swifter, sweeter sleep. She allowed none of those foolish thoughts to return to her: like challenging those Big-folks for supremacy; or asking them, kindly, to be quiet (or at least to ring the doorbell instead of trying to smash the damn thing down!). The music too could be turned down a notch. But the logistics of it all had wearied her.

I mean, what could she really have done? Purred? Meowed? Rubbed her frizzled furs up and down the House-owner's legs in an altogether unfriendly fashion? And what would she get in return… realistically now? A kick where it hurts if she were lucky; and everywhere else if she were not! It was, unfortunately, a zero-sum game, whatever that means.

Whining in the most pitiful tones, Laxative continued with her life-long laments, until the deepest sorrows of her soul, she finally concluded, would not at all be heard. Everybody has enough worries of their own in today's world, and let's be honest about it, cats don't figure too highly in the food chain. Pretty useless creatures they are; they just lie there and sleep, and wake up occasionally to eat. Kind of like why some of the guys called them Man's Second Best Friend.

Thus Laxative gave up, very dejected, but at least feeling a little better for her tears. Although not before the winds had again returned for another bout with the dark, solitary homestead.

*

A sudden gust of wind glanced off the door and soared backward into Elena's face, leaving Gee's precious demeanour largely unchallenged. Her face was left with the cold impressions of a storm whose epicentre lay somewhere inside the house, and its frosty chill became imprinted upon her peeling forehead, like an ailing snowman in the forlorn Autumn storms. There was no way that any sane person would risk driving home on a night like this, and Gee just about qualified as being of *compos mentis.*

With the lucidity of her mind's eye, she could plainly see that all things were not quite right. The unabated growling of the winds, the onerous thunder that stroked beneath heaven's dark ceiling, the groaning of some of God's creatures – all these things meant that the forthcoming day would be dark for the Syndicate. But what Elena perceived through her other, less known, senses was somewhat more alarming. Because it was only her Other-sense that witnessed the dull and sullen dawning as the dimensional wall closed again.

*

No matter how many times he had seen them, the effulgent glow from The Highway always caught him off guard. Gold, glorious and glittery, gorgeous was the scene and great was the setting he now found himself in.

He shrivelled slightly, unaware of how the others watched him coil. His eyes narrowed, no wider than the edge of one of the two flaming swords belonging of the mighty Keruvim. For he saw the two guardians dip their arms, thereupon permitting the virulent flames to ebb somewhat, so that The Escort could pass through.

They saluted Gabriel's guest courteously before the fiery wall conjoined again. It was then that the horrors started, all over again…

There were creatures above The Seat, which is sometimes called "The Hilasterion", on account of its prime usage. One by one, they were monitoring all the movements currently being made by the party. Their eyes were cast everywhere, upon those they knew to be unfriendly, and upon those who were known to be without fault; it made little difference. They guarded that throne for every second of every minute of every hour of every day, in all ages since the beginning of time, until the ending of time and afterwards. Save for their times of worship.

Presently, eyes bore into Satan like arrows dipped in molten lava, like darts that are laced in poison, like words that are tipped with the flames of requital, like bolts that are made for the bleeding of both traitors and foe-men. Even so, Michael 'The Bold' was there to keep him in check. He was the chief fighter anywhere within The Palace Gates, or indeed, anywhere outside. Then alongside him was Gabriel, their Chief-lord.

So they were put at no small ease. For even Dorian and Chrionious, two other notable warriors, surrounded the fell villain, who had, doubtless, come by with mischief in mind. Thus, the two illustrious guardians relaxed back, comforted at the great strength that was present. Any subsequent misdeeds were most unlikely to happen with such prestigious company around.

Meantime, those that could see but could not be seen were close to finishing their appropriated tasks. All they needed was...

A stray thought to pop into her head.

Now Jema-Jane had still managed to come to the somewhat irksome conclusion that something "...kind of" strange was happening, even though she was most definitively *not* a believer in bad spells or bad spirits (or bad vibes coming to think of it). Nothing fey or otherworldly mind, just something... a little out of the ordinary. It was the wind and driving rain that led to her assumptions, her company and their argument that sealed her fate.

She reckoned that by reversing their previous antics (and by ensuring that the latter was far stronger than the former – kind of a reverse-polarity-scientific bullshit, coupled with some more ancient, if you like "traditional" values), they could alleviate some of the evening's sour dolour. It seemed to contain enough elements of objective reasoning for a desperate young scientist to cling on to; it was near enough the real thing to be pursued.

So J-J followed up her hypothesis with rigour.

In such cases it was also patently obvious that two people were far better than one; which is why...

Yellow Eyes was joyous at his latest triumph.

'*Nearly there... I love you J-J!*'

He almost wanted to reach out and hug her.

'*Come on now, easy does it girl...*'

Presently, though none of the crew could see it, there yet remained an anonymous presence lurking behind the mirror.

The discreet figure stretched out his long, bionic arms and reached deep into her volatile brain. It was not so much to hug her, but to give her a bit of a stirring – a bit like a ribbing but of cerebral matter. So, without knowing it, she was soon to be in complete submission to his every thought pattern, even as the docile stared on in bemusement.

*

'Lucifer *mein-e* Keruv,' came The Voice from The Throne. 'Wo kommst du?'

It seemed like an awful eternity was spanned out before the other finally ceded to answer.

'Where have I come from? From running events upon Daearawd, of course, where else? Oh... yes, and from orchestrating the heavenly realms, as usual.'

'Ah, yes, I see now!' the first responded. 'And in your grand estimations you have obviously considered the army that I have ordained for this day? Would you not agree that they are a very great people, a worthy rival against any and all of the gods? Or perhaps you are not yet aware as to how they will triumph over evil across the face of The Earth, and over all that lies in your Ephemeral Kingdom – '

'They are arrogant and insolent my Lord, and that is when they are asleep! How much more hubris do they hold when they are awake? So if you have chosen such to form part of your end-time Forces of Destiny… then may *God* help you.' His laughter was coarse, a dry throaty chortle of evil propensity. 'And may *The Good Lord* have mercy on your souls! Ha, ha, ha…'

All those around the throne became tense.

Satan roared on with laughter.

They drew closer.

But then, as abruptly as he had begun, he stopped, as too did the guardians. There was presently little need for the aggression.

'I see Lucifer that you have grown none the wiser over the years...'

With a quick wave of his arm a huge video screen appeared from behind the gathering. All else seemed to fade away and the chance of any further distraction disappeared with it, before those who were gathered together had focused their eyes upon the images being revealed onto the screen.

Michael, Dorian and Chrionious withdrew some way off Lucifer, albeit for the merest of moments; but this allowed Satan to see, with greater clarity, the disturbing images that were about to be rendered.

Graphic patterns were displayed one after another in quick succession, in what on Earth would be fairly considered as a grand cinematic experience. But the visions herein were much more poignant, moribund even, although the characters and players who formed part of each scene, if seen by men's eyes or if perceived by women, would not be so real, for they were spirits and not flesh and blood. In truth, they caused the guest to suffer exceedingly, as was its intention. Albeit, none of this was because of any frail disposition on his part.

After the last picture had been rolled the visitor was held steady for a little while longer, so that he was well able to hear The Voice That Speaks.

'Shall I take it then that you have not yet heard of the latest routs against your princes?' boomed The Voice as Satan squirmed in anxiety. 'Well let me fill you in; it occurred only a short while ago over Sidon and Persia – across *The Aetherbelt* of the Middle East in fact – on Daearawd of course.

'Verily, I do believe that some of your greatest warriors were there, but that we were *propitious* enough to take some captive. Am I not correct…?'

Michael nodded. Gabriel continued in his place.

'I understand that Apollyon also known as Abaddon – who is perhaps one of the your greatest princes – without contradiction – was amongst these. Oh, yes… and I hear that I ought to let you know this also…' Gabriel glanced up towards The Throne, before advancing rather candidly. 'Thank you Almighty One:

'Two of your most noteworthy rebels are in chains right now for overstepping their jurisdiction, and they shall remain in bondage until the last week of your domain.' Gabriel's voice was filled with the power and authority of The Lord himself. 'Therefore, you shall not receive them back hereinafter until my master's say so, and then you shall only possess them for a short while.'

'Presently, as Gabriel said, they are kept in the utmost Darkness,' The Voice rejoined, 'for I can hear in Annwfn the pleas of the mighty. They cry in anguish and angst and they shall continue to do so both day and night, as an infant does for his mother or a child for his father, until I am pleased with the multitude of their torments. Their eternal dread is set, Lucifer, as it is also for you.

'You understand these things, just as I have spoken them to you, *Mein-e Keruv?*'

…

'Lucifer?'

…

'Lucifer?'

…

He knew well what it meant, for his mind was cast back to another date, a few thousand years prior.

*

It was the Day of the Deluge.

Some of his most dastardly immortals had been chained and dragged down deep into the pits below, whilst pleading in the most pitiful of voices for their clemency. Satan was still very greatly pained to remember such thoughts, particularly so as it was also around the same period when the floods had first struck, and the rains had first pelted, and the ground had first split open to reveal its watery depth.

Many agents of good were still upon the earth in those days, and indeed, many more proxies from the skies above had joined them soon afterwards. Most of his own however, principally those who at some stage had been involved in some form of unsanctioned relations with the humans, had been rounded up successfully, and thence, after a brief series of skirmishes, The Onslaught had started.

The mightiest warriors from the Celestials, Michael amongst them, as too was Dorian, had set upon Satan's forces and the latter's men were beaten badly and treated shamefully, as though they were the scum of the Earth, which indeed they were. Albeit, Satan winced violently at the irony of troubling thoughts that continued to plague him so.

And those who did not return to their assigned abodes quickly had been herded like animals and sent down in chains into the Blackness of Darkness. (These were, and still are, the most formidable part of The Gaols in Annwfn). Thereupon, each one had been readily sentenced to detainment at the Lord's pleasure, whereof the words of Jude do yet speak truth:

> *"And the angels who did not keep their proper domain,*
> *But left their own habitation,*
> *He has reserved in everlasting chains under darkness*
> *For judgement of the great day."*

For the crime of:

> *"...thoroughly corrupting the peoples of the World*
> *to the manner of them that would come after them;*
> *to wit, Sodom, Gomorrah, Admah, and Zeboiim;*
> *for causing them, without due warrant,*
> *to partake in the most insidious perversions known to man;*
> *... for causing them to taste in the great deluge of my wroth."*

[Words spoken by the Governor of the Celestial].

Whereupon these, the most heinous of the rebels were shut away, ready to be revealed only in the last time, unto them that should follow after the pernicious crimes in Noah's Times, and after the corrupt plots of Lot's Prime; if indeed they were lucky. If not they would suffer sentence forthwith, and each would be damned immediately.

*

So it happens, even to this day, that The Adversary can still sometimes hear the cries of their agony, of which it is often said, "… he will one day have to become a participant". Alas, for the fate of them who have fallen!

Nonetheless, a voice was still beckoning him:

…

'Lucifer?'

…

'Lucifer?'

…

'Lucifer?'

…

Oh yes, he understood well what it meant.

*

'Mark baby, come over here for a second would you?'

He normally obliged J-J with anything, so he could at least manage this much. Kind of sad, admittedly, but that's just the way it was when you were hopelessly in love.

'Just here…'

He stood by her side as the others sat by and watched on despondently.

'Come on guys get real,' Alisha urged. 'Don't be messing around with the mirror no more. Or else,' she continued, whispering into Elena's ear, 'not whilst I'm here!

'There's an unseen power behind anything that is treated as an idol guys... And that includes that mirror!'

Elena, too, was annoyed at the current goings-on. Both her parents, for once in agreement, had strictly forbidden her to dabble in any such things. And not yet being wise to the ways of the world, she took many things people said as gospel.

By way of biblical idolatry, she was only permitted to light incense to idols down at the local Orthodox (or at the Roman if it came to it). Sometimes however her benevolent father also allowed her to pray/chant/call upon certain fashioned mounds of clay and porcelain, to her heart's desire, though, only if the statue's name was prefixed with a "Saint – ". That, you see, was the magical part of the church liturgies, which made it for most people, okay; that is to say non-idolatrous. But you still weren't allowed to call the statues Buddha, Ram, Shiva or anything else, because that didn't count. That would then be idolatrous, unless, perhaps, you prefixed them with a "Saint – ". You see how it works now in the all-important name-game.

Not that Elena was overly interested in spooks, ghosts or anything else for that matter; but she was highly reluctant to go messing around with things that she didn't fully understand. "It's like most men…" her mother used to tell her privately; dangerous, foolish… more balls than sense. So she was advised to dedicate her energies to her main past-time of archery, which yielded far more reliable results anyway. Men would come and men would go, she was told, but Cupid's arrows would forever cleave to whatever target she aimed them at.

Culling herself beneath Gee's huge chest, the youngster managed to allay some of her fears. Gee, on the other hand, was snuggling up closer to Sash, and Sash was already looking to his black sister Alisha for comfort – the so-called "Mrs Maturity" of the group. Not that she really wanted anyone with her right then and there…

'J-J, what're you doing now?'

'To be honest, Alisha, I was kind of thinking – '

'Stop it right there,' Sash blurted, his eyes opening wider than an escapee's from Dartmoor. 'That's the problem right there – you think too much.'

J-J ignored him completely. 'I figure that if we brought an "evil atmosphere" into the house by messing around with the mirror – not that I've gone superstitious or anything like that Sash,' she added for clarity, engrossed in her own analysis, 'then surely if we played around with it some more things will sort themselves out?'

'What kind of rubbish is that J-J?'

J-J pondered quickly for the answer to her question. She didn't know why she'd said what she did – of course it was foolish – 'It's part of The Law of Reciprocity,' she lied, blatantly, though perhaps not so to her friends.

'Anyhow Mark, you're the one who's gonna have to return this place to Mel ain't it, so you really haven't got much to lose?'

'Oh come on J-J, we all helped to organise the party didn't we?' said Elena. 'So that's a tad unfair don't you think?' The storms continued to lash the premises without remission.

'Maybe. But at the end of the day, the buck stops with Mark there… Ain't that right baby?'

Mark was carefully observing the scenes around him, whilst trying to do his best to ignore the constant attention he was getting. The storm clouds were once again brewing, the winds continued to batter every known orifice of the house, the occasional streak of lightening lit up the distant skies. He counted about ten seconds before he again heard the dull rumbling in the deep blue vent beyond.

'Emm… about two miles out and closing.'

But he still looked unconvinced. 'Listen J-J, don't you think all of this is just cos of the wind? I mean, do you really think that…'

His voice trailed off when he caught the wicked glint in her eyes. J-J wasn't exactly saying much, because she couldn't – not in there with all of those uneducated buffoons around; plus, she didn't have to. But she was worried – Mark could see that clearly – and the present onslaught of winds seemed only to compound those fears.

'Yes, I do,' was her stern reply. She too, turned to face the windows.

There had undoubtedly been a "…slight change in the weather" – everyone at least conceded as much.

'Perhaps it's 'cos of unsteady eddies, which are created by energised sunspots, I think – you know, on the sun's surface like. But I reckon that the story may be true – not demons coming out and all that nonsense – that's clearly rubbish. But something's happened here for sure. In modern day physics most professors reckon that there are more dimensions than the four we are aware of; perhaps ten or maybe eleven dimensions in total!'

"The Funk" suddenly found it difficult to maintain his unequivocal coolness.

'J-J, baby, coming from anyone else, I'd say that they're stupid. But J-J, babe-y, what're you sayin', what you be trying to do to ma-heart.' Gee faded there and then for the second time that night. 'Why're you lie-ing?'

'Tell us you're joking J-J?' Elena pleaded.

'Nope! 'fraid not dear. No wind-up whatsoever. There really could well be something *unscientific* happening *out-there*! That is to say, outside the body of our current understanding.'

The Driver peered into the mirror, partly to conceal the smirks that had spread all across her face, but also because Mark was already standing there waiting for her.

'All I wanna know is are you down with this, because we need you Mark. I need you now Mark... Agreed?'

His heart was palpitating with increasing rapidity, but he couldn't let her see that. His temples throbbed like kettle-drums, but he could take the pain if he had to. His brow albeit showed evidence of dual affliction, a sight which he had to remedy immediately, before the rest of the gang caught sight of it and charged him with being uncool – an accusation hardy enough to break even the proudest homeboy.

He wiped his perspiring forehead mindfully: 'Okay then, I suppose we should give it a go. Because you know best in this sort of thing?' Markie yawned widely again, quickly moving his arm from his mouth to his forehead, where the beads of sweat just didn't seem to want to yield.

'We'll give it one more go then shall we...?'

*

Elsewhere, however, the scene made for grim reporting.

'These ones here are your heirs, are they not?' Lucifer shouted accusingly. 'These ones here, down on The Earth, they're yours are they not? Or do you now deny them as I sooner presumed you would? For you are nothing – '

'Yes they are mine, I do not deny it. Be quick and speak your piece.'

'Well, for your information, they have declared that they neither believe in the divers worlds or indeed in any of the lords thereof. Furthermore, they have laid claim to the ultimate presumption – that there is no longer any need to fear your humble *servant*; neither do they, it seems, fear you!

'Moreover, have they not said that neither you nor me are worthy adversaries and that their fate belongs to themselves and can be called upon and directed at a whim? Or is it because my *Lord* requires less from his servants these days, because he has gone soft, that he fails to hear all of these accusations himself?'

'They will be my sons and not my servants. Indeed, a couple may make it as friends of mine, so long as they follow my commandments and exercise their faith.'

'Servants, sons, whatever.' There was only the slightest reaction to the incessant goading. 'But what truly troubles me most are the things that I have heard from within this very camp. Am I correct in assuming that they have a destiny before them and that they have received A-Class protection for that A-Class Ne-Gro – the Black Watch! Or is it just my *vivid* imagination that causes me to greet such folly? Ha, ha, ha, ha, ha…!'

The Enthroned Ones now seemed more pensive. The one to the rear, whose face could just be made out, appeared to be lost in a world of his own. He shifted uncomfortably in his seat, heeding carefully every spoken word and weighing up its sum as he ought, to see whether or not there was anything that yet might meet the criteria. His present reluctance to respond was because he was in deep thought, as he was already in preparation against the challenge which he knew was about to come. And it was not because he was at a complete loss for words. Entirely.

At length Satan, The Adversary, spoke again.

'I have also heard report that they have taken it upon themselves to play the Mirror Game...'

Clouds billowed out from beneath The Hilasterion, in the various colours of the rainbow and many more besides, colours which cannot be readily discerned with the naked eye. They seemed to be coming from underneath the dais, from a place far, far below the Courts of the Worthy Dead. The Governor bided his time, scrutinising his visitor well, barely concealing his disdain, before sniffing up the fragrance drawn out from the prayers and praise of the perfected within other realms. Then he returned to face his scourge:

'Oh yes and from whom has this report come?'

'From some of my own that I have on the ground, no less,' said Satan, as he proceeded to pace around the courts.

'Now my Lord, do you not say that you are as your word, and that by the testimony of two or three witnesses it shall be a declared thing? And that your *Wort* is at least as high as your *Name*?'

Without awaiting a reply, he capitalised on his forging momentum.

'So therefore, *we* had the thought – '

'Yes, Satan, I have also just confirmed your *report*.'

'The Morning Star, if you please. You may address me as "The Bright and Morning Star".'

'I created you Lucifer, but you chose to become my adversary Satan.'

'Oh hush now,' riled The Adversary, pointing towards the thrones, 'for he, next to you, has been put above me. I was the highest in these courts before him, was I not?'

'He was found worthiest amongst Mankind. And that place was always reserved for the most honourable amongst Men; not for Elves, Dwarves, Beasts, or Angels, fallen or otherwise, but for him who was found the worthiest amongst Men.

'He was more diligent in manner than those from before The Floods, Noah and Job included (who was a valorous man, even for the bane that you afflicted him with). He surpassed even his own mother Mary for obedience, even though she yet has a favoured place in my Courts. He was more deserving than Daniel the Wise; more noble than any of The Prophets, that even Enoch and Elijah could not stand before him. He made more petitions than Moses, sung more hymns than Samuel, and he was even found better than Esaias – whom you caused to be sawn into two!'

'Yes, and I remember that wonderful day well!'

'So shall you suffer yourself… soon.'

'So all is well?'

The clouds were now grey and black, and the music wafting through The Throne Room seemed dulled and somewhat staid. The Adversary's ill presence was beginning to be felt.

'Nevertheless, Satan, there has been but one caught in this folly of dismal pretensions, so I have written those words against her… but I have not yet imputed them for your benefit.'

'My Lord, if you would just let me finish… I am sure that soon another shall join in J-J's evil folly and then the two shall both be in agreement.' There was a brief interlude as Satan the Accuser paused to consider the matter further. The other Enthroned One seemed to flinch at these tidings, albeit, only for a second.

'So verily, this is what I have come for…'

And while The Devil expounded his fell ideas, there was complete silence throughout the grounds for about half of the next hour.

*

Assuredly, I say to you, whatever you bind on earth will be bound in heaven,
and whatever you loose on earth will be loosed in heaven.
Again I say to you that if two of you agree on earth
concerning anything that they ask,
it will be done for them by My Father in heaven.
For where two or three are gathered together in My name,
I am there in the midst of them.

MATTHEW 18:18-20

'… So I gave thought of taking them over to the Seas of Turmoil within the Dreamscape and to the place therein designated as the World of Dreams. Perhaps to the Land of the Lost Souls? Or even towards the Sea of Blades? Maybe even to the Archway of Doom, which is in the land of Menifarl – that's a nice place is it not? A thorough testing ground for ones so confident?'

The abject cynicism came up against a stony silence.

'Perhaps you would even like me to take them over to Krandor, O Great One?'

Upon the mentioning, all quiet was swiftly broken. Querulous mutterings resumed inside The City's inner walls. The talk was thick and fast. The gabbling was full of evil intent towards the guest. Revenge was in the air, and the Devil could sense it. But he had done it now. The only thing he could do now was to sit tight and wait, and try to ride out the storm.

'Krandor, you say?'

Fortunately for him, the long line of warring-angels was ushered outside past the Outer Courtyards to continue with other outstanding duties. This Inner Court was now strictly out of bounds save for those that formed his escort. Their baneful guest continued with his parley.

'Unfortunately Lord, it seems as though you have not granted me widespread usage of those wonderful lands since the days of The Trolls of Nagéthâwn, who were before Adam. Hopefully though you are once again bold enough to take on the courage of your convictions, and perhaps, this time, you will adhere to your very own words? If so, speak thus against their folly and permit me the selfsame rights… Or has my *friend* now lost whatever strength he once may have had?'

Immediately, the defenders of the dais reached for their swords, and Michael was amongst them. He was the first to make the headlong dash towards their adversary. In a matter of seconds he was at his foe's throat with his hands hard upon his bolstered neck.

'With these hands I've pressed clouds – to release water, to break up storm clouds, to disperse the rays of the sun. Now it seems, that they're ready for you!'

'Michael!'

A terrible fear sailed through the soft luminous clouds, and with one movement a stern glare gripped the stolid warrior hard. The Archangel relaxed his grip before releasing it completely.

He cocked his head uncertainly towards the glorious beams, raising an eyebrow in an inquiring fashion. 'Yes Lord?'

'It is not time yet, my faithful servant, so let him go.'

The Archangel brushed himself down, before doing the same for their visitor; and then he took a step backwards.

'Of course, Lord.'

Promptly, he was summoned to appear before the Lords of the Realm, which he duly did, soon becoming encapsulated in a velvety white cloud that was floating about a cubit above the floor. He was carried briskly forwards, towards the footstool of the main figure in the middle. Then, he turned around to face the throne, to face the words and it was only then that The Adversary was left alone.

*

Meanwhile, somewhere else within the first heavenly sphere, the corrupted words of insidious *men* were once again being set in motion.

'Mark, are you ready for this?'

'Yeah, whatever you want baby. Whatever you want.'

'Okay, so you remember how it goes.'

'Just about.'

'Well, good then.'

'Someone count it down, would you?'

'Three, two, one...'

*

'I see you have trained your lackeys well!' The Fallen One stared closely at Michael.

'It is nice to see them behaving themselves so well – just as mine always do, mind! Well done Lord, I mustn't fail to congratulate you on your great achievements. It is all for the best I assure you. But may I suggest that you – '

'No, you may not,' The Governor rounded curtly. 'You shall watch your mark, even as I have commanded mine to watch theirs.'

Then Gabriel spoke: 'Or else I shall leave you to them here and now.'

'Oh come, come now Lord! A little banter? A little light folly never harmed...'

A dozen wingless creatures were promptly on the scene, as were the two creatures above The Throne, who each had six wings apiece. Between them they were more than a match for The Vile One, and they could capture him, punish him, and bring him to justice, with or without due process. It was those who were of the Devil who had defiled the flesh, defied authority, spoken evil of dignitaries; and now it was pay-back time – nothing more, nothing less. It was Chrionious who took the initiative.

He walked briskly over to the prized guest, his hand becoming stronger than burnished bronze, the anger upon his face masking that vast echelon of experience. Suddenly, and quicker than the eye could blink, he raised his arms in defiance of Lucifer's standing.

'Treachery!'

'Keep your rank and your position my brother!' The Archangel caught the fist from behind. 'The Lord has just commanded me as much,' resumed Michael with longing, 'so you'd better do the same. I don't always understand him brother, but we've got to listen. You know that much don't you?'

The saddened look on his face said it all.

'Good doggy, listen to your masters,' goaded Satan. 'There's a good boy…'

However, something from amid the clouds captivated Michael's attention.

'…I mustn't forget to throw you a bone next time,' teased the rebel relentlessly. 'I'll even make it a big one, on account of my inherent generosity. You'd like that wouldn't you boy…?'

While Satan continued to prattle on in the background, Chrionious' observance was gradually being consumed by something else. It seemed as though there was an air of approbation coming from the First Throne…

'You pups really are pathetic aren't – '

But before he could even finish, his escort caught a glimpse of their master's eyes.

Crack!

Lucifer saw the back of Michael's arm late, yet he still managed to block it. But the Archangel had already followed up with another timely blow, this time aimed with the palm of his opposite hand.

'Take that Devil!'

Thwack!

'And that!'

Whack!

There were two quick raps in quick succession. One was from Michael and the other was from Chrionious himself. They caught the Dark Man square on the jaw, bruising him immediately, the combined force of which was enough to send him reeling.

'Bastards!' shouted Satan as he fell back a dozen yards onto the gold-paved forecourt. There, he was laid out for quite some time, dazed and greatly disorientated. Moreover, he was hurt, and injured, and highly humiliated; he had little else to say at the moment.

'Get up, O Weak One! And try to pay due respect for those of a higher standing.'

At Gabriel's command, The Archfiend began to fumble his way to his feet, over by Michael's side. The Enthroned Ones thought it best to ignore the present fracas, and resumed conversation on the important matters that were just coming to a head.

'Lucifer, *mein-e* Keruv, you will now be pleased to hear that I have taken the time to consider your proposal…

'As you say, my word is indeed my bond. Know therefore, and be certain on this, that if two should agree on any matter, and in this case in particular, upon the dark matters, which you have…'

'Eh-he-hem…'

'…Brought to light, shall we say…? Then, I will surely give you my permission. But only if two or three should agree – and believe. That is all.'

He couldn't quite believe his ears, but he knew that he'd heard it all the same. There was only one more thing left for it. Surely he would be cast out, again, for this bold move. Surely, he would…

The Devil moved closer to The Ones upon the thrones.

'Skin for skin, Lord,' hissed Satan, his head sunken and his manner servile, as he rubbed his hands together in expected glee, his previous shaming already forgotten. 'Do I have permission over their flesh also?'

There was a short pause as the central figure made haste towards his right-hand man. But this one seemed to delay a while, as though he was emerging from a latent trance. Then, at his lord's insistence, he seemed to yield a little, releasing a painful sigh as he realised what the inevitable consequence of this fell encounter would be.

With a brief turn of his head he appeared to be indicating something, which caused The Adversary's countenance to brighten up somewhat, more than it had done ever since the Great Deception which had taken place on Daearawd, in the defining age of Men. Then his face appeared to positively glow.

'Are you sure?'

Lines were etched deep into his companion's forehead, which few if any ever saw. His face had become ashen, the colour of a wounded prince; and his breath was laboured, as though upon his shoulders was placed the whole weight of the world. Yet again.

'Yes…'

*

'Amen…'

*

In a quite unrefined manner, The Escort laid hold of their pejorative guest and accompanied him back towards the edge of the universe, which is also the beginning of the Second Portal. Some of The Devil's own were already there waiting, being privy to the brutal manhandling of their lord and master. They had approached the doorway leading to eternity but they were nonetheless shocked at what they were now being allowed to see with regards to their most eminent member.

Praus, who was the leader of the corrupted ranks, considered the affair gravely, but at the same time he had no way of truly knowing what was really going to transpire. Nor indeed was he aware of the gravity of the business in question, nor what they had agreed upon, his master and the other; save for that it was serious, judging by the number of warriors who made up the first and second levels of his escort. And there was absolutely no way that Praus could comprehend the course of events which was set thenceforward, even if it were to have been told to him by the gods themselves!

Presently, several mighty warriors came into view. It was not difficult to detect that Lucifer was the one in their midst.

'Listen guys, there's load of 'em.'

'Who d'ya see boss? Who d'ya see?'

Praus scrutinised the huge herd of angels for a while, before his sight zoomed in on the faces of those in the procession.

'Well I'll be damned! That's Tal there with Scion!'

'...Yeah, I see... but isn't Alphie and Moroni too?'

'Yeah, yeah, yeah, I see them, I see them. Motherfucker! What's going on here then?'

Then Praus, Baal-Rasdda, and the others from their ranks paused a while as they mulled over the possible implications of this entourage.

'Captain?'

'What is it is Bel-Gamon?'

'I hate to say this now, but isn't that Chrionious there coming out with Dorian, captain of the Seventh Guard?' Upon the saying, all of Praus' numbers gazed over through the thick spumes of cloud. 'Over there master, right before the Highway's Fourth Elevator?'

'You're right, shit, sheathe your swords, sheathe your swords,' Praus barked, turning sharply on his own retinue. 'I'll be damned if I'm going to face those two with a mere bunch of amateurs! This is some heavy-duty shit here.'

'It's true ain't it boss!' croaked his lieutenant. 'They take all our best members to Sidon, get slaughtered, and leave us with a sad bunch of miscreants. Then they say "Go over to the Eternal Doorway and guide the Prince of Darkness back through to his lodgings would you? There's a good chap!" – '

'Baal-Rasdda, shut up a minute... Who can you make out over there, by the captain of that troop?'

'What? Talking with the captain of the secondary guard?'

'Yeah, that's the one.'

'I don't know to be honest – but it looks kinda like...'

Then, suddenly, Bel-Gamon, who was ranked third in the retinue, popped up again.

'Master, master, have you seen him yet? Have you seen him yet?'

'What? Where? Quickly!'

Gamon sent a smoke-trail out towards the direction his troop had just come from, before promptly disappearing in a cloud of sooty resin.

'Gamon, you fucking coward! Come back here... or at least bring your troops back!'

'Master, look where the trail has ended!' gasped Rasdda.

'What is it Baal-Rasdda? Where did it end?'

They looked over towards the procession they had just been scrutinising and they could feel the agitation in their own ranks, which had not been aided by the swift departure of Gamon and about a third of his members.

'Hold on. What's going on here then?'

'Praus, I think that really might be...'

'Holy shit, if that's really who I think it is, I'll kill you if you say his name.'

'But it might be... Oh fuck!'

'I'm warning you Rasdda!'

But he didn't have to say it, because a spotter had just come flying out towards his gosgordd.

'Lord Praus, Prince Michael's a-comin'...'

*

The fearsome band of watchers gazed out into the dark empty space for some time to come, as the remainder of the guard put their swords away and returned to camp. There were many other engagements which had to be performed; they could not always fight, desirable though such a fray would have been.

'Would you just look at that, Michael...'

The bold warrior cast his eyes askance.

'They've now made Praus a prince – would you believe it?'

'Nice chap he was, but never had too much up top. But it looks like he must have come along a bit since then.'

'Or else they've lost too many of their lords to the Blackness of Darkness and Tartarus!'

'Yes, or that!'

They followed Satan and the rest of his fiends, through the matrix of dark-matter in the universe, until the tiny glimmers of light shone no more. Then there was no sound, no disturbance, nothing. The tiny specks of light had dwindled into a dull and hazy reflection of what once had been, which now was not, even though they were soon to be again, even if only for a short space. Thereafter, they petered out completely, obscured completely by the gloomy clouds surrounding them.

To some, that was the extent to which they had erstwhile fallen. But to Michael, even the most recent exchange of insults paled to insignificance, that is when viewed against the far darker backdrop that was waiting outside.

*

Alisha's pleas had fallen on deafened ears, much to her obvious chagrin. Her earnest sobs could no longer be heard against the muffled sounds of the distant melee; again, much to her blatant annoyance. Shit was bad and she didn't mind thinking it (if not saying it), which, because of the unique circumstances, she did in fact do – time and time again.

She came to a perched position, low behind the sofa bed, away from those two destructive dolts. She was feeling somewhat protected against the broody storms that were gathering outside for mischief, and from the fools on the inside who were reciting a blasphemous re-creation of The Lord's Prayer. Although she tried hard, very hard, she could not possibly have hoped to avoid them all – a fact that was not lost on the spectators.

Without warning, the wind and rain joined forces in one violent action, as they lashed against the house porticoes in their final attempt to drown the last stubborn dregs of resistance. They waited with yearning for the Two Foolish Ones to complete the fiendish mandate before releasing the full fury of their venom, like a monsoon out of season which had just remembered its rightful course.

Balustrades from the rear of the premises wobbled angrily until they buckled near completely, and a great clattering din quickly overcame the august presence of the storms. Alisha sobbed bitterly, her tears an avenue of escape, the dizziness currently about her head, a welcome relief at last. But even that was short-lived when every lug became subdued, as they became haunted by the dull ringing that was coming from around the kitchen.

A kettle began whistling unpleasantly, in careful synchronisation with the limitless wind. It rattled out a tune that was barely common with inanimate designs, though nobody was overly concerned with this fact; for nobody could actually remember putting it on in the first instance!

It bickered acrimoniously by itself for a while, shaking the foundations of the kitchen floor, whilst wailing heatedly upon its hot iron railings. Thereupon, it gave off that characteristic popping sound, which is not unusual in horror movies and sci-fi novels, the same that should not form any part of a true-life tale set in London. The sound occurred over and over again, and then once again for good measure, like there were many kettles, of all varying sizes, coming to the boil all at the same time. It was a phenomenon that caused the alarm bells to begin ringing. And they were not just the ones inside their heads.

Raging vehemently of its own accord was the rain. Its wrathful host was the wind. And their guests were the Lords of the Underworld, sprites from Uffern, characters from beyond the Dimensional Barrier. All were bent on entry.

The windows shook from the outside in, as the rain became more vexed at the displacement of its former position. This was evidenced best by its skilful angling, which was in a manner that was wholly contradictory to the current laws of science, just as the venom from its visitors was wholly contradictory to the ways of The Lore. This foul alignment, within the blustering flurry, was sufficient to punish any of those left inside and would do so promptly after the next erroneous transaction was stuttered. So *they* waited.

Meanwhile however, another glass portal withered, whilst others cracked suddenly, all doubtlessly caused by the high-pitched squeals that were coming from the alarm-systems, which, supposedly, had been turned off for the night. A new day was forming now, one with fewer rules than even the darkest of nights or the blackest of days; one in which all regulations were altered slightly. It was a day in which, whatever rules there were, veered towards the unsettling condition of anarchy.

Alisha cried again, angering the host, scuppering the prayer for a moment. Then, at long last, the angry droves of rain succeeded. The water, the first signs of the latter rain, began to seep through the home's uncovered orifices. All this occurred even as more of the prized inlets swung open. And Dread, at last, had found himself an in-road.

Other ominous sounds were soon caught coming from the rooftop and out back. Some were from the tiling that had previously been dislodged, which was now in free fall towards the ground in random doses. Then there were the survivors of Enfield's canine and cat populations, who had gathered earlier towards the rear lawn; they issued the remaining tumult behind their humble mistress, Laxative. The meowing was annoying and the barking was incessant, until one of the creatures aired an altogether more acidulous sound. That was because its time had come to be the next victim to the raging river outside. The sudden drowning of that singular schizoid Siamese submerged all other sounds insouciantly. And the noise made as he sunk within the foaming river was as disturbing as any sound made on that eve.

However, there was one peculiar wail coming from the front of the house that was particularly distressing. The continuos, chortled, icily-clad shrills, by virtue of the breath it came under, shook the foundations of the Syndicate well. It even took precedence over the asphyxiated gurgles emanating from behind the lawn. Shortly afterwards though, the very same noise seemed to alter drastically, and it changed into a piercing howl, like that of a wounded wolf. The turbulence was increased, The Friends were imbued with zeal, and their mobi'es were now dialling frantically. It was all enough to send shivers down even the most honest of spines.

*

90

One visit upstairs was now not enough for Alisha, and from where she was crouched, there appeared a long, smelly stream of protein-filled liquid. The crap behind the seat of her pants was not hers though – that was courtesy of Butch, the bitch-lover, who had forced his way in through the cat flap a minute or so before. Neither Gee nor Marcus jibed any longer, because none fared any better.

If, however, they had stood still a while longer, and if they could have been bothered enough to be a little more rational in their thinking, then they would have soon realised that those boorish moans were coming from their next door neighbour's feline. And if they would have inquired a little more deeply still, they would have quickly realised that, after such a horrendous night so far, the cat was severely pissed off.

She had been beaten, locked outside in the driving rains, was now very much alone and in a bad state of repair, had just discovered the body of her best friend, was very unstable and in desperate need of some tender loving care. The only thing that had cheered her up slightly was the grim fate doled out to that brutal beast, Rabies.

Alas! For The Friends were not so rational, especially after J-J's foolhardy stunt, which was now coming to a head and backfiring dreadfully. After that, what could one do? Therefore, that very sound was enough to complete a whole catalogue of lamentable activity. Which was, in fact, when The Lord's Prayer was ended…

*

'Quickly!' clamoured J-J. 'Everyone take cover!'

Acting rashly each one dived headlong into the falling pieces of masonry, the crumbling wall furniture, and the broken cutlery.

'Get out the way Gee!' exclaimed Mark, as his flight was all too suddenly interrupted by the Big Man.

'Get out my space yourself, bitch!'

J-J too was an anathema before his eyes; so that left Sash to search out his three remaining companions, who were all busy protecting themselves as best as they possibly could.

'Ugada, ugada…'

It wasn't working. His voice box had packed up. He wanted to find his voice, to cry out for help, to blast the Two Fools, J-J and Markie, for leading them into such perilous circumstances. He wanted to encourage the others to do the same. But while he was looking towards his boy Gee for additional support, he knew by the look in their faces that they could not even find their own tongues, let alone help him in his quest for his.

It seemed to have taken forever to recite the prayer backwards, but that, in fact, was the time taken for them to discern the immense changes in the atmosphere. For the winds appeared to recede quietly into the distance, as though it ought not to have been there in the first place, and the grievous howling of the tormented cat appeared, all too suddenly indeed, to stop. The bitter rains also seemed to cease somewhat abruptly at about the selfsame moment that the monkeys' eyes disappeared... although this latter thing was scarcely noticed by anyone. Shortly afterwards, however, the mood inside relaxed, because it was all now coming to an end.

Slowly, the two culprits turned to face the others.

In truth, they were just as surprised as everyone else, astounded even at what they had just witnessed; but their friends didn't have to know that. After such an inauspicious start they (and in particular J-J) were very quietly convinced that they may have fucked things up like Pol Pot, and doomed their gang, perhaps even themselves (which was worse!), to a fate worse than death.

Now though, or so Mark presently thought, maybe he was something greater after all, something approaching a god, as he had once believed in his teenage years. But who was he to say? Except, of course, Mark... of course.

There was silence.

*

'Who's the man?'

The silence repeated itself... which did little if anything to deter The Kid.

'I told you guys,' Mark resumed, trying hard to regulate his irregular heartbeat. 'I told you it would work. Do I deserve some respect?' A beam as wide as a townie's march was written all over his face. A right royal mess had been avoided.

'Yeah, well, it's about time too, Boyo!' Sash replied. 'Because anyhow my chief chav had – '

Gee made it more concise for him. 'Because any how... and I mean anyhow... annnyyyy-how things had gotten any worse my man, I would have brock you one-time serious. Seen? But big up the boy anyway... and J-J with her advanced ways of thinking of that reverse-polarity bullshit. Cheers girl!' He panted deeply, recovering his position slightly on Mel's favourite sofa-bed.

'Thanks J-J,' Elena added, still somewhat disconcerted. 'But I can't believe that your idea actually worked!'

'Yeah, to be honest Jema I wasn't overly impressed with your inspiration myself,' Alisha continued. She put her hands on her hips like a big black mama. 'For a moment, I thought that you'd really lost it there girl... and I would have been none to pleased if you did, I'll tell ya that for nothing!' She exhaled, wagging her finger at the insolent young upstart.

'And neither would I have been,' Jema replied, mimicking her actions in turn. 'But it didn't happen now did it my beautiful black sister? Next time, have a little bit of faith would you? And there's me thinking that that was the fundamental part of your religion – pardon me!'

The two girls laughed virulently, which soon turned into genuine fits of mordant relief, straight from the heart. The two friends hugged one another closely; it was the first sign of well-being after a hard night of stress and song and so it was nothing to be shunned, only to be welcomed.

'Keep your paws next time sis, or you'll do somebody some serious damage one day!' J-J then gave way to the leader of the pack, Gee.

'Relax dreaded Bros and easy on down my beautiful beanies, for is 'im not I and I's top boy?' acclaimed the black chief, beating his chest proudly with ardent passion. 'Is 'im not,' (*he pointed to Mark*), 'after yours truly – of course – d'article rudeness? Proper-man? *Roooood*...boy. Mash up dem bloodclart.'

Not even Sash appeared to mind the apparent stunt and the sudden relegation of his person, for a fair work had seemingly been rendered.

'An' all dem t'ing innit, Gee?'

Sash had to style it out for all to see, or perhaps more accurately, so that no one could actually see his obviously-well-concealed affront.

'Cheers guys, it was quite cool wasn't it though?' Mark said, disarmingly modest now. 'So this country fella now figures that if Jema-Jane and Alisha there can find ways to get us into the shits then an innocent little backwater boy, like me believe it or not, can get us all out.' Judging by his quivering hands, however, it was plainly obvious that the whole experience had shaken him.

'Imagine that eh g-guys, would you? Just imagine that...' He put his tremulous hands on his hips, hoping the extra support would help restrain its involuntary spasms. 'Just imagine...'

'Yeah respect due from the London Crew, to you know who, to Mark – the man with sugar, the man with soul, the man with spice. *Nice* one kid.'

Even Sash was now pleased. 'But not again, you hear me 'Leash, J-J... Mark. Not again. Because I'm not gonna be hanging with fools no more!'

But even as Mark's mysterious blackness was being adulated by the benign figure of Negroid charity, the Italian and Welsh Farm Boy stammered out another word, which no one wanted to hear; which Sash and the others, in fact, tried their damnedest to ignore. And it was all because of the next windy clattering that rapped hard against the doorframe.

Mark: 'Guys... I think – '

Sash: 'Oh-oh!'

Alisha: 'Ah man, that ain't right!'
Gee: 'Shit, that looks a bit like – '
J-J: 'Fucking hell, did any of you see that?'
Elena: 'See what? Guys...?'

*

Never would they have expected the eyes to manifest themselves again from the shattered remnant of the floorboards, and not in such a hideous fashion too strenuous for mere mortals to describe. Never was there the thought that anyone would have, at any time before death's final gate, welcomed the previous eve's torments over their present status, grim though all its tidings had certainly been. Thus, in effect, never would they have allowed themselves to be drawn into such disgraceful acts of foolishness, if they had only known what truly lay ahead. And it was only the grace-saving effects of the undulating footfalls that spared them from having to comprehend any further what it was they had just seen.

For when the massive single pane of unbreakable glass, shattered, and sliced thrice the afflicted feline into two dire halves plus a head, the five of them who afterward heard the god-awful sounds of its angst quickly passed out into an immediate state of unconsciousness. But they were not to be alone. Nevertheless, it was only when Elena saw the pair of grey scaly hands reaching out to drag her down that she too realised that what her friends had opted for, the place for which they were now headed, was by far the safest route.

So she hastily followed suit, quicker than the eye could blink, more confusion set in her face than the previous form of Alisha. But in so doing, she did not part from the place easily, because of the active fear that was clawing at her soul. Instead, she left there in a much-debilitated state of mind, as one who has just suffered the full horror of war. Though it was only after that, when the final forfeiture was at last received, that the silence again returned to haunt the empty room.

PART II

THE NEW WORLD

INTO THE UNKNOWN

And truly, if they had called to mind that country from
which they had come out,
They would have surely had the opportunity to return…

HEBREWS 11:15

His was a well-known face at all the sacred sites, from the White Temples in the southerly most parts of Elfdom by Josh's Clepa, which is one of the three principal cities housing Council members, right across to the sanctuaries lying in the far northwest of Goodlands. His was, undoubtedly, one of the most prized voices to be found anywhere within the plains. Moreover, concerning matters of wisdom and The Ancient Lore (which was first known to have been scrawled onto the rawhide of an antelope) there were few others among the gentry that entered into moot with him. For he was one of the most scholarly Surps anywhere within the realms and a testing challenge to any opponent of wisdom.

His skilfulness in disputations can be traced back to his early days when growing up as a lad in the easterly provinces of Elfdom, past the Colonnades of Gwalior's Teeth, by the mountain ridges of the Grey Snow-caps in Halifeyst. The 'Young Frydor', as he had been known in the period prior to his inheritance, had taken his seat readily at the feet of many a great scholar and prophet. Since the days of his cognitive incipience, it is supposed that his tutelage would have been principally in the sciences (maths, physics and earth sciences); philosophy (works from the great sages of old, including Baron Gogian Humboldt, father of the Stone Critics of Lladin); and the histories of Krandor. Even for the secrecy of many of these things, he was now regarded as an authority on much of the history of the Norsemen, the Jutlanders, and those who are called Kelts. He was also an adept on the records of Krandorians themselves. Pertaining to the customs of the ancient religions and laws, there was none better.

Albeit, the ways of his calling were strict and the fruits it bore, barren. His soul had been sorely troubled by some of the things taught him, and he had become loth to accept many a creed and doctrine without proof first. In truth, so the records tell, there was little to challenge the callow buck, apart, that is,

97

from the corrupt temptations that happen upon all elves at times. In times past such a one as Frydor might have been called upon to raise his blade in angry defiance against the rising tides of violence. But towards the ending of that era, such labour seemed no more, for peace abounded in Abundance.

Therefore, it came to pass afterward that Frydor began with his pilgrim ventures. He visited places far and wide in his indelible quest for the wisdom. His desire was to learn, to increase understanding, to divide the runes of the Elder-days. Such pursuits could only be accomplished by way of the Ancient Greats.

*

Amongst elves at that time, one of the more renowned insights belonged to that famous young professor, Brother Bob Lionard. He was a follower of The [Good] Way and a son to chief of the clans of The Light Elves, who had descended from Yesteryear. One of Frydor's worthiest peers, Rob the "Lion-heart", if it was not for his slip-up with men, would be reckoned to have an honour price (or *gradd*) matching that of the noble Surp himself.

Many called this elf the Lion-speaker, for the boldness of his great many words. Others, less inclined for the zeal expounded in his every utterance, remarked with some adversity about his nature. When he was gifted with his *awen,* few failed to be greatly affected. A great many sages pored over the ink-clotted words of the older manuscripts to discover whether or not this *wise-elf* was "The Chosen One". Was he the one who would arise in the last hour to stir the masses from apathy, before the great and terrible plagues of Mizraim returned to visit the lands in judgement? Even that notable scholar Midu, who at one time had been chief physician in the Great Castle Keep of Fou, admired his many words.

Nevertheless, we shall not dwell upon either at this moment. For no worthy wise-elf (as these two certainly were) can be excluded from any fair telling of Krandor. Albeit, 'tis needless to say that young Roberto was largely respon-sible for many of the changes which occurred in the early life of the equally fastidious youth, Frydor. Most of these changes were for the good, although some, perhaps, were more dubious to call.

Another of the aforementioned intellects was an old grey-bearded dwarf called Hek Nagin. Born hard by the White Plains of Harmswaith (which is also called the Valley of Shadows by some), he it was birthed into a land of disease, want, and turmoil. For dark were his early days and evil was the curse that had afflicted him. His name means, 'The Proclaimer Who Will Proclaim And Not Be Deterred', and as well as being one of the chief elders of his order (the same to which Lionard was adjoined), he too was a seer, and one of some credible skill. Or so say the loremasters.

At the time of these records his age was said to be more ancient than the oldest of all oak trees, south of Caer Bezaubern. But his eyes yet remained more piercing than any wild-eyed falcon, eloping on a searing summer's day. Uncertain though it was, the time of the *Nagger*'s departure was surely at hand. However, it is not quite yet. When he is gone nonetheless he shall be remembered kindly by most of those residing in Elf-dom.

In the days of yore before the falling of Queen Eliza, many said this of him:

"The counsel of the Nagger was as if one enquired at the oracles of the gods."

(Which, even in the day of the lords and the gods, was no mean boast!)

Also deserving mention are some of the Elders from Westerlings, who, ever and awhile, had striven against the forces of Tou the Bald-headed, son of Boto of the Cold-claws, King of the Wild Cravens, Lord of the Unruly. In the days of old, before Westerlings was renamed, the province had been known as Engels. It is these soils which make for songs such as; "Producer of many a noble warrior… More patriots perfected than Elfdom… More slain than any other rocky outcrop within the entire northern boundary!"

Their grounds at present are filled by a race of green-skinned dwarves called *The Little People*, who were originally from Bel-Monkfrith, which lies along the Dead Sea Coast. They then ventured westwards, marrying with the villainous peoples of the country, yielding vilified crops, producing villein for seed, who then ate from the villainous fruit of the vine. The round and rustic speech, which is now heard wafting through The Dales, is a testament to this.

*

It came about, towards the Feast of Scheusalnacht in the Era of the Forgotten Soldier, that two of their more prominent members were conceived, born of their mothers in the western part of Engels. Lily mab Dothas named her son Esi-An Drawn (which literally means: 'To Speak Softly And To Extend A Hand Of Friendship In Order To Gather In'). His father was Daniel the Dangly, son of Darius the Danngoly – a warrior descended from Otto the Slasher – that valiant hero in the Vile Wars of Deithcanyon's Creek.

The other spawn berthed was his distant cousin, Greenwood. Much like the fable of Miriam and Eliza, cousins, of whom it is told that angels flocked down from Heaven, conferred blessings, commanded that deserts should be their sons' dwelling-place, ordained one to speak and the other to heal, so was it with Esi-An and Greenwood. Both were blessed with divine seed, taken from the very depths of the Elysium Waters; both were hardened to the climes of Engels; none were they ready to oppose them.

It is now said that after such a life of piety, the like of which has not been seen since the days of Uncle Sid, Old-Thegn of Chard, Esi-An is still roaming the outer regions of Krandor, warning folk of the impending doom due to come from Dereden. The fate of Greenwood, however, is somewhat less certain.

He had been a seafaring man for much of his days, waxing most valiant against the Pirates of Penzance and The Plymouth Brethren, whom had banded together to wreak havoc across the southern seaboard. Bold and brassy with many a ribbon stuck fast to his chest for bravery, he it was called "Chief of the Mighty" by seafarers. Moreover, even in the battles fought against the Phantoms of Ben Carrock (when it happened that the lords of the Gejit clans made summons for denizens to rise up from Annwfn), Greenwood had waxed valiant in contention.

Afterwards, the sages say that he migrated to the Far North of the Krandorian provinces. Others pronounced that he subsequently returned to the cities of his ancestors, to a place of peace and prosperity in the Far North, where the vine grows abundantly, where scent is the spawn of the gods. Nevertheless, the Dark Elves of Dereden rumour that the sheer quantity of ale in his gut caused him to topple overboard in a journey from Port Carnyen one day. For, they say, he was a man given kindly to much liquor. Believe that one who will.

These, therefore, were the noble folk, who stood proudly against the Terrible Alliance. Such is their fame that their exploits have even reached the mouths of the famed Bards of Meréden. No mean feat is this...

*

Between the Mounds of Hope and the River of Peace lies the place called Se'kere, which means 'Expectation' in the old Black tongues. It is to this place that the elderly Surp travels every seventh cycle in the coldest month of the year. According to prophecy, this is the place where the Knights and Judges of the Laicar Noibla will alight onto the lands for the first time. These warriors (also affectionately called the Knights of St Andrew and St George) shall re-establish the Keys to the Kingdom coming, thus helping to usher in the new age of peace, reconciliation, and prosperity. That is the same day when the merciless shall be judged for their asperity, the blameless are commended for their virtue, the pure are honoured for their strength, the devious shall be undone; the humble are remembered for exaltation, the haughty shall be brought down, very, very low.

We now return to Frydor, one of but a few living who could understand these things. This elf was thoughtful in all his ways, clear as a cuckoo-call in speech, mighty as the Zaqen in deed. He had judged these prophecies many years (as one must), preparing himself fitly to receive them. Rigorous indoctrination, disciplined meditations, prayers, penitence, holiness, fastings, and many other such noble arts did he practise to purge himself of his sin.

Many were the ways of Surps, which few mere mortals were willing enough to understand. His stout legs once even carried him to the Hermits of Thurles by the border with Loch Abar, with whom he spoke for many days. They had exchanged oracles, received blessings, bestowed gifts upon those of higher rank – all the things that accompany such noble visitations.

Thus, to a wise-elf such as Frydor, the sight that was to appear before him should not have been as stupefying as it was. Alas! His discomfiture we shall allow for the time being; for it *was* a most curious affair which occurred on that grand dawning, sometime in the midst of Rhagfyr.

*

It was the wet season, mists hanging low in dark swathes of discordance, storms breathing heavy fumes towards the grey, gloomy mounds perched beneath the northern skyline. The skies were filled to the brim and grim was the colour cast across the surface of heaven. It was as though a weight was waiting in verdict, wanting to release judgement upon the grassy-green soils beneath.

Winds bore down in strong gusts from across the Waters of Temptation, gathering its rain together to form static sheets of pins that were prickly and punishing to the skin. It was this, so the gods thought, that would make futile any attempt of ventures through the fens on that particular day.

The hills were lifeless blobs of earth protruding from a dark green blanket that had been covered in sheen. The topsoil was variegated, its colour changing from the lush green of its leafy umbrella to the deep brown tans that characterised the barren soils. But, of late, few travellers were inclined to traverse the forbidding landscape. And none could blame them, as we shall soon see.

Heading northwards, ample lands stretched to as far as the eye could see. Rich, fertile soils lay to the fore and barren swathes of land – the result of disease in an earlier year – marred the opulent backdrop. This was, in part, due to excess erosion; but it was also due to the plenary villages constructed by skilled wrights, smiths and masons, each from his own hold of expertise.

Beyond the thick hanging soup, further elevations of natural beauty appeared for miles around. Ghostly some seemed; others sprouted suddenly, as the wavy lines of grey uncoiled themselves from about those habitats. Often, the lands were teaming with spores. There were wild things, both of creatures known and unknown. They came in all shapes and in all sizes and in every colour under the sun.

Hounds ran wild amid the logs recently felled by the adze of a woodsman's axe. Large pigs, whose snouts were dun-coloured tusks, snorted about in their swill, romped about in their feed and pounded out their forage into grime. Swift antelopes milled in the lower prairie – graceful as the silent wind to some, horned as the devil to others, with hoofed feet like his henchmen.

Heading eastwards the valleys opened up into verdant dales and heather land. Scrubland became the mane and a steep embankment was its forelock. Green hills compassed about the lovely green pastures, and they had been flattened more kindly into stepwise rolling ledges by the presence of brown-backed bears. The scene, without doubt, was spectacular.

However, when the first rumbling was heard, the light was short (to the throw of a silver-tipped lance in most places), and neither the sun nor the moon chose to speak cordially on behalf of the unwary visitors. Without fail, therefore, it was to be a most distinguished day of reckoning.

Some cite the despair encountered in an everyday life of wear and tear
And a being whose chief belief is in the futility of seeing and existing;
Though others say dolefully that this is a misnomer,
And lay blame at the foot of reason to explain all, any further.
Yet others lay hold of the dark powers and evil plots,
For it falsely gives the promise of a better lot,
And all ills forgot.

Reckon with this saying those who will. As it transpired the hills around the southerly town of Se'kere was the location for the initial encounter. It was the conjuncture for the first meeting between Men and Elves, between the Two Twin Worlds of Dreams, which have had their names since a time out of mind, since the Matrix first evolved. And it was also the first encounter between the Forces of Good and the Hordes of Evil.

Therefore, blinded though The Friends were for a time, there yet seemed a faint recognition that took place. It was not a familiarity by way of remembrance, but rather, as it soon transpired, it was a joining of spirits.

*

Elena was the first to open her eyes. She kept her hands raised to shield her face from the rainstorm which had saturated the skies in anticipation of their arrival. But its force pounded down too heavily upon her naked forearms and her exposed fleshy parts, quickly bruising the delicate skin she had been birthed with, whilst at the same time coarsely removing some of the tenderness that lay behind. She turned her head away from the prevailing gusts, as she tried with all her might to keep herself from the buffeting droves that blew onwards across the plains. Then, diligently, she looked around in search of her friends.

Elena prised her lids open, again, to peer through those elliptical cracks. Her eyes soon fell on something rather familiar.

'Arghhh!' she screamed, before the recognition of this new face had dawned upon her.

Then it was Aleasha's turn to sound off. 'Elena where are we?' she queried.

She peeled back the coverings of her eyes, clearing the grit and the grime that had collected in small, sticky packages in the corners of each visual orifice.

'I'm not too sure 'Leash. Where do you think we are?' Elena rejoined.

'Last thing I remember was… well… you know,' said Aleasha, sounding somewhat highly strung and sulking. 'To be honest, I haven't got a clue li'l sis.'

They yomped on further about a dozen yards through the boggy soils beneath their feet. After the short tab, the girls were in the mood for another question. It was Aleasha who posed it.

'Seems like we're in a swamp, doesn't it?'

'So where're the rest of the guys then, Elena?'

With her left hand, Aleasha brushed aside the sweat that had innocuously whetted her brow; with her right, she compelled herself to scan the present scene more carefully.

'I don't know. I mean, I barely recognised you until you stood right in front of me…'

*

Elsewhere, all corpses were commanded to rise, all minds were told to explore, and all eyes were granted leave to examine, until all things were fitted as they should be. The thrones were put in place, the hoary-heads were gathered, and the elders assembled together for judgement. It was the Ancient Lore they had come to examine, that ancient and most trivial part of that which is called "The Ten Principles of Justice".

I, Merwys, which means "Black-bird" (name correctly given for such an auspicious occasion), watched till the thrones were put in place, and the Ancient of Days was seated. His garment was white as snow, the hair of his head was like pure wool, but the buckle on his bronzed feet was gold, as too was the belt that he wore around his waist. His throne was a fiery flame, and the wheels that bore him were like a burning fire; a fiery stream issued and came forth from before him like the fires that the Sea-serpent spews when he consumes those great ships when they set sail to Narcissus. There was a thousand thousand ministering to him, great was he like the King from the Farthest Sides of the North, and mighty was he like one of his princes. It was then that

I looked and I saw many marvellous wonders displayed before me; for the courts were seated and the books were opened.

There were those around spouting out pompous words of self-gratification and sin which others around paid heed to. For times were dark and minds were foolish, and of those that were not altogether ignorant or base as the base-born slaves of Annwfn, they were somewhat weary in mind and wanting in their gifting.

It happened then that as I was yet watching, one with the appearance of a Zaqen of a great many days, bathed in blood, tried in battle, and victorious over the Dark-side, stood by. Then was he granted position before the throne that seated the gods, about which many a mighty man was to be found. It was him who was the mouthpiece of the other, mightier creature, who roared like a lion and spoke with authority. And it was a curse that I heard him pronounce upon all the inhabitants of the lands: both above and beneath, great and small, base-born and titled, bondservant and free, poor and rich, weak and strong, the wise, the witless, that he who is unjust, should be unjust still; he who is filthy, should be covered in grime; he who is righteous, should be adorned in white raiment; and he who is holy should remain safely in its stead, forever.

He spoke dark words – bold and brash, brash and black, black and brazen, harsh as the seas of Derwent, bitter as the judgement that struck the Cities of the Plain in the days of yore. (Were not those towns smitten for being lifted up, for having the abundance of food, and for being taken with the indolence of a tortoise which has been put to sleep for the night?) Verily, I say, as one learned in the Ancient Lore. Verily; for it is an undeniable and unmistakable truth. Therefore, such was the damnation he pronounced upon those that had gathered round to hear:

"Make the heart of this people dull,
And their ears heavy,
And shut their eyes;
Lest they see with their eyes,
And hear with their ears,
And understand with their heart,
And return and be healed."

Upon the hearing, all voices fell silent, and those before the throne quaked and trembled. There were great cries of lamentations and of woe and of grief, and mourning was rife as fiery white coals were cast upon all the inhabitants of the worlds. These were parcels of doctrine and deliverance needed for the last few hours of Sunlight, and it was Joel who was commanded that his sons might receive. For was it not the prophet himself who first spoke the battle-runes which was to be pronounced again in the darkest hours of man? Thus to him was given the charge of ordering the troops according to the counsel of their elders.

Then Phinehas was summoned to minister before the alter on account of his zeal shown in days gone by when he had thrust through his bastard brethren and his brazen bitch; the Apostate Zimri and the Midianite woman. His spawn were beckoned too that they might join in the foray. Then came the offspring of James and John – those who were called "Boanerges" – even by the mighty Zaqen – a name which means 'Sons of Thunder'. And as Time passed into No-Time, I could see these packets being warmly received, and those that grasped them and held them close to their bosom bursting into flames of a thousand beautiful colours. Likewise was utterance granted them that they should conquer the lands, undo the curse, and squash all foemen; for the earnest expectation of creation had grown great.

I turned again, and I saw yet another sign. A great and mighty beast was slain, and its body was destroyed and cast into the burning embers. It was a tremendous monster, awful and terrible, though as for its exact likeness, I was neither willing nor able to recollect. The remainder of the beasts had their dominion taken away, though as Grace would have it, their lives would be prolonged for a season and a time. For without this Grace would the worlds be rocked, the Seventh Trumpet sounding aloud to the accompaniment of noise from the Twelve Tribes who daily practice their war-cries before the seraphim, the cherubim, the elohim, and the hoary-headed elders (who even now I could see were lying prostrate before the hilasterion, which is the chief throne that all must come to if they wish to live). But before this must come the Two Olive Trees & Lampstands who stand between the Earth and Heaven.

In their speech is fire, the strength of the gods; on their backs are coarse skins and sackcloth and uncultivated wools; within their hands are plagues and prophecy, power and dominion over Faunus and the rest of his ungodly brood; and they bring with them yellow parchment from a time out of mind, upon which are written the sacred words of the Lore – The Ancient Lore. Time, Times and half a Time shall be their allocation; No-Time shall be their spell. Such was the Law all had come to examine that day, and it was Wyngod the Bard, the visiting saint, who was tasked with the detailed inquisition.

He opened his mouth and words were given him. From his word-horde he plucked forth his knowledge; from his heart he waxed bold; with all his sinew and might and courage, determination came forth that he might slay all foemen there that day, should there be any stray sheep in the congregation; or indeed, should those who were of the Synagogue of Satan wish to inquire too deeply into the truths which once they blasphemed. Moreover, of all the words that Wyngod the Wiself spoke, none were found to be wanting:

Righteousness – principles of right and wrong behavior; morals

Justice – the principle that punishment must be proportional to the offence

Truth – that which is true; the word of God; the Law

Humility – the state of being conscious of one's own failings

Judgment – an obligation arising from verdict out of the faculty of being able to make a critical distinction and achieve a balanced viewpoint

Equity – justice, fairness; the quality of being fair or just

Mercy – compassionate treatment of an offender, when it is in one's power to do so

Revenge – the act of inflicting equivalent injury or damage for injury, damage, loss or failure received

Faith – spiritual apprehension or voluntary acceptance of divine revelation apart from absolute proof

Reward – that which is given or received for [good] deeds done or received

Nevertheless, it was the Gang of Ten they had come to inquire of that same day, that all their foolishness, all their apostasies, all their adulteries, and all of their child-slaying antics might be made manifest to those around. The Sons and Daughters of Hades were these also called, a name fitly applied to the cave-dwellers from Annwfn; for it is they who had once belonged to the Council of Elders upon Daearawd, who were now loth to share in communion with those of the True Faith. For they had neglected the teachings of the Ancient Lore and were struck with a curse as a result, abominations and adulteries and apostasies being committed in consequence. Though none in truth knew wherefrom they had been sprung, widely has it been said that they were spawn of the Devil himself. Believe that one who will; if not without the fair witness granted.

So the Council was seated, and the Heads pored through the scrolls before them. All was written upon the hide of a dun cow, as in the days of old, which was also the days of the savages.

After some time, the Spirit of the Zaqen concluded their judgement to be this; that all, barring none, should be dispatched to the coldest, farthest and darkest reaches of Annwfn and from there, once their sufferings had been perfected, all again were to be sent down shackled into the deepest darkest holds of Uffern to make restitution for their sins, if that were possible. As was foretold by the sages of old, it was their fate that was to come after the destruction of Hacosh and Hannah, which was to occur on the darkest night of the year, by the perilous Banks of Ruin.

So it shortly came to pass that the Spawn of Satan (as they had come to be known) also fell through the arches which joined those two worlds together.

And they alighted upon a different part of Krandor, in an altogether different form.

What follows is the Gang of Ten, the "Tuff Talk" and their crimes.

Anus Hel-Yobo, chief son of Hell;
Kaitlan, son of Llawod;
Murtacuffs Williamson;
Ded Volga, having neither father nor mother or genealogy,
(but of hosts and cousins and foster-cousins, without number);
White-man Arthur, son of Records;
Black-man Eddie, son of Shadows;
Madguysa of the Light-fingers;
Karma Sven "The Mere Youth";
John-John the Carpenter;
Steve "Charlie" Brown.

Anus Hel-Yobo, False Priest – he is father to a whole brood of stragglers whose minds he has set against the Lore.

Kaitlan the Large, head of Tuff-Talk – that band of robbers, thieves and thugs, and more. The "Talk".

Murtacuffs of Brixton – one of the doppelgangers from Annwfn, with the ability to transform himself from a saint to a sinner, in the matter of minutes. Deputy of Tuff-Talk. The "Tuff".

Ded Volga, "Mad-Dog"…' Again the elf paused for a space whilst he summoned up the strength needed to continue. 'Master of deaths, depredations, and the degradation of men. Cultivator of the herb, carries the Turkin-blade, as Ottoman, chief of Trolls. Killer.

White-man Arthur – a deep-sea diver whose knives rarely fail to bring him into favour. A lifter of great weights. Once, so they say, he wrestled with a Grey-Bear on the banks of the North Pole, and overcame him, before plucking him spry from the earth with his robust arms, and casting him full-bodied, into the depths of the sea; though not before removing his ears.

Black-man Eddie – a hustler. He who was written in one of the books expounding the numerous errors of Babylon, guardians of the Lawless, after they had put four men in gaol, trolls, whom they swore belonged to ARIP (a band of lawless criminals whose sole fealty is after themselves). It was the Black-man who was mentioned for striking one upon the cheek during a game of pig's bladder one day. For he had set up a goal and was commended as a result, the kiss of fairies being placed warmly upon his hot lips. But within gaols, no man might kiss another without dire retribution, goal or no goal, which feat therefore Eddie duly undertook, landing him in deep mire with the spawn of ARIP who afterwards sought to take his life.

107

Then there is Madguysa – the friendly face of the bunch, much like Eddie, though with his light-fingered responses, not so nice. The "Guys".

Karma Sven – the leader of the Sons of Dogs crew and a rabid fornicator.

John-John the False Prophet – the crafty craftsman.

"Charlie" – the alcoholic artist.

*

Sashi and Gee awoke not long afterwards. Sash's head spun far too much for him to understand the general commotion; Gee, on the other hand, wanted shot of the whole new feel. He rather preferred the blissfulness they'd had earlier, when they'd been journeying through… God knows where – up until the time when they'd arrived at this God-forsaken venue.

Bleary eyes strained to see the diminutive figure upon the naked shoulder of the hill. The form resembled a mermaid skipping capriciously across the smooth green lawns. The outline formed a delicate shape, waif-like in appearance, almost like someone they knew. The bounding beauty drew a little closer still.

'You're all in my dream!' Elena cried, whooping with delight. 'Isn't it wonderful? Welcome to the land of my dreams... Oh my goodness me,' she resumed, bounding off the green turf like a kangaroo with wings. 'It's so great isn't it?'

She grasped hold of Gee's hand, for reassurance as much as anything else. He pressed her equally, sharing the same warmth, enjoying the same fascination. He caressed her skin tenderly, as he had done so many times in the past.

'What did you say girl?' Gee's response was matched only by the weariness in his eyes. 'What was that you said, Elena? – We're all in your dream?'

He looked at her sternly before allowing his gaze to become broken.

'But if we're in your dream,' he continued, letting go of her hand, thinking a little more deeply, not wanting to speak any negative words into her psyche, 'then… then that's cool then. Yep, that's cool, I ain't got no problem with that.'

'It's exciting isn't it? Everyone's always excited about being in a dream – remember us talking about it a while back… well, sometime back anyway. It was *brill* weren't it – I mean, we didn't get to sleep for ages!'

'Yeah, I remember – but I still don't believe it.' The Big Man looked sullenly at the forlorn skies, before passing his eyes over Aleasha's trembling form. Shortly afterwards, he returned them to Elena.

'Where did you say we were, my girl?' He wiped his tired eyes as the subtle downpour continued to breech his defences. 'This place looks a little messed up if you ask me… oh, and are you cold by the way, or is it just me?'

'No, I'm fine, Gee. How about you Aleasha – are you okay?'

No response was forthcoming from the Black girl.

'I mean, we're in some whacked out dream,' moaned Gee, holding fast to Elena's frail arms. 'We don't know where we are or what we're doing here... Anyway, while we are here, if you really are in control of things like you say, then it wouldn't hurt if you conjured up a couple of naked women with extra large breasts babe...'

'Or maybe a Hercules for the honeys, eh?' Aleasha rejoined, recovering her voice at long last.

'If anything goes wrong,' shouted Elena gleefully, 'then all you'll have to do is wake me up!...'

This was, most definitely, good. How many times had Gee tried to fly, to take off without wings and defy gravity by making his body lighter than air? In his dreams it seemed so now and again but the truth is he had never quite succeeded. His spirit, yes, but not his physical body. Yet. Some of the herbal weeds he used to smoke borrowed off some of his brethren from *back-in-the-day* worked reasonably well; but they never really allowed him to reach Cloud-9.

He concentrated hard on leaving the ground, just like Elena. Unfortunately, nothing seemed to be happening.

'I'll try again in a minute,' Gee murmured embarrassed and apologetically.

'After a few deep breaths you'll be okay Gee.'

'I know that!'

'I know you know, I was just saying.'

Aleasha looked at the pair of them and said: 'I give up... Anyway, it kinda beats me how all y'all are convinced about these strange new powers – wholly unexplained and totally inexplicable? It's a nice notion guys, don't get me wrong on this, but I just think the pair of you've gone to cloud cuckoo land that's all.'

They ignored Aleasha's obvious jest; because only The Foolish ever called their faith arrogance.

'Yeah, just another minute, after I've warmed up a bit... '

Soon enough, it was quite clearly evident that no progress was being made. Sashi, being the young man that he was supposed to be, strolled over to his three remaining friends. Haplessly for some, he was not entirely sold on the idea that he had fallen upon strange and foreign lands, in someone else's dream.

He made his approach over towards Aleasha, to see what her wisdom had to offer him.

'S-s-so...' he started, stuttering slightly as he spoke. 'So, we're all in Elena's dream are we?'

He glanced offhandedly at her round black face; then he thought of something deeper.

'Why are we all in Elena's dream, Aleasha?'

Then he thought some more, turning this time to Elena and then towards Gee.

'Why aren't you all in my dream?'

As if this wasn't already enough, he paid one last visitation to his mind. It was not, however, in Sashi's nature to push things like this, so he left it there for the time being, not really wanting to cause any more trouble at the present time.

'That's just dumb Sashi,' Gee pounced hotly. 'But no offence or nothing, Desi – it's just the way things are! Can you live with that?'

'Silly Sashi!' Elena giggled, taking her cue from Gee. 'You're too old aren't you!'

Somewhat humiliated, he went over to the adjacent hill and sat down glumly, where the mists were presently gathering around him, to dampen his spirits even further. Soon, the clouds began to thin out a little, and more understanding seemed to come to the Friends.

Aleasha wiped the sweat off Gee's forehead, and assisted him to his feet.

'Where're the others 'Leash – Mark and Jema I mean?'

Shrugging her shoulders, she looked towards Sashi for an answer to Gee's question.

'Aren't they supposed to be here with us in the dream – '

'Why should they be?' snapped Gee. 'They'd be here if they wanted to be! And personally, after the stunt they pulled… I don't want them here with me – get it chief?'

'Jesus, Mary and Joseph, I was only asking Gee! No need to be getting aggressive,' Aleasha moaned, taking a step or two backwards. 'Sorry.'

'Well… just don't do it again then. Those two fools would have turned up if they'd wanted to, 'Leash, an' I's got a few words to say to them when they do! And that is that!'

There was a short pause as a smile crept slowly across Elena's face. She smirked coyly before her faithful entourage.

'I'll wish them here shall I?' she said, her teeth beaming radiantly all the while. 'Then we'll all be together again won't we?'

She cast them all another radiant beam, which again, was a little too merry for Aleasha's liking.

'Why not?' Sashi groaned. 'The more the merrier.'

She pondered the alignment of her feet, lining them up to the angle which she thought would be most propitious, before carrying on.

'Well, here goes nothing then…'

Eyes shut tightly, her facial expression soon turned into a grimace. Her face began to contort, her mouth began to quiver, and her face took on the same colour as the bleeding sun. A faint wispy smile revealed itself on her lips, moistened by the descent of the soft pattering raindrops. She gazed intently into the canopy above, which was lodged carefully in the grey-auburn skies.

'There. I've willed them to come floating over those hills there,' Elena stated, pointing adamantly to a brow some way away off on a neighbouring mound.

'Sashi, Sister-'Leash, don't worry, this is going to be great! I can really feel the power in this place. This is absolutely fab!'

The clouds that had shrouded the various green-tops parted, leaving the four forlorn figures poised, much like four lost sheep on a mountainside. What little light had been remaining also left, taking the opportunity to realign itself upon Elena's choice mound. And within a short space of time, two shadows were seen to be approaching. They were thin and hazy-looking with no set contours; but they did follow the set path indicated by the young girl's index finger.

The next five minutes passed slowly.

Mark was the first one to negotiate brow of the hill. Gliding smoothly down its mane like a wily child does upon a slide, he drew fresh brown tracks behind him, which clung turbidly to the side of the knoll. J-J's own run was interspersed by a little light whooping and a few jigs for joy. She hurried down the remaining slope towards the rest of their friends, following hard at Mark's heels, trailing him by only a few yards.

Then came their two shadows. As one would expect, for a while they appeared to trace the paths nominated by the two lost comrades; until, that is, they had moved passed the nearest aesthetic protuberance. Again, the sunlight began to dim, barely managing to separate the two shadows into two distinct images in their own right. But that was at first.

Then another ten minutes passed, only ever so slowly this time.

*

'…Guys, did you hear me?'

Jema-Jane was somewhat reluctant to repeat it all again, but as the news she bore was quite important, she made sure that her comrades had taken in at least the main thrust of things.

'I think I've remembered everything, and haven't missed anything out. Cool eh?' She moved closer towards the two short men.

'This is Frydor the Elf,' J-J said, indicating the bearded old man.

'…And this is Flip.' Again she pointed to a form that was presently obscured in part, by the mist and fleeting rain. 'That's Frydor's nephew!'

The second elf paid a marked resemblance to the more withered form, although he was perhaps not so slender.

'They're here to help us, as I said,' J-J continued, ' – even offered us their services as guides, would you believe it? We met them over there, on the opposite slope of the brow there.' Her index finger, as Elena's before her, seemed to reach all the way to the other side of the hill.

'That's wonderful J-J!' Elena exclaimed. 'As far as I'm concerned, the more we have with us, the merrier…

'Welcome Frydor, hello Flip. We're all very pleased to meet you, I'm sure.'

She extended an arm of friendship to both elves and was quietly surprised at the strength of both their grips. Pressing her delicate, cream-coloured fingers into the palms of his hand, Frydor shook it vigorously before handing it over to Flip, who took to brushing his cracked lips just beneath the bend of her wrist.

'Ooh! Charming, I'm sure,' Elena mocked self-depreciatingly. 'But thank you all the –!'

But then Sashi interjected, unimpressed at the episode so far.

'Hello, er, Frydor. Er… P-p-p-pleased to meet you again,' stuttered Sashi before the strangers, rubbing the side of his head nervously. 'So w-w-w-where are we going to then? What I mean is…y-y-y-you're an elf right?'

The little man nodded.

'Yeah, sorry about that – just wanted to sort that one out – y'now get my head straightened kind of… I haven't really met many o-o-of them before, y'see. I don't actually think I've met one before, not even in my dreams.'

'So what? Are you like a dwarf with big ears then, or what?' asked Gee in the coarsest of terms, as was so often his manner.

The elves, not readily offended, smiled.

'All I really want to know,' said Mark, 'is how long are we here for? Oh – and by the way, as a matter of interest in fact – how did we all get here? And where exactly are we?

'…And someone please turn on the lights…'

*

'Can you feel yourself Mark?'

'I don't know Frydor. Why d'ya ask anyway…? Can you feel *yourself?*'

'I've never been completely sure how to answer that one. For we all have dreams don't we – but do we not feel things in dreams, sometimes? Are they not therefore real? On occasions, we even have visions – and do we not perceive something there too? So would that make them any less authentic?'

'So what? Would that make it all so then, if I could – y'know, feel something?'

112

'As real as you want it to be.'

Unfortunately, Gee looked confused. He went over to Aleasha and whispered into her ear:

'This is more than a little weird if you ask me 'Leash.' He blinked hard, opening his eyes each time to view, again, the same strange scenes in front of him. 'Same ol' shit's still here 'Leash, and I don't particularly like it.'

'I know what you mean – I don't rate it much either anymore.' The wind continued to chill her parched features, rallying as if in opposition against her every word.

'Bad things are always happening to me. It's gonna stop one day though – I tell ya that for nothing.'

The arch on Gee's back, the way in which his afro curled up tighter of its own accord, the manner in which his face managed to contort through odd shapes and sizes (rather uncannily for any human other than Jim Carrey), by the way in which spittle flew straight through the gaps in his teeth – all indicated quite strongly that the young black buck was getting riled.

He patted Mark on his shoulder, encouraging him to take what strength he may, and moved off silently to calm Elena down, if at all possible.

'This can be wonderful Gee, cheer up!' encouraged the youngest.

They were lost in a landscape, a beautiful wilderness albeit, but lost all the same. To add to their traumas there were two strange-looking guys with them, fellows who seemed to want to rub it in even further. Where they were, exactly how they had gotten there, or, more importantly, how they were going to get out of there, was all uncertain. All Gee was sure of was that he didn't like Elena bounding around like that, like a spring-hinged kangaroo with a spindle up her arse.

*

'With regards to the first question my child,' Frydor declared, observing his company closely, 'that is, where we are headed; that shall be made clear as we make our journey towards the city of Efas-Us. There we should be safe for a while.

'But concerning the time of your sojourn here; if you are who I think you to be, then:

> *"When the sun shall fall from the sky*
> *And the moon shall turn into blood*
> *Then shall the end gates open*
> *With an almighty and everlasting flood."*

'Moreover, all these things shall happen before the morning of Seventh Cycle of Sorrows, as told by the Ancient Lords of Rohanne! If you are not whom I suppose, then these words are wasted on you, until you perish on the fields of your choosing. Then shall your end be set, your lives lost, the worlds be plunged into darkness.'

Frydor chuckled darkly upon witnessing the glazed look that came over those surrounding him.

'Neither do I know where you've come from,' he resumed. 'I can only go by the teachings in The Books. But I can tell you where I was birthed, if that would be of any use to you?'

The gang looked miffed. It wasn't at all ideal, seeing they had come such a long way and all, but it seemed like that was the best they were likely to do for the moment. So they nodded, disconsolately.

'I am from the town of Mandoslern over yonder,' Frydor motioned, indicating a distant stony ridge, surrounded by pale hedgerows and shallow blue fords. 'And I have been visiting this site for many, many cycles in anticipation of you all, me thinks. I hope you may one day be able to appreciate this sacrifice… though I must say I am pleased at last to be making your acquaintance!'

Flip, who was the younger elf, was quite clearly uninterested in the whole sordid affair. His eyes rolled continuously at his uncle's speech, his skin colour flushed on his sentences, his heart throbbed painfully when the other stopped. He did not try to hide any one of his feelings. However, these visitors did seem a *little* more peculiar than many of the others he had seen in his time, if only for the small strange wraith that failed to appear in the least bit concerned.

Bowing down low, he made play of his genuflection. Paying homage to foreigners was practised frequently, especially at sacred sights, special hours, when the strangers they saw bore weapons. Therefore, there were no qualms concerning this appropriate tribute. Nevertheless, he would have preferred to be making his *own* way home. This would not do at all.

'Honoured to be in such distinguished company, me thinks,' lied Flip, winking over-casually towards Elena. 'Perhaps over time we might get to know one another better?'

'I am sorry to disturb your thoughtfulness, friends, but we must hurry!' Frydor interrupted brusquely. 'It is not prudent for any of us to remain here now.'

He turned aside to the direction whence he had just recently come, mimicking it seemed the very motions of his nephew, who was already traipsing on his way towards the cloud-covered wind-swept mound. But then, there was something else. From the very edge of his baldric came the dim glimmer of a sword.

*

Elena saw it first, and then Sashi, who had been following the frightful passage of her gaze.

'He's armed, people!' Gee yelled when he saw it. 'Watch yourselves!'

He pounced stout-heartedly upon the elf, arms before him, feet at the ready. The elf, however, countered his attempts by some skilful manoeuvres of his own.

'Uncle!' Flip cried.

Frydor side-stepped deftly, and lowered his centre of gravity to a height which Gee found difficult to contend with. The latter stumbled, upon a gnarled root which he should have seen protruding from the edge of the present path. It reminded him of that tune by Gnarls Barkley 'Crazy' which presently started to ring through his head.

Meanwhile, the elf reached out his small stocky arms, grabbing Gee by his collar. He knocked him further off balance with a well-aimed kick to his groin. The Big Man's ungainly floundering made the elf's task easier; and he landed hard on the turf with a bump, by the side of Flip's legs. Then, after the tune, he saw the stars.

The elf drove the tip of his Elfin-blade, "*Saiya*", hard upon Gee's jawbone, and brought it to bear in a highly precarious position for the newcomer. Tainted with the taste of crimson gore, cut by two quick lashes to his cheeks, the leader of the young band of renegades finally subjected himself to the inevitable.

'Okay, okay, what d'ya want boss?'

With this, Frydor sheathed the edge of his sword.

'Enough of these antics!' At once, Frydor extended his hand to aid the miscreant to his feet. 'We have much work to do.'

Then, turning aside to his nephew, the elf said: 'Dress him down son, for we have much work to be getting on with and the time is getting late!'

*

They felt the reverberation travel over the adjoining hillside area. Quickly, the sensation became spent, lasting only a few seconds, dissipating into that unmistakable hint of sulphur. The grey dusk light, that welcoming of a New World, was with them now. Tremors threw the lighter members of the company skywards (namely, Elena and the two elves) before Krandor's own natural forces prevailed again, and drew them all back towards the ground. There was excitement in the ranks as what had been hoped for had finally came to pass.

'This power's great!' Elena exclaimed, almost ecstatic with joy. 'Did you feel that lift? My goodness me, I am really in control, aren't I?'

Both Sashi and Gee looked at her, not in least bit willing to argue.

'Twice in ten minutes, this is brill. I've got the power! Wo-wo-wo-oo-o-'

'Might I suggest that you snap out of your delusions young sister,' Frydor said abruptly, as he plonked himself squarely down by the foot of a nearby apple tree. 'That was the Heart of the Dead Man...' He saw the glum looks on their faces.

' – He lies not far from this unchancy spot,' he resumed, 'but like most dead men, he does not rest easy 'neath the earth.'

The stillness within the camp became an heaviness.

'It may alarm you somewhat to know that there is a saying in these parts:

"Beneath the soils and beneath the dirt
Lies the Dead Man's broil with a woman's hurt!"

'It is one well worthy of note.'

The elf's eyes became stolid, as if suppressing emotions that would otherwise arise should he at all choose to continue. His manner also seemed to wane, as did his countenance, blackening as the skies above when broody flocks of geese hover overhead. Then his face cleared somewhat as he looked at the youthful innocence around him.

'It is not the best time to be telling you such,' Frydor started, before agitation cloaked him about again... 'But it occurs for his foul residence, which lies some way beneath the surface of Krandor.

'The grounds yield all manner of evil and turpitude, and from time to time, they even spew forth creeping things, unwholesome entities, disembodied souls, diseased spirits. And zombies. You are fortunate to experience these things early on, lest your heart should be soft for your future journey.'

The guys looked on in bewilderment; except for Elena that is, who was now close to tears.

'That was only one beat of his foul heart,' Flip murmured disconsolately, 'but we all felt it.'

His countenance suddenly seemed to age; 'But it is not good – for it means that even now it is swelling for the reception of many more souls from these lands. His stomach is always expanding to receive more visitors, before contracting again, forbidding any to leave, binding all of its captives in its wake, confining all who enter into the pits of his angry wroth.... Till the Days of Doom come upon them.'

The elf parried the curious stares with a disarmingly effective smile. 'Nevertheless,' he grinned, somewhat benignly, 'it should not bedevil us at this precise moment, as you are new here, and your sins here have not yet began to fester. But, depart from these sides we must, and forthwith! For there will be eyes here soon to assess what they may.'

He arched his fit, elderly frame towards Elena, before issuing a more direct appeal.

'Please my dear child come with us?' He reached out his arms to hold her by the shoulders. 'And do not try to delude yourself any longer, as it only causes harm in the long run! The Dark Lord will shortly have some of his Nightriders out in the skies, to survey the site of this latest tremor – lest there should be some war fought on his grounds that he knows nothing of.'

The elf called back impatiently over his right shoulder, as he made tracks before his nephew:

'Moreover, when he does come, woe to the ones he finds lingering! Indeed, woe and solemn grief!'

'Tis all true I'm afraid,' Flip confirmed, as he also made ready to leave once again.

'For the Evil Lord is sensitive to all that enter his domain, and all that enter into his kingdom he would like to examine, intimately. So you'd better come quickly while there is still time, for there is much still to be told you. More even than I understand myself which is no small measure I assure you.'

'Efas-Us might offer us a sanctuary,' Frydor yelled, beckoning to his nephew to hurry and catch him up.

'G-g-goodness g-gracious me – wait a second mister. Hold-up people!' The younger elf stayed where he was. He looked curiously at Sashi.

'So w-w-what you're saying is that we r-r-really are already a bunch of fugitives in dreams r-r-right?

'Rightly so, my friend. We are, indeed, in Dreams. In fact, we are in the World of Dreams and in the Realm of Krandor itself, which means "Doom" in the old Elvish tongues. It is well noted that all who set foot herein enter into their own reality, but that few having done so are able to withstand its unwieldy pressure and leave.'

'What do you mean?' sobbed Elena, who was now crying freely.

'Well put it this way; the transmutation, second only to death some say, causes folks' minds to bend, their innards to twirl, their eyes to lose their vision. We shall see if you can fare any better.'

Flip turned aside and at a swift pace headed northward to catch up with his tottering uncle, who was pressing on hard towards the honey dales of Hafod's Ridge, which lies by Mount Ys Synnwyrus. He was not much farther along before he turned around for one last time.

'Understand this however,' he hollered in tones that raced through the receding winds. 'If any of you do wish to live, then my uncle will have to point you the way. And only my uncle may do so!'

So with that last cry, those two were gone.

*

At length, having seen the two elves disappear into the hillside's murky mists, Aleasha spoke most candidly with her friends.

'So what do we do guys? I mean, we don't really know where we are right? And to be honest, as far as I'm concerned – and I don't particularly care about what all y'all think now – but they looked to be kinda okay didn't they?' She ducked beneath the branches of the apple tree to shield herself from the deluge, and nodded towards Gee's freshest wound. 'Apart from the swords I suppose?'

'I say we go with them too!' Mark added. 'I've been on a few trips in my time, gang, but definitely not on one like this. And, as Aleasha said, they're the only ones who seem to know that we're here ain't it?'

He drew a few sceptical stares, not least from Elena and J-J.

'And I know I ain't imagining this guys, because I haven't taken any funny stuff in a long time – I'm well clear of the thing,' he clarified, smiling pleasantly at his surroundings, quite unsure of exactly what he had just said. 'Well... the hard stuff anyway.'

Exasperated, they each looked at Markie.

'I think we have to go with them.' Instinctively, Gee tightened the reigns of his corset. 'Mark's right guys: they seem to be the only ones who know anything about us, and what we're supposed to be doing here. I reckon that if they were bad or something, then this mark on my pretty little face would have been a big ol' hole by now.

'Fuckeries,' Gee gasped, feeling the depth of his wound, 'I was really quite lucky there to be honest wit' ya, when you think about it and everything... But you've got to admit it though, that that was a wicked move I pulled there init – when I jumped on him!'

A distant clap of thunder, which resonated for miles around, was the first response to his braggadocio.

'Yeah, great move mate – you not getting yourself killed,' Sashi jeered, to the full approval of the others. 'Nice one Gee, couldn't have done much better myself.'

'Shut yer-face, Chief Running-mouth.'

The nervous laughter subsided rather quickly after that. Besides, Elena was not altogether certain what course of action they had decided on.

'So does that mean that we're going with them then?' asked Elena, piping up at last to speak some sense without the accompaniment of tears. 'I mean, what else can we do?'

There was another brief pause as The Friends stared longingly into the distance. It was a rueful moment that long held their gaze. Perhaps it was the magnitude of the ascent lying before them which they pondered or the storm-clouds brewing over the distant horizon. Nevertheless, they did soon agree that they didn't have anything much else to lose. So it was surely worth a try. Anyway, it would all be a bit of an adventure, at least, wouldn't it?

Biting her lip nervously, it was Aleasha who managed to find the words:

'Yeah, we do it, we go with them. Why on earth not...?'

118

BINAH:
CONVERSATIONS WITH AN ELF

In the third year of Cyrus King of Persia, a message was revealed to Daniel,
(Whose name was also called Belteshazzar).
The message was true, but the appointed time was long;
And he understood the message, and had understanding of the vision.

DANIEL 10:1

The visitors' response seemed to gladden the Sun, and it shone forth its approval accordingly. Not far off the two dainty figures tramped northwards towards the rolling horizon making good speed. Their hue, when set against the dimming void, was tanned, and their colour continued to wane as swiftly, they marched deeper into the dales, without pause, without reflection. Six furtive forms followed hard behind them, as Gee and his friends hoped to engage them further concerning the strange words that they had uttered some time earlier.

They passed close to the Fields of Awneduyne, where mighty men of renown had fallen in battles, back in times of greed and austerity. This was accompanied by the broad rolling plains of Gweaeryl, which some say is populated by ugly denizens, hosts from The Otherworld who have not managed to find rest since their untimely departure in ages past. Then came scrubland from the west, and a tardy heath which was shrouded by small knobbly protrusions lying only a few hundred yards to the fore. With time the unsteady silence held between The Syndicate and their guides was broken; but this it seemed only for the voice of larks praising, the lifting of the deep grey mist about them, the early glint of the morning air, the rich grey smile of the Sun.

Soon, the unchancy nature of the grounds became evident. The soils beneath their feet gave rise to sores, spiking the soles that had borne them well over the course of their hour's long trek. Furthermore, the sallow pastures ached limbs and strained bones and divided in twain the joints and the marrow, all in turn. Neither was the morning freshness slow in appropriating its assigned task; nevertheless, the tidings it brought was of cheer rather than discontentment, even for the small spillage that began to fall sporadically on the deep green meadows beneath.

Their route had taken them to the bank of a steep hill, whose skirts lay studded with a profusion of bright flowers. These were spangled as the backdrop which nightly sets itself above the same lofty mound and lovely as the sprite-maidens which are daily sent to water them. Time and again several heads of oxen drove on through the fertile pastureland, the Wood-folk with their kine beside them, doubtless being drawn to richer grasslands to fatten them up before the slaughter.

Upland appeared to bask in the songs of thrushes, the broad, sweeping paths of plovers. Only the hoots of owls behind them constantly reminded The Friends of the foreign spot they found themselves in. At the Rill of Rehythaine moreover, which rested near the adjoining swath from which they had just parted, Frydor found a quieter place for he and his companions to recuperate. Their exertions spent all were now ready to rest their aching limbs.

*

Not even a few hundred yards separated them from a cluster of elfish nomads who had camped further along the bend of the wide-berthed river. Frydor, having explained to the leader of his youthful entourage, Gee, the way in which elves conducted affairs with strangers, dispatched him with his nephew to obtain some useful wares for their present route. The feisty young buck was only too willing to oblige him. So they set off, without discordance, at the behest of the wizened elf.

Shortly, the two were back again, heavy-laden with coloured cloths – handmade durables which had been made by the Orange-bearded Dwarves of Styx. In their possession they also had oils and flour sprouted from the fertile grounds towards the south, for which but a few choice pennies were exchanged. Flip had successfully bartered for a trove of quail and bags of fresh herbs and vegetables, each by way of his skilful tongue, which was reckoned to be highly blessed amongst elves. This did not fail to bring a warming cheer to his uncle.

Then Gee produced hordes of silver-grey rags, all skilfully woven by the hands of elfish smiths and their maids. The elf produced some knee-length garments that were embossed with promising scenes for the coming days; and others that were marked with the cruel twists of war, and the ill names of their slain, and of the names of heroes and gods, held dear by the folk that had spirited their cloaks away. The vast bulk of their woollies were resilient to all but the most fearsome deluge of Uranus, when he, in anger, spews forth his venom to the accompaniment of spittle, which bleeds his mouth dry regularly and causes showers and thunderstorms to sound across the vast face of heaven.

Amid all this however, they had come by some simpler items. Some were intended for the clothing of bodies, others for the bandaging of wounds. A few had little more use than to line the forest floors about forts and keeps, especially when it is neither day nor night, but cold as the outer reaches of Annwfn. At such times, it was believed that the body might suffer no loss; thereafter, fate was to be left in each one's hands.

It was then that Frydor actually showed his true personage for the very first time, thanking kindly his brother's son for the deed wrought, and beckoning his gratitude towards the looming form of The Big Man. It was also then that the sullen alteration in the Friends' own attire became apparent...

*

At length Frydor politely asked Sashi to gather in some tinder wood for the fire that he was about to start. Words were few, but a murmur of approbation spread quickly through the friends. Elena seemed to be the most interested in the elves, and in examining her new environs. But Mark, too, was eager to prove himself more than able, as he busied himself with Flip in the preparation of their communal meal. This was by the Rock of Magron, hard by the bend in the slow-flowing part of the stream; a burial ground for saints in days gone by.

The mentioning of mealtime caused rapt expressions to appear on the faces of one and all, brighter even than the aspect of one privileged of sitting before King Morchyell the Merry. It is his court jesters who prance around in shallow, mud-filled pits with such rollicking abandonment, burping, yodelling and bleating all the while (loud as a ban-dog which has just become conqueror of his prey) that great and serf alike swore that the slaves of Yewffwl were bound by sprites of The Underworld. Hunger pangs tore away at the Company's stomachs, testimony enough that they were each in dire need of filling.

The elderly elf set fire to the logwood, promptly charging Flip to tame all things as best as he was able. For amongst his many talents was his proficiency in the crafts of preparation, presentation and perception of all meats, herbs, pastries, such as his great aunt had taught him before her departure at a ripe old age.

So the bird flesh roasted slowly, releasing many a trapped aroma, bringing to memory many sweet reveries of home. Presently, they gathered themselves together again in a circle and sat around the cruising flame. There they waited a while for the sooty black dust to disperse. Once the ash had begun to settle, J-J pressed the succulent greasy rump upon her delicate lips; and being The Syndicate's member best found with boldness, soon discovered enough muse to ask the more senior of the elves a question. And indeed it was the very first one of true relevance for quite some time.

'Please go through the whole story one more time,' she prompted, nuzzling away at her bird-breast, 'just so that we're all certain about what we're doing here – it's not really every day that this happens, you know?'

'If you are up to it, that shall not be a problem,' Frydor replied. 'But not before I have satisfied my gullet with the tasty barb of this morsel…' The elf loosened the sails of his baldric before attacking the food.

'The fact that you have become so disorientated,' he began, chomping away on his tender flesh, 'is really quite transparent… though it is somewhat understandable nonetheless. If the same transformation had so suddenly come upon myself, I dare to wonder how I would have fared! I'm sure it must be quite an unnerving episode to have one's life so abruptly changed, not to say the gravity of life's meaning thrust upon one's lap so forcefully!'

J-J's companions remained silent, not wanting to break the thread of his intimate narrative. Frydor's eyes were cast faraway, above fields that were gilded in the prominent hue of the Sun's glorious rays.

'Long, long ago (though still some time after the first of the worlds was made) the World of Dreams was formed. It lies in the Dark Caverns of Imagination, which is the current System. This World was most unlike any other place ever created, for it was made to subsist in all five depths of existence at once – that is five "Dimensions" as both Men and Dwarves call it. Verily however, this last depth, which is sometimes called the "Fifth Level", is still a mystery; but it is thought to contain everything even though at the same time reckoned to be contained in all – '

'Our sages say that there are three dimensions each for our bodies, souls, and spirits, that is nine in total; and one time dimension for the corporeal realm and another for the ephemeral realm, to make eleven dimensions in all,' interrupted Flip, not wanting to be judged as unworthy by the new visitors. 'But we call everything outside the first four dimensions the "Fifth Level." '

Frydor shuffled his position slightly, to coddle the ebbing flames with the end of his stick. Cold winds blew onto his kisser, smacking him hard on his pale and blistered skin. But they soon left for another face, close at hand. Elena it was with whom the wind played at buffeting, as she tried to peer a little too closely to Frydor.

The winds continued, the fires dwindled, ears pricked up at the deepening voice that beckoned them. Elena smiled at the beauty of what she believed to be her own creation. Soon regarding Flip, who was shielding his own aspect from the wind, she witnessed on him the same pure breath reaching for the long strands of Frydor's hair.

Its sortie was to separate his choicest locks with the same diligence as that of a gold-digger, who daily sifts his refuse in hope of those legendary vices.

But Frydor's appearance seemed to darken, though not to wane, as if solemn were the clouds that covered the lands, and unchancy was the intent whilst it lingered. Shortly, however, this black omen was passed, returning the elf to his aged, mortal self.

'Back in the dawn of time, preceding the days of Adam, the World of Dreams was created – a Matrix that was made to exist containing, amongst others, Daearawd, Krandor, Nef and Uffern. Billions of years before Man first set foot on The Earth, both of our worlds shared the same ingrained innocence. There were no wars either by the sword or by the spear, there were no rumblings, there was little burning… and few were the foes that plundered, such as besets the land this day; for pillaging was scarce. A few women were ravished, but few were hard pressed by mortals or those not possessed of the *Incubus*. Hence, the creation of this world continued to develop with Elves and Dwarves, Men and Animals, taking the central focus in all future proceedings.

'In due order therefore, in the current world, this grandeur was first for us Elves and then for the Dwarves, and then for all the creatures subdued by us, both great and small, so that none may fail to walk in the ways of their calling… Even if their commandment was solely from freedom to altar to food to furnish our platters, such as besets the boar!

'My friends,' Frydor continued with some gusto, 'some of the mythology in your worlds – namely that of the Norsemen and Kelts – these were derived from things which your folk have seen here. Have not some claimed to have dreamt these things via more intricate connections with the Fifth?' The elf glared long and hard at Sashi, as he attempted to gauge an answer from someone whose understanding might have been heightened by his various readings. But seeing no answer forthcoming, he soon continued.

'Although we do not dwell with your people, some of your cousins – those of the race of Mankind – and also some of your more itinerant creatures, have found their way into these doleful realms. Most accidentally, though some have located the still active portals.'

J-J raised a curious eyelid, not so much to scold Frydor's strange wisdom, but in patent disbelief of what he had just stated as fact. Her friends too, in their own way, voiced their own concerns about such advances. If, indeed, all things were as had been purported, and were true, and their experience was no mere mind-game, sent to spiral the sense of the worthy into oblivion, then his words would surely gain more credence within their hearts. They waited by silently, birds coursing through the open meadows, listening to the gently flowing waters of the stream, marking its meandering path as it petered out into the distance, hearing its roaring fall, which was taken up swiftly by the voice of an old, wizened elf.

'Likewise, some dwarves,' he rejoined, 'and even some of our own elves' – his nephew nodded – 'to mention but a few, have found passage to your lands, to the place which men call, the Earth?' Frydor glanced around for reaction which he soon discovered in the radiant eyes of Mark.

'So that's why some people say that they've seen fairies and angels and – ' Frydor felt the need to correct the Kid's youthful curiosity.

'Yes, that is partly it my boy – you've come close to dotting the I! Although if we here are after truth; angels and some of the more malign deities have been around since before there ever was a place to dwell in – and so one can say that they are, in a figure, more real than even we are – although by the looks in your eyes, I dare say that this is not the most difficult thing for you to conceive at the moment!'

There was a short burst of laughter as Flip mimicked Frydor in pinching himself and screaming.

'See there now,' the younger elf bragged, 'I'm real am I not? I feel, therefore I am?'

'Well-done young Flip, I am glad to know that you have been learning your books!'

The company, bar Elena, chortled for a little longer still.

'Nevertheless, even in our own eyes the race of Fairies is the stuff of legend and elf-youf's dreams at a troublesome age. For they were, apparently, small and defenceless creatures, wiped out when the tides turned evil and each dwarf took to his own rule, as in the days of Mydgaet of Godwfsyn, Old King of Syn, whose offspring (the flaxen-headed, pug-nosed barbarians of the east) give credence to the notion that he it was who was the forebear of the Vandals.

'Moreover, those Dark Dwarves who sternly opposed their righteous brethren of the Geditouann tribes – those namely of the Geditouaff – was it not their desire to kill all of the love which had at one time existed in this place? And then destroy our peace (which, in the days of old, had brought cheer to the hearts of many), and steal all of our wealth – which was vast – and plunder all of our God-given goods. Unfortunately, since the days of yore these wicked ones have been allowed to flourish in the Old-world. Their desire evil continually, their hope was to lay hold of The Keys, thus giving them the reigns to the Chariots of Nef itself!'

'The Keys?' Elena enquired inquisitively, picking him up smartly. 'What Keys are you talking about Frydor?'

Rain began to tumble from the sky and through to the soils that supported it, through wood roofing and big broad leaves with green veins and sticky protrusions, before subsiding again shortly and withdrawing into the wilderness some way beyond Bryn Owëin. Beneath the remaining canopy of water resided a party of men and elves, some of whom were pleasantly surprised by the fresh sensations they were privy to. The others were less keen, the rain wearying whatever enthusiasm they may have had for the coming jaunt.

Breadcrumbs and chunks of flesh stuck fast to red hot iron hooks, even as Frydor sensed the crest of a great story rising within him. He drew his face out of the covers shrouding his features. Come what may, he would not fail to quench either the constant growling of his stomach, or the bubbling muse which presently wanted to give rise to a story.

'In the beginning,' he started, beginning his narrative as all best tales do, 'there were the Ten Keys, all of which were entrusted to the peoples of the Lands. From the southerly most tip in the Land of Nod, where reside those of the Blackfaces, to the northern most outpost of Goodlands five keys were given to us Elves with the same number being granted to the Dwarves. We were at the time were the two most populous races. According to the telling of the Books, eight keys were used most widely.

'These were The Keys of Faith, Virtue, Knowledge, Self-Control, Perseverance, Godliness, Brotherly Kindness and Love. For it was written that:

"If these things are yours and abound,
you will neither be barren nor unfruitful..."

'The years soon passed. Then it happened that The Fallen Ones (The Nephilim), to whom time offered little comfort, began taking on the forms of angels and men, before gathering in these here provinces as spirits.'

The Syndicate and his nephew proffered him their understanding.

'Some of them came from the World Above, from Daearawd as it is now commonly known, although most ascended from the World Beneath, from the Holds of Uffern, and from the cold, clammy caves in Annwfn. But when the influx of those from the Nether-regions had come to exceed even the sand upon the seashores, then were The Keys moved, so that the Malignant Ones might be kept in morbid mystification. Alas, our very present hope – for most of The Keys finally ended up here in Krandor, the last outpost of light, where there is still yet hope for good methinks...'

Hung within the darkness of the weald was a stillness. It was a strange tranquillity that was poised as if awaiting the first splattering of raindrops to break the momentary peace, disturb the heavy topsoil, churn autumn's felled leaves one from another for use as forage. It was the commencement of some mighty downpour long past its season, but it did little, if anything at all, to deter Frydor from further articulations.

The elf tore at his bird flesh with teeth that had been trimmed to a razor-sharp edge over the years, and he bit out a generous clump of meat for his stomach to ponder. Thereupon, as further dark mysteries came back to mind, he swallowed the remainder of his chow with a few more obstreperous gulps. He adjusted himself favourably in front of his audience, and then continued with his narration:

'These Pernicious Ones then set about the corruption of the Ancient World. First the Dwarves were adulterated (as they were less astute than any other folk); but after that, the Ruler of the World Beneath furthered his fiendish plans, for the enticement of Women and then of Men. It is him for whom our lands hold this saying:

> *"He does not die, even as he causes truth to lie,*
> *Although his guise, a handsome reply to the wicked,*
> *May often, indeed,*
> *Or at least from time to time,*
> *Take on a cunningly altered style."*

'Finally, the afflictions were sent towards us Elves, as summing over the whole, We are perhaps the most virtuous.' Flip nodded his head in approval of this last remark. 'Even so, the seed of vice was also sewn into much lower organisms... animals, birds, giant mammals; beasts of the dark and creatures of the light; all were ill-fated at his pernicious hands. And so has the curse lingered to this day within Krandor's consummate bounds. Even the Orcs were – '

'What?' exclaimed Elena. 'You mean that you've got real dungeons and dragons type orcs living here – for real! Are we gonna be up against them Frydor? Really?' She increased her grip on her friend, Gee. 'I've seen them before you know, and they're really scary aren't they Frydor? But are you really being serious?'

All eyes turned towards Frydor; his face bore the mark of no humour.

'Yea, we have many orcs here and not a few dragons. Now as for the dungeons you perhaps refer to; we do indeed have some – dark and horrid places they are, the worst of which lie past the Dragon's Region in the land of Dereden.'

'I have reason to believe, Uncle, that there might be some darker gaols lurking in the north somewhere, in Badlands; perhaps some in Fou-ouls also,' Flip said, turning aside to Elena. 'But how are you aware of them?'

Elena replied, 'Oh... well, it was because of something we used to watch when we were younger – it was quite good really – but it was only make-believe.'

The two elves looked at each other quizzically:

'Unfortunately,' Frydor replied gravely, 'this is not the case here, surely as I breathe. The corrupt orcs and their goblin masters in these realms govern many a dungeon with total dominion. In comparison rarely do their vast hordes of evildoers face justice... and few shall do in this age. The Forces of Light have sufficient problems in protecting their own territories without resorting to assailing a foe so grand in numbers that of yore the sages reckoned them to be the promised descendants of the Black Host Of Nef, whose dwellings were once with the stars.'

For a moment The Friends pondered his words, allowing time to shape the understanding of the received reflections. 'So what you're saying then,' Gee surmised, weighing up the sum, 'is that we've had it?'

Frydor returned a blank look to his inquisitor.

'Well bollocks to that shit then!' Gee said, as he rolled back onto his side.

'So how did the orcs get here then?' queried Aleasha, somewhat more meaningfully. 'I mean, how did they get such a hold on things round here in the first place? I thought you said that all of creation was good to start off with?'

'Ah my noble scholar, you are not being as attentive as you must,' Frydor responded, in somewhat of a huff. 'You must listen to what is being said before you answer.'

Aleasha quailed back into her spot next to Gee. She too fell back onto her side, her arms as props beneath her body like those which support the onagers around Orphunk's castle.

'Orcs are a foul race, O Wizening Ones, created by the crossbreeding of giants and notable beasts. They are themselves the spawn of devilish seed, for long ago, after The Floods on Daearawd, many fallen spirits descended into Krandor to begin the next stage of their sinister plan.

'Unbeknown to those from the North, there yet remained some Evil Ones who prevailed in escaping from their clutches, some time after the waters subsided. (I have heard it said, in fact, that they fled far and wide from the Place of the Boat, which, according to our Lore, is atop of your mountains called Ararat.) Coming to the point: they undertook relations with some of your corrupted Males – some of the Qadesh as they are known here – and they enjoyed intercourse with your Females, so that an already decadent seed might soon be destroyed completely.

'Thus, in the days of old, Giants were born to these.'

'Giants? You're shitting me?' blurted Sashi.

'Yeah Frydor,' Mark added, without the smoothness which often set him apart. 'Surely all of that stuff is just a bit of mythology? Like wizards and witches and shit like that.'

Frydor looked surprised if not alarmed; 'I assure you – if needs be,' he started, almost spluttering the ice-cold water that had touched his lips, 'that they *are* not. And as they were full of iniquity, fearsome in countenance, and fearless, they had the strength to trounce much of the Old World, single-handedly, especially when petty rivalries further divided the Faithful.'

'Since those ancient times – times which even the stars have difficulty in remembering – these Fallen Ones have continued to be a blight on the lands, a terrible scourge upon our beautiful landscape, a blasphemy before priests and prophets alike. Moreover, none save the most valiant have ventured to quarrel with these Rapha, as the giants were termed… not in these lands anyway. And few ever will, and prevail!'

Frydor the Elf grabbed at a stray leaflet, drawn near to him from the flames. Ruefully, his consideration fell on the days of old, fire-lit eyes resting upon the animated streaks of the small inferno smouldering before him. Presently, the soft, delicate petal crumbled beneath his gentle press, dissipating, as he soon believed the worlds would be, into dust, flames, and emptiness.

'But now, such has the world become. Alas…!'

After permitting his nephew to rekindle the flames, it appeared as though Frydor's face fell victim to a sudden darkness, which wrapped itself about his demeanour, tighter than a smith enfolds his metal round the sheets of a famous sword. It appeared more sullen than it had ever been before.

'My forefathers frequently traversed the Great Heights, as they were a noble folk and were descended of the priestly castes… and their hearts yearned for The Truths which have been since the beginning of all ages. Nevertheless, many of my kinsmen (Elgather the Great included) were confounded by the severity of its ascent. They were further afflicted by an unchancy spell – that curse which meets all those who, having set their sails to the wind, were afterwards found wanting of strength to persist.

'Nonetheless, not all enlightenment eluded them, as some of these elders became the Prophets of Yesteryear…' A hint of pride echoed sorrowfully in his voice. 'Of this I am of course proud, as any elf would be. Though I very rarely attempt to remember such, for the price that was oft times paid.'

As Aleasha and Sashi watched on, they saw, not a wizened master of much age whose many accomplishments were made for the telling, but a lonely old man, not so in company perhaps, but in experience, in troubles, in turmoil.

A tear or two formed beneath his eyelids, a sultry appearance on a cool and grievous day. Many were the thoughts left to fester in the depths of his mental psyche, which had been forgotten in their brooding stilt since days gone by. Albeit, these he presently seemed to fling aside, though with no great ease, as he called back to mind his company, and as he bore in mind the magnitude of his current obligation.

*

The day became still but warmed with each exhaustive step, as the Friends made their way through the grey mist that hung about the meadows. Straddling their vision at regular intervals were hills, high and lifted up, trees lining the fertile soils of some, leaving other banks fallow for the uprooted logs that lay in possession of their skirts. The new band moved on in silence, the only noise the running of waters far off by the foot of their present spoor, and the faint humming of insects as they sought to recapture the breaking of the new day. All thoughts soon turned inwards and they fell on the words of Frydor's admonitions, which all hoped was but surely counsel, not relevant to themselves. But any respite was short-lived as they entered a high plateau, between the two large mounds before them.

The Friends, led by Aleasha, found themselves trudging across immovable granite boulders balanced broadly on soft, miry swathes of grasslands. Their purpose now was to navigate the banks of their current hike, until the opposing ridge, which was raised aloft upon three steep slopes of uncultivated red loam; then it was to touch the summit, passing along route the transient hamlets belonging to the nomads. After this they would descend again, seeing much the same as before, though with the added duty of sturdy saplings to grapple with and loose, trembling rocks placed there by the gods to cause a stir.

Most found the going difficult at first, especially Elena, for her tiny feet, small frame, little strength. But as her friends helped her and her bewilderment became lees noisome, she caught second wind and recovered a mighty surge of her own. Sashi held the rear of the train, his heart as valiant as any who trekked in the party that day. Nonetheless, his legs were in adamant refusal to journey any swifter than they must. It was he who struck up conversation again as he closed ranks with Frydor and Aleasha at the helm. He probed the elderly elf for more of his wisdom, having successfully taken the fern-strewn slope of Gwaeryl's broad shoulders.

'Frydor, where are we,' gasped Sashi, 'and where exactly are we headed?'

Upon the saying, the Desi withdrew again to the back of the party, mumbling uncertainly about the way the gods have treated him for too many of his days.

'And how many more hills do we have to walk over?' Elena enquired. 'My feet are killing me!'

'One at a time please,' replied Frydor dubiously; 'for I cannot speak to more than each one in turn... so then, who shall be first?'

He resumed his tread without so much as breaking pace. Mutterings of discontent arose again from the midst of his retinue, one grumbling about the venture thus far, while another's grief lay with the grim ascent that lay to the fore.

Aleasha however, being the one closest to Frydor, had little else on her mind, save for understanding the things which the elf had erstwhile spoken. It was concerning these matters that she questioned him further, as the cool upland air quashed voices and unblocked ears, causing each one to reserve what energy he might for the ongoing excursion beyond.

'...Would that it were so, my children,' mused Frydor, lamentably. 'But The twin Keys of Death and Hades were taken first. The Key of Death had been entrusted to the Dwarves and the Key of Hades had lain in Elfin hands.

'Back in the days of old, they were used for the castigation of irreconcil-able evildoers; even so, it was only on occasion and against the most scurril-ous that they were ever employed. And then only against the likes of witches, warlocks, idolaters, adulterers and man-slayers– those corrupters of justice and beguilers of the naïve, who, by their divers brands of wickedness, lead people, body, soul, and spirit, into the darkest pits of Uffern.'

Gathering that Frydor was already loosened of his tongue, Aleasha decided not to interrupt him in his flow. Instead, she motioned to her companions trail-ing some way behind to draw them in closer to listen. This they promptly did, raising comfort, narrowing the gap from one to the next, leaving orders reversed and Flip, Frydor's nephew, to bring up the rear.

*

'The Serpent's Men made use of sorry enchantments in his encounters with our Elfin-folk and made full play of dread to deceive the fearful Dwarves,' Frydor muttered, as if in deep reverie. 'Then his hideous cohorts – who were numbered by the thousand I must hasten to add – made an attempt on The Keys, murdering some of their keepers and leaving in his wake a slaughter so foul that even giants weep at the telling.

'Thereafter, he hoarded them all together and sent the former Guardians down into the dungeons of his master, who is the Lord of the Underworld, that he may detain them at his pleasure. And verily, as sure as the Serpent himself has a black heart, these foul designs pleased him endlessly. Alas, to this very day, no one knows whether those that were captured are still there, suffering those infernal flames; or whether or not, perchance, they have been delivered...'

They saw a glistening town before them, not far off on the wind-swept horizon. It was fashioned by the mouth of a river, lying close to its basin, and the rich lands bordering the plains at the feet of Gwaeryl were but its soils. The river itself coiled both this way and that, stretching its long, narrow claws far into the misty beyond. As Flip pointed out, staying his uncle's narrative for the moment, it was upon this present shelf that the Troll-kings of old had first gathered their armies together, after fleeing from tribulations of the South. This, the Friends heard well, and marvelled at the remainder of his interlude. Yet it was plain to see why such a place should have been sought.

Without doubt, the journey there had been long and hard and beset by many a trial and torment. But from that blessed spot they could see for miles around, and on a clear day, to the ending of the river itself, when it runs its final legs westward into the Kaspen Sea.

The level ground from which they had sooner parted bore no clue to the forts of days gone by, but for the odd scattered inscription upon tombstones which none were able to divide. Albeit, the rare cry of ravens and the occasional sighting of beasts so black that they blotted out what part of the Sun was upon them that day, rumoured otherwise.

The rising curiosity of the Company soon returned to grim recollections, of slaughters, of broken sanctuaries, of treachery and sabotage.

'So… are you saying that man might be burning down in some gaols somewhere, even as we speak, since…'

'A time out of mind?'

'Yeah?'

'Precisely.'

Frydor carried on his pursuit, oblivious to the flummoxed countenances around him.

'Well,' muttered Sashi disconsolately 'at least we got that one straight!'

*

Immediately ahead of them lay the faint outline of a track, which was hidden behind streams of hedgerows, and forested to the rear by trees of stunted growth and feather-covered bracken. It was on the other side of this trail that Frydor thought to pause awhile, allowing his company to gain their breath, and causing hordes of recollections to come flooding back as his own afflicted reveries. So there they perched their bottoms awhile, in the middle of a damp, grassy bank.

It was a hive for animals of all kinds. Gee started back as one of them, a goat of sorts, pounced in efforts to evade captivity. This carefree response caused Frydor to call to remembrance his last fair enquiry.

'Forgive me for not explaining myself as I should,' he stated, not at all rising from his spot.

'Not so long ago came a rumour,' he rejoined ' – not the normal hearsay of those who engage themselves in needless tittle-tattle, from the rising of the Sun to the going down thereof – but this word came from those schooled in wisdom, educated in history, who were also proficient in the sciences. (Otherwise, being the learned elf that I am, I would not have heard them so politely!)' He smiled at his not-so-veiled modesty, to which Gee, being the fellow that he was, responded kindly.

'Many of the sages – Josephus the Learned included, who was also called Josef Ben Iddew, Father of all Historians – many say that one Great One alone descended into the prisons, according to his own free will. In accordance with our forespeaking, he was supposed to be the noblest of all Men, numbering all from the first Adam even to the Serpent's son, the Antichrist himself, who by his guile, intrigue and treachery, will bring all forces of Daearawd under his sway from his base in what you call Europe.

'Anyway, this man was the leader of a ragtag bunch of rebels,' Frydor espoused, smiling knowingly at his company, 'but he soon whipped them up to be mighty in valour, by his holy spells, secret runes, and exemplary example. And they did wax great.

'Nonetheless, they say that his followers aided him only as far as the gates of the gaols themselves but that for the sake of the searing temperatures (which would have surely smote sore any elf's flesh) – they could advance little further. In fact,' Frydor murmured, 'some say that one of his comrades helped him a little more than the others...' A dark glint came across his eyes as Frydor shunned his profile from the sun, ' – in treachery indeed!'

Each of the friends shook their heads, all in agreement that the words spoken by the elf needed more elucidation. Either this fellow's companions were friends, those that would always be there for their comrades, or they were not. They understood little of what could lie between the twain. They drew nearer to the place upon which he was sat.

'Are all these reports not written in the Antiquities?'

'They certainly are uncle,' Flip said gladly.

'And rumour has it that whilst there he, with his sword in his hand, plundered the less evil parts of that city in search of those who had gone before him. Stranger still (so Josef later recalled), some of these bondmen rose up from their grave, unbanded their burial clothes, adorned themselves with the raiment of kings, before making their journey back towards King David's City. There are many that have spoken the selfsame words to give the selfsame testimony – both friends and foemen alike. All fitted accurately one with another, lest they who spoke should be found wanting.'

The younger elf allowed his head to bob along with the wind. Though he understood little of these things himself, he was a learned elf, what one may call a wise-elf, and noble was he with his learning. So far as he was concerned, according to his wisdom, these matters were found to be true. As for the explanation of these things, they must yet lie with another.

'Nonetheless, this same worthy man did not end the time allocated to Beelzebub for his exalted rank when he was flung out of Nef, but he left him to fester beneath the glorious bounds of Seren. So one can see, even in this day, the works of the Fly-Lord, which are clearly evident in the wanton depredations of Krandor. Moreover, the Lord of Dereden himself gleans his wicked way from this unchancy snake... he does not work on his own authority, although he does have several of his own guises.' Things were beginning to make some sense now, so the Friends consented.

'Therefore of all The Keys available, only these two are you barred from. For Death and Hades can only be retrieved by he who comes after you, who was also before you; by him who is now approaching hard on the heels of those Four Fell Horsemen and their fiery co-riders. With them,' Frydor added with sincerity, 'is a great and eternal power that none can truly fathom, not even by a Surp, but only by he who rides a short way off the Vanguard of Uffern's Steeds.'

'Would that I...' He reconsidered in mid-muse and sprung up from his spot.

Frydor turned his stare away from them now, and gazed across the dim outline of Demenuê, the range which they had just finished traversing. Above the peak of Gwaeryl flew the bleached-white swallows from Gothan's Ridge. White streaks coursed the greyness of the tawdry ether; hungry kites circled some way beneath them; gulls reached evermore into the firmament above, as with one tilt of their wings, their grace took them deeper into the solemn skies.

But before the hill itself trees bore semblance to the twisted forms of druids. Their branches were harsh, winnowed by squalls of the previous season. Nevertheless, for all his wisdom, Frydor presently looked absent; as though he feared the venture he had set himself on.

"If this person is but myth, mine kith
Then we are all but mortal-weeds doomed indeed.
And neither shall you return to the Land of your Fathers
And your mothers shall grieve, at their latest deceased
Before Death comes and catches up with the others
Diseased."

With this, Frydor chose another spot, his back taking the smooth part of a rock. Leaning upon the boulder, weakened some by his present sufferings, he gathered his breath from the four winds. Clambering again atop of his latent thoughts, he strove even more so to conquer the fear that wished to dominate, the dread that sought to usurp his soul.

'If any of these things are not, my friends, you shall certainly perish before the wrath of Lords from the East, just as I shall, which is the grim fate awaiting all who are caught dwelling in the mire of their own iniquity. Upon the fulfilment of these lands, all we hold dear shall be plunged into the deepest darkness, yea, not only of despair and solitude, but also of misery and torments with fires of molten brimstone for company. Then shall we all be lost forever.'

As if agitated by his own words or the new site he had chosen, the elderly elf rebuffed the persistent pleas in the look of his nephew, Flip, and made instead for the brake in the woods by the bending path. At once his company saw that it was his wish to move again and so did likewise. They collected up their purchased wares, creaked limbs which had just begun to set, and trailed the elves hard by their heels, into the weald beset by brambles and thorns.

They wandered on for some time to come, great bushes of fern there to thwart them, bristly leaves present to hinder their path. They could hear the rushing of streams that bordered the hillock, yet they continually chanced paths too narrow to tempt.

Soon, they were scrabbling down the slippery mounds, which had once become a snare to John-john the Late, who was called Conqueror of the Fallow-lands, Master-of-none, The False Carpenter. Folk speak of his retinue appearing ever and anon between the burping of the fish at Airam, when it happens that the two mermaids, Nhoj and Nicki, rise to the surface and spew up all of their noisome spawn (which would have provided for their seed in days to come), seeking redress for the slaying of their mortal forms. These were they cursed by the hand of Yah, for their foolish responses when questioned by Erynaidd, Chief Witch of Beguilement, when she tasked them to remember the Seventh Principle of Justice – that which is also called the Lore of Perthynas. Believe that one who may. They headed for the banks of the rivulet.

After some time the Sun appeared again, beaming down its love upon the battered forms of its visitors. It drowned out sorrows, suffused resistance, and if Pluto, god of the Underworld, had been present, then would it have also quenched his evil sting.

Picking their feet up for more toils, they traversed the Three Rivers at their confluence. Shortly, they were at a basin of slippery reeds, known as "The Wasteland of Costanne". For a brief while, they sought escape from the grasping swathes of grass, and they marched on together in silence. Cloaks were drawn close, heads were bowed, the Sun was pacified upon the hide of their last member, Flip. Despite this, cheer was good, though in Elena's case, it was somewhat frustrating. And Gee, grumbling all the while, failed to see the immediate end to their condition. Were it not for the Son's mighty berth, which compelled them through the Affliction of Adam, Son of Earth, Spawn of God, they would have surely failed their jaunt.

Once past those unchancy lands, they were sprung over the breached ramparts, which in times past had marked the boundaries for the floodwaters. Now, however, they housed little more than the drenched fields from the swamps at Nuahs to the Stone of Enaj – two stalwart giants who were once called Babbler and Blighted, before their times of condemnation. Nevertheless, the waif urged Frydor to resume his account pertaining to how, where, and why, the Keys held such importance. And soon enough Frydor the Elf heeded their voice to continue.

He stopped his entourage near a path juncture, beckoning them all to be seated.

'What I can say is this, however,' the elf observed somewhat mysteriously. 'No one knows the exact location of any of the Keys.

'Some of our Krandorian scholars suggest that their precise whereabouts may be concealed in lines of code buried deep within the Books of Antiquity themselves, but few of these ancient writings have ever been divided accurately. (This is the book that has traditionally been kept in three parts: to wit, the Book of Knowledge or the Book of Law, the Book of Understanding or the Book of Prophets, the Book of Wisdom or the Book of History, all of which are sectioned and split accordingly). Concerning these books, has it not been said by a dwarf-maid of old?

"All that has happened and all that will happen, are written in the Books."

At that point his nephew also joined in, not wanting for any of his own great learning to go unnoticed.

'It was she who also said:

"What has passed will be what shall come to pass
The sole lasting difference being the recurrence of the last.
Though oft times an illusion it may most definitely seem
The confusion will nonetheless vanish as we conceive what indeed can be."

'However,' resumed Frydor, allowing no time for his nephew to relish his famed reputation, 'I shudder to think what the state of this world would be like if this wisdom was well known.'

*

The afternoon light had dwindled and the pale morning hue had passed, but the Daystar, with Her soft yellow fingers, caressed the brows of Her faithful. As the moon on the blackest night of Rhagfyr, so did this brilliant orb brighten the entire extremity of the sky: from the Gwaeryl's Lofty Peak right through to the Three Rivers and the grounds that bound them at Her foot. But this sallow virgin was not shy in exposing herself through the grey-mantled cloth which trussed Her up. As a maiden in her bower when she first learns the art of allurement, so did this beauty bathe Her body in the cool naked blueness of the sky.

Comforter of the day, Lover of fields, grasslands, and the work of farmhands, Loather of all things black, She unfurled more of Her charm to the warriors that walked beneath the gracious scent of Her smile. Like the words of a virgin when she succumbs to the temptations of love was the play of her breathing within them, or like the soaring sparrow-hawk that roams freely across the expanse of heaven was the lightness of Her touch upon the heart of Her believers. Nonetheless, She yet demurred somewhat; for the prospect of such words spoken by the elf troubled Her; and so She failed to reveal all, even though all were longing and in dire need.

Cocks the colour of Uffern's Host sung jubilantly in exultation, their rejoicing one of gladness at the sight granted them for Her glorious disrobing. The Company lifted their faces at this, making joyous their arduous trek through the woods. Notwithstanding, trees emerged from either side to shield them from Her full seductive splendour, lest each one should be smitten with Her hot looks and not be able to continue. To the less charitable, this was a welcome prospect indeed – but to those charged with great things, it was fit only for the walk of fools.

The light of Her being sat atop of the canopy, at times making its presence felt on the matted floor of their tread. But for the most part their feet were taken with hardy logs, felled at the blade of a woodsman's axe; or slithering snakes returning to their lair; or the rustling of leaves as animals, more bashful than the Daystar herself, sped hastily from the attendance of the interlopers and from the wiles of the Sun, returning to the dark, unruffled caverns of the woods whence they came.

Tight on the heels of the doughty elf, each one was soon freed from the darkness of the weald that had cloyed them about. They bounded the last stretch of their shadowy encounter, and one by one, emerged into the full abundance of Her comeliness. Yet against the lowing of kine and the distant soundings of horns, as shepherds gathered their flocks together in search of new pastures, and even for the merry shouts of the Friends while they sought to comb their way through the tangled enclosure, Frydor's choicest articulations were still to be heard above the rising din.

The wise-elf stood and watched his companions rollicking through the last dregs of gloom, and he could not help but wonder if these juveniles were indeed the ones he had so dearly sought after for so many of his days. He kept his thoughts to himself for the moment, until, at his behest, they were all again seated.

This time they were by the sharpened staves, which bore the names of those that have sacrificed their lives in lieu of their friends. One such rune simply read:

> *"Mafa Hasleg, King of the Injuns, Lord of the Battle –*
> *The prince who, in days gone by,*
> *waxed boldly in the face of his treacherous brethren,*
> *who had turned to smite him when he was come of age,*
> *and when the battle had turned grim –*
> *Worthiest of all known Rebels."*

'Oral tradition holds that the Key of Love is hidden in the East,' Frydor re-joined in dark tones, as though recreant were the ears that espied him ' – some-where in the realm of modern day Dereden. Fear and Torment behold this key, and have done since a time out of mind; even as their clansmen Death and his co-rider Hades have drawn their own keys, following the Troubles of Yester-year. With time I shall let you all know the remaining prophecies concerning the Key of Love, but as of yet I am unable to talk more, for little has been revealed even to me!'

Moving on swiftly, he quieted the murmuring that had arisen:

'Silence my children, for I have still to mention the others, such as the Key of [Brotherly] Kindness, which is reputed to be in the Land of the Wicked.' Frydor lowered his arms again, in a slow and deliberate motion, and all noise died with him.

'Long, long ago, in the days of King Mathär, the Key came under the stewardship of the Keepers of the Good – these were they who, through their fastings, prayers, and penitent hearts came to be honoured by worthy folk everywhere – even by the fearless Zaqen – and frowned upon by the corrupt and greedy alike. However, soon after the lands produced their first chills, the Serpent took it upon himself to seduce these venerable folk, by promises of restitution a hundred fold in this life, with bounties and mansions to boot, and the service of fair wenches in the life which is to come. With such extravagant promises,' Frydor added, almost heartily, 'it is nigh easy to see why even some of the most contrite were beguiled...'

He sighed loudly before pronouncing; 'And so happened these sins upon all. To this day their order fails to follow the true path of enlightenment, but they have followed after their own pernicious ways. Their way has become entwined in the heathery lair of the Snake himself.

'It is their damnable heresies which have destroyed the hope of some and contaminated the faith of a great many others. For from these came the No-midniacs, and their cousins who follow the creed of the Sejutis (those equivo-cators of truth, beguilers of justice, lovers of the perverted, defilers of innocent little elves, women and children). Alas, even now, under the directorate of their Papa, they reside in The Monastery of the Upturned Cross. I believe that they are aware of the correct whereabouts of the Key of Kindness, but are not letting on.'

His kinsman gave out a long extraneous sigh, swiftly followed by fidgets unnumbered, as time began to catch up with him.

'Whether or not it has been given to others more sinister, only time can tell.' His weariness gone, Flip also nodded at the recollection of his uncle's words, as though summoned from the depths of his memory, funnelled through his the dark crevices of his reason. Aleasha, too, seemed to wax curious, and

J-J and Elena also. Even so, their male-hearted, bull-headed companions, of which Gee was chief, appeared to grow all the more sceptical.

'Another of the Keys has found it's way northwards into anarchic and proud lands. The Antiquities state that the Key of Godliness was located in the Badlands, at the time of Old Queen Palmer of the Swan-witches. After *Dera-denu*, as the Ancients called it, and Krakôuz, this is perhaps the third most ungodly place in all Krandor. But we, like the Forces of Darkness, know little more than this.

'As for its precise location – no one knows save for the wise, and I'm afraid that I don't yet count myself as prudent enough even to search for this one, though it is surely my calling. For the Key was hidden when the hearts of many began to falter and turn cold, for the evil *gosgordds* that encroached upon the regions...'

It was long that Frydor gazed upwards at the naked breasts of the Maid, and longer still that he meditated on the songs of thrushes and the limber lays of larks. He bore the message of his ancestors well, grievous though it appeared in his eyes. Not even She, with her buxom yellow sails, could brighten up his withered countenance. Birds from by the forests came and perched close to the old elf, issuing the quarry of their breasts into the ears of he who beheld them. But neither could they, with their lovely voices, lift him from his melancholy.

'Many of the Good-Folk waxed brave in that day,' remembered Frydor boldly, heartfelt waters coursing down the lines of his furrowed face. 'Therefore in honour of them, it is our tradition to speak this saying at times such as these.' He rose in his spot, and sung:

> *"As they fought, so shall we fight*
> *As they wrote so shall we write*
> *As they battled, so shall we strive*
> *As they died, so shall we rise..."*

> *"When the time is right, all shall be revealed.*
> *Many shall be set alight but the True shall be healed.*
> *Those that hungered shall be filled,*
> *Those that did not shall be killed!"*
> *...Amen!"*

He permitted tears to flow down his coarse, cotton garment without encumbrance. This bore the warmth of his body between the heavy layers and his skin, cleansing along route the parched naked epidermis that once seemed that it was spun in silk, and moistening, without contradiction, his solemn poise.

Again She threw off Her covers till the Friends basked beneath Her afternoon glory. Again She brought weeping to the faces of Her faithful. And again the elf, like Sashi when in new company, stuttered, uncertainty gripping him like the paws of a brown-maned bear. Though of the remaining keys, he in no wise failed to deliver; at least in speech.

'Some of our brethren residing 'neath the shadows of the Eastern Warlords have spoken of the Key of Perseverance being on their mainland, at some place near to the Sea. But no living soul knows any more than this. That is not to say that in days gone by our fathers did not try – '

'But in all honesty,' interrupted Flip, 'few hardly knew where to start the search!'

'True O kinsman. 'Tis a good word you speak. But there are some now (the estranged sons of Gaylord of the Bends from Hores) who are now in league with them that are good, namely the Manchumen. Under the auspices of the nobleman Caradoc, they never fail to resist the evil tides of dissent from Montgomery of the Long-shanks, son of Gwynedd jon Gurujon, as he is called by some, or Gwyneth mab Belial as others call him.'

'Then again,' continued the elf confidently, 'going by the Book of History, the Key of Virtue is probably the safest one of the lot! For it lies within the realm of His Excellency, King Anthony the Younger of Elfdom, lying perhaps in the more venturesome spots by the borders of Abundance, where the fires reign supreme.

'(But Anthony is a worthy king, with a stalwart guard of elves for his protection – even though the commander of his troop is a dwarf! – and dour do they remain until death). His is one of only a few kingdoms yet to succumb to the manifold swarms of evil. Moreover, should the Great King continue to show his favour, neither shall he yield.'

Enamoured with nostalgic propensities, however, Frydor slurred his next few lines:

'...The Elfin-Priests, who used to perform the sacrifice in those parts, hid the Key at the report of a highly distinguished prophetess in the days of yore, the Seer Adiaha. They say:

> *"Her skin was after the blackness of onyx,*
> *As those from the tribes of Geneors."*

'For word had drawn near that the beasts in search of Virtue were held up hard by the ancient borderlands. *Alltud* were with them slaying all those who withstood them with impunity, leaving behind them a trail of strewn destruction – hacked limbs, broken bodies, and so forth,' he gushed as torrents flowed down his mane. No longer was his seat a bed of downs, fit for a king.

So promptly, as the comfort of his place had worn thin, he was up on his feet and in the hunt for another favourable spot.

THE KNIGHT'S LORE

*

God sets the solitary in families;
He brings out those who are bound into prosperity;
But the rebellious dwell in a dry land.

PSALMS 68:6

*

The stifled warbling of the mistle thrush made for enticing listening, ringing across the fields called Nostrum Arran in honour of those slain at the foot of the mound. Champions were buried there: from the Troll-king Blathmac, who with his iron spear thrust through upwards of one hundred Men of the Rapha, before being smitten by a pebble flung by one feisty lad, whose mother was ravished by Blathmac in the days prior to his infancy, after a worthy bout of feasting amid the Kalan Yule; to Eochaid, son of Domnall, who perished on the Night of the Savages, when Knight-orcs had raided the frontier villages, violating their more comely maidens (a frightening prospect even for ones so grim), killing their callow brood of whelps, before putting to the torch their elders, who had once given birth to the noble race of troll-warriors; and then again, to Arran, who was perhaps the mightiest of the lot.

He it was who butchered around four hundred men with his arsenal, most of whom he slew with his trusted mace. But even when his fight turned grim in the early years at the Battle of Trum Gath, he feared not, but took to ravaging his assailants with nothing more than his bare hands, his spittle (which survivors swore was like that of a poisonous lizard), and his razor-sharp teeth, which he had kept in good stead even since he was a minor, under the care of Volo the Fat, his mother. He was also a predecessor to Shaul Lahn – that gentle troll-giant, who is cousin to Bonetee. Nevertheless, of his cousin Shaul, some speak of him being:

"…The most gentle giant of the lot,
save for when his foot is stung by a nettle-bush…"

Frydor paused for a trice, whether it was to listen to the distant humming of the birds or to the present carolling of the wood-plover, his company came to a standstill beside him. Their talk was at length deemed fortuitous and so Frydor followed the route to which they beckoned him, through the cloyed covers of foliage and across the long, broad tongue of raised soils.

So comely were the lays and songs that many creatures assembled together from the depth of the thorny weald. Beavers from the waterside and badgers from their holes, wild-cats from the trees and carrion-swooping kites wheeling high above. None failed to cease a while from their manoeuvres, in order to examine the strange rejoicing that passed on through the spoor beneath, as the company of two Elves and six Men, trundled on into the darkening woodland.

At length Flip found shelter beneath a tree of some great height, gesticulating with his hands the most favourable sight for his uncle. Thereupon, he allowed himself to slump against the selfsame tree and wished for the others to do the same. One after another the Syndicate followed in turn, leaving Frydor alone to remain on his feet.

'...And as the tribulations...' Frydor continued before correcting his phraseology. 'As the slaughter, rather, swept over the lands encompassing, many commoners (or *serfs* as men call them) were quickly removed from the sight of the evil Goblin-lords of Krakôuz. However, dark sayings emanated from some of the Elders, leading us to believe that the Key of Knowledge is well, having been buried in deep vaults cast in iron shafts in a secret location in Fou, by the White Wizard Cain, who was born son to Adam the Madman.

'It is enough to say that a great many elves died and that many more suffered as a result... more than is pertinent to tell of at this moment. But let this, my friends...' Frydor raised his head gravely, choked back the tears, lifted his voice above that of a moaning dove-bird; 'let it be a testimony to the fortitude of our forefathers and their maidens – for even to this day, the Key of Knowledge has never been found. For, of them oppressed, neither widow nor orphan yielded up it's knowledge.'

None of the Friends seemed embarrassed by the Elf's show of emotion. Indeed, they rather seemed cheered by it, and encouraged, that perhaps they too might show their true disposition should the time ever arise.

'As always, when things are at their darkest, there came a great light,' remarked Frydor. 'And this was to be no exception. Following the days of the Eastern Onslaught many a great seer was raised up. My forbears, Jude mab Jonah included, took this as a sign that good will eventually triumph, and that all was not yet lost.

'Representing prophetesses were two of the fairest damsels in all the Old-world – the elf-youth Savannah and her elder sister Georgia, daughters of her who was called Enekkear, of the clan of Davies – those who first became known across all Krandor for their skill in songmanship, artistry, and all manner of knowledge. Representing prophets there were the giant-men Malachi mab Midu (Crowned-prince of the Dréds) and his brothers, Aaron and Benjamin, cousins to the clan of Davies. All three had been mighty men of old; born to brawl, fight, and make war. For one thousand pounds of muscle they shared between them but only one pound of flab.'

Flip also smiled as he reminisced the songs sung of those noble warriors.

'But by way of charlatans there were a great many, all out to gain what they were able, with scant regard to anyone else. Chief of these was that old witch Oanshagh…'

'Mistress to Áed Sláine, the first Songsmith of Waemorg!'

'That is correct my son. So few were they that promoted the era of *Harijan*, which is the name given to those periods of collective restoration, which literally means; "Them That Followed After Him Who Must Be Followed". But a small number of the fairer maids, by virtue of their inward beauty, fitted kirtles, and shapely countenances, stirred even some of the doughtier Knight-orcs by their feats of integrity, even when the war-bands of Dillon mab Delaware ran riot. This was a most commendable work indeed, as rarely do Knight-orcs have a heart even to stir!'

After this Frydor waved his arm for his companions to draw in close:

'However, for not revealing the place of the Key,' he resumed tersely, grappling, and then losing that fearsome contest to restrict his emotions, 'there came a mighty vengeance which led to the destruction of many of our brethren, wiped out cruelly on the hills near Brae Bannockburn.'

'Wallace of Braeheid – '

'And Bobby the Bruce,' the older elf added.

'Kaitlan of the Kembers, son of Alistair – '

Frydor cleared his throat loudly, prompting his son to allow him to continue unimpeded.

'And the infamous Robert Ros, husbandman, sages say, to her who could transcend both space and time – Genie Ros – kinsman of the House of Beakerskara. (He was the foremost Whiteface ever to inhabit the land.)

'Nevertheless, all of these folk perished on the slopes of the same mount.'

There was silence as each one did his best to soak up the tears.

'Nonetheless,' Flip sparked up, bringing animation back to their ailing demeanours, 'they succeeded in culling the baneful of that day, at least for a while, until they either died in the ensuing fighting or were taken prisoner in Englewood by the armies loyal to Lord Sackville, Arch-villain of Skara, as he was known for his unrivalled feats in bloodletting.

'Albeit, all the praetorian fellow ever gleaned was that there was a key called Knowledge and that neither he nor his captives would ever behold such splendour.'

'Then he smote them cold with the edge of his sword, isn't that right uncle Frydor?'

At this Frydor the Elf rose up from his seat and glared upon his nephew in anger. It was no ordinary glower, but the poison glance which may do an elf great mischief. Therefore, it was good fortune for the younger elf that he managed to recall the memorable exploits of the Blessed Elenwydd herself, for she had been amongst the slain at Englewood. She it was who, with her valiant will, had summoned up courage from the grave in the form of

Goodwin the Giant, and had questioned the troll relentlessly about former times. Thereupon she had issued command to him that he should stay a while and help protect her little ones from the onslaught of the dark dragon of Daearawd.

Clearing his throat rashly, Flip thus surmised; 'It is true then O uncle that these noble warriors were dispatched with more honour than I, pray tell, may give them at this precise moment.' He sat down and scowled rudely at the black-crusted beetle on the floor before him. '– And that all would no well not to forget such – present company included.'

The elf sat down morosely, not daring to look up at his uncle.

'Hmm…' Frydor breathed, withdrawing his deadly glance, loosening his sash.

'Yes, yes all right. But now I must continue regardless.'

'Of course, Uncle.'

'Faith is a mystery to us all,' observed Frydor coolly. 'For back in the earliest age when both Dwarves and Elves followed the way of devout pilgrims, there was no fixed place for one to alight to meditate on this noble key. But those that parted on such a venture normally fell on a place called Hope, or the port thereof (which lies in evil hands now), although some meantime came to Expectation – Se'kere, the place whence we have just come. It was upon these sites that they worshipped, so that, if fortune should have been granted them, those of their number who were deserving of Faith might be given some of its goodness…'

As the Sun drew herself behind her grey-coloured cloisters, Mark made a pertinent note:

'So where was the Key in the first place… And who kept it?' His friends beamed broadly, thinking, it seems, that they had caught out Frydor the Elf.

'Elders say that there was never a keeper of this key, my boy,' the elf clarified, 'as there was never anyone to offer up sacrifices on its behalf. But its secret was intrinsic, in itself that is to say, in a way not readily discerned by those lacking wisdom.' He looked candidly towards his company, with the solemn indication that they still had much to learn.

'Pertaining to this treasure, was it not Tino-costa, son of Eric of the Masabamen (he who had beforetimes dwelt in the Heinigwlad), who uttered:

> *"He who believes must believe that it is,*
> *And that he will be rewarded if he diligently seeks after the same…*
> *Or else let him part after the ways of the Infidels and the Fandals,*
> *Whose ends shall be in fire, whose death shall be in pain."*

'Many were the priests interrogated for this key, and several were the souls slain, and without numbering were the widows made. Even so, there was scarcely one that knew a great deal about the key!' Once again, Frydor fell into melancholy.

'These days, much of that wisdom has passed away. So that even now, there are none too sure whether it was fashioned in gold or silver or costly jewels, or whether its presence was a figure, not meant to be seen by the eyes of elves.'

Stirring uneasily in his seat, Flip was unsure if he should speak his mind, not wholeheartedly believing these things of yet...

*

But it was Aleasha who caught his flitting eyes and they seemed to draw her straight into the depths of his inner being. For a second it was as though she was trapped inside his small elfin body, in a dank and sombre tomb somewhere, within a darkness more oppressive than death itself. It seemed there was nobody around to help her and that she lay half-ensconced within his mind with no way of escape.

The feeling of a painful inevitability slowly crept over her, but at best she could only cower away in a corner of the gloom elsewhere. A last avenue of hope, the window of his eyes, appeared to recede, vanishing under the great inundation of saline water, while more yet came up from beneath her, to flood the plain around her feet. The throbbing of the mantle beneath her soles vibrated with the racks of his wailing. And, for these things, no few tremors grasped at her carriage.

Then, however, just as the crushing weight of despondency had almost entirely smothered her, the girl managed to squeeze herself shut, parting his psyche not a moment too soon. Returning swiftly to her own soul, she found herself looking at their new elder even more intently than before. Indeed, she found herself hanging onto his every word. But the latter at least was pleased; because he had at long last found someone else to share his burdens.

*

'What about the last key then?' Jema-Jane urged. She looked up eagerly, availing herself of the lull in discourse. 'I'm only asking 'cos I thought you said something about there being ten of them... and I've only counted nine that you've gone through so far?' she added slowly.

'Yeah, that's right, you've only talked about nine of them!' shouted Gee, somewhat more coarsely. 'What's the beef on the last one then, chief?'

'That would be the Key of Self-Control,' Frydor replied curtly. The sound of ruefulness was no longer to be heard in his voice. He dried his cheeks with his handkerchief, before revoking his gaze from Alisha's direction and sending it to the woodland beyond.

'According to some older sources, the Key was entrusted to the High Trolls in the hill region of Abundance, some time after Qaeda Singh, King of the Sevens, had migrated with his couth-cousins, the Masabamen. However, it soon came about that those in league with the enemy ignited many fires, burning up most of the trolls and their forest-dwellings, so that the whereabouts of this most prized key might be made known.

'Indeed,' railed Frydor bitterly, 'the flames were so powerful that there is even a remnant to this day, for they were concocted via devilish sorcery taken from the most dastardly runes available at the time. (Even the infamous Shailash, Troll-knight of Yesteryear narrowly escaped these flames, when word arrived from a seer, foretelling that the coming eve would be a night of sorrow for his household, should he not seize the moment. This he duly did however – being a man known to fear the Impending Word – ending his spell of lovemaking, dragging out his goodly whelps, before fleeing with his mistress into the far-clung caverns of Trol-land, accompanied by those of his Trolliégion)!'

His company smiled kindly at the elf's obvious turn in humour, though not broad were the smiles, not wide was their aspects, not loud was their laughter, lest the dead think themselves mocked and the haunting grounds of Rhûn come alive again.

'Few are the trolls that now exist in these parts,' Frydor began again, albeit tersely. 'There are still some nonetheless, descended of a long and noble line. The *Nocsies* I believe they are now called. Their two most prominent members today are husband and wife, and if my memory serves me correctly, they have the names of Saspion and Fels'noc, who is her husband no less. (For *trols* are generally called after their wife's names, as is common for the race of Iwys, in honour of those bearing the offspring, as it were). Companions of mine say that if any were to know the whereabouts of the Key of Control then it would be them. For they are truly of priestly stock, and are of a caste directly descended from the Great Troll-kings of Tara.

'At first the enemy had tried courting these *troll-knights*, to gain knowledge of the Key's location. But having failed miserably in his quest, he drew upon the more deceptive charm that he stores in his deadly arsenal. Thus, he took to possession through magic and wizardry. But he succeeded in his evil only in part; for to this day, only a few of the trolls remain hexed.

'Somewhat predictably perhaps, things took a turn for the worse when this key vanished. Thereafter, ill-discipline and anarchy sought to have the reign…' And as the elf yet spoke they witnessed a struggle in the forest afar off, in which a black-faced kite swooped low upon some scurrying little thing, digging its evil talons into its furry hide and springing it clean from its earthly abode. An abhorrent silence then followed, which was taken up quickly by a great rollicking of other sky-creatures, as they heeded its screams and saw their venerated member come out the victor.

'But some reckon there yet remains a goodly seed within the troll-couple, and that perhaps, with time and the restoration of all things, they might one day be saved...'

Upon speaking these words Frydor stole away from the abhorrent mutilation they had just observed, and glanced about himself for a second or two, as if aware that something greater than his company had indeed been listening. The pounding of his heart, the throbbing of his temples, the damp sheen of water which lined his brow, the cruel exultation of the sky-beasts – all told him that his terrors were not wholly unfounded. But a stout-hearted fellow Frydor was, or more so than most at least, and it would take more than fear of the unknown to quell his unsullied orisons.

Thus, he spoke his last for the time being, before the cloud that had been following their every movement, returned to cast them back into its ashen blanket.

'It is to this key we go to first,' Frydor mentioned as if in passing, rising up out of his dry spot alongside his new acolytes. He clapped his hands upon his nephew's shoulder. 'That is the whole, and I think I have left nothing unsaid!'

Little more was uttered at present, Frydor beckoning for his friends to bear with him a while, until the gods saw it fit to return his composure. So for the time being matters required that the children let it be. And so, for a short space in any case, they each obliged him his wishes kindly.

THE FIRST SUPPER
&
THE FIRST LORDS

Foods for the stomach and the stomach for foods,
But God will destroy both it and them.

1 CORINTHIANS 6:13

These are the Twelve Lords of Krandor, who govern northwards of *Elfery* (formerly Elf-dom) and southwards of the Black Seas and all across the Eastern Worlds. In due order therefore, in the Realm of Dyngwr, under the regency of the Prince of Gwr himself, their names are: Fléichïor the Fat, co-regent of the Northern World; Drygiöri of the Blackfaces; Pedéyrôr the Elf of Meréden and of the Eastern Seaboard; Alex de Vitaz of Anbad; Digwïlydd the Ogre from Iniquity; Galeg the Large of Giants; Cèrïdyn the Crimson from El (and the northern parts of Fou); Badred the Rouge from The Two Dark Valleys; Malebö of the Ugly-faces from Harmswäith; Llöhwryn the Virulent of Krakôuz; Yorath mab Grêyndrwl from Hores; Suntribo, Goblin-lord of the Dark-skies. These are they who, either through their accomplishments in wisdom, craftiness or ruthlessness, together with slaughters unnumbered, have been greatly honoured by the Prince of Gwr and have excelled under his reign. They have even been granted fiefs within his Dark Kingdom that they might show him true fealty, undertake homage, pay him tribute, and so forth, until such times as the world is conquered and the rumour of the Surps is put to rest once and for all.

Like a select handful of his Dark Lords, The Prince himself is a man. But no ordinary man is he who sits between the Two Balls Of Faith. In season, when the Sun meets her bride in the Eastern Skies, and her presence is blotted out by that glistening white orb, the highest tides are loosed, the numbering of years is divisible by fourteen (to mark the Twelve Dark Lords, their master, and The One Who Is Yet Unmentioned), some say that it is then that he comes under the sway of him who, by many, is called The Unmentionable. For dark are his ways, evil his tongue, and great is his power, mightier even than many of the Men from the North. Albeit this sorry enchantment works once only every thousand years or so, when all stars are aligned, as they ought, the moon is in her place, the puff of Neptune's nostrils is unleashed across all the oceans of the world.

*

So the mightiest of these is Fléichïor the Fat, chief counsellor to the Prince of Gwr. As in the fullness of time Beelzebub himself shall take on the reins of the whole universe to become Arch-lord, and the Prince of Gwr shall become cloaked in the powers sent to exalt him to his ascendancy, so is it destined for Fléichïor to become ruler over all Krandor by the staff which she carries with her at all times.

Rarely given to anger, she was trained in the foulest forms of sorcery by the Black-witch Merthatch herself. Few are there anywhere within the lands who have endowment such as she. For in an instant she can alter her form from the blubbery body of a female hag and take on the comely appearance of a virgin wench, and then again of a mighty man, some five cubits tall, fully adorned in the raiment of war. All this according to whether it was required of her to strike fear, seduce, or slay her foe-person, as was befitting the moment.

Wise in her counsel, even as Wyngod, chief of all wise-elves, she was also gifted in spell-binding, even surpassing the mistress who taught her. Those who know say that she will one day be anointed by the Druid Blakthawn to be adviser to Him Who Sits In The Chief Seat. But evil was she in all her ways, especially against those who fail to do her bidding, either through refusal or through want of trying. Malicious is the judgement she then often sets.

*

Then comes Drygiöri of the Blackfaces, Regent of the Southern Seas, from the Land of Nod. So black is his countenance that on a moonless eve he cannot be seen but only detected. For his evil surpasses all those of warlocks and he exudes a murderous reek not at all fathomed by those who have not sold themselves to the Devil.

Nevertheless, his strength is great, lying first and foremost in battle-cunning, and his skilfulness, in the conduct of his realm. In the dark arts of interrogation he is perhaps the most proficient in the kingdom, seldom failing to extract a guerdon where gifting is necessary, or to wrest confessions where guilt is due, or indeed bones, when he himself is wracked by the pangs of boredom. His particular enchantment is with the spear and vats of boiling oil, which tribes of his dominion are known to make play with. But brave is the heart which refuses to seize its blood-pumping when in view of his war-band, in full-array, when they bear their instruments of death.

In the feat of fell forespeaking and sorcery Drygiöri was marvellous, none more so than when he is under the influence of various herbs snatched from the lands of his origin. Of his splendour, nevertheless, this is seen most befittingly when he is swayed by the chords of a ballad, to wit, those played as his chief minstrel plucks a fair note, causing a ripple in his heart, flowers to blossom, women to bear children everywhere. Then does he go into a trance and speak of all ill tidings to come.

He for his wisdom will become advisor to Fléichïor when the Sons of Nef are smitten at the hands of the Hosts of Hell, and the Prince of Darkness has risen again. He it is who works tirelessly to this end, that when the time is right, he might not be found wanting.

*

After him comes Pedéyrôr of Meréden, High Elf, High Priest, and king of all the lands in the Eastern Seas. Too great is his astuteness to be spoken of in the ears of Men or Dwarves, that only a few of his own race understand the depths of his visions and various promptings. Indeed, for the greatness of his calling, he is almost considered *alltud* even by those of his own retinue.

His delight is in divinations and all things of dark interpretation, as well as all secrets, rumours, and wisdom, even after the knowledge of the Surps. These folk Pedéyrôr admires, even though he often refers to them in a less than gracious fashion: "A doughty race of ruffians" they might be, or so he often told his war-band, but they were worthy of his full attention, lest their wisdom overcome his might.

His kills of elves number no less than two hundred and sixty-three. Albeit a great many more have suffered starvation and doom at the hands of this godless captor, but sages are not agreed as to whether these unfortunate souls should be reckoned as part of the count. Nevertheless, there was little querying his valour. For even one day, in the midst the snowy season by the brown hills of Waemorg, when he was but a mere child, he slew the Twelve Hags of Heisenberg, single-handedly, with nothing more than his trusted selection of stones. (It is said that he afterwards stole up to these twelve witches and discovered that one of them still sought to breathe. Thus, removing his hunting-knife, which his father had given him for such occasions, he slit the throat of this two-faced vixen, followed swiftly by other barbaric acts which remain untold even to this day. Then he drained them of their blood, deprived them of their organs, and washed himself by the rivers of Dunsdale, which flows quietly in the south-west of Erriémor.)

Flesh ruddy and raw, with long and spiky ears, some say this was so that he could hear all reports at all times, whether intended for his hearing or not. And his head was large as a melon, to trap the mass of his brain. In his following come the hordes of Wardael, Dark Elves, in whom reside no goodness whatsoever. Their weapons are triple-pronged tridents, swords forged in the darkest holds of the land in Kasjmör, over in the East, and their stony hearts with which they might take a maiden and ravish her, before slaying her mother the very next day for not relinquishing her rights in like fashion.

But Pedéyrôr was of a pleasing manner, even to those he is about to slay. For his way indeed is with intricate books of learning, and not with the strength of his arms – a quality which the Prince of Gwr seldom failed to admire.

*

Then is Alex de Vitaz from Anbad, Second King of the Realm, loftiest, perhaps, of those who sit around the Prince's table. In his dominion lies Drwggwlad, in the heart of Krandor, and his harem is in Saenned, in the heart of the Black Hills of that place.

Some tell of Alex springing forth from the depths of the earth, having been conceived by men enslaved by evil beasts before being sold into unlawful intercourse. But his present tyranny is said to be everlasting. When his chief harlot (whose name is Aural) lies by his side, it is supposed that he then has the ability to speak ill of all people at all times, in any language underneath the sun. For it is then that her awen conjoins itself to his, and their fluids combine, and their groanings are heard all the way across the deserted regions of Anbad.

Afterwards, those privileged to be spared by him have their faces removed with a hacksaw or with the trusty edge of his sword. However, seldom is this blessing bestowed, as most foemen are smote at dawn after many hours of painful torment. Thus, for his baneful ways, folk do not cease to speak perversely of him.

He received his current spot albeit for the quality of the slaves he trades in. There is no place sacred for the King of Anbad, even as there is no place to shelter from his slave-bands. Neither after wars, famines, or pestilence was there a sanctuary for The Poor, a domicile for The Feeble, a cave for The Oppressed, an orphanage for The Bastard (or an hostel his mother). Though at times, being a foreigner himself, he did sometimes furnish his gaols with the bread of affliction, on behalf of The Stranger.

He it is who attends all Council meetings, lest he should miss out an opportunity to increase his parsimonious gain. So of all the Lords therefore, he is the most feared by The Commoner. And why not? If they are fit and healthy, with a few more years left yet to run, then shall they fetch him a handsome price at the market; if they are young, they might serve him well themselves. But if their legs are spent, their breath laboured, or their minds taken with infirmity, then will he end their task of all ages there and then, lest space should be wasted on his baggage-trains. Such is the command given to all in his labour, whether slave or free, man or beast, or *Belfrog*.

*

Digwïlydd the Ogre, First Prince of the Realm, resides upon his stone-crafted throne in the Land of the Giants. He holds a mace of some considerable weight in his right hand and upon its spikes are the remains of men, elves, and dwarves.

In killing delight is borne in his eyes, in maiming, joy, when his face lights up brighter than the midday sun, revealing features common to any giant: coarse hair which line the sides of his head; dark eyes and bushy brows; scars that criss-cross his sullen demeanour like the grooves on a freshly-furrowed battlefield; warts so evil they pay fair semblance to the hills of his forgotten wasteland.

If one requires trusted counsel then little reason will any find in this fellow. Sages speak of his mouth opening but once a year, when it is his month to appear in person before the Prince of Gwr that he might narrate to him an orderly account of all deeds wrought under his lordship that season, and to pay him full tribute. Insiders at the court suggest that it is Blakthawn, Druid of the Keep, speaker of all tongues (broken and otherwise) when he is risen from the Black Couch, who is given the task of interpreting all manner of gabble that comes forth from his imperfect embouchement.

Nonetheless, in war was his way is perfect. Set him towards the enemy with whatever tools at his disposal, and he would surely dash towards the fray, arms flailing, with a heart bent on violence. Though seldom was he dispatched without a number of trusted counsellors. For at any time when he is taken with the need for blood, after he has smitten all his foemen, it is not unknown for him to start ravishing his own great warriors. And so is this testimony true; for Digwïlydd was truly a most abominable creature indeed.

*

His cousin, also a prince of the realm, is called Galeg the Gaul, prince of the New-Dogs – that foul race of savages who were first sprung from plains by the Port of Wreckers. He is another giant whose strength lay in his forearms, biceps and thighs, with strapping great veins protruding through his feet. But contrariwise to his kinsman, of reason, he registers, conducting all his affairs with chief nobles with somewhat more restraint and much less bloodletting than Digwïlydd himself. Beneath his mud-encrusted mane is hair so golden as to make even the Daystar envious of his covering; around his face is hair the colour of a winter's hayfield; and so thick is this beard

151

that his kinsman say that the remnant of dwarves can be found buried within its deepest parts.

Perverse though it may seem Galeg was best at ease when in the midst of battle and pitted against hordes of enemy hosts. It was at those moments that he might set his mind adrift, being heedless to all the formalities of courts, ladies, nobles, peers and so forth, and accomplish what was intended for him since birth, which is to ravish all about him, until but one man was stood. Then would he add a notch for his great conquest, either upon his left or right breast, or upon the fleshy part of his face somewhere. And he would leave the scattered remains of hacked limbs and chopped bones as portions for the circling jackals.

Thus, tremendous was he in the eyes of the Prince of Gwr, not least for his fortitude when warring. And great would he forever remain.

*

Cèrïdyn the Crimson rules the northern part of the Land of Fou-ouls; some of the southern and eastern provinces however lie in the grip of local warlords and orc-handlers. Crimson stands only three cubits tall, has large hands and feet, a huge forehead, is as ugly as a pug-nosed beetle but constantly lusts after women nearly twice his height, knows no words of flattery. As wanton as he is though, unbridled desire is still only his second greatest fancy.

For he is leader to all men of stunted growth within the central part of Krandor. As such, brawling is his hobby and fighting his skill, making war he does as often as, if not more so than, he makes some godless wench pant like the comings of a roe-deer in season. No pleasing spectacle was either, however.

In the north they call him Prince of the Bloody-hands (after his great, great grandfather Cèdrïc), for none loves to wage war more than he does. Indeed, this truth was shown one day, in the midst of the warring season, in the year of Baal-Casgé, in the battle for the Molug swamplands. For that day, when he was injured in fighting against some rebel *machog* he refused to leave the battlefield but stayed his ground and compelled his war-train to bring him some prisoners, that he might smite them in fair combat, single-handedly, lest the tally of those he had slain began to wane.

Therefore, 'twas a true word that many younger dwarves held close to their tongues when Cèrïdyn was mentioned in their hearing. All sought to emulate him with great exploits, bloody swords, and lustful ventures, that both friend and foe might remember their inborn defect no more.

*

First of the lesser lords is Badred the Rouge, who has the lordship over the Two Dark Valleys, which are also known as the Twin Valleys of Corruption, which lie westward of the Waters of the Gods in Badlands. His spouse is Neomè, distant cousin to Saspion, who reigns as queen over the central district of Trol-land. "Transtrol" is he called by many, for the defilement of his line by men; and bent is he by nature, for his liking towards big, beefy trolls, either male or female. Moreover, for the unhallowed temperament that often caused him to mutilate himself with a machete, he was deemed as unstable as the court jesters from Yewffwl.

But his hands were lethal with the javelin which he likes to hold by his side, and, more importantly, his war-band consisted of around one hundred thousand *Balrogs*. These were doughty men, ready either to draw their swords in defiance, or take on a most sinister appearance, no longer to be descried in the eyes of men.

Some of their mightiest feats were the darkest episodes known to man, even the massacre of scores of elf-maidens when his stomach was hungry and his pouch in sore need of spilling. This occurred during the Times of Ys Nos Lleuad.

When he ravishes one can see the coil of a deadly snake unravel in his eyes, some say like the sorcery that struck many a heathen king in the days of yore. At such moments his savagery was known to become all the worse. Bold were the men able to withstand him at such times as these and rare the maid who was not then violated.

*

Not for the blemish that waxed sore upon her skin was Princess Malebö chosen but for her record as administrator while she had grasp of the helms of Harmswäith. Beforetimes, she had acted with such shrewdness against her former lord Ullembö, that she was snapped up promptly when Fléichïor noted a need for a change in rule, as the accounts of that precinct did not add up as they ought. Now Goblin-mistress and leader of the largest band of the Gejit clans, she commanded high respect around the table of her peers, not least for her worthiness as a triple-breasted beast who yet compelled herself to the fray at all times.

Soon after the Uprising of the High Elves was ruthlessly crushed, the Prince of Gwr promoted her to his courts. At this time the number butchered by her hands was one hundred and sixty; before, that is, the steward to her chief counsellor, Dymbô, ceased counting for the weariness that had come upon his eyes. (He was subsequently hewn asunder on the railings of her gilded courts, upon which she and her Inner Circle took it upon themselves to make a feast with the remains of his body. They sampled the delights of his blood, and drained his urine from goblets, before taking to the warm, stringy taste of his innards, which to them was not unlike flour and watered dough when fashioned and formed into long tasty strips.)

But Malebö was faithful in all that she set herself to do. In murders she spared not one; in raids she looted even the beans set aside for babes; in torments without mercy; in ravishings with wantonness, to the accompaniment of laughter. Her husbandman now was Suntribo, who was part orc-goblin, part man, though rarely did they ever consummate. The hideous wailing that was required, before all organs were satisfied, all desires were met, all war-bands might rest in peace for the night, prevented such loving from the Two Heinous Beasts of Harmswäith. Nonetheless, her followers still loved her dearly.

*

Llöhwryn the Virulent is Third Lord of the Realm and sovereign of Krakôuz. Now of this man were there many sayings. Some reckoned he too timid to sit at the Table of Lords, in the presence of such warriors as Drygiöri of the Blackfaces, Digwïlydd the Ogre, and Cèrïdyn the Heartless; others whispered that he was as ambitious as Malebö herself, but wiser (which the latter always frowned upon), and that he, for his understanding alone, let alone his power over the mind of others, should have been granted higher standing within the courts.

Nonetheless, though some of these sayings were in fact true, it was the Prince of Gwr himself who at times waxed fearful of this man, lest what he could achieve he did. However, it is always better to keep one's rivals close at hand, rather than allow them free reign of their own fiefs, Gwr was reputed as saying… until the right time was passed, if there ever should be such a propitious moment.

Over two hundred thousand men were reserved in Llöhwryn's pastures, all mighty men of valour. Forty thousand were skilled with the sword; the same again with the mace and with the twibil; and more still with the quarterstaff; fifty thousand were adept at use of the flail. All were twisted as Fyck, Demonlord of the Eastward Seas, which was in no small part due to the abundance of opium covering his lands from the Eastern Waters to the Dead Sea. And of his dreadful retinue there were none less than four cubits tall.

*

After him is Yorath mab Grêyndrwl, Lord of Hores, Fourth Lord of the Realm, the eleventh ruler after Fléichïor the Fat herself. He was a *manelf* – that is to say, his father was a man and his mother was an elf from the area around Bryn Grêyndrwl.

It was Yorath who served his master loyally, always, paying him full tribute, adding tithe, dividing his spoil with his master to a berry. Neither was there a task too difficult for him, save for the needless slaying of innocents, which more often than not he allowed his retinue to proceed with, rather than participate in such depraved acts himself.

All would agree that he was young, talented and ambitious. His icon was the lordship of the Southern World, his desire to rule all south of Bryn Corff with impunity. This would he accomplish by his meticulous planning and handsome demeanour, through which he had already found favour in the sight of the Prince of Gwr (and, of course, Badred the Rouge).

In the days of yore, when the Dark Ruler was still in the lookout for men – men in whom he could put his trust, men who were cunning, men of intelligence, men who also had a port available for the shipping of illegal commodities during the Blockade of Dôr – he had come across Yorath mab Daefhys. He was subsequently promoted. Presently, having found favour in the sight of his liege, he was given complete dominion over the unchancy Land of Hores.

Nevertheless, his grip is not as stern as it might be and the dour forces of Audrey, Queen of Goodlands, and her daughter the princess Crystal, have restrained his evil claws from snatching away the greater part of the lands. Some say that any female is fair play to him and that he can beguile them with one look of his eyes, one swish of his locks, and his eloquent speaking of either prose or poetry, for which there is fair evidence to cite.

Failing this, which was rarely the case, he too has a mighty army of some eighty thousand souls. One-fourth were pirates, another quarter were machog (that is to say, Knight-orcs); the rest were either deranged elves from the east, or the daughters of the Fandals. They helped to ensure that Yorath never had an empty bed during the war-seasons.

*

And vassal to the Prince of Gwr was Suntribo, Hobgoblin, Goblin-lord, Orc-goblin (so some of the less charitable called him). He was also human in part, although he never would be fully. Nor would any of his ungodly brood, until many successive generations had been purged by the interbreeding of their seeds with eggs drawn from the fairest maids of Avalon. His hide was black and scaly, his face the ugliest of all those exalted by the Prince of Gwr, even more than Cèrïdyn (so much so that Yorath rarely looked upon him above his neck), and his evil was tremendous, less than none save perhaps for Digwï-lydd the Ogre. He it was, Leader of the Orcs and Restorer of the Faithless.

But be that as it may, to the learned man he *was* still occasionally struck by skilful cunning; although more often than not he was found to be wanting in his manner, being as dumb as an unbroken mule when the fancy seemed to take him. Great was his power nonetheless and unswerving the warriors who had made troth to him, through all campaigns thick and thin. However, the talk that came from his mouth, without the unction of his unholy master, was merely the gabble of the unformed tongue.

The wind to this one was as a swift-footed steed. Ever and awhile (or so was the rumour within the courts of his praise) he even had the ability to vanish from view for a while – a trick taught him by his ancestors in whom had lain hosts of rueful spirits since birth. Albeit, Black Lord of the Sky, Goblin-lord of Hosts, Rider of the Great Black Beast, whatever worthy appellation was bestowed, little made difference to his manner.

Amongst his retinue were those fell creatures of the Näzgrîl. Now it was their appearance which struck fear into the hearts of all those who saw them, save for the noble thegns themselves, their chosen entourage of handpicked warriors, and the mighty Zaqen. Nonetheless, many who met them rarely failed to make crude aspersions from where they were perched still in fear. Woeful were their deeds upon the battlefield; woe betide the man who rose in boldness against this lot; woes all round at their mentioning!

Yet there were even greater abominations amongst Suntribo's accursed gathering, namely those of the war-band named the *Crowlags*. These fell beasts followed him stalwartly wherever it was he wished to go. If into the skies of Heaven, then they would tuck in tightly to his tail; or towards the Gates of Hell, they would plunge down willingly into the depths of the earth itself. Into combat, they would roar with the sound of a thousand men before joining the battle. For those who accompanied Suntribo were noble and faithful; save, perhaps, on this one single occasion…

*

Not far above the spot from where the Company had just parted, another creature hovered motionlessly amongst the many birds. Like a mighty kite with its wings stretched out broad and its tail, the talons of its work, it prowled the open skies preying for lesser creatures than its grandiose self. Often times, as in the aftermath of a great battle when scavengers come alongside black-eyed ravens, they like to gather themselves in ordered collection atop of forts and above the bodies of the slain. Their meal is for those weaker, their hunt is for the feeble, their taste for the blood of the living. Therefore, just as the raven sends its croaking cry to boast of its presence, before swooping down and glutting the dead of their bellies, so does this bird make it's own dash for those they leave behind.

Not any of God's fair creation was this beast. Its black body, ill contours and dark, dusk-lit eyes failed to bring any form of grace whatsoever; and the hooks it contended with was to provide foul recompense to those bold in battle. The sky's remaining denizens made haste to scatter themselves, even its heroes: falcons, larks, and so on. All provided a path for the Black Rider and its Beast.

'H'wat d'you t'ink my bew'ty?' growled the Black-rider. 'D'you t'ink I should go down to se-ee what dese foo-ools're up to?'

Scrupulously, he followed the jaunt made by those whom he had been watching for some time.

'D'you not t'ink that the *mast-ter* would be most interested in dis curious affair?'

With his gnarled hands, he stroked a solitary black feather, one of the many belonging to his ride, but was careful not to rend a tear in the muslin-like fabric. Lazy clods of mist peeled away from before him, leaving him to appear as a dark blob against the Daystar's lavish bosoms.

'I shall tell the *mast-ter*,' he confirmed, patting his faithful carriage on her mane. 'He shall know h'wat to do. He always knows h'wat is best.'

At once both the bird and its rider turned away from the scene, and they headed upwards, soon disappearing into the cool, blackening aspect of the evening Sun.

*

Before the eve had come, however, they were at the slippery marshes of Awn-dynedhèlle. The elves had made a raft large enough for the eight of them to stand in. This they boarded wearily, each in his turn, as the Friends were somewhat dubious as to Frydor's proposed skill with logs and (unsmoked!) hemp.

They took the craft through the towering pinewood trees which reached up to the belly of the sky, touching it once, twice, and on each successive occasion. The sun did it's job as it peeped through the foliage of the dense swamplands. Once settled, they navigated the cypress knees which propped up out of the marshy swamps all about the place. One in particular gleaned more of their attention, as coiled up within its bark was a cottonmouth. Its lips crackled and its tongue spat forth venom, whilst it made itself ready to exact sufficient tribute from those whom sought to pass it by uninvited.

Alert as ever Frydor was not oblivious to the new threat. Upon seeing the reptile recoil its gristly length and extend, ready for the pounce, the elf took his oar in hand and positioned himself carefully within the boat. Then he smote the thing unkindly on its head. Once, twice, three times, until it slithered down into the depths of the murky swamp. Thereupon a crocodile of great size set upon it immediately, ravaging the serpent so fiercely it left it no room to manoeuvre.

Scarcely ruffling the floating lily-pads, Flip steered their raft away from the scene, not wanting for its fell fangs afterwards. Shortly, the alligator moved away, in preference for its usual forage of bullfrogs, fish and young, lonely relatives, who were void of parenting. He looked back at the scene and smiled inwardly when he saw another form, which bore an uncanny resemblance to the first, smothered by the grisly green fins of the gator.

'That's the way it should be!' he murmured, thrusting in his oar into the fresh hairy depths of the water-weald. 'There she is...'

They found a place to moor some time later and as evening drew near and the dusk light dwindled the elves began the task of hunting for the morning's meal.

The search in the woods around them was far from easy for the terrain they had found themselves in. Huddled trees, scrubby heaths, coarse swathes of grass that reached up to the elves' jawbones; none made it easy for the Company. So they kept to hunting rodents, snakes and suchlike, although no overt restriction was placed against the slaughter of any; even a brawny brown-backed bear would have gone down a treat, as too would have a mud-nosed mire-swilling boar, if given the chance!

The most astute amongst the tree-rodents sensed death creeping near and so kept themselves apart from the hunters, merging carefully with the fog-bound goutweed which had been blackened further by the grey-bellied clouds. There they remained until the Friends had passed, longing for a better end to their days. None wished to journey unprepared to whatever realms lay beyond death's final door, whether beast or animal, and so each one remained careful and on guard.

*

Flip packed his hand inside the scarf, placing himself unobtrusively before the pines' looming shadows. He was successful in concealing his key instrument of destiny, lest his meal should shrink away from before him. Wise was this elf, not only in words, but in deeds also.

Sinking back into a low squat, he wrapped his heavy garment twice around his torso, and remained still, only his flitting eyes betraying evidence of the hint of life. Thus he remained, unflinching, interposed between the sombre colours of the forest and the gloomy-grey disposition that marked the eyes and ears of his friends. His presence was concealed from his prey, as was intended, though some further boon yet remained with him as the chills from the nightly winds squandered all about his fearnought.

An unwary *squish* (part squirrel, part fish) mistook his still form as part of the evening's backdrop. Its eyes were still cautious, however, as it approached from the bank of the forest, pausing every so often to clean its paws and feed on its package of food. From the brown barks of trees to the open glades in the timberland, the creature drew sinuous curves in the dusty heather.

No sooner had she seen the bait dangling invitingly before her, amid a haven of dead leaves at the foot of a blossoming conifer, did the backdrop of the bustling weald fall forwards before her very sight, with arms as thick as trees. These reaches wrestled the stunned creature to its back.

Then there was a brief tussle, lasting only the instant thunder races from the bellows of Neptune, when he is taken with his gallon-glass of bitter. In this contest, one writhed whilst the other wrenched, both dutifully using the implements at their disposal. But Flip, being more familiar with his hands, dealt a sharp final blow to the rodent, which, eventually, put her out of her misery. The crack was clear although muffled, leaving only a small trickle of blood to leak through the thick, rugged cloth.

'There, that makes two,' Flip said gladly, pleased at his latest catch. 'That should be enough for breakfast. But I wonder how uncle Frydor fares?'

*

Frydor was about a half-mile downstream, not far off the sedge-infested banks, the dwelling of bobcats, green lizards, and mermaids of all shapes and sizes. The trees moaned at the sight of their guest as each twisted branch sought to reach one past the other. Cold drops of vigour soaked the skies to completeness and from the ford sprung a rising mist spreading its tentacles high above the valley floor, stretching far as the eye could see.

It was through this grey blanket that Frydor the Elf stumbled along, being guided by the perceptiveness of his pointed ears and the keenness of his elfin visions. Frydor was yet to fathom the latest conquest of his nephew for the mists forged of primordial sinew that hemmed him about, even though his kinsman's cries uprose in great bursts through the green upper layer of the overhanging canopy. At length however, he found his spot. It was a quiet and unruffled place, backed about by some flowerless fern-bushes.

Slowly, he lifted his sombre aspect, until he was facing the coiled constrictor. The inky void became less of a hindrance and activity round the woods soon aroused this most accursed of beasts. Eyes, white as snowflakes fallen upon the Great Heights, pierced through the murkiness towards the Elf's heart. His venomous hiss made for the terror which lies bound in each and every being, a sound as evil as the first unchancy words spoken in the Garden. Frydor needed no one to remind him of these things, for well did he know the ecstasy of the hunt to be vanished. In its place was a window of foaming toxin up from an earthen crag.

'You people have taken my cousins, my favourite uncle,' railed the snake, 'and my sister Boa-Louise, but you won't take me.' He rattled on a little more as he proceeded to realign himself for the task at hand. 'No sir-ree... you won't take me, even if it's the last thing I do!'

Nevertheless, Frydor stood poised in his spot, with little time to rub his eyes and even less time to pounce, so he thought.

'I am the l-l-largest and l-l-longest in my vast line of snake-species...' stammered the snake in parsel-mouth, a tongue too forgotten for Frydor to be weary of. 'And I am also the l-l-last.

'Therefore, I will not y-y-yield to your desires, so that you may satiate your carnal l-l-longings with my succulent flesh, no sir-ree; but indeed, you shall become my f-f-f-... grub!'

The proud snake slithered through the thick of the undergrowth, disturbing the leafy-green foliage, demanding deference and discharging its waste. It opted for a path close to the elf but it maintained its distance well, keeping his eyes constantly upon his new foeman, in anticipation of any hostile movement. When it came to it Frydor was an elf both bold and grim. He was much too strong-willed to be confounded by any lesser creature.

The elf resisted tensing his muscles lest this should slow his movements. With only his elfin-blade to succour his comfort and his learning in battlecraft to quieten his soul, he steadied himself as much as he could without freezing. He was prepared for the attack, ready at any moment to bound from his spot and smite his disputant cold, with any one of his implements.

So, with his left hand still confined to his neck-scarf, he grasped the dagger with his right, setting its edge to the ground and sky, nib settled towards the hissing performer. He let slip a few nervous chuckles from his carriage. Only part of the elf's arm peered through his scarf; there was nothing beneath the elbow lest he should have chosen entanglement with a poisonous breed. Frydor trimmed his eyes further, regarding the dim contours of the snake through the narrow slits by which he perceived the outside world, but the snake kept its distance well, abiding by its moment to strike, living by its own rules, which is the Law of the Jungle.

The stare that drove nails through Frydor's core was cold, cold some say as Iesous mab Dyn who bore the affliction of many upon that one sorrowful day. Stung by barbs with evil lashes, split by a hedge of thorns thrust upon his crown, pierced so that all the waters of the worlds might be cleansed and the bleeding of all elves everywhere, healed; little was spared this one. Save for the breaking of his legs by rods, his soul by words, his spirit by the fell clutches of Baal-Zebub, Chief Regent of Annwfn.

'If you're not going away,' Karoas hissed arrogantly, 'then perhaps I'd better help you.'

With this he lunged forwards with a sharp, sudden feint which he suspected would take the elf by surprise. Glands broad as the hide of a mammoth, teeth glinting of previous triumphs, tongue spitting venom, all at once things bode ill for Frydor. It was a manoeuvre designed to test the old elf's reaction – whether or not he was a worthy enough match for Karoas, last in the line of

Boas. And well was this move designed. For Frydor hesitated, and for almost a moment too long it seemed. But he quickly came to his senses again, in no way perturbed by the elaborate dance.

Karoas, assuming a dearth of mobility in the Surp, was at it again, sudden as its smaller cousin the cobra, but with a thrust more cunning, with vengeance most deadly. At once there was scuffle, in which, for a short space, no party appeared to fare the better. Even as folks tell of the Wars of Pendragon's Wilderness which raged for nigh on two millennia before there ever was resolve, likewise did this contest continue undetermined till evening had again smothered the broken tranquillity.

In a while, it was silence that held the reigns. The evening weald was come, the battle was won and was lost, black birds had come in to squabble over the remains of the day. Presently, it was one party that prevailed over the other. And for his lack of guile, it was Karoas whose recollections of past and distant things came flooding back to memory.

The next thing the snake did recall was viewing the lower part of his body emitting a warm sticky ooze into the dark alluvium soils. But he felt little discomfort as the gore trickled out from beneath him. Surrounding trees seemed to hold deference only for themselves, and refused to ponder the curse of the snake smote before their very eyes. Indeed, all power seemed vanished from the clearing that eve. The plight of those under their boughs was their charge; weaker beasts who daily paid homage, gave thanks, bowed before its proud branches in longing. These were the ones whose keeping lay in their barks and in their skins.

Karoas was at death's door – that much he knew at least – but try as he might to feel the sorry sensations so commonly associated with one's untimely demise, he in no wise felt a thing.

This all came as a bit of a disappointment to him. He saw no spirit-guides come out to collect him, as his head fell down between the bushes, nor was he able to view the studded stars fixed upon the dark raiment of heaven. (This thing in itself was somewhat more of a setback for him as he had always enjoyed star-gazing, especially when he had been a youth in the care of his guardians, for they had lain on their backs contentedly at times of such mystification). That glory was now gone, however. He joined his kith in the lonely grey loam.

Frydor gathered the pieces of his catch together, right down to the last paltry head, which was still squirting spit and venom. With some evident greed, he stuffed it all into his satchel.

'That will make good soup. Well done Frydor!' the elf said, obviously pleased with himself. 'Just you wait and see my good fellow, just you wait and see.'

Such is the account of the death of the last snake in the line of *Anak-Boa*.

Breakfast was a rather quaint affair. The Company found itself near the skirts of Mount Derwent, on the other side of the river away from the hamlets. The trees had little of the foreboding they had held the night before, neither did they seem so tall in the shimmering daylight. The air sighed as it had always done, the sun rose, and birds gathered cheerily together, singing songs of gladness for the breaking of a new day.

It was not long afterwards that food was served in a clearing by the Afon Mon. They were a little way down the weather-beaten track, which was littered with brittle boulders and stones, all strewn desultorily about the place like the patch upon which a child plays its marbles. The fresh morning breeze wafted an uncertain aroma towards the troop, filling the air with its own brand of fetors which none failed to notice. Whether by wizardry or by some culinary lore known only to High Elves, the Syndicate was not to be disappointed.

The evening's catch had been fair. Carrion had been altered into a mixture of meats and stewed soups, all blended with newly ground parsley and peppers. Vegetables had been garnered from the surrounding weald, fresh and hearty as any found in the heart of Abundance. This was taken aside freshly made poppadoms. The entire concoction soon found its way through to the empty stomachs of the Friends.

'Got any more?' Sashi grunted, cleaning the last of his snake-soup. 'That was pretty damn good if you don't mind me saying Frydor, specially the bits and pieces you put in there... what were they again?' he quizzed uncertainly.

The elf whom he addressed was busy himself, with his head buried deep within his own bowl.

'Oh and them poppadoms – great idea – wicked mate!' He then belched a smelly though somewhat sonorous burp.

'More, my Indian friend? Well, of course,' replied Frydor. He guzzled the remaining 'bits' that had collected towards the bottom of his container. 'Here you are...

'But you must try to drink this soup sparingly, for it is of the type Anak-Boa, which I fear causes one to open the bowels all too regularly!'

He poured more liquid into the smooth base of the willow.

'It is good, isn't it?'

The rest of the friends were no more encouraged by Flip's vibrant remarks.

'Perhaps I might have some more after this bowl-full, Uncle?'

'As you wish, son, all to his own... or hers,' piped the elder, looking at the glum faces of the three young women. 'I really wish you would try some young fellows, for it is really quite pleasant...'

Nonetheless, it was not for his insistent goading that J-J, Elena and the others proceeded to lick their vessels clean. Food had been scarce all the while and each was hungry (a thing which frequently worked against them when it came to moments of resolve); so they soon found something of a solution to their quandary.

Imagining the culled snake to be chicken (which worked well for Gee) or a fresh hide of meat stripped off of an 'healthy' British longhorn, the Friends closed their eyes, opened their mouths, and prayed…

*

It was early the next day before the sun made another welcome appearance. Bursting gloriously through the grey misty sky and unveiling her portly stomach, she granted them their first daytime viewing of Efas-Us. And what a sight it was!

Before them were Hovsepian's Marble Gates, named after the Worthy Elder of that place, who had been the leader of a rebellious band of rioters. In a time before records began it is believed that they had taken to speaking darkly of Men from the East, though fondly of those from the North. But in that day, as in many others, such talk was forbidden and such deeds were deemed to be heresies worthy only of either the pyre, plundering, or persecution. Nowadays, folk gathered there daily in their quest for trade and barter, scant heed being given to the noble things of the past. Springing items from weary passers-by or transferring wares from those who were slightly more dubious than themselves was the sole call of such noble environs these days.

Now the men in those parts were lanky. Tall as trees, most were lean as the Spear of Iselgod, which fastened him to floor by the hand of the Eight Mighty Dwarves of Gwynedd (who thereafter prised open the giant's mouth and thrust through the poisoned tip towards his foul gut, losing one of their members in the doing, however, after they had overcome the beast so valiantly). The sight of dangly arms poking through sullen garbs was common as too were the skinny legs, slender shanks (stout to barely hold a chicken in famine), and scrawny necks, upon which their sombre faces rested. It was all the more menacing when they appeared ghost-like, moving through the streets towards the Friends. Each one had a pipe of some description hanging inanely off his lip, with black puffs of smoke shadowing his worn visage. It was a sight greatly dispiriting to the strangers.

The women were even less prized however. It is true to say that most ate less than their destitute male fosterage, yet for some reason, they still bellowed outwardly at the hips and thighs. Vast swathes of flab were held in by little more than stitches of reed-fibre! Breasts bounded about in brown beaver-skins, fitted by the weavers of the animal skins. Bones knocked unkindly against one another, all in an instant it seemed, rattling joints and fusing marrow.

Their raiment appeared as plain, drab even – impoverished material, too coarse even to clothe a black elk before the celebration of the Kalan Larc. On their feet was either cheap leather or wooden clogs, some of which were fashioned by smiths on their benches. Others, however, were crafted by wrights of the G'ladhrim Treku who reside over in the south. But their frugal attire had a simple attractiveness to it, which was very much becoming to the younger elf; though not perhaps in the eyes of those who had been spoiled since their earliest days on Daearawd.

Some way up ahead, mules were towing carts heavy laden with loads which were suspended from their backs. One farmer in particular herded his cattle onto one side of the road. He waved at Frydor in a courteous manner, though not without prodding the head of his flock with the end of his shepherd's staff. Seeing yet another elf, Frydor broke off for a quick discourse. He was somewhat disappointed when, for some considerable time, they failed to move the chat on past the weather.

Nevertheless, they did touch upon the health of the good bishop, each one saluting his very existence as indeed all should. Frydor then rejoined his nephew at the helm, leaving the other to return to his cattle, his life, his pot-bellied wife. The hard effects of life working the land had weathered the farmer's face. The Friends saw as much and vowed never to allow themselves to fall victim to such relentless toil. Asides from that his face was cheery enough, though there seemed to be scant matters to be cheerful about on that particular day.

Farmer Lomu continued with his tracks, guiding his husky head of kine up towards the market. He prodded, poked, and pushed the slower ones, though he still found the grace to nudge the very youngest more tenderly. Hard on his heels was his charge-hand, who, with his sweaty palms and large forehead (enough to gather up all the grime of Abundance Flip joked), the elves recognised to be a dwarf.

His hands albeit contained a friendly press, and he had a pleasant enough name to boot. It turns out that at their time of meeting, Young Mallory was in the midst of contemplating life's alternatives to free-loading, which usually meant stealing to order. It was an occupation he had never previously given thought to, prior to Foxy Biblo (a trusted family friend) approaching him earlier that month.

Alas! Times as they were. The youthful Mallory would have to weigh up such an exacting option with his fair damsel, Marion, whose main occupation was filling yard-arms behind the local bar. She was the one he had been waiting for all of his life, that he might sweep her off her feet, consummate their lovemaking in an orderly fashion, before going on to produce midget dwarves when they were fully established.

Coincidentally, as the Friends were passing, she happened to be bringing her beloved his day's worth of sandwiches. Quite attractive to most, even

164

those not of her own kind, she appeared to take an avid interest in Markie. They walked along the uneven tracks barefoot, Flip spending his time admonishing the younger dwarf as best as he was able to stay on honest ground, but thanking him all the same for speaking so candidly.

Soon however, the cattle and their masters turned towards the Seat of Coma and the outdoor market, which lies westward of the Gate. It was there that the two dwarves bade the Company their last farewell for the time being. Now, too, they were gone, from view and from memory.

*

They drifted around for much of the remaining day. Only when the evening succumbed to the final night chills of the cold season did the Company find a place to put up in for the night, hard by the bounds around Efas.

Roofs thatched with reed, they opted for a lowly-hung daub-covered tavern, over a dozen bedrooms in total, each one of its own size and standard. There was a plethora of washrooms, each of which was in a good state of repair. And there were plenty of cubby-holes, for… well, for the necessary!

Perhaps what was most in favour of "The Highwayman" was its size. Its ceiling, granted, was lacking in height and its walls in depth, and both sometimes stunk of rotten summer kine-fields. However, much of the insides were spacious, large enough to allow an average-sized man to manoeuvre with some ease. And below the ground there were hives of chambers and passages, all of which predated Efas-Us itself.

Most of the rooms and hallways were adequately furnished, to Flip's best estimation, as he examined the dressed walls and the priceless carvings that were mounted upon graded oaken stands. The adjoining encumbering walls were studded with paraffin lights, and all were set at generous spacing to highlight the pitched gloom. These ran almost the enitre length of the open floor-space from one end of the quarters to the other. The earthenware, though not lavish, was ornate, enough to draw a second glance from Mark, and the rooms within were pleasant. But few rooms could be considered as opulent, save in the eyes of Gee perhaps, whose beginnings were in somewhat more humbling surroundings.

Space inside the rooms was an invaluable commodity. Relatively sparse in decoration when compared with the hall outside, they still contained enough utensils to provide a functional, perhaps even a contented welcome for any distressed visitor. Two beds could be strung together if necessary and the combined spread lay beneath the brightest paraffin lamps (which were somewhat adept at casting ghastly shadows across the entire length of the room). Moody spectres danced eerily amid the murky lighting, like the eyes above the shadowy form of a Crowlag – those dark beasts, descendants of the *Clawrender* and of the *Näzgrîl*. But the Friends paid scant heed of them at present, tired as they were, and welcoming as the place at first appeared to be…

*

Dinner was served later that evening. In the normal pattern of things guests would start off at the bar an hour or so before the outset of the first course. Then, regardless of whatever dishes may have come prior, the final evening spread would be sealed off with a few douses of half-pint ales and a generous selection of Farmer Delaley's egg-encrusted pork pies, which had been selected from his farms in Elfdoslern. The evening of the Syndicate's arrival was to be no different.

The day's speciality had already been set by the head chef Antonio: buffoon loins (from a creature that was new to the Friends), carved from a highly reluctant creature; generous measures of sprouts; butter-laced warm carrots; roasted yams and fried onions. All were drowned in an abundant flow of thick gravy. There was also the rump of a succulent pig to keep its company, which was laid next to the cold platter of asparagus, lentils and mellifluous roasted chicken. The Syndicate ensured they were not too late for the evening's most lavish serving.

Opting for a table at the rear end of the inn, they soon found that they had chosen an ideal spot for themselves. Where they were benched they could peer through the large east-facing windows, and contemplate, each one to his heart's content, the eve's beautiful resolve. They might even be able to drown their bevies in peace and devour their meal with a modicum of privacy. The issues they needed to speak of were too deep for any idle lug to overhear, so caution still held the moment.

'So, Uncle,' Flip started, casting his eye around at his new comrades, 'what's the story to be from here on in?' Unfortunately however, he could hardly be heard for the jeering people.

'Uncle?'

Several of the tavern's residents were making merry with various wines, port and sweetened mead, while others danced with spontaneous exuberance to tunes sung by the resident troubadour. It was Grahymlawd who was at hand to provide jovial songs or melancholy dirges, according to the manner of mood for most. He was a songsmith of great word-horde, so folks tell, even if his voice was not all that he cracked it up to be.

The light from the lanterns barely made a dent in the heavy smog. Pilasters of light were in place but little difference did these ornaments make to the settings. The sounds of guzzling men soon drowned the songs of feasts and the tales of heroes and eroded much of the rapturous applause which, out of tradition if not courtesy, had been directed towards the scop.

166

'Did you smell that, Sashi?'

'Did I fuck!'

Sashi tried following Mark's glare, but the herbal leaf burning somewhere in the vicinity seemed to want to spread its tentacles between their conversation.

'Smell's like weed to me.'

'Skunk you mean?'

'What else?'

'All I smell is trouble, Mark,' Aleasha interjected. 'It beats me why anyone ever takes that stuff in the first place – must be mighty boring down there in the West Country Boyo!'

And it was all rather dull in Efas-us too. Smoking at the pipe was an extraordinarily popular pastime amongst the young and paltry in these parts, so much so that they even had competitions to see who could draw down the longest breath of soot.

Presently, the accentuated smoke uprose from the herb higher and faster than the steam from the boiled gravy broth. It was a dwarf-maiden who carried this brew, which she had balanced delicately upon the crown of her head.

'Well, my good people,' Frydor said, chewing on some hardy gristle once his meal was set before him. 'I do believe we shall set out from here within two days, for time is not on our side.' The elf lowered his head and continued gnawing at the rest of his bone.

'But we shall need to equip you all for the journey first.'

'So is that it then?' Sashi enquired attentively. 'D-d-don't we have a say in the m-m-matter?'

Frydor was curious, certainly, though not enough to restrain himself from his devouring-feats.

Sashi peered closer; 'I mean, I know I may not exactly be the quickest tool in the box but have I missed something here?' The inquisitor looked half-heartedly towards Gee to sort out his confusion.

'I mean… what are you on about Frydor? We just want to g-g-go home – and that's it – why's that too d-d-difficult to understand?'

'Yeah, Frydor man, what you be saying chief? It's home for us not some silly adventure…'

'What kind of stuff are we looking at then?' Aleasha rejoined eagerly. 'And where exactly are we going if you don't mind me asking Frydor? Because the way I see it is like this: why don't all y'all elves get some of your own folk to do your work, you sort us out, and we'll be kindly on our way?'

'Yeah, stop picking on us?' added Elena for clarity. 'It's not fair.'

There was a curt nod of a head.

'If I may, uncle…' The younger elf pushed aside his platter for the moment. 'With your aid,' he resumed, 'perhaps we may see a beneficial end for all involved. A Win-Win situation I believe it is called.' Flip looked longingly towards the far end of the bar where youths were busy making small talk with their female cousins.

'Now I do not pretend to fully understand all the things which my uncle often proclaims and I will not make any unworthy assumption that I ever shall, fully anyhow. But the evidence is in my own experience, as it is now in yours – a thing no elf could rend asunder. And so I believe that the moment holds it for me – therefore, I also am ready to go forward with The Oath. I shall swear the pledge!'

At this, Frydor raised his head and looked at his nephew. Perhaps he had the slightest sniff of bemusement about him, as was told by the light smirk that found its way to his face, but not blatant was this mocking, not loud, not obtrusive.

'Some change in you young Flip?' Frydor said after pondering his kinsman for some time longer. 'I've known you since your mother first wrapped you up in swaddling clothes, and I have truly recognised your interest in these matters; but as for accepting them as they ought, you've been no closer than a white-maned bear to the Sun!'

'Yes, Uncle, but now I do not jest!'

He lowered the lip of his frothing goblet.

'On our way here something inside me warmed to the words you had spoken earlier. I cannot readily explain it all, though as you well know I would dearly love to try. But, Uncle, surely you yourself know that many things cannot be defined in the words of even the most enlightened elves – and with all of my ability, I jest not, I have sought such solutions. To no avail however. Thus, all I can really affirm is this; your words and your philosophies were but mere fantasies up until this very day, even after seeing the queer sight of these strange ruffians appearing out of nowhere...'

Rebuffed, Elena stared at him irately.

'Now however (and hereafter, if the gods should smile on our passage!) only a fool would say that you speak anything other than plainly, truthfully, and honourably, difficult though it may be to always comprehend the fact.' The younger elf gave Elena a broad smile.

'I have seen many mysterious phenomena in my time uncle. But I have never counted any as far beyond the normal realm of things which science, numbering, or reverse engineering could not possibly conjure up, given enough time and wisdom. Nevertheless, the things I must bear witness to over the past few days have blown me away, loosely speaking. Therefore, I was compelled to make my choice, which, thus, I have done!'

'Pray tell, Father, what think you your brother's son now?'

Frydor perused his younger sibling up and down. But it was another curt retort.

'And a brave and noble choice it is too, young Flip. Cheers, all!'

Frydor raised his goblet to his companions and saluted each one in turn, beginning first with Aleasha, who was sitting under his left wing, and ending up with young Elena on his right-hand side. Then he took another swig:

'And to you too, my loveable rogue of a nephew. Cheers, and all the best to your days!'

'Aye, brave...' Flip replied, somewhat discordantly, 'and perhaps noble. But let not my friends think that I am too young! Do you not remember my uncle – I have reached my hundredth cycle this week and am therefore come of maturity! I hope you have not forgotten these simple things my good uncle and ignored, amid all the excitement, the reason for my coming in the first place?'

'Forgotten? Me...?' Frydor dove straight into his awaiting pint-glass. 'My goodness gracious me!' he said, as he came up with froth on his lip. 'I had forgotten, to tell the truth, with all the excitement of the past few days... One hundred and one pardons I beg of you my young cousin, one hundred and one pardons! It all comes back now... one hundred and one pardons, I beg of you my nephew? Granted?'

Mumbling quite cheerfully beneath his now foetid breath, the elf still managed a jovial smile.

'Then all is well – and congratulations Flip! Compliments to you on your coming of age. Now you may live as you ought to, and die as you see best – according to The Lore that is. For you are now responsible for your own ways!'

'All is forgiven, my good father, and I thank you for your good wishes.'

'Ah, so all is truly well.'

The elf gestured towards a pretty young dwarf who was serving drinks at the main dining table.

'Over here my good maid – a few more bevies if you please.' She caught site of Uncle Frydor, dressed herself down accordingly, and hurried over.

'Ah, the best-looking dwarf in Cakewall's Inn!'

'The *only* dwarf in Cakewall's Inn!'

'We should like a gallon of your best ale if you please, as we are celebrating the hundredth passing of young... *OOPS!* ... Well, perhaps not so young, Flip over here.'

The dwarf-mistress permitted a loud, broad grin to polish the elf's vision. It was a rather gummy smile, though it was one filled with much warmth and kindness. And as she leant over to pick up his goblet, it was Flip who was forced to reconsider his previous estimate of her. Her two prime melons could fetch a fat ransom at any market-stall he had ever been to!

*

The atmosphere quickly sparked up as news of free ale reached the ears of the hangers-on. And all this for an elf who had been sitting quietly on the end of the table in the middle of the hall.

His attention had been drawn to the duo of elves who were sitting with the men-folk. In turn, this bystander, who was a smidgen of an elf himself (with a pink face and ears nearing the size of his feet) fell upon the feeling that his friend, who happened to be perched next to him, ought also to be privy to this information. This fellow's name was George. And George was always trying to get his leg over. On this occasion however, as on all on the others indeed, he was not having too much success.

Now something had attracted him to the pretty young maiden sitting to his right. Unfortunately however, throughout the preliminaries of the pre-meal banter, and despite the fact that he had stoked himself up with half a vat of mead to entertain his courage, he had not yet chanced upon the nerve to engage her in full moot. Therefore, the saying that he soon heard from his chum was his perfect moment, and make fair use of it he duly did!

And so was the news dispersed round the table. From mouths to ears to clamours and shouts, through all manners of wild gesticulations, all eventually returning to the eavesdropper himself. All this in a matter of a few short minutes – just in time for all to rise, and toast the celebration.

'Cheers, and happy *berf-week* me old mate Fil-lip!' Peregrine mispronounced, already half-stoned from his dubious smoking habit, the stale liquor not aiding him one tittle.

'Many 'appy returns me old codger; and may the gods bless yer wonderful soul!'

His cheeks lit up rosily while the rest of his company stood to their feet. They beckoned a most pleasant compliment towards the young elf as is customary, and in chorus chanted:

'Cheers again, Old Boy, and may the gods show you favour all your days.'

'But how about a little share in your good fortune, for me and me few friends 'ere?'

Peregrine tottered slightly before keeling over to one side.

'Blow me,' he mumbled to nobody in particular. 'I've almost had enough already methinks…'

'Looks like your birthday was not so much of a secret after all,' Elena whispered merrily, still picking at the generous portions of food which had been all too much for her tiny stomach. 'Well at least not a private one!'

But the jeering and coarse banter drowned out any kind of response from the popular elf. Flip looked to be quite contented as he was. He beamed at her broadly.

Meanwhile, Marion returned to the table with the requested vat of ale. By this time, Elena had finished mulling over the remaining scraps on her plate, dubious as to whether or not her stomach could take any more, and doubtful as to whether or not she should actually press the matter. She shoved the dish towards the flowers holding centre stage.

It was Sashi who saw it first, followed quickly by Gee (who was the stronger and the hungrier); but Mark was closest to the dish when it rested. And as the three lusty lads fought over the leftovers from her platter, a keen-eyed observer raised his voice in rapturous cheer:

'Giddy-up, folks, it's a free for all!' Peregrine yelled gleefully, before he dipped his arms into Marion's brimming jugs...

THE KNIGHT'S OATHS

Fools and blind! For which is greater,
the gift or the altar that sanctifies the gift?
Therefore he who swears by the altar,
swears an oath by it and by all things on it…
And he who swears by heaven swears by the throne of God
and by Him who sits on it.

MATTHEW 23:19-20 & 22

The Troop awoke early the next day inside one of the annexes of the dusk-lit tavern. Mark was already sitting at the dining table when Gee arrived to join him; the others gathered their senses some time later on, after the weariness of sleep had parted them for a new day. When Flip finally arrived, they at last got down to the business of discussing the hour's most important decisions.

'I'm glad that everyone is here right now for we must speak in absolute privacy,' Frydor said, keeping his volume low and his pace quick. 'The huge quantities of alcohol for each of our visitors turned out to be a grand idea Flip. But let us yet hope that they do not soon stir!'

'Thank you, Uncle. We are now at liberty to talk as you say, but for how long, who can tell? So, Uncle, as we now have the place to ourselves, let us make the best use of it as we can.'

Aleasha fancied neither the whispered tones of secrecy nor the present darkness that was lurking around Frydor's eyes. What ought to have been glorious rays of light seemed rather to be something grey and foreboding, which added to the dank and cramped feel of the morning room. But the moon did her best to remedy things, shining through the rafters in uncannily bright beacons, giving daybreak a new meaning, suffusing flowers and wakening hearts.

Oft times at such an early hour in these parts both the sun and moon were visible. The decree had been made certain by the Sorcerers of Thurles, those magicians of the Forgotten Era who had waxed bold in both their charms and magic. Be that as it may, however, when Frydor leaned forward to speak, resting his upper body weight upon his elbows, he shunned coldly the temperament of the day outside. Instead, he chose to share his arcane thoughts somewhat more candidly.

'I think we must leave this place immediately,' he said, eyeing his company tensely. 'Our weapons are in need of collection, and we must be prepared for the long journey ahead of us. Time is never for the lacklustre or indolent. Much rests on our own conduct – lest we should hope to blame someone else for any future ills!'

'Er… excuse me?' queried Sashi. All eyes turned towards the Indian. 'What's this business with uzis and weapons, Frydor? You never said anything about weapons... and fighting? There's none – '

'Yeah blud,' Gee agreed. 'What's with all that shit?' The others too were acquiescent.

'Uzis? What are uzis?' queried Flip, looking flummoxed as his uncle made pains to answer. 'As for weapons; almost every elf, dwarf or indeed, man, owns a sword, for it is the custom of our lands. It provides some sort of recompense against muggers, free-loaders, evildoers, and those in the service of corrupt magistrates, a great many of whom there seem to be at present.'

'Nevertheless, we have no guns in this land,' clarified Frydor. 'That is a barbaric weapon of earthly invention. Nay! But we have need of special weapons – '

Ears pricked up at the mentioning.

'– tools that have been crafted specially for you, if I may say so at this stage, to assist you finish the tasks at hand. It is armament which no *gun* or man-made weaponry could match, primitive though they may seem at first.

'But be that as it may, you first have to grow in the wisdom of your spirit to utilise our weaponry most effectively, and then perchance, you shall be able to rent in twain both the natural and the spiritual. If not, then that is how they shall remain – barbaric tools of yesteryear, with barely enough credence for our own self-preservation, let alone qualify you as the legendary Zaqen.'

The Syndicate looked baffled.

'I don't like the sound of this Frydor,' replied J-J. 'What is it exactly we've got to do? And how can anything possibly be better than a nuclear-tipped warhead… except perhaps for one with added biological and chemical compartments, which filter out before, during, and after the main explosion…?'

She shoved aside her cornmeal porridge and fixed her stare even more guardedly upon Frydor.

'I don't know about the rest of the gang, except maybe for Gee, Frydor, but I'm not gonna be any "follow-follow" girl – ain't that right Dog?'

'Damn right girl,' said Gee.

J-J the parlance-poocher looked around at the others.

'You see Frydor – and no offence or nothing – but we are not… how shall we say… down with this. In fact, I'm sometimes almost like my girl there,' J-J said, nodding towards Elena. 'I sometimes don't even think I'm here at all!'

The crew creased up to Elena's obvious embarrassment. The feigned African vernacular, the slickness… all that shit went down like a pint of water after a marathon. Soon however, the somewhat capricious chaps were compelled to regard the present situation a little more seriously. They had to regain their composure if for no other reason than to quell the elf's swelling irritation. J-J had voiced enough of their heart-felt concerns for the elves to get the picture.

'Have you finished yet children?'

There was silence. *Children? Here we go again*, not a few of the Friends thought.

'Exactly what is laid upon us, I know not myself, though I can hazard a fair guess. Even so, such that I do know I cannot even tell you, until you swear The Oath. But I shall tell you this – it is serious!' Frydor's tone was calm, his voice collected, his speech unequivocal. He cast his eyes squarely upon J-J and then gazed upon Sashi and then the others.

'So what say you now?'

Discomfort raided Flip's private seclusion causing him to shuffle his feet from side to side in a rather aggrieved manner. Presently, he left his place by the tableside and walked around a little, to ease off the decidedly frosty atmosphere which had taken both the room and his ageing joints, all too suddenly.

Frydor turned to his nephew, ailed by his sibling's agitation.

'Flip, my weary son and foremost acolyte. Perhaps you could fill in these young initiates on a few more of the prophecies pertaining to themselves? Let us see how well you recall the schooling of your youth?' The Surp also needed to relieve the pressure on his lower back. So he stood to his feet and followed Flip's pattern, letting out a most healthy groan as he did so.

'Ah… that does me nothing but good,' Frydor sighed, his back creaking audibly. 'There, I can feel my bones falling back into place now!'

'Nah! Hold up dread!'

Both elves stared implacably at Gee.

'What I means to say… oh whatever – this ain't funny any more chief! All that style and pattern fuckery you be coming up with about us collecting some keys and saving the world… man, what do you take us for? Now I know we might be a bit green under the gills here, but give us credit – p-l-e-a-s-e. You're in trouble. You need our help. We die… and you still don't get what you're looking for because it just can't be gotten, because you've tried it all before. Am I right?'

Flip was the first to break his stare. He stood still and cast an all-too-obvious glance at his uncle, who in return chided him with no mild look of his own.

'Yeah, begging your pardon and all that,' Mark added, struggling to raise his voice above the background mumbling coming in from Gee's direction. 'But what I think my friend is trying to say is that – now don't get me wrong or anything, because I may have misunderstood the brother – but I don't think that he wants any of his crew to be trekking around the wilderness after monsters, orcs and someshit.'

'Damn right! I ain't gonna be trekking after no foolishness!'

'I'm sorry Frydor,' Mark rejoined quickly, 'but I think you'll do better fighting your own battles. You see, we're just happy as we are – like in one piece and everything.'

'Can we just go home Frydor?' pleaded Elena. 'Please? We've really enjoyed meeting you but I think that I need to return home now – my mum will be missing me. At least, I hope she will be.'

Frydor looked at her, confusion set amidst his furrowed brow.

'Honestly, it's been interesting… almost fun,' she plied on sheepishly. 'But I need to be there for my little brother – we're really close you see, especially because of the divorce and everything. Anyway, all good things must come to an end – just as they say...' Everyone felt really sorry for Elena.

'Especially when things have turned pear-shaped, right guys?' Mark said, about three seconds too late. 'All good things I mean and not your mama!'

'Nice one Markie,' Sashi spluttered, trying to ignore the fact that The Kid still did not have the hang of Mama-cusses. 'Let's have another one then… on second thoughts, you can keep your humour to yourself Boyo – I think I'm just happy as I am.' Sashi's head slumped forwards until it rested in the nook between his arms.

'Anyway, Frydor, how about it?'

'How about what, Mark, my friend?'

Elena said, 'How about telling us how to go home and leave this nightmare? Please?'

Her mind vied in and out of the present day reality as it had done ever since her first setting foot in Krandor. It had not yet settled into any one state, partly because she was young and confused, and also fairly innocent; but mostly because she was lost and hurting badly. The rest of the guys did their best to comfort her, however, reassuring her with words they didn't quite believe themselves and extolling the virtues of such a venture, should they really be forced to undertake it; lying through their back teeth, generally. They were adamant of one day returning. All things said however, little seemed to draw the youngster any closer to reality.

'You need some waking up little girl,' Flip said, slapping Elena once round the jowls, before following up his efforts a second time. Nonetheless, Elena was no more willing to accept the reality of her current lot than before.

"One for All and All for Each Other"

'That is one of our Surp sayings,' resumed Frydor the Elf. 'Now I do not pretend that your adventures will be without perils, but you are more than able to overcome them, methinks. Just keep your hand upon your chest and your eyes upon the prize and the world will turn…'

*

The moon cast sinister shadows upon the forlorn figures of the Syndicate. Outside the inn and shrouded in the expressionless constant of grief were the repine lights from the rising sun. All glory cowered above the slumbering town as was befitting the moment; all held their peace, none was left in a daze.

Gee leant over to Elena, his dear friend, and cradled her in his long, expansive arms. She began to weep softly into his chest, consoled a little by his protective custody, but longing it seemed for something more.

'I just want to go home!' she wept silently, onto his breast. 'I just want to go home Gee. Please take us home?'

'I'm so sorry,' Frydor replied tenderly. He reached past Gee and touched her lightly:

'But, if the truth be known, according to The Holy Books, you found yourselves in this mess for the foolish games you engaged in whilst you yet resided on the other plains. You opened the door to our world and all that lies herein. It is not from myself I am glad to say. No reproach lies with me. So any charge that must come lies squarely at your feet.'

Elena looked glummer still.

'All I wish for you now is that you return to the land of your fathers. Though if at the same time you can help us to fulfil the prophecies of old, which happen to be inextricably linked, then why not let it be so? Smite two birds with one stone, as they say?'

But Gee reared up menacingly. 'Yo boss!' he roared belligerently. 'Tell us what you want us to do to get out of this place and we'll do it. But don't expect us to believe it or even to like it. 'Cos as far as I can see, you're just some fucked-up little munchkin whose got lonely in his old age and has lost a complete grip on reality! And yo' mama was probably a loner before you too…'

As the amiable dwarf-maid approached from the kitchens, Gee gradually relaxed his grip on Frydor's scarf.

'Well then, Gee, you'll just have to learn to look a little deeper then won't you?'

*

Shortly, the moon disappeared and for the rest of the morning it remained hidden behind the stout presence of the glistening daystar. The embers of the rising sun suffused through the morning breeze bringing cheer, happiness and freedom of expression. Butterflies swept past the misty windows to the tune of dragonflies singing noisily in the fields. Insects hopped dizzily around, crickets mostly, joyous at another day's worth of dancing and singing, which lay before them. Momentous was the day, wonderful and bliss, more gorgeous than the first day of Mai.

They could hear the plodding sounds of a cart trundling along the byway some way out behind the rose-garden. They were most likely attached to a prime set of horses or maybe even a couple of *buffoons*, especially adapted for their new role. There were traders and merchants there too, in abundance, most having started off their long day's work by marching the distance towards the town-centre to peddle their wares. Rams' horns, goats' heads, cows' ears and feet, all found their use in some way or another, even if it was just in a witch's brew.

Nonetheless, it was not before the day was a quarter spent that most of the folks inside the inn began to arouse from the night-time's slumber. To all intents and purposes it had been a good evening all round. Even the gossipy chatter which most elves had been privy to had been all rather interesting, especially with regards to those men-folk... Not that with the first rays of light anyone was vaguely interested in the previous night's discourse.

Around the dining table, Frydor was currently preoccupied explaining the situation somewhat more coherently.

'It is for your own sakes that I hark on as I do, J-J. Today, we must head for the lodgings of one of my most trusted friends, the Surp Byron DeBecks, a resident of the Eastern Quartier. There we shall talk more.' The elf glanced around artfully. 'It is not now a good thing to be talking about such matters in front of strangers. Is that not so my nephew?'

'You'll be right there, my uncle, as usual. Especially ones given too kindly to the drink such as these. Loose tongues the lot of them if you ask me!'

Now Aleasha had long accepted the need for at least some guidance, courtesy of the withered elf, but she was yet to be fully reconciled with his dour pledges and solemn words. If indeed his words could be trusted, how much more had he not told them?

So she queried him: 'What about the oath thing?'

Her friends mumbled in general concordance.

'I kind of see why you'd want us to swear an oath – almost makes sense. But I thought you'd been waiting for us anyway... And if it's us who are going to fulfil your country's history, even though the big-head Gee there reckons it's implausible, then why the need for any further troth? Besides, I already have a pledge to my God, so I don't feel I ought to swear allegiance to anyone or anything else. I hope you understand.'

She turned aside and sat down.

'We'll soon see how strong your fealty was my dear,' Flip responded flatly, as though the words of *men* counted for nought. 'Then shall we see how noble was your pledge.'

*

The roads were dusty and hard worn, resembling wider versions of old country lanes which had been cracked and disfigured for its age, a commonplace feature back in the Real World. Amongst the littered alleyways were gathered large numbers of street-sellers, hustlers, donkeys, asses, elves and not a few dwarves. The elves were the ones who brought some cheer to proceedings as the Friends passed by, for their friendly countenances, which some say was fashioned by the gods themselves solely to bring cheer to men. The dwarves albeit seemed somewhat more staid than their fellows. Rarely was a midget given to smiling, and certainly not unless he had coaxed some poor soul out of his hard-earned wares.

The Eastern Quartier, which was the place to which Frydor's company ventured, was the newest sector in this ever-sprawling metropolis. It had sprung up after most of the troubles of yesteryear had died away. So dark were those times, that many gave thought to spare loved ones the full horrors of the world by not giving birth to them in first place! Folk nowadays were filled with more hopeful verisimilitudes for forthcoming cycles, and many more were gleeful now that the approach of the New Millennium was upon them. Evidence of this were the seemingly endless numbers of religious freaks who seemed to be popping up out of the woodwork!!

The Company neared the house in question. In colour it was red and pink, with ghastly floral arrangements laid out towards the front of the domicile and inside it was totally lacking any Feng Shui. The building itself was fashioned after the manner of a townhouse, though with a little more carriage space towards the fore, but its size was sufficient for a small family to reside within with some comfort. It therefore offered enough space for the noble Surp and his wife, ones whom Frydor himself had not seen at all in almost twelve cycles.

In former times the two noble elves had entered into an odd dispute over some of their more arcane doctrines. This, amongst the more usual contentions connected with *gradd* and status, had conspired to drive a spiked prong in between the two kindred. Things had mended a little since then, albeit, for these were pressing and difficult times which they both had to face, together, if they ever hoped to triumph over the evil within the lands. Go-betweens sometimes ran errands for the Surps, relaying messages of brethren trapped within the shires, bringing wines to weddings and books to feasts.

So Frydor was presently on more amicable terms with his cousin; lest pride should have destroyed in hours what it had taken lifelong diplomacy and study to construct. Nevertheless, the news which Frydor now bore threatened to drive a wedge into their fragile stand-off for one last time.

*

Tock-tock-tock!

The door opened slowly, perhaps somewhat *too* cautiously but a wide enough gap was created for a head to pop round the doorframe.

'Who's there...? And what do you want?'

'Is that anyway to answer your cousin, Maid Byron? Open your doors immediately and show my visitors some hospitality if you please. Or have the elves in these parts lost their manners altogether as some dare to say!'

The door peeled back further, the figure inside slinking back into the hallway's sullen gloom. Two pale eyes appeared glowing from within the blackness, timidity already set in their midst, but a welcome sight they yet remained for one so burdened with unanswered anxieties.

'My goodness me, Cousin Byron, you look like you've seen a ghost? Is there anything the matter?' Frydor hollered, altering his vernacular suitably. 'Cat got your tongue missus?'

She goggled at him as if she had just seen a spirit rise out of Annwfn.

'Am I to stand here on the street outside fore'er, my dear cousin, or do you not recognise me since almost yesterday? And wherefore art thou not hither...? Cousin Byron?'

'Keep it down Frydor,' Maid Byron said at last, the shock of his appearing at last wearing thin.

'Well, I suppose you'll want to come in then...? But know if you do, I'll have no more of them foul disputes or the like behind these four walls – not even a mention cousin. You understand?'

Frydor the Elf smiled back at her, as she, rather unenthusiastically, turned back towards the main stairway.

'Byron, cousin Frydor's 'ere,' the maid yelled. 'And he's brought some... some queer sorts of people with him it seems.' Turning aside to Frydor; 'So what are yous up to then, O crafty elf?'

'They,' replied the wise-elf, with what one would suspect was his deepest most heart-warming pride, 'they are my company. Men and women of destiny these are,' he furthered, stepping out from the direct sunlight and into the shadows, to reveal a dubious collection of shapes and forms.

'Well, that's nice, Frydor,' Maid Byron choked, 'cos we don't get too many of them around here... do we hubby?'

There was no reply yet from her husband.

'Tell him that I bring the Knights of Fable – the harbingers of doom. The ones who shall help *us* fulfil the final end-time prophecies.'

J-J, presently the only member of the Syndicate inside the house, stared hard at Frydor.

Knights of Fable? Harbingers of doom...? Just where does he get off?

Nevertheless, she kept these and many other thoughts to herself for the time being, for she had indeed helped to make their present bed; and so now it was just a matter of learning how best to lie in it!

'Yes, we know about them already cousin Frydor,' the first lady continued. 'Byron had a dream last night that told him you'd be turning up on our doorstep... with some street urchins if my memory serves me correctly...

'Anyway, I'll let him fill you in on the rest of it, lest I should miss out anything noteworthy.'

She examined the remainder of the Friends as they filtered through the doorway.

'Yep, by the looks of 'em, these are the ones he dreamt about. It's just that we never thought you'd be turning up so soon!' said she softly.

With rather gifted promptitude, it was Byron the Surp who came in next through the backroom door. He walked straight up to his cousin Frydor.

'Pleased to be making your acquaintance O Wise One and couth cousin,' Byron cried, throwing his arms around the two elves. 'And these must be your companions I take it:

'Gee and Elena and Mark and J-J and yes... Sashi,' Byron stated, nodding at each one in turn. 'It is a very great pleasure... oh, and I mustn't forget Aleasha – it wouldn't do me any credit at all to forget 'Leash!'

'Pleased to meet you too,' Aleasha returned. 'But how did you know...?'

'Ah, we have our way. But the secrets of the Surps would not remain secrets if everyone were to know now would they...?' said Byron, concealing the grin that had developed upon his mien.

'Nonetheless, the things that I am to tell you will hopefully throw more light on the matter.' He reminisced for a while. 'Or else, as much as is needed at present.'

Thus, the Company was welcomed in the traditional elvish manner, before Byron the Surp made each of his new acquaintances roll out a seat before him. But even as they began listening to his every fraught word, the Friends could tell that it was a grim picture being painted. Only then did they truly realise the extent of their current lot.

180

I was in the midst of dreaming a dream when I looked up – and behold, I saw the sky.

The uninhabited landscape stretched from vastness to the distant shores, whereupon the sun shone high atop of the land. Its brightness was after the likeness of the sun of yesteryear, when the aether did magnify its glory, and its light searched the whole land so that no darkness was left concealed in any part. And the heat thereof burnt up all the weeds and all the dross that was found upon the landscape, so that what was once an extended bundle of debris was now made fine and plain. The dust blew gently in the coming winds, as a shadow flitting through the velvet darkness.

I continued to watch and I could perceive the shadow coming in from across the skies, from the direction of the east. At first it was nothing more than a blotch in the sky – a flock of geese perhaps, or maybe even a stray cloud, lost without the accompaniment of screaming denizens. There were thunderous bellows, the evil laughter of Kronos when he cackles his evil glee. But then the sight did come into my vision more clearly and I saw that the gathering of dust was indeed very heavy with rain. It was full and fit for the bursting.

Thereupon, several more clouds began to envelop the sky, not just the one, until all the land was covered in obscurity and the sun was all eaten up. Then was the sky rent asunder releasing tremendous measures of water from its belly. So did it rain, and it rained hard, till all the ground was of mire and the silvery rain began to reflect its gloom.

It came to pass that afterwards I turned my face towards the west and lo, I saw there five vagabonds entering into the lands from out yonder, from upon the other side of the distant mountains, which lie towards the Shores of Hope. Yet still they remained beyond the hills, behind the valleys, hidden from the darkest rivers of the land, though they seemed to know these things not. Nonetheless, they did see the plain about them, though neither did they figure that any further. But there was a sixth form with them, a female of their kind. She it was who had the appearance of one of the knights of old, a grand rider of comely appearance, even to the honour of them that had once sat at the tables within the courts of St. Andrews!

This one was a dark and lovely figure of a most handsome appearance, which no elf could possibly deny. But she also had a fissure in her armoury, a hole in her shield as it were, which seemed not to be befitting of such a noble warrior. Moreover, the five that were with her were adorned in the most basic of rags, which were enough only to cover only their shame but little more after that. For these ones had the likeliness of street-people: they were cold, wet, hungry, destitute, and more beside. They appeared as though they were doubled over with nothing but the weight of emptiness upon their backs.

But then I looked again, and I saw one of their faces – and ghastly it

181

was too. There seemed to be mocking on his lips, which twisted his face like the court jesters of Yewffwl. Indeed, he seemed to be riled at our very presence.

So to him did I put the question:

> *'My lowly fellow, what is this that thou now jests of,*
> *seeing that thou be ignoble*
> *and that the look of a degenerate seems to cloak thine person,*
> *(Albeit, seemingly scarcely at that)?*
> *Speak now my good friend and share with me thine good episode*
> *That perhaps this noble one can also simper alongside thee!'*

But all he could do was laugh an evil laugh and spout an evil cackle. Moreover, he grinned an horrid look which truly galled my soul tremendously, seeing that he lacked even The Commoner's most basic courtesy of goodwill and generosity. Nevertheless, him did I press further, lest the telling of this strange episode should make a worthy tale, and inevitably, he told me some of this narrative which I now tell to you...

Throughout his dismal life he had been beaten down. He was one of those who had been tormented by both those whom he could see and by those whom he could not bear witness to. The Afflicted, The Stranger, The Poor, The Bastard – the Son of a Widow – his was not a life one would have wished for, stout though his frame yet appeared. He told me again that he was a lonely wanderer, dwelling outside the city walls as no one would dare receive him within its lofty embattlements. Now there were others beside him whom he wished to show to me, so then I looked past the knight once again and observed them all closely.

Observe – Such a pitiful sight what greeted my eyes!

> *How the young had been brought so low and wretched!*
> *Woeful because of their less than homely attire*
> *And for the debilitating aura about their shoulders!*
> *Lo!*
> *For the times of the end must surely be near or else all is lost!*

Nonetheless, I gave ear to all that he, and indeed, they, would tell me, for that is the manner after the Surps:

> *"To give of oneself to one that has lost self."*

For the most part therefore each one had but a few chances in life, but of them they were not able to use, as they ought, for they lacked the wisdom with which to accomplish these things. They were foolish in their ways, blackened in their every futile thought. Perhaps one of them may have been received back into the king's service as a guard tending to the city walls – for this one's crimes were not as weighty as the others, neither was his manner so uncouth, and his shoulders were broad, as I have already made mention. Nevertheless, he would not advance therefrom, and only if Fortune were to bless him would he remain in the king's service for life. Thus, even this one, of them the most propitious, was subject to a miserable existence, of lack and of longing rather than of love and fulfilment.

So I turned again to understand better the manner of these sorry people. They seemed so abandoned, so alone, almost as some of the wayfarers within our great lands, that my heart pained me sorely to see such things.

I confronted the courtly amongst them, to wit the knight, that she perchance might elucidate the way of her acquaintances. For I was greatly puzzled as to why such a high one as she was should be seen in the company of such servile companions, who were dressed in her presence to an even baser degree than the least of all bondservants!

They were mere street-urchins – children with no name. They were the ones for whom there was no fixed dwelling, and nor would there be until the times of the end when all things have come corrected; save, perhaps, for a cold, dark, dreary dungeon, in the midst of the Serpent's estates in Dereden. Hence, I compelled the knight to tell me her story...

They had once all been friends, companions lost in a foreign city. In that day they had no employment and therefore little wherewithal with which to become citizens of the land. So in order to keep themselves they had turned to scrounging.

They harried those whose fate was less embittered than their own; they sought out the benefactor, they cherished the rich, they hounded the merchant. Moreover, because they had met earlier on in life and had formed themselves to a motley band (one in which they went around terrorising the good people of the city), they remained in its stead, that they may continue to prevail against the goodness and charity of the city's kinder folk.

So they stole anything they could and everything they would lay their hands on, from the unkempt wares of normal folk to the finest raiment lined in gold. Whether it was to clothe the sores on their backs or to sell on further to them that were corrupt, these things they did, and oft times made blameless profit.

For want of a complement to their persons, if indeed it may be seen as that, they initially were loth to violate another man's person in order to satisfy their own carnal appetite – a noble virtue amongst ones so base. However, even as the times regressed and the land began to go into receivership, they soon became forgetful of their one sole ethic, and, thereafter, neglected any decency whatsoever. Thus they eventually became as the Dark Dwarves of Dereden, resorting to any means necessary to accomplish their aims.

So it happened, one day, that knowledge of their operations came to the ears of the King, that there were such pestiferous delinquents in his kingdom that were even now a scourge to his blue-blooded subjects. Consequently, he sent out his guard to arrest them and to bring them in for trial, that the plagues of the land might be greatly reduced if not ended altogether. This they duly did, without too much obstinacy. (For there were few brazen enough to shield their evil exploits).

So the King himself was to be their judge; and the jury consisted solely of the King and the Word that he had acquired. Thus was the date was set for their hearing.

In the questioning and torments that followed, one of their members, the knight in question, appeared sorely contrite pertaining to the crimes that she had committed. Thereupon, she made pledge to His Majesty the King, to honour and obey his laws, to follow his kingship, to bless his fellow servants, and to seek out those that had once been as themselves – The Damned. So it came to pass that the King, being greatly aggrieved at the harrowing accounts of their rearing since their earliest days, was moved with compassion. Indeed, so much did her story stir him that he even granted her a place within his household as an equerry.

Now the others were not so repentant. Wanting in forethought, they seemed to pour scorn on the very inquisitors that punished them, even as their limbs were racked far beyond the bounds of reason. At length nevertheless (perhaps after six inches or so, so they tell) they did submit themselves wilfully to the King's clemency. Thus they made a rash and hasty oath to purvey his name from that time forth and forevermore, though at the time it did seem solely to save their own skins.

It was during their time in custody that they witnessed some of the wicked, smitten by the King's executioners. Now these things bore more than a little affect on these stalwart evildoers.

They saw other wrongdoers who had once been as themselves – the Iniquitous – being hung slowly by the neck, seemingly unto death. But it was not so. For a little time afterwards the felons were cut down and disembowelled, with tools too olde to peddle. After this, their innards were burnt before their gaunt aspects, till the look of horror uprose upon their faces. And lo! The fear of death did far more to quell their humour than any of the torments which had previously been rendered. For the friends were a formidable flock – foul, foetid, flagitious, though they were too, fearless – the usual suspects pertaining to any mischief perpetrated upon the kingdom's more favoured souls. Yet the King still offered them leniency, in lieu the sorry dirge they had earlier told him.

Nevertheless, the ones whom the Friends had witnessed, well, they were not so fortuitous. Because those of these – The Crooked – who were still alive after these things were dragged into a bath of thick oil, and if they survived for too long afterwards, they would most certainly meet a grisly end. Was it not then that the executioner put his torch to the bath, in lieu of those that did not soon drown under his morbid hands of wroth, that they might perish in the ensuing flames that engulfed them? So the friends indeed bore witness to the sorry expiration of the lost, lest the darkest of all fates should come upon them. Having been reared in a reverent society, the Five Foul Friends yet maintained the Faith.

Thus, they bemoaned their sins, as was expected, upon which the King cleared them of all their evil crimes. Indeed, he even offered them a place in his guard and household, till such times that they satisfied his officers that they were fit enough to leave and rejoin the lands gentler folk. All truly hoped that their good deeds would be as noble and numerous as the dust that blew upon the four winds of The World.

To begin with then, they had been good and studious workers, managing their own affairs well, and the avocation given them by the King. But then, as the seasons progressed and rainfalls increased, they again began to become wanton, and it was not long before they rediscovered their olde and destructive ways. Before long, the King had gotten wind of their new transgressions. So they fled onto the streets without, making their homes with The Profane and the Perverse, with The Nasty and with Ragamuffins; with Whoredom. It was there that they remained until one day; and in the dream that day seemed like only yesterday.

Meantime, their olde companion had advanced much through that selfsame period. Her master, the King, had even bestowed upon her the highest honour of the garter, and so was she the first knight of St. Andrews since the days of Tonian Dulcy – that infamous hero of legends who with one hand, smote many a foul foe of the kingdom, and with the other, healed them that were sick. All the same, after hearing their fate, the knight was filled with infallible feelings of compassion. And so, like a mastiff-bitch tracks the scent of blood, she trailed the ruins of her comrades.

It came to pass that some of her servants with their ear close to the ground told of some trouble that had recently sprouted on one of the King's walls. Many an item had gone missing from goodly residences, including, to wit, five of the King's trusted servants. The knight, quick as a flash, sought the gods on this matter, till her spirit grew cold and her heart waxed heavy. Her former spars had done such deeds that ought not be done, for they were once again caught in the web of corruption.

Hence she set about finding the new lodgings of her olde pack, that they may return, give an account of themselves, pay tax and full tribute, and if, perchance, her petition was heard, that they may set out again to exonerate themselves by way of exemplary example. So she searched for them far and wide, high and low, until somebody, whose dwelling was nigh by city's gates, made mention of an ignominious band of rioters. They had torn apart the northern walls to the city before fleeing through the gates and leaving behind them a wake of appalling tribulation.

Thus she tracked them down, and so here they were, together again, in the dream.

Again in my night-visions there was a moment of complete nightfall – and I, too, thought that I had been sucked into a bleak world. I faced the east to see what had become of the sun and it happened that as I did so, the fullness of the light began to reappear. My heart began to cheer and my eyes beheld the splendour of the coming day.

But then lightning and thunder and thick vapours of smoke started a-coming from the sky and the grounds. Hideous beasts began flying out of the dark and greying clouds, night beasts, who have no part of the daytime, gruesome to behold, awesome in memory. Yet they soared across the skies, one after another, towards where I was standing.

Behold! What a terrifying sight it was! For it made me cower and search diligently for a hole in the ground, that I might hide myself in it, curl up and shrivel into nothingness, for the sheer terror that was before my eyes. But there was none there that could conceal me, even as there was none there to hold my hand for comfort!

I looked again in desperation, and again I perceived the dire band of criminals. Amidst all of these tribulations, their friend, the Knight, appeared to be granting them sympathy, even over the fears that presently lay without. She went to pains to explain them the very wrongs of their doings, which affected them in no small way, as I could tell (wise as I am) by the change of their demeanours.

Soon enough then, some appeared to pay heed to her speech. Queerly however, as I yet faced them, I could see a bright shining sun emerge from above their heads like the tongues of fire which crowned the first disciples at Pentecost. Albeit, this seemed not to come without its troubles.

Scars began to form before my very eyes, as wounds that had festered began to heal, ears began to open, sight beyond sight was granted. But when I risked a glance elsewhere, utter darkness and ugly beasts continued to come, flying atop of the land as the chief of the corrupted lords themselves.

I ran for shelter behind the feisty Knight, my courage, for the moment, having failed me, and I was very much afraid of what would come next. Open-ing my eyes a peek, I looked up again and behold, I saw something new.

This time I was watching and I saw six knights whose swords were raised proudly towards the coming Hosts of Heavens and I was listening as they de-clared war upon them that drew nigh. Then they set about hewing down many of the fowls of the air and the bodiless spirits that came with them, all the noi-some hosts, who had come to cause mischief.

Afterward, I was watching these things closely, when I saw a giant advancing inside the land of what I presumed was Abundance. It was a great giant with a homely countenance – a stern figure whose nostrils were as those of a tiger – fierce and unrelenting, as that of a fire-breather.

At first then the brute seemed to be friendly, if somewhat panicked by events. And by his side was a female troll. They held hands together, as each one sought to succour consolation from the other. Meanwhile, others like them seemed to be traipsing at some speed away from the wrath emanating from the east, and by the looks of them they could in no wise escape fast enough.

Moreover, I was still there when I saw, out from 'neath my field of vision, a serpent arise, with a deadly glint in its eye. It leapt up quicker than the eye could blink, deadlier than the cobra, and it lunged at the foreword most troll. The selfsame soul screamed aloud in pain and in angst, to which the others responded with shudders and tears. Then I heard a cry as of one on the bat-tlefield in the thick of a slaughter when the battle has turned grim.

'No my sister, run!' he shouted. 'Get away thither!'

But she too – that is the one to whom he spoke – was bitten by the serpent. Shortly, the two of them were stopped dead (that is to say the two that had been smitten). There they remained as if in a trance and I could tell by their eyes that that is what is was – a known brand of wickedness from the dark lords of the Zju-Zju Lands. It is these masters who keep many a terrible soul in captiv-ity, numberless soulless forms all housed on the borders between Krandor and Annwfn, betwixt the time of life and the days of death.

So I looked closer still from the midst of my position and I saw fires and great turmoil erupting on the surface of their vision. It seemed as though I was looking at these events through a looking glass, albeit one with devils dwell-ing behind the screens, mocking, prancing, and cackling like the evil hosts of Uffern. But then my mind closed again and I returned to my body, wherein I remained in fear of my life, greatly apprehensive of the witchery that had hexed my acquaintances. Still I stayed, remaining where I was, behind the King's servants and away from the heat of battle.

Nevertheless, the visions ere my eyes did not yield until I saw the shield of the first knight healing itself of its wound. I understood little more of the things of which I had been privy, even after all of these matters had transpired;

although I did remember something else noteworthy. And that was a tune that played the pipes of my soft inward organ, that I might hear its soothing lullabies and my muse might return.

It was as though a voice called me that I might hear him speak. An ominous tongue of great stirring which lodged itself into my mind. Indeed, I saw again (for my eyes were opened and the image of the King came to me in a dream), a marvellous thing indeed, one which is well worthy of note. For he was kin to the King rendered in the night-visions, but he was also very different, more natural it seemed, even though his speech was in matching fashion.

Thus he (for it was a man's voice) began to articulate the following:

'Byron, Byron, hear ye, my son. Remember the words that the elders spoke:

"...But if they cannot exercise self-control, let them marry.
For it is better to marry than to burn with passion."

'My son, recall also the words of the prophet, which are written in the Grecian scrolls:

"But know this, that in the last days times of stress will come:
For men will be... without self-control...
Lovers of pleasure rather than lovers of the King,
Having a form of goodness, but denying the power therein.
And from such people must you flee!"

'My son, I have given wisdom, for it is the wise who will understand.'

The dream ended there and I was trembling greatly and deeply disturbed. Thus, I have told you all things and left nothing unsaid.

My Friends please help me to understand the full meaning of all my dreams and visions. You would do well to suffer me patiently and render unto me the interpretation O Young Ones, that is if you are to fulfil your calling which was prepared beforehand that you should walk in them.

May the gods give you wisdom. Amen.

*

The aroma of warm honey-laden pastry wafting its way through the arches joining the kitchen to the dining area was as pleasant a smell as any that day. Flakes crumbled delicately as they were placed upon the pastry-dish and there was a tempting array as Maid Byron laid bare her hand. It was not only mortals who swore to the fragrant smells of her cooked savouries, which had succeeded in whetting the Friends' appetites – more than a story ever could – but the gods also more often than not proffered their gratitude! They say that fairies from time to time were seen to haunt the recesses of her kitchen and pantry-board, evidenced, so they say, by vanishing articles before the main course.

The roof of the elfin-home was oddly shaped, being loftier towards the rear end of the domicile than towards the front. Nonetheless, the all-round aspect was high enough for each to squeeze through comfortably. The corridors too varied, leaving Flip with the impression of an aged premises, whose dating would revert back to the period before modern craftsmanship. For the passageways were narrow and confined mostly to ground level, and there was scarcely enough space between chambers for somebody large to squeeze through with comfort. The décor of that drab place, though recently redone, smelt dank and musty. All was painfully evident as they hobbled after Frydor through to the adjacent quarters.

Ornaments lining the walls of the Surp's home were scarce. A small collection of books was stored in the library raised well above the fireplace, parchments of use only to the learned. Very few were the volumes of light reading: a scroll of cooked recipes borrowed from the nunnery of Yves; children's books; texts on the history of art. The remainder were books on the peoples of that place and their religions, their gods and their customs.

A gammon table doubled as a study desk, atop of which flared pine torches kept in their sockets held tight by the wall. These were so that the avid reader might pore through the sacred words more easily at any time of day or night. Several bland logs were sitting close to the fireplace on the rugged hearth. It was to this pile that the hostess was headed, having become aware of the sudden chill that had descended to fill the room.

'Are you cold there, O Plump One?' The blazing hearth played unkindly on her features as she lowered herself to kindle the fire. 'Might I add a few more logs to the flames without adding to your discomfort? By the looks of them, your friends could do with some warming. Believe you me, you get it where you can these days?' She gave Sashi a deft wink, which lasted a little too long for his liking.

He altered his gaze and beheld the dream-teller, who was standing in a daze, contemplating the words that had flowed forth from his awen. Even now they conjured themselves into repeatedly shifting shapes and forms and pictures, creating scenes of other lands and distant shores and strange races.

As he watched, flames puffed out large and angry, like the breathing of the Draig of Nosnef, whose sparks it is said will do one of two things: either consume the world in its fall; or stoke the smouldering embers of Uffern's deadly blaze. The sooty fireball, for a moment in time, seemed to swell out of control, but then, as if reneging in its anger, made surer promises to those that looked on, dying down again soon after it had inflated. A murmur of appreciation set Maid Byron to other tasks, the fierce eyes of the fiery hearth reminding all of her scorching presence. As the fire dwindled and eyes became accustomed to the moody gloom, the room ebbed a shade darker.

'So where do we go from here? I mean,' railed Sashi bitterly, 'we all know that Aleasha is the "Brave, Bold Knight" in the story, so where do the rest of us fit in then? Why don't we all just bugger off home like we'd prefer to do anyway?'

He peered up towards Gamine and then Byron, her husband, who was now lain back half-sleeping, stroking his soft white beard reflectively. He had the hope that either one of the two strangers would be able to enlighten his present confusion.

'I mean, yeah, nice dream and everything – I'm even half-impressed that you know all of our names... like your cousin Frydor here. But as Gee said, it's a fix isn't it?'

Gamine looked morose. 'Well the bare bones of it *luvvy* is that you are going nowhere sharpish,' she said quite unexpectedly. 'Cos as of yet, all but one of you are useless to the hopes and causes of our beloved Krandor – ain't that right hubby?'

She parted forthwith through the opened door, not awaiting the response of her mate.

'Of course she's correct, Frydor,' Byron agreed, whilst leaning forward closer to his kinsman, making pains to whisper further words into his ear:

'Frydor, your people are a ragbag bunch of criminals whose only fealty is towards themselves – not entirely their fault it must be said, but how can we entrust them with something so great as the duty set before us?' Seeing no response forthcoming, neither fair nor foul, Byron resumed: 'Meet some of the prophecies though they may do, cousin, but something still needs to be done with them all the same – lest we waste our efforts... and endanger our lives.

'Perhaps we should wait and see if others will step in to fill the void. Perhaps –'

Frydor's very look cut him off. 'Without me they cannot, without them I dare not!' He shifted uneasily from his stance, his nephew Flip, noticing the apprehension that seemed all so suddenly to ail his aching limbs.

'You know what needs to occur, my cousin,' resumed Byron, 'if we are to progress, as we ought. So what say you? Are you too in agreement with my interpretation of events hereunto and that they must first be initiated into the sufferings of the good folk of Krandor? If so then it is with the Blood Oath that we must proceed, and quickly, for time runs ahead of us!'

Frydor replied, 'I have already– '

'I get it now,' J-J shouted irately, interrupting Frydor's thoughtful response,

'... you want us to make that pledge you were on about before we get any weapons and get us into some sort of bind or agreement. You want us to sign away our lives don't you?' She looked around towards Flip in the hope that his countenance would shed more light than his uncle presently was. 'You're really serious about this stuff aren't you?'

'If we do get the weapons, can we finally get out of this nightmare then Frydor?' Elena inquired naively. 'Can we really go back to where we came from?'

Imperviously, the two doughty elves nodded towards the youths.

'And what if we don't?' asked Mark grimly. 'What if we don't want to fight your battles for you? What if we just walk out from here right now and try to find our own way? Why should we do something for someone who's done nothing for us? We'll do it all ourselves, or at least we'll go down trying. Besides, how do we know that we can trust you?'

'You do not. Nevertheless, if you do try to go it alone, you shall fail, and miserably,' said Frydor, his voice turning into a low growl as he sought for a more favourable spot. 'Where will you go and how will you get there, since you are all strangers in the land? Moreover, who will guide you past the sulphur pits, through the valleys, in the midst of the waters, across unchancy lands too cruel to fathom? Who will speak for you when your language falters?'

As the words fell from his mouth, the greying elf became even darker in disposition. His eyes transformed into falling mounds of black coals, two bland orbs set against a blazing holocaust that roared tumultuously and his skin was darkened till they too blended insouciantly with the fires.

Another piece of firewood cracked amidst the smouldering flames, distracting each one from the elf's disconcerting gaze. It brought to life the uneasy silence that presently held the reigns. Animation quickly returned to Frydor's antiquated carriage. At once, a second tinder-piece burst open, sprouting out a dozen smaller fireballs iridescent, stinky-smelling, bright as the Four Moons of Jove, king of the gods, who nightly accompanies the Great White Beast on his journeys across the heavens. The tiny orange-yellow sparks lit up the room's walls with a flash.

'There should be little doubt in your minds that each one of you would be captured,' he said, observing the caustic phenomenon taking place by the fireside, 'then you would be taken prisoner by those who are loyal to the Crown of Tyranny whose stronghold lies in the east.'

Frydor glowered when he spoke next, 'And needless to say they would force you to confess your crimes – '

'Crimes? What do you mean "crimes" ?' yelled Mark. 'We ain't done nothing yet!'

'Mark, my dear friend, things do not work so smoothly or indeed as fairly as they ought here in these lands; that is partly why you are here.

They would reckon with you a while, lest you should be willing to spill the beans, and if not, then they would torment you till they knew of our current whereabouts.' Frydor shot a desperate look towards Aleasha, as if to implore her to understand. 'Either way, they shall afterwards use you for their sport, as they take great pleasure in afflicting pain in those weaker than themselves, counting such evil acts as game. And we cannot possibly allow that can we?'

'But who'd be interested in us? And why is everyone after you guys Frydor?' Elena's voice trailed away as she felt half a dozen pairs of eyes penetrating her nucleus. She quailed away completely when she perceived the closest set, which was borne upon the head of Byron.

'Aleasha, you are the knight in the story…'

Though not unexpected, a murmur of appreciation nonetheless ran about the house. Gee and his friends glanced up eagerly at the wizened elf to hear his remaining words.

'It is written that you must come with us and so indeed you shall. In the land whence you have sprung from you have already made worthy enough vows for us to trust your honour and so we require none further from you. Save for that you adhere to your new name, which you shall swear to – the name that you received before your birth. These things shall suffice.

'Of late, it must be said, you have lowered your guard, allowing all sorts of mischief and misfortune to haunt your every waking step. Your shield has fallen somewhat, but we, being noble, shall show you how to carry your weapons properly, with boldness, courage, with defiance! And that we may do for each of your friends – as many as may *wish* to accompany us on our travails?'

'Er… do I get a say in the matter?'

'None whatsoever, Aleasha.'

However, all did not rest easily with Frydor. He paced up and down nervously until once again, he had become the centre of attention.

'Perhaps we should give her a choice Byron, cousin,' Frydor remarked shrewdly, now uncertain as to whether these saplings could deal with such liability. 'For no prophecy has, or ever will come into being by the will of us elves. Perhaps we should allow her the – '

'Nonsense Frydor! You feel the burning within your bosom just as I do.' He cast his eyes askance to take in his couth-cousin's countenance. 'Even now, as I yet speak, I feel the touch of grace rising up from within. So Frydor, let's to it! Time and eternity await no elf, so we must make best use of what we have!'

He backed away from Aleasha and Frydor and turned smartly to address her companions.

'To be honest, your remnant have all… er… how shall I put this without dampening the point?' There was scarcely a broken moment before the elf plunged in there with his caustic observations. 'Well not to put too finer point on the matter – you have all lived a worthless existence up until now! Physical yes, mental to some degree, emotional in the wrong way, but not at all spiritual.' He saw Frydor visibly flinch.

'Here we provide you with your last opportunity to do something useful, something bold, something noble, something you can be proud to be remembered by after you breathe your last breath... and you wish to refuse us? And me – Byron the Surp? Oh, how dismal! How low! How profoundly base!'

With further shrieks of desperation the podium was eventually handed back to Frydor. But before doing so Byron did call to mind this one last thing, wisdom from the gods instilled into every wise-elf, which, for the Friends, seemed to seal the moment:

> "Success in life should not be judged by the amount of things
> one can accumulate in the process of so many years;
> A better measure would be the kind of people that, afterwards,
> one leaves behind –A somewhat more humbling experience!"

'I perceive that my cousin is right, Aleasha, Gee... O Syndicate! But perhaps what is more is that if you do not submit to our current demands – fond of you as I may be now – we shall have to ensure that you are all killed...'

*

Sweet was the smell of sugared pastry, more lovely than the scent of blossoms given to the princess of Avalon, by Adam, prince of the Injuns. So blessed was this reek that men tell of the borders of that land being taken with the whiff of roses, the sweet smell of beeswax, music played on the organ of Veer Noc Seren, prince of all pipers, chief of all players, Zaqen. It was a tempting fragrance if ever there was one, though for this uncertain moment, it failed quite miserably in stopping the sudden descent of Gee's chair, before even the final syllable of Byron's last thoughts had parted his kinsman's mouth.

The chair soared high, the seat crooked upon the head of his target, clammy hands grasping it as firm as a dog's jaws on a feline. Gee saw the exposed destination, which he reckoned was wont of some major alteration and some added wisdom – the rear of Byron's balding head. The stool fell fast, blistering, blinding, belting through the air like one of the Eagles.

Gibbering ceased for the moment as the Surp allowed the chair to fall nigh upon his sconce. Quick were his reactions at that precise moment, lightening quick. Quick as the mind of Grach of the Gloved-fingers when he is questioned on old science, quicker than the feet of Caleb of the Long-storks when his friends are caught in the fray. In a defensive manoeuvre fit only for the gods to view, Byron unravelled his feet so quickly, they found their way to the

Dog's midriff without even a soul seeing. Catching him square in the midst of his expansive chest, the leader of the Friends was upon the ground without ever feeling discomforted. The Surp then pummelled him relentlessly whilst oblivion took hold of his senses.

It was all far too quick for any of the guys to jump in and help Gee out of this unnecessary fracas. Decisiveness had eluded them at this time, and by the time their wits had returned, Gee was already sunk upon the loam, heavily bruised and verging on unconsciousness.

'Oh no, not again,' mumbled Gee to himself.

'So you ask yourself: What happened?' roared Byron. 'Is that right boy?'

There was not even a whimper of approval.

'Well, this is what happened,' (hitting him hard again); 'I am skilled and highly trained, just as you are, Dog, but only better! Far better. Though the Books doth speak of your prowess in places, in the days of thy youth; how you did love to fight for all – justice, injustice, sport...

'You were one of the originals in your town, in the place of your dwelling. "The Foremost Amongst The Bad" or as others told "The Original Gangster", if my memory fails me not.'

The others looked at the Surp in amazement. 'But how...?'

The elves completely ignored The Syndicate.

'You turned many to violence and ill-gotten ways,' (Byron said harshly, slapping the Dog round the face again, albeit this time to wake him much as to wound him). 'But mercy has been with you for such a time as this.

'Now, therefore, please decide for yourself what you should do. But please choose wisely, as today, I fear, the power of life and death has been put into your hands. And not only yours but the souls of many – some who have not even been born as of yet. It is left for you to decide. But as for your friend, Aleasha, she shall certainly come with us! Though she may not know it yet, her vows taken in the Other World require her, implicitly, to come with us, even before she does anything else.'

Byron's palms caught the leader of the pack a further three times before he continued:

'And to the Remnant,' he cried in dire tones, unclasping the collar of the felled six-footer, 'it is for each of you to choose your own bidding. You are all of age. You may, if you wish, die this instant with your comrade here,' Byron said, throwing back his cloak to reveal an elfin-dagger which he placed close to Gee's throat. 'Or you can help us and yourselves, by swearing allegiance...

'Do you comply?'

As for Gee, the knife was pressed somewhat too tightly against his jugular for him respond in anything other than in the affirmative. He nodded, his head dazzled, his pride wounded, but his injury was by no means unaccompanied.

Only when Gamine re-entered the room from the pantry did Elena too step forward to confirm her life-long solidarity.

'We'll do it then, Frydor. We'll go with you.'

'Yeah, okay, we'll do it,' added Mark, reaching for the warm, fluffy cookies that were thrust in his face. 'We'll take The Oath – So what, are these chocolate or coconut…'

*

Some time later in the basement of a house on the outskirts of the same town, an arcane ceremony was underway to honour the five new initiates of the Old Way, before they might commence the pursuit of excellence towards the conquest of all Krandor. All of those that had been invited showed up; moreover, only those who would turn up had been invited.

The location of the house was unknown to the noviciates of the new order, for they could not yet be trusted, even as they were yet to swear The Oath. However, once The Oath was sworn, they would then be bound, not only by word but also by blood. Then, as much as was pertinent to them, they could hear.

The words they were compelled to speak took on the following similitude, which was first avowed by the people of the Lore in the days before the Forgotten Era, by the good folk who once resided in the Hornbeam Glades in the Everregions:

We have received the seen through our eyes
And we believe the unseen through our hearts.

We believe the past,
We believe in the present,
And we accept the hereafter.
We believe that our words bring us life
And not the fools of laughter.

We shall call upon that hidden name,
The mystery with the prize;
The enigma, the riddle,
The words of the wise,
Shall yield to us eternal lives.

We shall then believe yet again
The thereafter.

This again is the same oath that is sworn to the good king who governs beyond the Land of Angels, by those few that are accepted into his formidable company. Thus it happened that the Syndicate, save for Aleasha, testified to each of these things, with understanding, and that every member of the Syndicate again made a tiny nick on the little finger of his or her left hand, so as to ratify that these things were sealed in blood. Afterwards, one pinch thereof was dropped into the Krandoric soils without, so as to signify that the spilling of blood might indeed be necessary to save the Good Folk within its bounds. But the last act in the rite, which follows after the traditions of the Elders, was this:

That those who were entering into the covenant should eat of the bread called "Pain de Geraldine" and drink of the liquor "Creme d'Irlande" as a memorial to the friendships that were certified there that day, as they had entered into the strivings of the bold. This part for most was reminiscent of some of the Communion Suppers in which they had been forced to participate while back on Daearawd. Nevertheless, the gravity of the things attested to here were much more poignant to them than ever before, if only because they swore to these things as willing adults, and not as unwilling children. At present their understanding was just beginning, and this fact is doubtless reliable, but to the degree which they vowed, they were also ready. Moreover, the tit-bits from this contract tasted rather nicer than the crusty old wafer-bread used by the Catholics.

Soon after these things the ceremony was cut short for time was not with them. Weary eyes even now wandered the skies and the shires in search of the things foretold by wicked soothsayers of the East. The time was upon their kingdom when a challenge from within and from without would beset their darkest realms and such advances would seldom be without wrath and righteous retribution.

Therefore, no more than an hour had transpired before each member of the Syndicate was made a full member of the Fellowship of the Troop, so that they too might partake of the sufferings which one surely must for eternal glory. To conclude these times of avowal, the tyros were grouped together into one place to hear the words of instruction that needed to be spoken over each and every life.

*

So in the dark and dusty confines of one of the chief Surps in all the lands, an elf by the name of John-jay, the evening climaxed with the handing-over of the words and the giving-up of the weapons and the summary of the keys. This was to be the final act before the group was sent on their way.

Inside the basement, as was afterward recorded in The Books, a vast scroll, scribed carefully in the ancient runes of the Manchu-G'ladhrim who were from the Hornbeam Glades, was unfurled and prepared, ready to be read from. It was Shaun albeit, Senior Elder of Abundance, who was given the honour of interpreting the runes etched onto the papyrus.

To the six, the Kings and Queens,
The Apprentices of St Andrew and St George,
and their faithful companions,
you shall let it be known that:

To one and all is given a shield.
If the shield is used in the appropriate way shown,
it shall afford the bearer protection against all manner of attack from the
weapons of the enemy, whether it be in the natural or indeed, in the spiritual.

To one and all is given an helmet.
This headpiece shall afford both natural and supernatural
protection to the pilgrims,
lest they should be enticed by those who are able
to travel and perpetrate wickedness within the Fifth.
It shall also serve to remind them of the oath sworn here this day
and the goodly outcome that shall surely follow,
whether it is in death or in life.

To one and all is given a sword,
whose blades are even more deadly
than the Toledo and the Samurai combined.
Moreover, in the hands of a skilled soldier,
even as the Prophet has erstwhile predicted,
they are well able to hew asunder the direst blades,
even the brawniest of the old elfin warriors.
These distinctive elven-blades are the most
devastating weapon in the armoury
and therefore must be kept sharpened at all times.
The handler is instructed to always keep it at hand,
lest evil should come upon its steel,
or worse still, upon the bearer himself or herself.
Go forth and scour your path void of all evil.

And all those, of whom a response was demanded, affirmed these things
under the weight of an anathema.

THE KNIGHT'S LORE

"To the six new initiates; to the reformed youths;
to the warriors of the new way;
to the believers in the olde and the authors of the new;
to those who shall originate much style and a-pattern..."

To Mark, who is now Marcus, whose name is also "Warlike":
You are given the *"Breastplate of Rectitude"* – for you are now chaste.
And we bequeath you a battle-axe for hand to hand fighting.

To Jema-Jane, who is now Jemimah,
whose name also means "Handsome as Day":
You are given the mail-cloak called the *"Armour of the Gods"* –
for you shall be well tended to,
and you shall blend into the background when your beauty begins to birth.
Also, to keep your enemies at bay,
you are given a slingshot with seven smooth stones.

To Godwyn 'Gee' N. who is now a Nwydogn or more simply Nywdog,
Your name in the Common Tongue is "Enough Gas":
You are given one of the Poles of Light, *"The Search-Finder"* –
for you, once being an Original Gangster, did know the ways of the world.
You were once as a dog but now you are not.
You once spoke in vanity,
but now you shall speak forth Wisdom until your very last breath.

To Elena, who is now Eleanor,
Your name once meant that you were a "Light", a beacon to those all around,
but now your name means "Mercy";
for you shall have pity upon all those to whom you are sent.
You are given bows and arrows befitting of *"Harvey"* your quiver –
for you shall shine on like the Moon.

To Sashi, who is now Sascha,
whose name originates from "Defender of Man":
You are given the *"Club of Fools"* –
for neither do you nor shall you ever rest easy with fools,
but you shall beat them down by way of your tools.

To Alisha, who is now Alicia,
your name once meant that you were born of a "Noble Kind",
now it means that you shall, in all your pursuits, be of "Noble Cheer".
You are given the Boots *"La Chaussure d'Evangile"*

and "*La Chaussure de Paix*"
which will grant you God-speed.
Also, you are given a copy of the "*Books of Antiquity*",
which thing contains both the
"*Book of Knowledge*", the "*Book of Understanding*"
and the *"Book of Wisdom"* –
for your feet have erstwhile brought good news;
your manner has brought peace;
and you have already begun to discover what wisdom is.

So was it written:

And so The Friends received their new names
As it was required for it was seen.
Upsetting the prophecy of The Just
Could not be, nor has ever been!

"And to the two elves who shall accompany them on their journeys
from Efas to Everlasting:"

To Frydor the Elf, whose every manner is after that of the Surps,
(save for the occasional excess of alcohol);
You are also given the "*Books of Antiquity*".
You are also to be granted some *geld,*
which has been collected since times past for such a day as today;
and the *deschoses*
[which literally means some pertinent things for the journey] –
for you are responsible for those in your charge.

To Flip, whose manner at present is after a Surp's acolyte;
You are to be given the *"Belt of Truth"*. Wear it wisely.
Know thou for certain however
that the dark days that lay behind lie forward as well;
but, read and understand all things well,
for is it not so written on many pages of these Books?

"Four horses are also given you for speed of travel.
For time is not redeemed in this age."

They have the names: *Pegasus, Tapfer, Vol,* and *Schatten-Flug.*
They are amongst the swiftest and most loyal of all steeds

in the realm of Krandor, and so shall they be of service to you;
if indeed, you are of service to them.

Even as Shaun spoke these last words, he motioned to Jay to prepare all things sufficient for their journey.

*

'Time is of the essence,' Shaun stated solemnly in the hearing of the faithful company. 'Hurry now Cousin John, for they must be on their way soon...'

Then he turned back to the face the new disciples, before saying:

'Dost thou understand all things that thou hast sworn here this day?'

To which thing the group replied, 'We do!'

'Has anyone compelled you to speak things that you ought not speak?'

To which thing the group replied, 'No!'

'Rememberest thou that the full grace of thy names and the full effect of thy weapons shall surely be witnessed, albeit at divers times in your forthcoming journey and in accordance to thy need. Moreover, the true meaning of each and all shall be hidden till such a time.

'Rememberest thou also to call out for the name when the time draweth nigh and the shadow from the sun no longer falls where it ought. Then shall you be in grim need for it is then that the saying will speak true, that:

"The truth shall be revived and the dead shall surely die!"

To which things the group then replied, 'Amen!' which literally means, "I am down with that" or "That be cool" – or, as in some of the older tongues, "So let it be".

Thereupon, John swiftly returned to the basement where the sacred observance was being held and he brought out from his person the official maps and translations of Krandor.

'Here are your papers,' he said, handing a half to Flip and the other half to Frydor. 'But make all haste for time is now against you and the clock is running. Soon the first clock will stop though the second watch shall follow shortly afterwards – that is Time and No-Time as the soothsayers so declare. You must part forthwith. And may God be with you, O Faithful Apprentices!'

Then all those who had been invited said, 'Amen!'

When each of the protocols was satisfied the new Acolytes of the Surps sorted out their own belongings and said their last farewells to the Good Folk of that town. There were many tears, tears of joy mostly as many reckoned these souls to be the answer to their prayers. But there were also tears of sorrow, as some of those present, prophets mostly, knew what the forthcoming journey would hold not only for the new followers, but also for all those that had backed them.

Perhaps some of them would see one another again, perhaps not; but be that as it may, even if they were so fortunate, for the most, it would have to be at a different time or indeed, at a different placing altogether. But the scope to speak of such is far beyond the bounds of this book.

Therefore, with all things now settled as they ought, the Troop parted from the main assembly and headed off with their stomachs filled to contentment. Albeit, it was only into the searching darkness, which John-jay and Shaun knew only too well.

PART III

ZONES OF CONTENTION

A TALE OF TWO FIENDS

"Hypocrites! Well did Isaiah prophesy about you, saying:
'These people draw near to Me with their mouth,
And honour Me with their lips,
But their heart is far from Me.' "

MATTHEW 15:7-8

Daybreak came in only a few hours. The dawn sunshine clambered slowly over the archaic hills beyond bringing a new ray of expectation for the hastening day. Thaelomir's steeds, the Etheldorians Bold, grazed freely upon the greensward upon the furthest sides of the meadow, where was found the tributaries joining the Afon Ellyllardd to the Afon Caniad, which sits by the tail of Bryn Gollam. There they remained, docile as the day was at ease and contented with the few pressures of their current lot. There they would remain until either their fodder became famished, the confluence of the rivers was run dry, their itinerant masters bellowed loud upon their clarions, loud as a warbler in its prime.

They cropped under the freshness of the morning sky, free of the burden of their riders and filled with the extent of the grasslands spread before them. They were also glad to be freed of the weighty saddles that had clung fast to their backs. The steep inclines which had tested their footing and the oppression of the night-time course made their present status a treat. However, reveries returned of wide open pastures back in the land of their cradle. Such sentiments only fuelled the horses resolve to return one day, for the beauty of the greensward in Etheldor was no small thing.

Breakfast for the party consisted of a healthy measure oats, which each duly took; one or two boiled fruits per head, together with some reasonably fresh milk purged of bug and tick over a smouldering flame. There were also slices of day-old bread, laden with generous measures of mellifluous ointment. Other than this little more was there to consume. In truth, at any moment in Krandor, one might expect to face the challenge of unplanned flight,

204

away from forces of an alien race perhaps, and so a full quota of nourishment was not always the practical alternative.

Diversions were a common occurrence within even the most tranquil sites in the land. Often it was forced marches, the slaughter of men and elves (in these parts) or the pillaging of livestock. Devastation spread from one town to the next without so much as the sounding of a conch! Among the party of wayfarers even Eleanor was becoming wizened to the cruelty of the land they sought; for she had already begun to discern a darkness trailing after them, though it was not presently searching them out and even though it yet lay some way behind.

Frydor the Elf took the lead with his partner in the pylon, Alicia 'the Wise', younger acolyte of the ardent Surp. Nywdog rode offside to cover the Troop's rightmost flank with Eleanor who was holding on tightly to his waist, her face fixed starboard, her eyes beacons amid the sideling grey skies. Further along the trail and still finding it a little difficult to keep apace was Marcus and his ally Jemimah, and they too rode uncomfortably on the inside of their double saddle. Their expedition was bumpy, jarring at bums and unsettling hides to increase the pain of the afflicted. And that, when tolled aside their patent lack of equine experience, made all things seem folly in the making. Indeed, try as they may to bring the reigns under control their golden stallion yielded them few favours. Sufferings aside they defended port as best as they were able as failure to pay due regard to any hostile war-bands might propel much more than their ailing ribs into grim jeopardy!

Bringing up the rear on his dappled grey stallion was Flip who was currently engaged (or enraged as it was soon to be) in moot with Sascha his cohort. They covered divers topics which distanced themselves from the here and now. Prime amongst their banter were subjects such as: local ethnic delicacies, pertaining to foods – which ones were tastiest and whatnot; religious parlance and dubious mentions of forewarnings by folk deemed as wise – including the vague prattle of Nostradamus from Sascha, and the words of Ivan mab Bellicose, an elf from Hores, courtesy of Flip. They also touched on personal matters, which held the sway of their remaining colloquy, and the narratives were relished with great savour. Nonetheless, fluent though their parley was, they kept the line from first till last as they meandered through the dense thickets.

Tall boles and felled trees jutted intermittently into their path to thwart them in their adventures. The steeds opted for the muddier tracks which they gaited upon sure-footed as Îsenhewr the Dwarf making choice their chosen ascent. Though worn and ragged the paths carried the shallowest slope of the lot and so their purpose would be served well enough without the rise of too much sufferance. There were no major snarls when they enjoined themselves to the route upward; and then towards the glades where trollish hamlets were spread few and far between. It was not long afterwards before their masters saw the first streams of troglodytes descending abreast upon the other steep shoulder of the hill.

*

Marcus remained caught in deep reverie for much of the ensuing ride, pulling forward his hood over the furrowed lines of his brow that perhaps by this motion some of his rising disquietude might be quelled. As he steadied the gait of his horse, he perceived that he too was alarmed for the recent turn of events.

Who was that old spinster that had approached Flip over by the Brook of Solitude? And what was her relevance to their present cause?

With such questions in mind he quietly spurred on his faithful steed Tapfer to regain the trot as he and Jemimah passed on through the land of low hills and pleasant dales lining the broad fertile borders of the Woods of Trol. For a long space afterward fear descended upon the ongoing company upon whose heads the width of the sun had earlier found its mark through drowsy leaves and felled bracken. But foreboding aside, their pace continued unbroken, while they yet found surer footing upon the solid grounds leading into the Vale of Ysgawennen.

Upon the left of their course hung many a mile of dense timberland at which travellers glanced ever and awhile in fear and in trembling for the unsavoury beasts that roamed thereabouts. Of no less dread were the creatures of Haleg's Forest who were reckoned to be *blaidd* for the most part. They say that wolves were required long ago to keep watch on the old castle at Riéms and so bloodsucking vermin and holy-horned horses were enchanted with one of the spells of the Black Witch of Babylon. And so their forms were altered into the accursed beasts of today, an unchancy spell wrought for aiding the Surp-elder Coblyn Llefennewn in his interrogation. Men say that it is his groanings and lamentations which is the cause for many a downfall of evil in the desolate regions of this weald. A piously afflicted soul indeed.

Was it not Erynaidd herself, queen of the wooded groves, whose beguilement by way of the Virgin-spells achieved such ends? And are not her incantations still heard to this day and on all moonless eves upon which birds flock gingerly through the begirding ether? Thus, many were the marvels which the forests held close to her bosom, not least the old wooden shack of Erynaidd's most mighty fosterage, the Old Woman Ceriddenne.

*

'A pitiful beast that is with you, O Flip, son of Costa the Lost One, Crowned Prince of Darkness! How you have tricked your company and friends!' crowed the voice unexpectedly from downriver, the same by which they had taken early meal together.

'Where are the Mighty Men of Seven's Dream? What then is this foul numbering that appears before me?' Her voice seemed to hiss as she dipped her linen into the quick-moving stream. She plucked her crankly fingers, counting from her left thumb to the middle finger upon her right hand;

'You are *faitour* are you not, elf? A Grey Wolf?'

Nevertheless, when the elf had reared his steed to question the old hag's impertinent manner, it seemed as though vanished was she altogether, for which he was in no small measure flummoxed. At length however he did find her again, deep in the woods before a hut construed in elm and rotted bark, from which a banner of smoking fumes seemed to emerge and alight heavenward.

He moved closer to her, her form soon paying semblance, so he afterward swore, to a single-horned beast, the like of which according to elven-lore was accursed. For was that not the form of the unicorns which used to roam the wealds, imparting wisdom unto all those with an ear to listen, all those with an eye to see, upon those men whose hearts were not yet hardened, whose necks were not yet stiff? But it was Old Woman Ceriddenne's line indeed that had made them abominable as they are at present and had smitten them to rove as bloodsucking scroungers all the days of their walk.

But soon her worldly carriage appeared again before his mien which brought a somewhat more soothing tranquillity upon his inner being.

'Who are you that know of our doings?' Flip had cried, in angst and in alarm, to which she offered no sure reply. Thus he repeated, drawing his trusty blade *Cheaef*, 'Speak now, woman, or be thrust through with the nib of my steel.'

'Aye! Like many have been beforetimes: young wenches, both the broody and the inviolate; babies of pale sheen and whelps of darkened colouration; and women so old that they bear their weight upon a stilted rod rather than their frail old shanks. Aye! Such an elf as you were... and indeed are! Now you wish to do the same to this worn vixen, an harmless spinster who has no arms to her name?'

'Ah but what vixen is harmless when robbed of her cubs, wrinkled as the Old Grey Oak though she may be? Likewise, what wench is caulked when robbed of her dignity?'

At this pert reply she pondered awhile, as if lost for the skill of his fine retort. Thereupon, her tiny feet carried her towards a pollard hung low with leafless branches, whereon she fixed her clothing to the side of the tree and fastened them tight with an awl. She finished with the clothing she had erstwhile dragged clean of the river, paying neither heed nor attention to his continual flurry of examinations, even though hot was his temper and hot on her heels he yet remained.

Then all at once a stern breeze rocked through the tussocked reeds by the river-mound and uprose to the old hovel of her dwelling, bringing forth gusts errant as a wayward plover strayed from shore to sea. It seemed as though with one slap of her elf-locks her head peeled this way and then that and a terrible storm brewed of evil nostrils was borne so fierce that all trees appeared polled and all thickets were made void of the livid shrubs that had composed them. And as her face was raised to set about the task at hand the tresses of her hair were bound together in fashion that even the most gnarled roots would envy. Then a growl, low as that of a brooding mammoth, emanated from the tiny slit through which she daily consumed her pottage.

'So you are as they say, an elf of some schooling? Well see if you understand these things then, Flip mab Costa, husbandman to the White Witch Shiavette…' Upon which she promptly proceeded to devour the winds with the Seven Questions of the World Above and the Seven Questions of the World Beneath, culminating with the most important of all enquiries.

'According to Men, Seven are the Sins Most Deadly, elf.
Name them in *rank* order if you are able:

'*Pride* comes first because it is the sin
for which the Morning Star fell to begin with;
Then comes *Lust*
for its taste has ensnared many a captive with her wayward ways;
Covetousness is next,
for 'tis the last though not least of the things inscribed from God to beast;
Then *Envy*, as to desire and not to have is almost equal to that above;
And of course there is *Anger*, for it says to elves,
"Be angry and do not sin",
Lest its puff cloud your judgement and your words breathe wind;
Then *Sloth*, for will not an idle person suffer hunger,
if indeed he is given to slumber,
And will not a lazy man go without for he says, "There is a lion outside"?
Lastly, peradventure, *Gluttony*,
for does it not say, "There can be much evil in too much good"
(And some good in that considered evil),
But the wise will judge it all, for it is the wise that will understand,
But the glutton will consume it all and fall for is not that the fool's call?'

At this she looked to fare no worse and wondered off deeper into the thorny weald, which was beset by many a trial and torment. Twisted arms reaching down from treetops, high as the sun, dark as the moon in its newness; tangled tresses and roots grown haply that its shoot might make mighty press against the buffeting strokes of the wind; clusters of yews through which both fox and foumart have their dwelling; thickets of no mean bramble to scour the visitor clean of his sin as he passed.

208

He held hard by her path, which took them along a contoured cascading stream, and they soon alighted upon a mound which stood by the base of the broad river called *Nweidd* for the name of the nymph reputed to have its abode therein. It was here that the witch spoke her first words again after the initial, swiftly discouraging the rising impertinence of the feisty young elf.

'Let not your pride rise above what it should O Callow One, for 'twas an easy saying that which you have spoken. All know that there is both a time to be born and a time to die...'

'Though few also know that there is a time to kill and a time to heal,' came Flip's favoured outburst.

'Ah! Again have you uttered a truth which all *ellyll* know. But what say you of this?'

'Seven are the Hills that trap Babylon in the evil World Above.
See if you can name but five or six or seven indeed to do the trick?
And what is the meaning that what has been planted
must also be plucked up?'

And the elf too observed:
'Have not the stones of the Babylon of Olde been cast away
And gathered to a newness of form in the Land of Lladin?
Thus, in the ordering of our letters:
Aventine, Caelian, Capitoline, Esquiline, Palatine, Quirinal, and Viminal.
Indeed, this new Babylon in the heart of the hills,
The place of the whore, the seat of the kings.'

With this, the decrepit old lady looked astonished if not puzzled. 'What knowledge have you of things fey from the World of Men?' she riled. 'And if your knowledge is good, then what make you of this:'

'The Seven that were for Thebes!
And what manner of verse shall accompany these things?'

'Do you question me or do you demand a response of some deadwood?
Seven captains there were led by Adrastus, King of Argos,
place and land of Hera's Birth.
His retinue formed was with Amphiaraus, Capereus, Hippomedon,
Parthenopaeus, Polynices and Tydeus.
Their call was to snatch the Seven Ancient Gates
from the hands of Eteocles mab Oedipus,
For the man, Polynices, who was of the same birthright,
But such was their tragedy when the brothers did fall,
At each other's hands beneath the Theban Walls.'

'And what was the manner of its success?' the witch responded angrily.
'The raid I speak of?'

'The same as that of a white-maned bear in Uffern I dare say!'
(Flip, in turn, provoked.)
'But as for its wisdom:
Is there not a time for war, even as there is a time for peace;
As there was certainly a time when the brothers were in love,
Before at the gates, gave it way toward hate!'

With this pert remark she smiled, a toothless gummy grin that smirked of all things foul and horrid. She then set about to beguile the elf of what knowledge he knew pertaining to further understandings of the World Above.

It was as though her countenance took on the rapt expression of a princess, whose fortune has just been restored by the sweet lips of her saviour and she fixed him a comely stare which any fair elf would do worse to squander.

'Now then, what of the Seven Land-masses of Man? Tell me all you can...'

'But why do you question me with such trivialities?' pounced the elf hotly.
'There is of course:

'Africa for the Black Man,
Europe for the White Man,
Australia for the Native-dweller,
Asia for the Brown and Yellow;
Antarctica which are cold and barren,
North America, which was taken from the Indian hands,
And South America, the greatest gathering of Catholics,
That are upon the world and within "The Mix".'

'And I suppose you too have *read* the words
that were spoken into the depths of the sea,
To caulk the dimming void and to loose the brimming waves?'

'Did not His hand command that all men everywhere should:
At one time weep and at another, laugh,
And that in the time of sin, all men are to mourn
And in the time of clemency were all men to dance?
For was not all underwater when His Spirit hovered above the waters?'

Old Woman Ceriddenne was again set standing in startled shock and in scorn did she totter as an ailing willow blown by Pan's broad nostrils or by a squally come in from the western sea-marge. But she regained her composure quickly lest any of her accompanying spirits deride her wisdom as being easily quashed by an importunate little babe.

She harried further through the woods, drawing the elf smartly behind her, muttering strange things into the bubbling ether. All seemed to reform and enclose itself above her words even as she hissed further dire venom. They headed towards the blackened dale, away from his troublesome Friends, and away from the Surp, of whom her kin did truly enjoy smiting his kinsman in the selfsame test in days of yore, before even the Storms of the Rising Winds had first come about.

Not far before them was lain an obfuscated headland, shrouded against the gloomy screen behind it. It was towards this darkness they headed, eyes cast downward for the sorry aspect that trundled along upon the vast horizon. Grey rain-clouds, the colour of winter skies, trailed their bobbing demeanours, as spoor became slope, slippery for the coolness of the previous eventide. However, not alone were the uncluttered eyes of strangers which seemed to pass over them as they penetrated deeper the depth of the dank, darkening forest.

A copse of tall trees stuck elated into the falling skies, past which they ventured in silence, her brooding swiftly taking charge from her sullen string of anathemas and their crowns soon fell upon a rugged hearth. This position swallowed them up easily as a silky gossamer a fly lost on its bearing.

The toil soon increased upon the elf, as though she fought not only a battle with wits against his person but also a struggle of stamina, that he should fall by the wayside, lest any more of her prudence become undone before *their* ears. But brave was the *ellyll* which the feet carried along, through the ruddy glow of petering light, which lay diffused for the many branches thick with the season's lush sprouting. And large was the plain she led him to, that he might be questioned of his learning further.

They stopped by a tangled trestle of leaves by which she impressed a large circle upon the ground. It was back to the World Above for the elf, in a way more taxing even than the journey that had spirited them to that unchancy plot.

'So what make you of this?' she rumbled, thrusting her stick into the concentric circles below which were written the words:

"Sheba,
Teras,
Tebel."

And by the look on his face, she thought she had him with this one. For sweat peeped down his brow, the likeness of which he had dared not brake since the beginning of her questioning, and bright flushed his cheeks, the colour of an amber moon.

'I may need a-a l-little m-more time,' Flip stumbled finally, as she set task watching him quiver before her very eyes. 'I s-shall have it soon, not to worry,' he rejoined stubbornly.

'As much time as you need, O Haughty One,' the witch added.

(For she liked to see him tremor at the onset of the shakes which comes upon all those who, having begun to answer the beldam's fell inquiries, were, before the end, unable to continue.)

'Now, *cousin* Flip, do you yet feel the quivering upon your hand?'

At this Flip became enraged at the swindler's inequity. He scowled at her rudely knowing accurately the things of which she spoke: for wise though the witch was, unfair was her treatment of him; and elderly though her frame yet appeared, few vixens of this sort can be trusted within the sweep of a bow's range. Moreover, he was not to be beaten by any aged spinster, evil-looking beyond all those called to spellbinding though she may well have been.

Presently, a volley of black-chested sparrows swept across the heatherland, birds that are as supposed inconspicuous to the normal viewer. Nonetheless, the elf deemed it an omen come to help him in his time of need. For their pattern was not after the normal form for birds of their kind, but they mapped out a familiar pattern against the greying skies above.

And the points that they etched he imagined to be the surface of the World Above, and as they whirled round above their heads, he saw that it was none less than Deaerawd, and its Seven Key Points, circling the Sun-god Mabon.

Thence the elf cried aloud:

'Ah! Now do I understand the runes well it seems…
The Pyramids of Mizraim,
The Hanging Gardens of [Olde] Babylon,
Phiadias' Statue of Zeus at Olympia,
The Temple of Artemis at Efas-Us,
The Mausoleum of Halicarnassus,
The Colossus at Rhodes,
And the Pharos of Alexandria…'

He pondered some more before embarking upon his even greater insight:
'And lest you should query me for more;
These are those places that are good to embrace for their comely aspect,
But when the storms do fall in the rain of judgement,

neither shall one stone be left upon another.
For rent shall they be from their former glories,
And sewn to the Four Winds held by the Four Watchers of the World.
For as it is written,
"There shall be a time to cast away stones,
and a time to gather stones together."'

'But what calumny is this!' screeched the old wench. 'For that was an easy
one,' she lied, through teeth gritted so close so as to prevent the retreat of her
breath. 'That was one for mere babes yet unlearned of proper foods. Though
perhaps now you can help *us* with this one?'
Moving on swiftly, she muttered:

'How many eagles are there,
messengers from that foul god of the Northern Rock?
And what is their being that they fly both high and low
in the airs of the winds?
Is this not a matter for Surps only, or those learned in the Ancient Lore?'

'Try this then, witch:
Their bread are snakes by which they increase their sight awake;
Their means is the aether, through which they fly;
Their convocation is themselves, Seven Strong,
in whose company they speak forth wisdom;
And their task set, from Heaven's arm, is to seal all serpents' lies.
For does it not say…?
That by their worship they shall break down the bulwarks of the East
And build up a banner for the North.
And does it not also say…?
That there is both a time to keep silence and a time to speak,
That when these things are ordered so shall there be peace!'

And the hag cried in wonderment, 'Nigh on perfect are you, O Callow Elf;
For you are correct in this matter –
seven shall certainly seal the Eagles of the Skies,
That before possession comes shall the end draw nigh.'

But then the woman turned about on herself, drawing nearer to his aspect, and
then seemed to walk straight through his withdrawn features. The elf blinked
rapidly, greatly distressed for the moment at what had just transpired, though
he did set himself the chore of keeping tight on her spurs lest the other should
abandon him quickly as she came.

She chose a yellow coloured hill by the downs of Llanereig by which to continue her upward ascent towards the crest of the local peaks. They journeyed along in silence for a while, save for the occasional foreign mutterings of the crazed old wench. Her movement too was fey. At times it seemed as though she struggled as one would with the appearance of over-ripened age; at others albeit it was as though no obstacle was too difficult for her, no slope too slippery, no path too cruel.

They travelled past an escarpment formed upon a narrow ridge and with time the elf began to feel the detachment from his friends. He knew that they were likely to be seeking him out, even then, and beckoned the hag to tell him clearly whereto she had chosen to lead them both (for he perceived that it was her *enaid* that steered them both and not her *corff*). But silence remained on her lips for the time being bar a few unkindly cusses; until, that is, they came to a long band of serrated potholes, just before the peak of the nearby cluster of hills. From there they gazed longingly at the neighbouring wilderness beyond, as Flip's belt throbbed with warm relief.

Though the sun had remained with them throughout, she preferred to face him in silhouette form (supposing perhaps that her natural dreaded features carried no great fright of their own!). It then seemed like an heavy grey cloak came about her visage to cloud her face and further darken it against the looming backdrop of the fair-skinned sun. It also looked as though ribald forms compassed her about, dryads taken from the woods they had just left, that had stolen with them a privy.

All at once the denizen of the evil woods cackled a fell laughter that all weald-beasts that heard it scurried off as black-faced bats from the sunlight.

'Let me then ask you this O Wise One,' she gibed, 'and answer all you are able.'

She stole a step closer (and he, without hesitation, took a pace backwards).

Then she spoke in dark tones that were grievous to his ear:

'But know this also for certain, and figure this last one who will:

'Then shall The Holy Convocation of Seven
Speak of Six-signs, Six times,
After the evil chime of Jacobi's last rhyme.
And then shall there be Seven Keys yet to bind.

'For there is yet some of your company that must be gained,
And then some thereafter that you most lose;
Some afterwards you shall keep;
Others, at times, will you choose to throw away.'

Thereupon, the withered old shrew shuffled closer to view his dark countenance, pronouncing:

'But regard yourself, O Ellyll of Prudence,
For though wisdom is a choice purchase,
with it comes an haughtiness unknown
Even if one's standing is as the Great Fallen Beast.
But let this wily old shrew see what your *ysbryd* might find,
Before the Valley of Hinnom's last bind?'

The elf shuddered as she made pains to continue, uncloaking herself from the bands of darkness that had earlier hemmed her about, neither giving him chance of recovery. And evil was the look she sold him.

'Therefore, answer after all these things, elf,' hissed Ceriddenne, her face etched as though deep in contemplation. 'And tell of all these things as you may…'

'The Seven Signs of the Times. What are they for?
Break it down and tell me more!'

So with a little thought, Flip answered as he was tasked to do:

'Before 4004 B.C. was the Pre-Adamic Kingdom or "No-Time";
'Between 4004 B.C. and 4 B.C. was "Times";
'Between 4 B.C. and 30 A.D. was the Day of the Messiah or "No-Time";
'Between 30 A.D. and 2030 A.D. is "Time";
'Between 2030 A.D. and 2037 A.D. is the Tribulation or "No-Time";
'Between 2037 A.D. and 3037 A.D. is [The Millennium] "Half a Time";
'After 3037 A.D. is the Post-Millennial Kingdom or "No-Time" '

'Thus, as you can see, No-Time stretches from Eternity to Eternity… but the time allocated to man is a mere seven thousand years. That is to say, six thousand years are given unto man alone, and one thousand years to the man under the Messiah's reign!'

Though she was somewhat diffident in admitting it, the witch was impressed with the facility with which the elf had responded to this last query. Nevertheless, she vowed, under her breath, to make whatever enquiries that followed more taxing than the ones which had passed.

*

His eyes flinched open at the remembrance of the elf's cagey words, but within his mind he had grown none the wiser. Above the hymn of the humming of bees and beneath lowing of kine in the fields came curled leaves that were dewy with the oppression of raindrops upon their sheaths. Each one rattled as cold streams of air made light their touch upon the glistening green sheen. Loud was the noise of the sun-dappled meadows that coursed through the bush from the hoots of owls and the singing of larks in the lower air. But louder still was the carousing of friends that made light the elegy of the *callow* elf, as words far too strange to fathom were bartered.

It was only when Jemimah prodded him sharply that the young Breast-plate-bearer stirred from his musing. No need was there for further awakening as he saw, with his friends, the grey-green skirts of Bryn Gyrgon, in which lie the bones and tombs of deceased warriors, all slain by the hands of the Eastern Lords. Passing overhead lay a sledge track that girded its shoulder, broad-breasted, beautiful and full. And its mark descended in a coiled manner from the nape of Gyrgon's neck towards the jaws of the coomb where resided denizen's of death, alone, and in the musty darkness of the crest-studded crags.

Presently, cowls were closed and all breasts were girded for the buffeting breeze which swept wildly across the climbing track. A smattering of wetness spread across the mound from fore-rider back towards the van. Rolling clouds were cloyed with the goodness of hazy mist, their fat undersides sending out searching blue talons which sprung lithely into the distance. Sounds of lightning struck some way yonder out by the heatherland, several leagues away by Flip's dead reckoning. Such threatening omens caused Frydor to blow hard on his horn, loud and clear as once the day had been, and he gathered in his charge to escape the coming deluge.

Shortly the friends were drawn together and ordered themselves accordingly, as the path became a narrow spoor barely sufficient for the passing of one beast at a time. As more heavenly vibrations sounded the company quickly filtered back into array, Vol after Tapfer who was riding hard behind Schatten-Flug, which left Frydor once again holding the lead.

*

The whole of creation was still, save for the gentle flow of streams far beneath, by the foot of Caer Gyrgon. At times volleys of birds swooped and spun some way in the distance, but never so much was a solitary mound on Urien so silent as it was early that eve. The Friends waited by in peace, charcoal flotsams of cloud stealing up from the ankles of their charges to shroud the entire company in its gloomy-gray velvet. But there they remained, rallied around Flip, reflecting on the words of the elf, waiting to receive his further insight, the last fell questions she had asked him.

Using this tranquil moment for its own gain, ghastly images returned to the elf, reminding him of the final few inquiries that the old beldam had thrown him. He looked frail as a leaf at winter's end, whose veins were all that remained to be seen. Cold was the air he was caught in and dark was his present memory. Though there yet came a time, eventually, when the rest was broken, taken up quickly by murmurs of appreciation by the accompanying band, and it was at that time when the elf turned about on himself and smiled.

'Not to worry my friends, I think the last one has come back now to haunt me!'

Sensing a good tale in the offing, Sascha inquired attentively whether her final questions were more trying than the others which she had asked him, and if so, in what way.

'Trying is not the word, my boy – never so easy. The matter of this inquiry was deep and mysterious as any wisdom spoken by the Greybeards…'

'So what was it then,' cried the excited company, stirring the wildlife into action around them.

'Yes, what fell question did she put to you, that it should send tremors about your bones, put sweat upon your brow, cause you to look like the top end of a mountain peak in the month of Y Mis Du?' questioned Frydor suggestively.

The elf sat there brooding over his uncle's question, whilst Sascha was at pains to gauge whether or not the sudden interest had put him off, or whether he was even now reliving the torments of the damned old hag. Nevertheless, his concern was greeted with a stony reception, as Flip stole away on foot towards the crest of their present hill. It was there that he looked upwards and cried aloud in fearful tones and an unknown tongue that none of the beasts of the field understood.

Some said afterwards that he had cursed himself for becoming entangled in the web of the Black Widow herself. Others hold that he had done no such thing, but had summoned the gods to the mountainside, that by their presence the fullness of wisdom might return to him. Whichever was true is of no account here. Suffice to say that suddenly, thunder broke the roofs of the sky and lightening played all round. The belly of heaven was split open and out poured rain the curse of the gods; globules of ice so thick as to cover a man's hand even before the crack of Juno's whip could be heard, after he is seen casting his wares onto the world beneath. All took what cover he may before the elf finally resumed his tale.

'It was on a hill much like this one that Old Woman Ceriddenne questioned me on matters pertaining to the Ancient Lore itself,' Flip said, scanning the horizons. 'Dark questions, riddles, enigmas; matters of wisdom and understanding, much of it too involved for youthful ears to comprehend…'

The young elf's memory appeared to be leading him aloof, as if recollections of this sort was not what was intended. He grasped the hilt of his sword as if to succour what comfort he may. All noted him striving for mastery of his blade, as though trying to rectify a misdeed that might well have cost him dear.

'…Never should such questions be asked of mortals, unless they be descendant of the gods themselves. Unfair, unfortunate, untimely. Woe to me for the Black Witch from Erynaidd's breed did me ill. Woe to me for my pride! Woe to me for my accursed responses. Woe to me, for the gods themselves bore witness, and it was I who was found wanting.'

With that, he delved straight into the recesses of his troubled mind, leaving others to unravel what esoteric wonders they may.

*

They had been spirited to a terrible place, a realm of murk, dread and loss. It was an unwalled kingdom, a resting-place for sea-hosts from the deep. Black were the clouds that spread upwards from the ungodly forest floor, and black, beastly and fog-bound was the domain upon which it held sway. It was the land beyond Dreams they had come to, a region without enclosure. Peopled by men in the grave, populated by twisted multi-limbed deformities of all kinds, proud were the unkempt barrows of Gwidiwr. It was to this outer realm that the wise (or the foolish) were taken, when tasked to answer the sorcerer's most solemn inquisitions.

As all men know, dour must the heart remain if it is to triumph against the Unknown. For who can call the things that be not as though they already were, save for the gods themselves and for their spawn; and who is he who might enquire of the gods, save for the one who is drawn, either by Wisdom or by Fortune. Still, thoughts of the Glorious Unknown lay many years of ahead of him, who had been taken to that unchancy spot. Once or twice only did he fancy the veil between his world and the one beyond torn – whichever world that was – for he knew not even which world he was in. But no image remained clear when his mind converged to grapple it, no picture remained undissolved, indeed, no words remained at all.

A small gully ran beneath them, lost beneath the rock-face, itself held firmly by the Rock. And without this Rock, not only would this spoor come cascading down the mountain-side, like the waters that rush off the embankment into Mêr Cyswllt, but also the trees by which the rock was bound, the birds that perched in its leaves, the sky within which they flew their daily course. Indeed, little might remain, as she told him to his horror, should but the Word be rescinded, or should a man slip and break his neck!

So strait was their spoor that no two beasts might walk abreast at any one time, not in this world nor in the next. The sorceress led him onwards as always, her foaming mouth a sign that her *awen* was indeed being renewed, that blazing look, by which she lit up the dark wilderness, dreadful. He ventured as he may, close to her skirts, into the clouds that were broken only on occasions to reveal a panoply of stars set amidst the glistening array of heaven.

Trembling as men ought not, Flip soon found himself taken with fantastic visions and a oneness with nature that even Faunus himself would have envied; which indeed he did, slinking down behind the weary duo, his host of assistants trailing behind him, as wits became dulled and bodies tired; which is when they sat down to rest for a moment.

'*Gwyddbwyll?*' asked the witch of the elf.

Upon these words, the thunders cracked, the lightening charged, and the earth shook.

'Will my part be played whether I choose to or not?'

"As sure a certainty as you breathe
The air that comes forth from the leaves!"

Her brief sally ended, he replied, 'Well play then I must; lest I trust in the Unworthy Dead to make my moves for me. For it is written, "There is a time to embrace and a time to refrain from embracing", and my time is now come.'

She nodded curtly, knowing full well that he too was learned of the books of the *llyfyrion* – texts which only the wise ever pored through.

'So then:

"Magical night, magical wind
Let us see what this game will bring." '

With that the dark, dusk clouds became a sea of faces, about which noxious, reptilian fumes ebbed and eked. All of a sudden, it seemed to the elf that swart imps, green-eyed goblins and faceless wonders of the Otherworld were sat reclining amidst the bush-rows, all keen to observe what was about to transpire. Fear crept close to the winds causing Flip's inner man to wane in him. He who had once stood fast against the dark-skinned vassals of Drygiöri of the Blackfaces was now at ends to quench the unconquerable cloud that grappled sternly with his soul. It was then that the game began in earnest.

'So let's to it then, proper, O Elf! – The Law of Perthynas –
as scrawled upon the dun hide of a cow.
What are they Elf?'

She fell back into position beside the hedgerow, letting neither weariness nor brambles discomfort her hold on current events.

'In the Law of Kinsmen, first comes Man's responsibility to God;
 'Then comes his responsibility to his immediate family – that is to say:

> a... Wives to Husbands
> b... Husbands to Wives
> c... Wards to Guardians
> d ...Guardians to Wards

'Then comes his responsibility to those that believe the same as him,
to those who are of the same creed or lore – his Faith Family.
'Next comes his responsibly to his close relations, namely to his parents,
once he has left home and has a life and a wife of his own,
'And then to his [other] relations – his father's family, his mother's family,
his brother's family and his sister's family.
(Thus, summing up these matters,
his responsibility then is towards the family of all his immediate family).
'After that come workplace relationships,
namely slave to master and then master to slave.
'And our neighbors – both those we like and those we dislike –
assuming there are none who straddle the spike.
(For, as it is written, those who are not for us are against us
and those who are not against us are on our side.
So one's responsibility to his friends comes before
one's responsibility to one's enemies.)'

The witch did all she could to bridle her anger before moving on.

'According to Elves now, friend, Seven are the Sins Most Deadly...
arrange them in order if you are so able'

Without hesitation the Elf replied...

'Treachery – such as Breaking the Vows of Wedlock,
Hypocrisy – such as Neglecting the Teaching of the Ancient Lore,
Pride – such as the Daystar once had,
Lust – such as Violating Holy Virgins before their dads,
Greed – such as Absconding with Church Valuables,
Envy – which, more often than not, ends in infamy,
And Slander – or Blasphemy.'

Expecting her to praise him for his wisdom, he left his cocked head with his eyelids half-open and gawked wildly upon her hideous face. But tired was she at such trivialities, aghast was she at his ways, but gutsy was she against such stern opposition. Now must come the deeper parts of the Lore.

'The Gifts of Grace,' riled the witch. 'What are they...
and who are they for??
How can you show mercy to both the guilty and innocent;
upon both the good and the bad?
Clear now my confusion elf, and there may yet be reward in it for you.'

'Keep your reward for yourself, witch, and I will buffet your inquiries just as easily as the rest! Though we wise, vixen, may plant knowledge, it is you and your kind who will pluck it up.'

The elf's pert response hugely delighted those that had gathered round the gwyddbwyll board, and many peeled their forms away from the dreary backdrop, edging their way ever closer to the stage that held their attention. Even those from *Huan*, both golden and glorious, and those from *Lleuad*, crust-covered and grim, moved forward to the edge of the clearing, storing up knowledge which by now they ought know. Not lightly was this knowledge esteemed; for any clever dictate was wont to be repeated at feastings of the Unworthy Dead. Though clearly, it would take more than simple recitations to catch this cunning elf. Presently, even the rocks themselves seemed to reveal faces of their own.

'*Prophecy* must be done in proportion to our faith,
Ministry shall be accomplished once we have therein bathed;
Teaching, only when the teacher has been awakened,
Exhorting, once the exhorter has the appropriate words to say;
Giving shall be undertaken, with liberality – so shall be his pay.
The *Ruler* shall lead with diligence and not in dismay;
And the *Mercy-giver* shall do so with cheerfulness every single day.

'But ought not one have compassion on the innocent first, and if there be any strength left, understanding, where understanding is due, for the guilty?'
'So what does it mean then:

"Love your enemies.
Bless those who curse you.
Do good to those who hate you.
Pray for those who spitefully use you and persecute you?"

A rare beam of light appeared to emerge from her face, as she laughed and gibbered, croaked and spat, glad was she for her own astute observation. It seemed like not only those upon the chequered board took to this humour, but those all round: the molten-covered, mantle-ridden forms from Annwfn; the melted-faced, moaning-tongued minions from Uffern; even the Fair Folk from across the waters of Nef allowed a wry smile to encompass their miens. All appeared gladdened by the mocking verse of the gray-whiskered spell-binder.

'But why do you laugh, chief witch?' growled the elf. 'Do you not see the ending of the verse itself?' Thus he continued:

> "Therefore you shall be perfect,
> even as the spirits of Just Men made Perfect."

'And few are there in this walk who can lay claim to such goodness!'

With this, the witch marveled; 'Not in many ages have I seen one possessed of such deft wisdom as you, fiend.'

Without awaiting his reply, however, she made move her black queen, and she sailed along the long dark line that stretched cross-wise across the chequered board.

'But it is not all over yet, O Child of Calamity,' she bellowed, laughing loudly. 'See there, I have your king in check!'

The elf hesitated – not for the first time that rise either. He could see her bulwarks built up around the board: her castles spanned North to South, East to West, her bishops were sentinels guarding their sees, her knights were *Zaqen*, warriors of the Ancient Lore, her black queen, a heavy keystone within that dark enclosure. But he could not see her king – that prized piece that was surrounded about by his pawns.

> "Black is the day, black is your heart
> Black is the way, dark is your part
> Black Thegn *of* Costa, the Dark and Evil One."

Again, he glowered at her hotly, moved by the impertinence of the gaunt old wretch. Ill though his family name was, scant repute did her own line have since a time out of mind. He could see that her liking for him was little more than that which a Bugbear has towards a child.

'Have you not read, O Witch, where it says:

> "Renew your mind with words of Truth,
> that you may prove what is good, acceptable, and perfect"?

'If not, then let me remind you:

> "Therefore I exhort first of all that prayers, petitions, and intercessions,
> With thanksgiving be made for all elves,
> for kings and all who are in authority...,
> That you may lead a quiet and peaceable life in all reverence and dignity.
> For this is *good* and *acceptable* before the Lore."

> The witch stopped smiling.
> 'But then what is *perfect* Witch?'
> Silence.
> 'What is it that is perfect, O Vile Daughter of Erynaidd?'

'I know not, elf,' she fibbed, seeing his hand stroking the veins of his sword, evidence if one needs of a desire to undertake some throat-slitting.
'Pray tell?'

> 'Do you not know that He who wrote the Lore,
> raised up Judges also, mature and obedient men?
> These were able men such as fear God,
> men of truth who hate covetousness.
> Hence, if all His works are wondrous, was this act also not perfect?
> So what example should we therefore follow?'

Loud and long was the Fair Folk's exultant laughter. Shrill was that of their accompaniment. Fiercely proud all those round believed of Flip, but there was none who could find fault with his wisdom.

*

Of a sudden, there then appeared in the midst of their company, a man dressed all in white; white cloak, white hood, white sleeves; all was white save for his golden-belted buckle and the sandals which he wore. His skin was burnished bronze, however, brighter even than the crafting that marked Zeus at Olympia. And there was yet another.

Now this other fellow was not so cheery looking (not that the other was any more so). Black, black, and black. Blacker than the Seas of Derwent, darker than the throne of Dereden, without colour, without looks. He kept his head cowled in his hood, as he shuffled into position amongst the rest, sparing a moment to lay down the triple-pronged trident at his feet, albeit keeping his sharp scythe in his hands lest it be needed in the near future. Few were there attendant that resisted this untimely intrusion, mighty were the members that joined. The sky roared, the birds chattered, and once again, Hell's fickle host were sent squealing with delight.

'Likewise, not all is always perfect. But what we can, we achieve!'

The witch looked determinedly angry at his response. Without pause she pressed on.

'So now then, what of the Seven Chief Priorities,
or have you forgotten them as I presumed you had?'

'Nonsense,' replied the elf.

'The Passover of the Lore,
being the blood of the Lamb;
The Festival of Unleavened Bread,
being fellowship and communion with those of the Lore;
The Festival of First Fruits,
signifying the resurrection from the dead and the continuation of life;
The Festival of Pentecost,
being the coming of the Ghost after 50 cycles;
The Festival of Trumpets,
which is the heralding of the Good News;
The Day of Atonement,
being the cleansing of sin via sacrifice;
The Festival of Tabernacles,
being the return of the Ancient Lore and of the Zaqen.'

Again, Ceriddenne was set standing in amazement. She stood aloof, seething, teeth chattering for her anger, flummoxed by the cheek of the bold, brash elf, who had but half the days of her broomstick. She raised her grim countenance slowly, and when she did again peer at him she wavered neither a jot nor a tittle. Nevertheless, a clammy claw yet made pains to grasp at his piece, and he ripped her sentinel clean from the board.

'There, I believe the tables are now turned; see – now it is I who have you in check! Your straits here seem narrow as the bridge we earlier traversed.'

The imps screeched with delight and there arose a brilliant barrage of burps, a great fanfare of farts, and a noxious gathering of vermin jeering aloud without abashment that all the leaves of the trees parted and the birds within the leaves fell and the worms in the mouths of the birds, which was to be their feed, dropped to the loam as the rain which descends in Dere-den.

'It is your move, O Nag,' Flip charged further, allowing a coy beam to brighten the depths of the meadows. 'And I'll advise you to make it good!'

She rose from her spot, jowls becoming gaunt like the ruddy cheeks of Yseult, mistress of Mark, lover of Tristan, who was once called "Captivator of all Romantic Hearts". Indeed, for she was like none other since the Princesse de Galles, noble Queen of Daearawd, who had fallen foul of evil men in the days of yore. And in like manner were her words crafted…

Then came the final and most significant of questions, ones that all seeking passage must know and be familiar with. Or else one must be a youthful babe, innocent of sin, to have any chance of standing.

'So then, *elf*,' crowed the witch, 'at the juncture of Time and No-Time,
when the Tribulation begins with its signs,
what shall be the Seven Seals for judging sin,
who shall be, who shall have been?'

Thus replied the elf, fixing an evil stare upon the haggard old woman before him:
'I saw when the Lamb opened one of the seals;
and I heard one of the four living creatures saying with a voice like thunder,
"Come and see." And I looked, and behold, a white horse.
He who sat on it had a bow; and a crown was given to him,
and he went out conquering and to conquer.

'When he opened the second seal, I heard the second living creature saying,
"Come and see." Another horse, fiery red, went out.
And it was granted to the one who sat on it to take peace from the earth,
and that people should kill one another;
and there was given to him a great sword.

'When he opened the third seal, I heard the third living creature say,
"Come and see." So I looked, and behold, a black horse,
and he who sat on it had a pair of scales in his hands.
And I heard a voice in the midst of the four living creatures saying,
"A litre of wheat for a day's wage, and three litres of barley for a day's wage;
and do not harm the oil and the wine."

'When he opened the fourth seal,
I heard the voice of the fourth living creature saying,
"Come and see." So I looked, and behold, a pale horse.
And the name of him who sat on it was Death,
and Hades followed behind him.
And power was given to them over a fourth of the earth,
to kill with the sword, with hunger, with death,

225

and by the beasts of the earth...'

The dark man bearing the hooked tool saluted those around him, lest any should forget the authority he wielded at all times in this age. Nevertheless, he kept his face cowled beneath the coarse, dark material of his hood. He it was the destroyer of the dead, the collector of souls.

'When he opened the fifth seal, I saw under the altar the souls of those
who had been slain for the word of God
and for the testimony which they held.
And they cried with a loud voice, saying
"How long, O Lord, holy and true,
until you judge and avenge our blood on those who dwell on the earth?"
Then a white robe was given to each of them;
and it was said to them that they should rest a little while longer,
until both the number of their fellow servants and their brethren,
who would be killed as they were was completed.

'I looked when he opened the sixth seal, and behold,
there was a great earthquake;
and the sun became black as sackcloth of hair,
and the moon became like blood.
And the stars of heaven fell to the earth,
as a fig tree drops its late figs when it is shaken by a mighty wind.
Then the sky receded as a scroll when it is rolled up,
and every mountain and island was moved out of its place.
And the kings of the earth, the great men, the rich men, the commanders,
the mighty men, every slave and free man, hid themselves in the caves
and in the rocks of the mountains, and said to the mountains and rocks,
"Fall on us and hide us from the face of Him who sits on the throne
and from the wrath of the Lamb!
For the great day of His wrath has come, and who is able to stand?"

'When he opened the seventh seal,
there was silence in heaven for about half an hour.
And I saw the seven angels who were to stand before God,
and to them were given seven trumpets.'

'Then what?' cried the witch.
'After what likeness are the sounds of these trumpets...?'

Upon hearing the affliction awaiting both the Sun and the Moon, all those around the chequered board kept their silence. For with the closing of the seasons and the catastrophe that was lurking in the shadows in expectation for the king of Nature, there was very little to celebrate. The dark figure pointed his scythe suggestively towards the elf beneath the glare of the white-decked warrior, as if daring him to continue with his proud antics, double-daring him even. With this last question, the temperature of the inquisition had just been turned up another notch.

'Then,' replied the elf,
'another angel, having a golden censer, came and stood at the altar.
He was given much incense,
that he should offer it with the prayers of all the saints
upon the golden altar which was before the throne.
And the smoke of the incense, with the prayers of the saints,
ascended before God from the angel's hand.
Then the angel took the censer filled it with fire from the altar,
and threw it to the earth.
And there were noises, thundering, lightning and an earthquake.
So the seven angels who had the seven trumpets
prepared themselves to sound.'

'Go on! Tell me what you have seen, show me what will be.'

'The first angel sounded: And hail and fire followed, mingled with blood,
and they were thrown to the earth.
And a third of the trees were burned up,
and all the green grass was burned up.

'Then the second angel sounded: And something like a great mountain
burning with fire was thrown into the sea,
and a third of the sea became blood.
And a third of the living creatures in the sea died,
and a third of the ships were destroyed.

'Then the third angel sounded:
And a great star fell from heaven, burning like a torch,
and it fell on a third of the rivers and springs of water.
The name of the star is *Wormwood*. A third of the waters became wormwood,
and many men died from the water, because it was made bitter.

The mention of Wormwood struck fear into the hearts of Faunus and his reti-nue. Never before had they heard the Last Days expounded in such convincing fashion. Never before had he seen such wisdom reside in the soul of the living. Dressing himself down, he flitted over towards those representing the dead, and within a short while, he was in deep discussion with the leader of their host.

'Then the fourth angel sounded:
And a third of the sun was struck, a third of the moon,
and a third of the stars, so that a third of them were darkened.
A third of the day did not shine, and likewise the night.
And I looked, and I heard an angel flying through the midst of heaven,
saying with a loud voice, "Woe, woe, woe to the inhabitants of the earth,
because of the remaining blasts of the trumpet
of the three angels who are about to sound!"

'Then the fifth angel sounded:
And I saw a star fallen from heaven to the earth.
To him was given the key to the bottomless pit.
And he opened the bottomless pit,
and smoke arose out from the pit like the smoke from a great furnace.
So the sun and the air were darkened because of the smoke from the pit.
Then out of the smoke locusts came upon the earth.
And to them was given power, as the scorpions of the earth have power.
They were commanded not to harm
the grass of the earth, or any green thing, or any tree,
but only those men who did not have the seal of God on their foreheads.
And they were not given authority to kill them,
but to torment them for five months.'

Flip cringed at the very idea. *Imagine,* he thought, *suffering pain far beyond the threshold of endurance yet not being able to pass out, or not being able to pass away.* Such was the fate of those who did not seek the answers of life before the turn of death, of those who shunned the wisdom of the Surps and the courage of the Zaqen.

'Their torment was like the torment of a scorpion,' he resumed,
'when it strikes a man.
In those days men will seek death and will not find it;
they will desire to die, and death will flee from them.
The shape of the scorpions was like horses prepared for battle.
On their heads were crowns of something like gold,
and their faces were like the faces of men.
They had hair like women's hair, and their teeth were like lions' teeth.
And they had breastplates like breastplates of iron,
and the sound of their wings

228

was like sound of chariots with many horses running into battle.
They had tails like scorpions, and there were stings in their tails.
Their power was to hurt men for five months.
And they had as king over them the angel of the bottomless pit,
whose name in Hebrew is Abaddon, but in Greek has the name Apollyon.
One woe is past. Behold, still two more woes are coming after these things.

'Then the sixth angel sounded: And I heard a voice
from the four horns of the golden altar which is before God,
saying to the sixth angel who had the trumpet,
"Release the four angels who are bound at the great river Euphrates."
So the four angels,
who had been prepared for the hour and day and month and year,
were released to kill a third of mankind.
Now the number of the army of the horsemen was two hundred million;
I heard the number of them.'

Now it was the Reaper's turn to make preparations. He had just heard the
prophecy confirmed regarding the final flurry of the End Times and Rapture.
Shortly, many will be due for the gaols below the surface of the earth and beneath the mounds of Krandor, the area of his jurisdiction, and cursed would he
be if his groundwork fell short.

'And thus I saw the horses of the vision:
those who sat on them had breastplates
of fiery red, hyacinth blue, and sulphur yellow;
and the heads of the horses were like the heads of lions;
and out of their mouth came fire, smoke, and brimstone.
By these three plagues a third of mankind was killed –
by the fire, the smoke, and the brimstone which came out of their mouths.
For their power is in their mouth and in their tails;
for their tails are like serpents, having heads; and with them they do harm.
But the rest of mankind, who were not killed by these plagues,
did not repent of the works of their hands,
that they should not worship demons,
and idols of gold, silver, brass, stone, and wood,
which can neither see nor hear nor walk.
And they did not repent of their murders or their sorceries
or their sexual immorality or their thefts.

'Then the seventh angel sounded:
And there was a loud voice in heaven, saying,

"The kingdoms of this world have become
the kingdoms of our Lord and of His Christ,
and He shall reign forever and ever!"
So, for the most testing of inquiries, the seer sung her song.
And it was Flip who was, once again, given the task of a smart rejoinder…
or a callous failure.

'To rend or to sew?
The bowls, the final goal;
Why, who, what, where, when, and how?
Tell me the substance of all these things now!
End the prophecy,
Finish what you see,
Speak of the Zaqen
And talk of the King.'

'The first angel went and poured out his bowl upon the earth,
and a foul and loathsome sore came upon the men
who had the mark of the beast
and those who worshipped his image.

'Then the second angel poured out his bowl upon the sea,
and it became blood as of a dead man;
and every living creature in the sea died.

'Then the third angel poured out his bowl on the rivers and springs of water,
and they became blood. And I heard the angel of the waters saying:

"You are righteous, O Lord,
The One who is and who was and who is to be,
Because You have judged these things.
For they have shed the blood of saints and prophets.
And You have given them blood to drink.
For it is their just due."

'And I heard another from the altar saying, "Even so, Lord God Almighty,
true and righteous are your judgements."

'Then the fourth angel poured out his bowl upon the sun,
and power was given him to scorch men with fire.
And men were scorched with great heat,
and they blasphemed the name of God

who has power over these plagues;
and they did not repent and give Him glory.

'Then the fifth angel poured out his bowl on the throne of the beast,
and his kingdom became full of darkness;
and they gnawed their tongues because of the pain.
They blasphemed the God of heaven because of their pains and their sores,
and did not repent of their deeds.

'Then the sixth angel poured out his bowl on the great river Euphrates,
and its water was dried up,
so that the way of the kings of the East might be prepared.
And I saw three unclean spirits
like frogs coming out of the mouth of the Dragon,
out of the mouth of the Beast,
and out of the mouth of the False Prophet.
For they are the sprits of demons, performing signs,
which go out to the kings of the earth and of the whole world,
to gather them to the battle of that great day of God Almighty.

"Behold, I am coming as a thief.
Blessed is he who watches, and keeps his garments,
Lest he walk naked and they see his shame."

And they gathered them together to a place in Hebrew called Armageddon.

'Then the seventh angel poured out his bowl into the air,
and a loud voice came out of the temple of heaven, saying, "It is done!"
And there were noises and thunderings and lightnings;
and there was a great earthquake, such a mighty and great earthquake
as had not occurred since men were on the earth.
Now the great city was divided into three parts,
and the cities of the nations fell.
And great Babylon was remembered before God,
to give her the cup of the wine of the fierceness of His wrath.
Then every island fled away, and the mountains were not found.
And great hail from heaven fell upon men,
each hailstone about the weight of a talent.
Men blasphemed God because of the plague of the hail,
since the plague was exceedingly great.'

The witch stood up, a diminutive figure dressed in ghastly rags, but a formidable opponent to the best of them. Her wisdom had been grafted into her psyche over many a year to qualify her current status as chief witch. No few trials and torments had beset her paths in the early days, as must come upon all those of her calling. She lifted her voice, as if pleading with the gods for their answers.

'Now then alongside all these things –
When creation is covered with calamity,
When the earth is flooded with iniquity,
When the globe is drowned with His angry wroth –
Please go ahead and tell me…

Who is the Dragon?
Who is the Beast from the Sea?
And who is the Beast from the Earth?
What shall the name be of he who is 666 –
Bring me joy and make my mirth?'

She waited a trice for the resolution to the riddle that one either knew or did not know, for there was little learning that could prepare one to answer such dark mysteries. Only that which is revealed by the gods would suffice this query. But as she stood, the elf's face withered and stretched, all in a moment of time. His eyes grew dark, his face featureless, and his wisdom had become defunct. Thereupon, his pride fell to the ground as the landing of a stone upon the Seven Hills surrounding Dereden. It was then the witch saw that her decisive question was in no way to be solved…

'O Ellyll, ellyll, what shall become of thee poor *ellyll*?'

Flip leapt in – 'But do you know O Witch – what is the answer pray tell. Do not keep such wisdom from me?'

'Who said I knew?' A last fell cackle fell through her cracked lips, though not before she had moved her last black piece in their titanic struggle of wits.

'It is not for me to know such things, seeing that my destiny is already set. It was for you, O Elf, that you might have full counsel before embarking on your unchancy expedition. It seems therefore, that your fate is marked also.'

'If iron sharpens iron
And man sharpens man
Is the man that sharpens the iron
The iron that sharpens the man?

So shine and spark all you iron
Rise and shine all you men

Glow like coals in the darkness
And subdue all you who are sent.'

This the elf heard whisper from the cloying grandstand of bushes and brown-backed leaves.

'Mated,' mocked a voice, as invisible hands felled his king. 'Your *Brenin* is now mine!'

Then the clouds also vanished, she and the faces about her, gleeful in the knowledge that at last one of their own had finally entangled him.

But then came the dawning as the sun burst her glorious carriage through the tree-rafters. And the cocks crowed and the birds sang and the animals of the weald returned to their haunt. Too late was this, however, for poor old Flip; for the foreboding encounter had left the elf shaken and lost and in dire need of his friends.

*

After many leagues of hard riding the veil beyond which the trees succumbed was parted, and distant hives of life and activity once more greeted the ears of the company. Above the panoply of sedges and the smart plants of the *beggar-weed*, sewn to increase the crop of needy natives, there lay, almost perforce, a miry lake running close to the rivulet alongside which they trailed. But fronds fallen to the ground off ferns was yet behove for more news; for not afar north-ward were the grey-crusted mounds of Coed Wig.

Twin to Gyrgon, with a fresh-water lake sleeping below and thrushes carolling tribute to the feeding prey, the spectacle was very great to behold. From this vantage point they would circle in search of a scavenger's meal while the joyous sounds of their neighbours soared high through the ether. The Friends had just traversed this plot riding upon the backs of their faithful mounts and glad were they for such a viewing.

They drew closer towards the next small hamlet, which was blinded by the sudden appearance of stout trees and snaking ridges that skimmed the edges of the earth. But Flip's eyes were opened now and he saw the semblance of men albeit grander in portion and heavier in trunk than even some of the Men of the North who few folk ever saw. He weaned his horse carefully between the cultivated outgrowths lying either side of the road, trying as he might to keep his manner calm even though his heart pounded fiercely.

'Trolls!' he pronounced, pointing indecorously before his companion.

'Cave-dwellers, those ones over there. Probably just finished visiting their cousins dwelling within the hills,' he added, marking out the two locations of which he spoke, the line upon which the troglodytes were carefully descending. 'They look like large ones my friend.'

The elf's own sturdy frame barely stretched past the withers of Vol, to make semblance against the grand creature beneath him, of but the tiniest wingless insect before the glorious moon. Little effect did this have on the beast's steadfast response to his command of authority – for this steed rarely failed to honour the voice of kindly masters, whose persuasion lay not in the gallant thrashing of a horsewhip, but in the gentle, unbroken speech of an *el-lyll.*

Harsh shards and gruesome whips often lay contrariwise to their manner of rearing, having been raised without the flagrant lashes of brutal reins. For it happened that Etheldorians broke their steeds after the manner of their most famed son, Thaelomir the Great, who once dwelt in the sunny provinces of Etheldor. Then, as now, they believed that both mares and stallions, and indeed all manner of bestial quadrupeds and feral birds, were once well able of communicating with the likes of wise men and the more learned of elves. So it was on this basis that Squire Monty the Horse-breaker, a man of some renown, set about subduing the astute creatures by the power of the spoken word which was seldom not accomplished quicker and more effectively than at the hands of the brutal spur.

Believe these things he who may, if not without the fair witness granted. The pair peeled away quietly to the left, Sascha also becoming privy to the horse-runes which they were not reluctant in hearing.

'Easy does it boy,' goaded the elf further, his mind lost on the recent events he had scarcely had the time to talk of in detail. 'Come on boy, the other damned nag is gone now, and with it too her corrupted skill with words. There's no need to worry now, it's all going to turn out just fine,' he whispered soothingly into Vol's right earlobe. 'Trust me...'

He leant closer, his lips falling upon the long, flowing forelock of his steed.

'Easy now, boy, easy. Let us not make more meal of this than we must!'

THE LAND OF THE TROLLS

Nevertheless man, though in honour, does not remain;
He is like the beasts that perish.

PSALMS 49:12

Following the encounter with the witch of Haleg's Weald, their journey through the upland courses had been surprisingly swift. Words were still exchanged but laughter was little more than comfort for the soul, as the horses trundled their way through the ferns and the upland forests. Ice lined the paths of the closet dales, the remnant of the previous winter's chills which had claimed the lives of upwards of twenty trolls. But happy were the hearts as talk drew away from Ceriddenne and her conjuring tricks, Sascha doing his part along with the others, vowing to perform what impossible feats they may to quell Flip's frayed nerves.

After a space in which few words were uttered, the companions fell to complete silence. Their charges took to brooding for all as they continued upon their present winding course. To the east, woodland tumbled away in sheer abandonment, balanced, it seemed, upon a thin wisp of fog sprouting from the furnace of Llöegr and its Three White Lakes. Soon afterwards the scene was replaced with activity as the first trolls appeared, and what a formidable sight they were!

The stuff of ancient fables, a baneful race the Syndicate had only ever heard about from the legends of loremasters – Frydor being their chief exponent – was now revealed before their very eyes. From afar they paid close resemblance to the barbaric cavemen in the days of yore. As they drew closer, however, some seemed in possession of their wits. The Friends rode on at a steady pace led by Frydor the Elf, glancing at the trolls ever and awhile to see if their presence there would be a welcome one.

They were stalwart creatures for the most part. Beneath their brusque manes of hair, their hirsute skin, that wart-laced body of crinkled covering, lay between four and five cubits of green flesh, mostly muscle, by which they crushed men, fought bears and held at bay intruders from behind the dark hills of Dereden. The elves, being fully knowledgeable of these facts, paid due diligence not to rouse their hosts more than was necessary. Their gait continued at an even tread.

'They look quite big from over here don't they? I mean like kind of threatening if you ask me... So what, are they friendly people then Flip?' Sascha nudged his helmsman for a response.

'To call them *people* my dear is a bit of an overstatement,' Flip replied in no uncertain terms. 'No, but trolls are unique in their own right,' the elf resumed, relaxing back on the reins as he spoke, seemingly recovered from the frightful encounter which he'd had not so long beforehand. 'They are a strange and varying breed. Some are good, some are bad, but most, like with any people, are indefinable.'

They rode alone along the spoor, through the dingle, allowing Vol to navigate his own way across the tortuous trail. He read the lie of the land as easily as he could the sullen clouds which lay overhead.

'In truth a few of them were good once, great in valour and mighty in deed, rendering many a worthy exploit from shore to shore. Much evil blood was shed, even by the ancient ruins of Caer Gyrgon, beneath the Enchanted Gates herself.'

'So what became of them?' Jemimah called back, having overheard what was said. 'Why are they all cooped up by themselves in the middle of nowhere then, living so base and unsophisticated lives?'

Knowing her mind beforehand, the younger elf smiled inwardly. His way was clear, with the open-bracken hillside extending towards the wasteland, and at once, his horse broke into a cantor which soon became a gallop. Jemimah, in no mood for missed responses, soon had her charge on the go also, levelling similar inquiries to the fleeing elf. It was only at the Ford of Eïswr that he slowed again, until it seemed that the lightness of the steed beneath him could not be maintained.

'Is that not it then, Jemimah? You have the answer yourself, do you not?' Flip said encouragingly. 'For over the years, the number of them who were corrupted by the temptations common to man increased greatly...' Sascha looked back on his horse, smiling irritatingly as though such knowledge, though of no great consequence, he would in no wise share. It was something he knew that she did not – and rare was it that such grounds could be claimed!

Presently Jemimah's rosy cheeks became flustered, as she flung them a whole host of new problems. 'Flip!' she cried again, not wanting to lose her momentum. 'Talk to me.'

This time the elf did slow down, if only to put her out of her misery.

'Of course, however, those that were neither good nor bad, but fashioned their behaviour as was befitting, were by far the most numerous – like the numbers of any folk. Save perhaps for the dwarves – they seem to carry more than their fair share of the Sons of Belial, believe you me.'

'Son's of Belial?' queried Jemimah, a blank look inscribing itself like ink across her face.

'Sons of... Sorry, I assumed I was talking to Alicia. Sons of Belial – What you may call Sons of Bitches basically. Anyway, we cannot afford to harbour such fears, if we are to make this adventure a success...' But she sensed that he had not ridden so hard and so fast to escape her petitions, probing though they were. Indeed, she saw him withdraw into the cloisters of his habit, his face first and then his mind. Beyond them, an immense mountain towered upwards into the clouds above, where she thought Flip's memories lay at present.

Frydor caught this also, letting rip his reins as the rugged chain of rocks fell away to his right. 'Yes, my nephew is correct. Pluck up your hearts, let us neither faint nor fear, for the time of fulfilment is near.' He allowed his kinsman to recede back to that place of dread – whether in life or in the Spirit-world he knew not, but he reckoned it good medicine whilst the pressures of battle was not yet upon them.

'We venture this route out of utmost necessity, and not for any vainglorious institution it must be said. And forge onwards we shall, deep into the hinterland of these here timberlands, until, hopefully, we meet with our desired troll. Perhaps then we elves shall meld our hand a little more clearly...'

The groans abounded within the company, Nywdog taking the opportunity to pluck the boils that had developed, rather uncomfortably, between his groins and beneath his armpits.

'Know for certain, my friends, that there are many reasons why trolls may wish to live out here in the wilderness. Not all of them I am proud of as an elf, I must say!'

Ears pricked up as the youngsters, by now becoming aware of the cursory nature of the elves, sensed another good tale in the offing. Eleanor asked, quite sensibly, whether or not he had ever had any dealings with the trolls and, if so, whether or not he would mind sharing such an occasion. Frydor continued on past the present hamlet, driving Pegasus, that sure-footed steed, out onto the floor of the mountain canopy, into the midst of a narrow vale, which was roofed over by a dark, hanging mist.

When he was sure that no idle ears would be listening he pulled back on the horse's bridle, bringing his petulant mare to a standstill. By now she too had perceived the onset of austere weather before them, and indeed, the stringent hands that were beckoning them on to challenge it was she eager to refuse. Frydor, however, regarded adversity as little more than adventure, obstacles as mere building blocks of character. He would not be hindered so early on in his pursuits. Nonetheless, the elf proceeded carefully, fuelling their desire all the more, choosing the ascent which soon became rough and rugged, so much so that for a space of an hour or so, they were obliged to dismount and heave their charges upwards with what valour they may.

Accepting the gauntlet lain before them, the rest of the party followed at a more grudging pace. Clouds seeped heavy at the seam, brims filled to the bursting, bellows billowing with fullness. The sky was ashen, the embodiment of a bitter season, suspended in solitary clusters compressed somewhere in the Middle-sky, Frydor guessed. It was not an immediate threat, he reckoned, but it was something yet to watch out for.

Winds blew frostily from the east and south, rearing a fresh ticklish bite, which was raw on the skin, cracking blisters, patching faces, though scarcely enough to prevent the diligent press onwards. Those marching forwards were a brave folk, none more so than Frydor, who understood well the magnitude of the ascent laid before him. But they forged on as a company past the maze of winding narrow glens, through endless swamplands, eventually falling upon the large lake at the base of Bryn Golan – those clear blue waters, which every season, does not fail its full quota of salmon and flat-backed fishes.

After another short space they came to within sight of a small collection of hamlets. Frydor took hold of his horn and placed it to his lips, sounding a long clear note, whose echoes sailed gladly through the winds, cwm to cliff, crag to crag, all about the mountain-side which now hemmed them about. The sounds died away in the distant crevices, corries that existed passed the woods amid the Dales of Eryione. Hopes were high at present as thoughts quickly turned inwards, away from the buffeting strokes of wind that played unkindly upon their pockmarked skins. At present, none was there who would refuse any feed for their famished stomachs.

Anxious glances continued to attend their journey for a good while to come. Trembling at the unwanted attention, the Friends yet managed to trudge a few paces further, steps unbroken, monotonous, sparkling white precipice on the hinterland fixing gazes and chilling stares. They came off the grassy hill-side, curiosity it was now, more than anything else, gleaning unsubtle gazes. A company of men and elves was not always welcomed in the Dales of Eryione, or anywhere adjoining the Fallen Ridge. Jaws dropped, limbs ached, hearts pounded faster, and the sheen on the swords began to glisten.

Jemimah trotted on briskly, Sascha hard at her heels, hooves kicking up swathes of mud from the once dainty grasslands. From all around came the sounding of horns and the baying of hounds, as if the quarry had just become the prey. But the path towards the centre of the village remained unbroken, with men, bold and battle-scarred, standing aside the slippery path to allow their weary visitors to pass on through unhindered.

Pegasus, however, was in no great hurry. She led her company to the lush wayside grasses which provided foliage for their empty stomachs, before passing on through the conflagration of stern faces. Sustenance ended, she knew what was required of her. She drew her equine retinue near to the largest and most prominent hut.

*

Standing on its own isolated mound before them was the hut, and outside the hut a pair of trolls, and inside the hut and warmly wrapped in a hide skinned of a roaming boar, was another dour troll, garbed with a poisoned reek of death, cunning in design and fearsome in strength. Behind this setting was a trailing skirt of rain, closing in on the homestead. It was towards this scene that Marcus presently cast his stare, thoughts of the vales of his origin freeing him from the stifling stench of his company. After the heavy meal of the previous eve, his bones were already weary. And as he, too, approached the wooden stockades which fenced in the coop, it could be seen that his spirit was also dulled; all results of the arduous trek which had not yet ended.

The remainder of The Syndicate was even more reluctant to move at present – the hundred squalid souls before them made for no enticing prospect. Nonetheless, as they gazed in wonder at the splendid spectacle afar off, atop of the Fallen Ridge, they allowed their charges to be guided to rest by the hands of the village stewards and attendants, some of whom carried tilling-forks, others wielding brown-bodied herfs, sharp as a blade.

Judging by the huge mounds of flesh tucked coarsely beneath the garments of those around them, most of those arrayed before them were females, but it was not always easy to tell. There was silence outside the house as the horses finished their last few treads. The last scuffling footsteps could be heard closing in on the friends, as the giant form of a debased man unwound himself about the earthen mounds about his pen.

'And w'at is it you want, elf?' scoffed the portly troll, turning sharply towards Frydor. 'Why 'ave you and your retinue chosen such a fair day to visit us with your troubles? And w'at ails you dis time dat you and all these mice should be taking an interest in trollish lands?' Frydor paused, allowing the indolent cloud which had accompanied them for much of the journey to lull overheads. Then he, in turn, addressed the gathering.

'We were travelling through from southward out yonder and for the *sturfiness* of the day became dazed in the trail by the Brook of Salmon's Ridge. Then we lost one another for a space, alighting afterward in the midst of some thorny brakes and trestled thickets and dense leaves so lush that men with it could line the ribs of a great coracle.'

'And therefore w'at?' remarked the other callously. 'The Brook of Salmon's Ridge lies over ten leagues from 'ere, over 'ills and winding tracks and across the Waters of Brythan's Neck. I t'ank you for telling me da truth, O Elf. But come to it now Puny One; w'at is the reason for you visiting our 'umble dwellings in this part of the forests, elf? W'at is it you want? Come to it and 'astily and do not make me weary with your presence!'

'Ah, I desire no less!' the wise-elf returned quickly.

Turning slightly askance from his inquisitor, he motioned generously with his hands, so that any perceptive viewer might see that he bore no secret arms. Elves were long suspected of being able to perform curious arts, and such wisdom was graven upon the pages of "The Art of Trollish Warfare". But Frydor was wont to continue;

'It happened upon our venture that we came upon the Old Hag of the Forests, Ceriddenne the Conjurer, Queen of Evil in Haleg's Weald, and she challenged us in her corrupt ways, with the Seven Foul Questions of Passage. Well, perhaps not myself, but my nephew there certainly, whose word I can generally trust as my own.' He nodded towards Flip who was even now drawing his horse up alongside.

'Such and such went the encounter as he searched for herbs for our friend's tiredness…' It was then that the trolls first took in the poorly condition of the Breastplate-bearer. 'This all left us at a bit of a loose ends, for our souls were spent for the amazement of his telling. So we thought perhaps of chancing upon some friendly trolls in these here lands, than the uncouth barbarians who resided in the darkness of the weald out there…' The wily elf winked at his nephew; 'We have needs that you may be able to fulfil, my friends. Perhaps you can aid our passage northward? But first we should need to replenish our strength after such an engaging tryst!'

Tension mounted amidst the trolls as few there could remember the last time when an elf had been so bold in his speech towards them. Many were the relations, solemn were the oaths, and great had been the revelries between men and elves, trolls and Surps, since days gone by. But goodly receptions nowadays seldom brought about lasting kinship between the two races; seldom and at great cost. Therefore the troll looked disturbed.

'W'at?' he cried aloud. 'You try to fool us with the myth of that old nag… and count us less savage dan the barbarians of da Weald? Say dat dis is not so elf, that such a distinguished one as you appear could make such a false assumption.' Gjugg, the troll, appeared to be almost insulted. 'I defy you to say such a thing again!'

Observing his ungodly surroundings edging closer to their steeds, Frydor, politely, declined. 'I could never be so hasty, Master-Troll.' Instead, he dismounted Pegasus and made swift his hands upon Nywdog's shins and Alicia's shanks, whose dark presence had not gone altogether unnoticed. His poor mind weary, he still possessed wits enough to use the same hand, unbuckling the strap that kept tight his sword before laying it down gently in the dust.

'Forgive me for my impertinence,' Frydor added again, a faint smile on his lips.

'Well… just be on your way den, Elf – no 'arm done, eh?'

*

Busy beneath the broiling stew, the mistress of the chief trollsman, Miche, withdrew a lethal dose of her mortal concoction, quickly emptying the contents into her large, voluminous mouth. To the broth of hazel-leafs and skinned swine had been added a clutch of lentils and basil, plucked from the forests of Gwyn. Words of Blessing had not yet been pronounced upon the foods so it was not safe to chew even a mouthful in the presence of strangers. But once the holy utterance had been invoked, the cauldron would then be as plentiful as the meal made by Joshua the Jew, when the fish and bread were multiplied for five thousand folk and their kinsmen, and as choice as the meats of the Elysium Fields, which is the most blessed of flesh anywhere within the world. Without disturbing further her molten froth Michelle hopped over the hedgerows, rather nimbly for a troll, and was presently to be found in the company of Frydor's distinctive white-locked mount.

At once her eyes filled with admiration for Pegasus and her wonderful pale mane of hair. The mare, in turn, was not loth to such due deference, allowing her neck to sag in honourable appreciation, receiving the tribute not far off from the bear-breasted, beer-bellied wench. Raising her eyes a few more times, she welcomed the gesture for a short space, though it was not too long before she felt cloyed by this licentious welcome.

'We don't want you 'ere, elf, so kindly be on your way. Your folk have brought on us more adversity than ever a demon could even wish!' Two fit guardsman raised aloft their hefty cutlasses, which immediately brought wave upon wave of regret returning to Frydor for having earlier laid down his own trusty side-piece. 'And make your journey quick… and take your silly brood of falsehoods with you, O Calamitous Elf.'

'That's Frydor, please, if you don't me interrupting!'

'I couldn't care less if your name was Fels–' Hushed whispers rose from the gathered faces. 'Well I couldn't care less anyway.'

'Frydor the Surp, in fact.'

There were more hushed whispers beneath the leaden skies.

'Frydor you say? A Surp?'

A lightening streak, equal to the first bolt that divided the waters from the waters, sliced across the heavens.

'Yes that's right,' Frydor confirmed. 'At your service,' he said, proffering the larger man the clasp of his hand. He bowed down deeply upon feeling the touch of the troll's grimy skin. 'And on behalf of my party many apologies for arriving so unexpectedly. I am sure…'

'Well… Surp or no Surp, you're still not having any part of our possession,' Miche growled hotly. 'You're lucky even now to still be alive! I do not believe the foolish rumours, Frydor, that it was once *your* folk which fought valiantly amongst our members unto grim death, indeed, that it was one of your forefathers who led the Slaughter of the Orcs' Nest about the hills round Englewood.'

'For afterwards w'en da dust had settled,' Gjugg resumed, 'we suffered such defeat and continued misfortune not ever seen in dese 'ere parts, and yea, certainly not by any weedy elf. An' some of us even believe that compared to us you elves 'ave 'ad t'ings easy!'

The Syndicate looked to be all rather confused at this last statement. Scant was their knowledge of such events, past distant horizons, preceding time's beginning, before life had begun for most. Presently, in his exile of despair, he gazed upwards and outwards, so that the tears, which soon coursed down his face, were found to be indistinguishable from the rainwater that plashed about his puckered cheeks. Yet seeing himself in such stern company (let alone the shameful eye cast him by his wife), he set himself to quelling his rising tides of emotion.

> "Does a troll make a choice on what he has not heard?
> Or does he permit them a voice so that perhaps he can learn?"

This unwelcome interruption came from another striking troll, a rare match to Gjugg-trol; in fact it was Gjagg, his half-brother.

'Gjagg-son, w'at is it dat you want, undoing my sovranty in a way befitting of fools. You have shamed me in front of da people and have done a t'ing that ought not be done. Explain yourself, my kinsman, lest my wroth boil over.'

Even now the cursed Gjagg-son was enumerating the numerous transgressions of his brother; an act which was to prove greatly displeasing to the village chief.

'My brother, do you not remember the wise saying of David-son, king of the Iddew:

> "Does a troll make a choice on what he has not heard?
> Or does he permit them a voice so that perhaps he can learn?"

'Of course I do, Gjagg-son, but to speak thus before my people embarrasses me; so for dis cause, I pronounce your home desolate, your seed degenerate, and your wares departed.'

To which the wiser made reply: 'And to you, little brother, may the pride about your neck choke you.'

Gjugg-son: 'May da bard of Dogfael order a satire of shame, stain and blemish upon your name, both now and forevermore.'

Gjagg-son: 'May the wizard of Wardael do likewise, beginning with the crown of your head unto the soles of your feet, taking in all the fat, blubbery bits in between.'

Gjugg-son: 'May your face become dat of a swinging-ape, and may your stomach sprout udders.'

Gjagg-son: 'May the orcs come from out yonder, and remove your wife, your children, your mistress' (at which point Michelle looked decidedly alarmed), 'your host, and your leadership – if the word should be deemed fitting.'

Gjugg-son: 'May your body be mangled by your enemies, your limbs be spread across wastelands, your bones come food for scroungers, and your flesh become forage for birds.'

Gjagg-son: 'May swine come to your grave at the appropriate time, and dig up your remnant in an inappropriate way, and chomp on your pieces till their teeth all but fail.'

Gjugg-son: 'May your body suffer bloating, bursting and disfigurement, all at da selfsame instant.'

Gjagg-son: 'And the same upon your mother when she gives birth to her next alien.'

Gjugg-son: 'May your daughters be infested with leeches, your wife with worms, and might demons bedevil that old witch whom you call mother!'

Gjagg-son: 'Hum kah chan.' (Death to your family!)

Gjugg-son: 'Chao ni niang de zhu zong shi ba dai.' (Go have sex with your ancestors, grandmothers and great-grandmothers!)

And this, amongst the Troll-folk, was one of the Seven Ill Curses.

Therefore, to show that this mar was not to his liking, Gjagg-son returned in anger and in wroth from whence he had received his inspiration and sat down in a daze, contemplating angrily how he might deface the name of his brother whilst at the same time, nullify this grim cursing. Choosing wisely a servant whom he kept bound in chains, he ordered her thrashed mightily with a cat of nine tails, her nipples squeezed of her milk that she might no longer give suck to her spawn, her hairs plucked out from her private bits, and her arms pierced with spears, so that, by this pious affliction, the last blasphemy upon his name might be removed, never to be recalled again.

Nevertheless, Gjugg remained confused for his brother's lofty counsel. His reverie soon turned to more trivial matters: the earlier days of his im-maturity, before these ill times of waste and travail when times were easy as their lady-folk. *Why, why, why O Gods had I not been astute as Gjagg-son in those intimate days, and understood more than the elementary principles of* finger-and-toe *arithmetic.* The villagers along with the Syndicate were await-ing his final decision.

He had made it to village chief, at length, which was no small honour for the bitter rivalry which often took hold of such crafting. Through an amalgam of his uncompromising attitude, not to mention the strictly limited intellectual capacity of the other hundred or so souls in his village, he had excelled above his peers. Even his brother, whose distresses were now being comforted by the reverent screams he heard of the wench, had failed to achieve as much. But within this fair vocation compelling decisions did still sometimes have to be made.

The Chief peered at the expectant faces of the onlookers, who gazed back at him with no less vigour. They looked to him to be wise – or at least wise as a *trol* could be. Or else they would look to his favoured brother, Gjagg-son, for the leadership which ought to be both wise and fair. He was the one to bring laughter to the sad, joy to the maid, babies to the impregnable; the one who at times got them through the miserable moments by raising one or two chuckles, sometimes. And he looked again and saw Marcus, limpid as sallow waters, the run of some disease or other coursing through his veins.

Such great men need not know all that must be known, but only that which passes them on from one moment to the next. He could sense an atmosphere of unease about him on the glade, and this murmur stole upon him like Modd the Light-fingered, whose stealth they say was borrowed of Lucifer, formerly the Light-bearer of Nef. He saw that his moment had come and if he did not achieve his calling now, would he ever? He must consider all fairly, without sway, without partiality, before arbitrating on Trollish law: then must their food be shared, their swords be sharpened, fresh staves be hewn asunder, and whichever one, according to the truth of their telling. Not even their Most Wayward Brother would miss such an occasion for sport, if it came to it. At the moment there seemed to be no need to kill them.

One shouted, 'Master Gjugg, what of the Great Code of the Troll Most Learned?' which thing each was expected to have learned in his youth. His face became flustered again, pink as the setting sun. And it was at that time he caught his brother emerging again to cause more mischief:

"Does a troll make a choice on what he has not heard?
Or allow them a voice so that perhaps he can learn?"

But before his kinsman could speak another word, Gjugg had already decided.

'Prepare them something for the road,' he snarled. 'But no chicken. There shall be no chicken for the falsifiers!'

And with that all thereabouts, even Gjagg himself, lauded him greatly for his wise resolution.

*

The wind was stilled in another part of the world, for as suddenly as it had arisen was it gone. In its place came a thick bank of fog rolling over the battlements in between the Seven Dark Hills of Dereden. With it came screaming hosts of The Otherworld, as men swarmed howling over the ramparts in multiform devil-hosts. Drills for a real campaign were taken seriously in these parts as, all too often in these worlds, one's life and honour oft depended upon such outcomes.

One band tore through the barriers of the eastern gateway, penetrating the labyrinth which hemmed the kitchens about and their roar clashed with another host who were gathered to the sturdy column beneath the central tower. And it was below these tall pillars that dawn ever failed to break, so that Oppression seemed only to marvel at its own handiwork.

Grey fog encircled those palisades from dusk till dawn, all year round, and will do so from the beginning of time even till when the world has its ending. And no goodness shone either from within the castle grounds or from without. Dark, dank and dismal. Whose were the walls in the lowest keep in all Dereden? What were the tall black buildings that brought birds to bear? But beneath the grey loam, a most important meeting was taking place.

'So how many did you see then slave? One? Two? Three perhaps?'

'Eight in all *mast-ter*,' the messenger hissed.

'Eight? – The number troubles me! What great mysteries have been unravelled by use of the number eight?

Thirteen often on evil days
Twelve even at our hostings of mighty warriors bent in depraved ways
Again sometimes to draw the sword in defence of their Lord
The thirteenth noble Son of War.

Ten with which we count
And ten with which we number
And seven the cycle of men's recital
The days of graft and slumber.

Six, the number of days for travail and toil
The sum of millennia from dust to soil.
But eight? What means eight?
The figure of eight, which I hate, what means the number eight?

'So what say you, Fool?'

'I do not know *mast-ter*, for your wisdom is too great for me.' (At which the other looked pleased at his servant's obsequiousness.) 'But one had the likeness of a Surp, two were elves, and three were *womb-men*!'

'So why did you not bring me this news sooner, knowing these things are for certain?'

'*Mast-ter*, as soon as I was able, I came into your presence with my report. And indeed, did I not sense them carrying harsh weapons with which to deal justice and exact retribution, such that I have rarely seen in all Krandor? Moreover, there is nothing anywhere on our records of the Surp and these, his *fool-lish* associates. Nothing *mast-ter*, absolutely nothing have I seen!'

The master was not pleased. He was not pleased at all. He wanted to know more. He needed to know much more. As he pondered the mysteries held within the cage of his servant's bosom, his heart began throbbing as a thousand tribal drums out on the plains of Blacklands, at the mere mentioning of these strange curs. But for what fey reason his nerve galled him, he was not yet able to perceive.

'So what did they look like? Were they valiant? Which ones failed to have the mark of corruption upon their brow? Answer me slave. Perhaps indeed they were religious mongrels from the Northern Shires, as those perfidious Manchumen who dwell to the east of the Mainland? Speak, fool!'

But even as the goblin began to speak, his mind was cast back further still, till he began to view once again the things he had previously seen…

*

The discussions over dinner were varied, if not always trivial: What had caused the upsurge of violence in Yesteryear? Who was ultimately to blame for it? What had become of *their* troll brothers who had hidden themselves in the outlying regions? Such were the questions thrown into the air for moot. There they sat, the other relevant line of prattle, which was the responsibility of the Elves towards the Big Folk, becoming apparent by its omission by those of all sides. None were there able to talk on such matters openly lest the response yielded cast shame and blemish upon the accuser.

So great were the persecutions of those days that even the Light Elves from Hafgod, under the command of King Elffllyn III, fled far and fast in the thick of bitter conflict. Like summer locusts was the manner of their decampment, in numbers far beyond reckoning, from the shores of Medennin to the Land of Engels and its Two Dark Valleys. They had spread out north, south, east, west, the land becoming a blur of bodies, a blight of fear-stricken elves, whose valour was seldom doubted by their foemen. Nonetheless, those who did reach the coasts without the stain of blood on his hands were soon labelled *alltud* – a dark and unkindly term for true, blue-blooded elves.

It was a long hot evening, beset by many a trial and torment, before they gained one another's confidence. Both Frydor and his nephew, Flip, posed neutral questions to Gjugg and his brother Gjagg (who were still barely able to tolerate each other), and the trolls did likewise. Apolitical inquiries lacking the power to indict any particular race as the guilty faction became the norm:

neither the Elves, nor the Dwarves, or even the Men Folk. Over the process of time however this line of prattle began to ripen, whilst the sweetened mead began to loosen tongues and lessen inhibitions. Then came the drink a snare, arguments swiftly ensuing with blood-feuds till the third and fourth tenth generation being established at the mere tilting of a goblet.

Time passed, the lays of larks resounding quietly in the soft auburn breeze. The distant humming in the weald of Merdoch lay at odds with the festive board bashing of the revellers. At length however a rather unseasonable question asked by a troll of Flip roused further the dying embers.

It was suggested that the elves should consider somewhat more earnestly the fate of their most famed king, Elffllyn, and whether, at the time of the famous battle of Ypresein, he was, in fact, up to it. Now this unfair inquisition, by way of Calhavar the Carnal (who was highly ill-favoured, even amongst the trolls), insinuated that not only did the Elfin-king fail in his duty in securing the victory, but that he had absconded for a pretty wench kept sealed in his cloisters in the heart of his Castle at Anglesey. This trite saying brought much ill-repute upon the Elves as a race of noble warriors. The King did not flee, according to Calhavar, for the overwhelming opposition he was facing. Apparently, he had sworn an oath underneath the *uchelwdd* at the passing of the previous Kalan Yule that he would return to this wench before any foul injury might blemish his skin or restrict his movements beneath the bed-covers.

Calhavar continued in his guttural; 'Was it not merely an elf-youth that led one of your fiercest armies, and as such a mere child not properly weaned in the ways of war, one who was taken easily to the care of white-limbed, lily-livered damsels, who like to play at footsie beneath down-sheets?'

Nevertheless, it happened, when asked to spell out his inference and explain this mar upon the king's name (whose appellation is praised in courts all round Elfery) that the rambunctious old troll in no wise responded adequately. Instead, grasping at the leg of a roasted boar with one hand and obtaining purchase over a slightly-less-hideous-than-average troll-woman with the other, he made stern efforts to consume them both while gesticulating wildly that he was in no fit state to answer such banalities, and that the elves themselves should consult the constellations, spill their own entrails, or pay for the service of druids, a few of which he might be willing to recommend...

*

Aside from this restive creature there were a few others around the table who were worthy of note: the two mistresses of Gjagg and Gjugg, who were summoned daily by the names of Michelle (Miche) and Lindsay; Calhavar's fair minx, Ebola of Hores; and there was a *transtrol* whom the others referred to as Ottoman the Wise.

It was he who soon gathered that Calhavar, his warrior friend, had earlier been jesting when he mentioned the name of Elffllyn, although not without serious intent. Thereupon, such responses befitting a potentially ugly incident were made, especially upon seeing Calhavar maintaining his foolish guffawing about the revered former prince of Elfdom. With wily teases he made good semblance to a rowdy troll, showing himself to be but a disguised wolf-hound dressed in a bear's outfit, to which not a few of the visitors applauded his creativity with rapt applause and keen expressions.

Then upon seeing the gaiety of the newcomers and Ottoman's twisted countenance, and being that he was somewhat slower than the other head trolls about the festive-board, Calhavar mistook his company greatly. For he assumed them to be cheering for some ready wit proffered by the unseemly form of Nywdog, who, also with goblet in hand and bones of shank spouting forth from his mouth, made fair semblance to a mongrel trained in the hounding of friends, the devouring of fiends and the defecation of premises.

Now being somewhat more astute than his younger brother, Gjagg did not fail to encourage him in such beliefs, lest the combination of wine and wench provoke his friend towards even greater indignation. Then they would really have it. Tables would be upturned, knives drawn, he would thereafter slay each of their guests, making spoil of the food in the process; a matter which all would sincerely hope to avoid.

Thus of all seated bar the two elves, Ottoman was doubtless the most learned. For he was a *transtrol*, which meant that he was at least one-fourth troll, the rest being a mixture of all hybrids beneath the sun, whether fair-weather or foul. In this case his part was human. (It is said that a marauding band of troll-mistresses, banished by their husbands for some unproven infidelities, or indeed for their failure to ever please their masters when offered the chance, ravished his father!) And so it happened, at the time of life, that his mother gave birth to him whom was sat there that day.

But be that as it may, the days from his abandonment till his early manhood were still mysteries at present. They say that the Surps of Pöesy-Gothan had found him, wrapped up warmly in swaddling clothing by the great river-lake Hafren. Thus it was from them that he gleaned his eminent understanding of the Lore. Albeit, others yet maintain that a coven of spellbinders had discovered him in the Year of Arreg Yr Laith, in the month of Ebrill, which happened to be the correct month and year in which all black witches anywhere within the shires swear to do only good to those whom they encounter. And had he not been found on the last day of that month when the sun was setting for the day? And fortunate was he again for seldom has this solemn event transpired since the beginning of Creation.

But conjectures aside, those that knew Ottoman well said that his skill with the broadsword and his way with words were no less than a Man from the

North could exhibit in battle. Therefore, it was held by some that it was one of them, a Man of the North – who come in oft times surreptitiously to protect The Foreigner, The Oppressed, The Needy, The Widower, The Orphan – that found him. They say that these *men* tended to him kindly, teaching him the ways of his goodly ancestors, both troll and man.

For Ottoman nevertheless these things were still as a fey dream with many ghostly players. At his own telling, he had the misfortune of suffering an accident in his early manhood years when he fell off the back of a griffin which he had found napping one day. Sustaining grave memory-loss (and not a few broken bones), he was soon transported into the strange world of Dreams and Visions.

There had been an up-side however. To further apprehend the trollish ways he had chosen to live the life of a hermit, living off the fat of the land and off the flesh of sheep, and off other four-legged quadrupeds which he sometimes managed to pilfer from careless herdsmen. After another short space he was embraced as a novelty by a good-natured bunch of trolls, the like of whom he had never before had the pleasure to dwell with. Then, having been accepted into their fold, he subsequently rose high in their regard, displaying such bold exploits against the orcs and other fell intruders that made trolls wonder at his origin in amazement.

Moreover, Ottoman truly was far more perceptive than the normal serf could fathom. For even now was he suspecting of the Troop's visitation. They were not just "passing through" as they had theretofore affirmed. Nonetheless, for the sake of the idle ears still present, he had kept his peace for the moment, choosing wisely to keep his observations to himself. But his heart waxed warm for the eating of the Elves and the feasting of their Friends, as though they were friends of a forgotten era, who had recently strolled back into his presence.

There was a world beneath them he could see, and one high above which they hoped to attain; and not without his help would it come. He lingered after every word spoken by the noble Frydor and laughed heartily at Nywdog's buffoonery, who continued to act the idiot by way of his shameful consummation and base mannerisms. But it was not without reason that his breast responded kindly to their unsightly ways.

A FEAST FIT FOR KINGS

And I say to you that many will come from east and west,
And sit down with Abraham, Isaac, and Jacob in the kingdom of heaven.

MATTHEW 8:11

Another feasting, meanwhile, was attended by the noblest magnates from within Krandor's vast bounds. Those lands represented stretched from the Port of Wreckers right through to the northern shores of Krakôuz and the Isle of Syn which lies eastward of the small colony sometimes called The Fateful Islands. Its breadth was measured from across the plains of Badlands with its Two Evil Valleys right through to the double doors of Dereden. Presently, many were they who gathered to sit at the table of the Great Lord of Wroth.

They were men mostly that had the honour of sitting at the table of the Prince of Gwr as he was most commonly known, but no ordinary men would he allow to frequent his inner courts. Of winters there was none with fewer than fifty to his name. Of battles the least of them was Yorath mab Grêyndrwl, who slew one hundred and seventeen men at one time when rebel Clay-orcs had penned him into a field of lilies, and only ceased from his slaughter when his hand clung fast to his sword, by which time his army had returned to plunder. Of evil him who was considered lowliest was Llohwryn the Virulent by whose hand upwards of five hundreds chaste mothers met their death and their young ones with them for not dashing their babes against the Rock of Lleidr – and some of these even within the womb. Of rank there was none less than the one for whom was ever a place reserved, though seldom was it in occupancy, for the blemish that waxed sore upon his skin. For this one was three-fourths goblin and one-fourth human which made him unsightly as a warthog, and so would his line be till at least the twelfth generation of interbreeding between his spawn and the fairest dames from the Regions of the Blessed, whose lands begin northwards of the Waters of the Gods.

Thirteen was their number in all, including the warthog, Suntribo, sooner sent on errands upon the back of his fearless black-winged creature to espy those things he ought to know. Nevertheless, that numbering included the Prince of the Courts himself, who is the one who sits in the chief seat between the Two Balls Of Faith: one being *Ty Gwydr*, the other actually bearing resemblance to a weathered skull, which resided as rests for his stout arms.

Thus eleven were there presently found before him round the table which could at most hold six and twenty (for the Council members and their partners). And of damsels there were none, save for those of the fosterage of Carilorhn the Monk, and those altered into the guise of women by Blakthawn, Druid of the Keep. Their sum numbered five or six depending upon whether Sofia, Daughter of Runes, as she had come to be known as, could be accredited with sufficient feminine virtues.

Of face there was none more beautiful than her supping through mead-horns at the high-table, for rosy-coloured and fair were her cheeks when the morning chill brought blood towards the surface of her skin. Regarding breasts, there was none so lush and none so large save for that of Baborina whose bottom was perched opposite, who fortunate men swore was not born of any known seed, neither man, nor elf or dwarf. They said that it was she whose bosoms had pummelled the potholes deep in the road running course to Styx, when rear-venturing escorts climbed aback her for a long night of seedy lovemaking beneath the moonlit glades of Meréden. And of acorns was there never a smoother entry than the passage into Sofia, swiftly followed by a most succulent embrace.

But of shanks and lower-limbs was there never seen skin so green, scales so harsh, and boils so wanton of dispersion that men who ever sought to suckle upwards from her legs towards her golden arches, amid a cruel and stormy night blackened for the shadows cast of the bower, were quickly drowned in trauma for the taste hastily bestowed upon their tongues. No few men suffered their death in this manner.

It was said by the sages of yore and by erudite loremasters that this came about for the drowsiness one day of the druid Blakthawn. They say that, at the end of a long and arduous day of tutoring some would-be magicians and wizards and sorcerers in the pagan arts, he had made haste to convert the foul form of a beast presented him for punishment into another comely wench to be housed inside one of the king's harems. Nevertheless before his incantations and screaming and bloodletting were through he had fallen asleep in the bush past the approach beyond the moat, underneath a sacred mistletoe tree. When he had come to moreover he could in no wise remember the formulae which he had conjured about the indisposed creature before him. All wisdom had vanished, and no amount of diligence could bring back such knowledge.

Thus what was once a *bwystfil* was now a near *alltud* condemned to walk, bathe and make love with the hem of her kirtle never raised above the floors of palaces. And it was only in the deepest darkness that she parted her legs at all!

*

At the lower board men made merry with their maids as serving wenches passed between seething cauldrons and guzzling snouts, carrying upon platters of finest gold and choice silver loins and rumps and shanks of roasted boar, and for the lesser, hooves and peppered tripe, stripped from inside a head of oxen. Valiant was the talk as gobbets of pig carved from hogs spitting in the middle hall were consumed amid large quaffs of mead and ale.

Goblins, proud of neck, were sat in the northwestern corner of the hall, and mighty men gathered amongst themselves making joyous the sounds of their swilling. Nevertheless, it was not meet that the two muster in one sitting, for the foul facades of the goblins was nigh unto the limit which men might endure. Albeit, virgins snatched from their mothers' sides were upon the arms of one and all regardless of injury to face. Indeed those barbarians that had come with Malebö of the Ugly-faces from Harmswäith had cropped their share of the Kingdom's favoured hussies.

Neither did haughty pride deter men from growling out songs of dark intimation before the colossal auricles of those from far off. Only Badred yr Rouge, from between the Two Rivers of Corruption (which is the place betwixt the Valley of Corruption and the Vale of Shadows), and Drygiöri of the Black-faces, from Nod, which is across the Black Seas and stretches to the other side of the world, had come further than the Bugbears of Bosom's Lodge, so-called after the manner of their feasting and their way with wooing maids. For it is said that they enjoyed nothing more than the flesh of succulent elf-youfs and the large breasts of homely women with faces too repulsive to describe. Not few were the numbers of these godless wenches!

Many were the tales of valour and the songs of the slaying of Surps, more even than talk of ravishings, cattle-raids, raising of homesteads, and slitting the necks of innocent elves or puny little children. Such ill gabble came in thick from the retinues of Galeg and his cousin Digwïlydd the Brazen, who, for the deformity of his mouth-piece since the day he was conceived of giants, found the parlance of the unbroken Common Tongue rather too difficult to master. Nonetheless, they impressed upon their listeners their yarns of fortitude, mimicking pregnant women hewn with the edge of the sword by coarse dissections of the meal set before them, and the pleas of mercy that had come forth from their captives by use of garter stolen off a maid's breeches, made fittingly into bonds of affliction.

The Heinous too joined in with their own accounts taken from the northwesterly provinces of Krandor. At length moreover their ill words, once understood, gleaned them such a respect that had been erstwhile lacking round the tables of the feasting of the Kings of the East. For amongst them was one called Gallembö, who set about persuading listeners of his greatness by telling anecdotes of butchery so foul it made many men weep; though the better part of the gathering wept tears of pleasure. Indeed, for he spoke of slaughters so numberless that many thought him to speak on the offerings yielded up to dark gods at the Feast of Yule-logs, the Kalan Yule. It is at this festival that men, beast and goblins alike give presents to one another in remembrance of the past year.

But neither did he vacate his spot without calling to mind The Three Foul Things of Triumph. That is: the eating of their foemen's flesh, even if it be orc-flesh, whose meat had been bequeathed by owners smitten with boulders taken from felled keeps and tenderised, before having their gore drained of its pugnacity and their flesh fried over a searing flame; the drinking the blood of the same; and the last – bathing in the urine of their princes, in full battle-gear and head-dressing, as a sign of utter defamation to their enemies' laws, customs and values – as well as, of course, being an easy way to shower for the goblins.

However, over the process of time at least one of these tales made spew a mighty man in the war-band of Pedéyrôr, for the sheer horror of its telling. That was a man of some one hundred and one kills to his name in total (not including women and children), a warrior also known for his chivalrous deeds across all the regions of Meréden. No mere weakling was this.

*

Therefore, all was in due order at the banquet of Prince Gwr, also sometimes known as the King of Dyngwr, who was presently inviting his resident spellbinder, Blakthawn, to come and sit by his side. None of those about the table, even to the men dressed in drab browns and the hags adorned in black attire, were unsuccessful in noticing the summons for his appearing before the great king of evil ascendancy. But save for the Prince of the Keep and his Eleven Nobles, and of course the druid himself, none were allowed purchase upon the couch about the King's Black Seat.

A troubadour too was called. He came running in with his lute in hand and sweat upon his brow and cheek, gasps of breath escaping from between his collars like the panting of a roe-deer in hunting season; the evidence, if one needs, of an interruption to the bard's gentle caresses upon some ungodly wench or another. So he approached the high table trying to forget the things behind save for that his faithful friends were obliged to maintain his lavish guerdon for his returning, which he hoped would not be but a short space off.

The minstrel drew near to the Table of Nobles and dipped his head solemnly before he who had brought him to such improvident surrounds, Drygiöri of the Black-faces, and then again before the Prince of Gwr and then his titled. It was claimed by most (save for the peoples of Waemorg) that he was the most gifted poet anywhere in the uncivilised world. And of players, so all men ceded, there was none better.

Thus to show this calling was indeed true he gently placed his Five Fair

Fingers upon the Five Strings of Pleasure and tenderly he drew three of the same cords back away from the others. The tension of both strand and spectator was immeasurable, told only by the rapt faces that spoke solemnly of strange auguries to come. A fair twine, a tingle, the unleashing of a voice that told of the loveliness of the Court's maidens, Baborina and Sofia included, as would the knights have sung themselves if they had ever been blessed with such gifting. At once Effyllawd seemed to receive his *awen* – the thing which caused his tongue to be loosed and his mind to become light and his heart to throb desperately, the results of whose labour was not to be lost upon his huge sable forehead.

At this voices became hoarse, held tight at the prospect of such fair accolades being rendered upon their own strumpets. One by one the bard versified first the ladies of present peerage before turning his attention upon the lesser and then, finally, upon the nugatory – minor clerics and stewards mostly, assigned to sit at the feet of the Prince of Gwr for this most auspicious of occasions, once they had served him to his contentment.

Each one did he call by name, first the court-labourer and then his wench, a feat that even the most skilled prophets have trouble in attaining. In fact they say that of these, perhaps those who are kith to Wyngod the Bard or those of the elder, Mahesh the Brown-legged, do call such things accurately every time, a testament to their virtue so all kings, both fair and foul, bear witness. Nevertheless, at length, the numbers within the scop's repertoire became too great and no small stir was caused for this.

It was murmured by some that perchance it would be good for the bard to leave them now that he had spoken well of all their ladies, their aunts, their mothers, and so forth, but that conceivably, his particular anointing for prophesying the useful unknown might perhaps be in the wane that day. Indeed, another of much lower standing, present for his father's skill in tasting wine, called out something far ruder as the troubadour reached the crest of his piece. But he was quickly thrust through with a poker, gleamed from the embers upon the hearth.

The saying afterward was that young Malcolm, having been somewhat of a help to his father earlier on in the feasting, had become rather taken by the wonderment of his future calling and had thence dared to call out something foul of the poet's great grandmother. Now it was also reported by the monk Carilorhn that the musician had been particularly fond of this old hag, before that is, she was haplessly run over by a chariot, raced by two young elves intoxicated by the sweet yellow muse of warm mead, one of which had his first name given as Malcolm. Though, in fact, it had been another.

Nevertheless, after the body was cleared away and his blood licked clean from the rush-strewn floor by a pack of roaming mastiffs and some goblins (to which the men of Krakôuz would have surely yelped had they not been so high on opium), the songster did indeed heed the common voice to retire. But not before something else had come to him.

And this thing pertained to a certain troll (and, of course, his mistress), both apparently living wild in a certain land called Trol-land; so he thought. Though at the moment the highly revered bard could remember little more than this...

*

The troll the acclaimed bard was actually referring to was in fact Fels'noc the Trol, meaning "The Troll Is A Low-down Hag". He was descended from a long line of ape-men, who had been smote by the sword, cursed by witchery, and persecuted, ever since the days of Elgathar I. It was he who was under orders from him whose courts we have just visited, who had issued forth the command that all Fair Folk in the Hilly Lands of Abundance should be sought out and smitten by blades trimmed by the Gofs in bygone days. And a breed of murderous, brown-thighed orcs, who called themselves The Kyarfddmtrol, joined forces with King Elgathar in pursuit of the beleaguered trolls from sea to river, from valley to hill, and across divers mountains. The trolls had fallen upon many a mound, perishing in valiant contest, as was wont of all worthy warriors at the time, losing their lives to the dark forces of Dereden who were there to lay siege about their hamlets.

Nevertheless, not all of their numbers met with grim death. Nay – nor could they if the prophecies were to be fulfilled. But a few of the more noble managed to elude the fires, undoing spells by rune-crafts, deflecting sword-thrusts by faith and spear-shots by hope, hiding themselves in the darkened weald, as much of Trolland was in those days. Some ran to the plateau hard by the vales of Ypresein upon which plain they withstood their assailants several days. Through intrigue, escape through trees, and slaughter most foul, they kept at bay many an unwelcome intruder. Testimony to these hapless victims was the decoration of scalped skulls piled high upon the Stakes at Ypres, a sickening sight even to ones so grim.

Times and seasons as they were, few could keep the godless cacophony of trolls from producing more of their ungodly spawn. The present descendant of Noc was even now still alive, though living the life of a vagabond and a hunter, moving restlessly round the local villages in the raw rugged regions of the Midshires. Betimes Fels'noc was moved to gather his brethren in from the dales, that he might visit vengeance upon the remnant of his bastard kin – either those who did not adhere to his savage ways, or those who had failed to offer succour. Compelled would he be to exact damage, raise tribute, and leave behind a trail of strewn bodies well-pleasing to the eyes of a vulture. Sure it was said that the numbers within his company, at any one time, were small when matched against the people of the shires, yet none failed to live without constant dread of his terrible retinue.

Hardy, bold and brash – so men reckoned of the troll-folk. For few of them feared, much less ran from the enemy in battle, thus true was it said that their real threat came from within and not without. Nonetheless, the uncouth manner of Fels'noc brought uncertainties to the reckoning, he being, as was supposed, possessed of certain deft accomplishments that living souls ought not possess. (He was reputed as having the endowment equivalent to one of the mammoths from the Llomahr Falls, which is on the eastern fringes of Giants in the domain of Galeg the Gaul, as folk said it was he who killed the White Bear of Dothan with a single swipe of his forearm. Indeed, with his right hand some say that, one day in the midst of the snowy season, when the air was cold and the blood ran dry, and the songs of thrushes could no longer be heard coursing the blue streams of Gyrgon's Fields – which was also the day that a close female cousin of his had died – they tell of Fels'noc crushing a rock-bullox, barehanded!) Thus, even to this day few were they who dared approach him openly or alone.

If this 'Son of Night' ever has need of someone, he himself shall make the first approach, after dark, and his favours are not to be refused. Moreover, if he should choose to chance a raid upon any village, or hamlet, or even a small town for that matter, then all the trolls in those parts would flee, without fail, and not afterward return till all the damage was wrought and their lands had been plundered. Even the most dour and ugliest of trolls among the tribes feared him greatly. Some were seen to blanch even at the mere mentioning of the Mighty Noc. They too left for him their choice pickings, lest, without a treat, the trick of the trolls be enforced.

However, to many unlearned of all these things, the troll's great presence was no less disturbing. Fels'noc had sooner been a good trol, helping the needy in their times of trouble, filled with emotional depth and care for others' well-being, willing to share in his plunder, his wine, his women. Then it happened that one day, the curse that was laid down upon his ancestors, arrived abruptly on his doorstep without warning, and the power to resist its ungodly wiles was lacking. For the spirits of his forefathers had completed their cycles of walking through dry and dusty places and had come to inhabit him that they might find rest. So that from those afflicted days till this, the resident evil found within the mighty Fels'noc had flourished.

*

In the meantime, the rumour that the Syndicate was an itinerant band of treasure-seekers from the far south of Krandor, searching far and wide for old buried loot, saw no let up. With interests in the purest quarts of gold, fresh

256

ores and precious stones such as the diamonds bought and sold by the Iddew, and also the swarthy onyx and the dwarf-stone (a gem in scarce supply back in the South), the one who had commissioned them, a one Mister Schmidt, was terribly keen on laying his hands on the goodies as quickly as possible. That is before much of the lands' wealth vanished into avaricious hands. An affable solution, some may say, to the problems facing the world; but Schmidt knew of no good reason why anybody should deprive him of even a mere ounce of wealth while he was yet breathing. A crime worthy of death to one who enjoyed his overflowing coffers.

Nonetheless, there was little to be gained by the trolls in probing too deeply for the truth. They had heard of this Izan, Schmidt, and of his dark affiliations with the regent of that rebellious province King Alex de Vitaz of the Olive-faces. Both were merchants, both were self-proclaimed kings, but both were under the rule of women. It was Alex however who often forewent his ethical boundaries if the price was high enough.

At present most of Gjugg's band were happy to tend to the needs of The Troop until last light later that day but on the morrow their guests should be encouraged to leave. Failing this civil route they would let Calhavar know of The Troop's irreverent laughter at his buffoonery the night before, explaining away their own transgressions as a minor misunderstanding. Then they would hand him his broadsword (and an extra skin of mead for their sins) and then step back, and watch the ensuing affray unfold with delightful glee.

But it was Ottoman who held more affinity for the men than the rest of his comrades and it was in his mind to work fast. Though he would wait for a more prudent time before voicing his opinions, lest any foul urging be stirred that ought not. Frydor was indeed weary of such discriminating prudence emanating from the wizened troll and for that he was in no small way grateful.

*

At length the sun became fatigued by its daily exertion. Not long afterwards Gjugg and his homely wife Michelle found some fitting excuse to leave, and they were closely followed by Gjagg with his strapping great mistress, Lindsay of the Long-thighs, daughter of Cainan. Neither were they alone. Tottering quite deliberately from side to side to indicate how lethargic the spell had been and how he had quite suddenly been taken with weariness, Calhavar the Carnal soon discovered similar reasons for early retirement. Besides, it was long past the twelfth hour and his soft straw bed would be lain out and his pillow was stuffed, and waiting would be the two dire wenches he had accumulated from the neighbouring villages, one of which was Ebola mab Aidshiv, diseased daughter of Eciv of the Four Winds, from the Land of Fou-ouls.

Not long after savaging his last shank of boar Calhavar fell into a solemn trance, the like of which was not uncommon amongst bloated trolls with swollen guts, where some say the individual's gods resided. His lips muttered fey sentences, varying between the pursing of a great thinker who was trapped for the snarls of his latest problem, and that of an inebriated bearded dwarf, whose spittle ran course along his fluffy white mane. Hands not willing to accommodate the off-putting sight aroused him shortly after the drooling had become a barrage but upon leaving he uttered the following words:

> *"The rains are coming alongside the fires of gloom*
> *All must make haste or all will be doomed."*

With that he sprung up from his spot and left, spitting some other nonsensical insults. He spoke of the presence of Night-raiders upon the eastern winds, the greatest winds that were in the world, and the restoration of some of his own brethren. Then he mentioned the taking into captivity of others, who, until that time, were not known for their brawling skills.

As the embers dwindled and eyelids were shut it was Ottoman who was left to tend to the baffled company that evening. For he, as all would soon know, had been granted somewhat greater insight. And make full use of this wisdom he did.

*

Grey clouds closeted the vales of Gfynwreid like the fat-bellied Cherub of Nef the sons he tends, before another glistening prominence shed the last reams of its daylight upon the green northwards of where the Company were sat. The odes of dark ravens and the haunted hooting of the owl played upon the ears of its nocturnal listeners, soothing moans floating through the meadows coursing like a daisy-leaf across the inviolate breezes.

A colourful hawthorn came upon the moonlit soils, caught amid a flurry of cold watered air. It shed some leaves into the dying embers of wood. Some flew haplessly away, thrown skyward to oblivion; others fell onto the laps of both Sascha and Jemimah with the weight of concern stroked delicately upon their backs. A yellowish-white flower had befallen Sascha leaving a pink one, wrenched of the same stork, to land upon the lap of Jemimah. Quickly, the two tender petals were snapped up, without so much as a solitary glance.

The young man regarded his for a space, wondering why it was that it appeared so heavy in his hands, even though to the touch it was as soft as pure silk. He returned his gaze upwards, taking in the mesmerising detachment of clouds that had gathered to perpetrate some moist mischief. As he watched he could see the rain above the undulating borderlands creeping ever nearer to the sodden field.

So this then was the day before the dawning. Brave thoughts came to

Sascha and vain imaginations of glory, of honour, of immortality. His mind for a trice was incapable of calculating complications; his heart was filled with steadfast zeal; his desire was to soar above the elements: it was the state of great men who go on to achieve many a worthy goal.

*

Times as they were it had been a surprisingly good evening all round. Yet troubling thoughts continued to snag both Jemimah and Marcus. He was astonished to find himself understanding why it was that all would one day be consumed in anger. She was addled: surely that would be when the Sun-god Mabon burns up and Krandor with it, when too the tides shall come in from the coasts with a mighty deluge worthy of the god Neptune. And the sky, seething with anger at all the transgressions wrought beneath its vast berth since time immemorial, will split at the seams and cast down many a host expelled from Nef. The two flowers, one pink and one white, were released together into the consuming fires, where they burned till all that remained were scattered ashes and a searing flame.

With smoke in their nostrils and stomachs filled to bursting, Marcus was the first to get up from his place, and he headed for the charred log-wood. He steeped forwards and with a gust of his breath he blew at the coming flames. But this time, the embers were already kindled by the winds dashing about him and no blessing chanted by the Breastplate-bearer would they again savour, whether for better or for worse, for fair or for foul. Time now would bring its own judgement. Again the warrior stood by the flames, his hands cupped around a most pitiful gut, skin sagging beneath him and fit for rupture. He made his way back with Jemimah and returned to the generous, drunken hosts.

Wistful groans of air rubbed against the backs of ferns lower down in the vales. Squally rain-clouds tangoed for approval with the belts of fog hanging heavy upon the Ridge of Trolls. Dark though it was, resolutions were still held high. Talk came afresh with new avenues of implication for the elves and the trolls, depending who was dispensing the chatter.

Some herons had besieged a brake of nearby brushwood before taking to the skies again by the waterside, where the water runs stagnant and slow into a small peat-filled bog. Their long-necked skinny-bodied bedevilment seemed ungainly, nothing like the glory of swan-birds when they are dressed in their fabulous white-plumes.

There were more slanty-eyed trolls drawing closer to the festive party now, with their wares by their sides, and their snouts sniffing for the message brought of these eight strangers. A word from abroad maybe, or perhaps some new bargain-hunters out to secure a deal, who could tell? But news was news no less and it was good for gossip.

A few loggers were outside to collect some firewood for the night; hunters who strayed but a short way off towards the neighbouring streams where the run of fish was good. There too were night-owls with big, beady eyes, watching all, observing all, that if need be, word may be sent to the care of passing eagles in hoots or fulminations.

The truth be told however, by the time Ottoman asked Frydor the first question of any true importance, the cinders of fire-ash had reduced themselves into a silent fizzle, a soft parody of those others surrounding them. Then, the troll lifted the silent scrutiny which he had held over the friends for a long space and averted his eyes from the quickly dying embers.

'So, will Mister Frydor talk to me or not?' asked Ottoman gravely, considering the dark expression on the elf's face as a reflection of the black-faced sky above. 'Talk to me, friend. What is it that brings you here? Why did you come to this part of Trol-Land? Are you,' at which point the troll leant forward, 'hunters or scavengers? Which one is it elf?'

'We've already said; the stones in – '

'No!' shouted Ottoman suddenly. A few trolls stopped in the woods nearby, stirred by the new zeal that their adopted kinsman had shown, but none for too long.

'What is the *real* reason for your abrupt appearance. Not in many days have elves intruded into these parts and rarely with men at their sides. So then, what is it? What gain are you now greedy for? Perhaps you really are noble, one of the Surps of Renown?'

Marcus panicked first, glancing around neurotic as a fox with its tail alight, casting his agitated eyes towards Nywdog before taking in Alicia's lumbering frame. Neither did Eleanor rest easy. Ottoman's terseness had gained purchase over whatever mettle she had managed to bring to the fore, and this lack caused her to fuss a tremendous fidget with Sascha's clammy hands. She played with his fingers as though her own and she scraped the skin off his dried backhand even whilst the other trolls looked on. The depression of the image made was as of a graven tablet, like the first laws that were given to Moses. Unfortunately, the onlookers drew nearer still.

The wizened troll shot her a poisonous stare, one of those looks which often did one of two things to white-limbed maidens: weaken them at the knees accompanied by the loosening of bowels and bladder; or else it overcame them with such infatuation that they fell into his arms, having already became enamoured with his love, and carried him off to bed with no mean struggle until fully experienced of his loving. The word in the dales was that Ottoman was as good-looking as it gets, and beneath the yellow broom-tree there were few more accomplished in love-making!

260

Through handfuls of wood-ash the Troop could almost sense the mountain of unsolved dilemmas lying ahead of them. The more curious amongst the trolls soon parted, which left only Ottoman's grubby features remaining.

'Ah... By the looks of your company, I have chanced on something Frydor. But what?' he murmured, almost to himself. 'Ores you say, perhaps even gold? You are, of course, aware of the many leagues lying between these hills and the mines in the south-eastern part of Fou-ouls... and harder lands are there still before one alights on the prized rocks northwards of that place. And if you really have come from the south like you say you have, why did you choose to venture through the unassailable regions of Hill-Land and not skirt them about like any wise-elf would have done? I think, therefore, I am at an advantage, Frydor.'

'Well, we...' the elf hesitated in his response as he saw the troll's demeanour change. 'We...' Should he give him the benefit of the doubt? 'I...' Frydor the Surp was stumped. So he yielded.

'As you rightly suspect we are not traders of the kind described.' So he went for it. 'However, we are indeed searching for hidden treasures, though not all of them fashioned in gold or indeed encrusted with precious stones. To be honest with you I do not know what they look like for the most part. But we seek for those most sacred treasures of aged standing, sealed since the spells of evil Morgwyd fell upon this place when under the rule of his evil master who resides in the place the *Bearded-ones* call *Dera-denu*.'

There was a tremendous judder as both the elves and the troll recalled the two dread names mentioned in one sitting: Bearded-ones, which is what some called the Ancient Knights and Judges (that is to say the mighty Zaqen); and Dera-denu ('She Who Is Enticed By A She-devil'), which, since the time of Athelwyss, had been dubbed Dereden.

He peered at Ottoman square in the face, looking for any last signs of disapproval, lest he should withhold the crux of his being, but he found none. 'We are in desperate need of the Key of Self-Control, if I may be so truthful with you, but we think that one of your more wayward fellows has chanced upon it. So we come to seek him out, to see whether or not he might be able to aid us in our search.'

All at once Sascha reached for his club, Nywdog his stick, Eleanor had an arrow trained towards the lumbering trolls traipsing in the distant, while Jemimah and Flip unsheathed their swords and laid them straight at the stranger's neck. All movements, to their surprise, came naturally, all actions were fluent. Well had they been gifted! And well had they been trained!

'Uncle, I reckon that if we dispatch him now we might make the path in the woods over yonder,' Flip blurted pointing hurriedly towards the thorny brake past the nearby bracken. 'Then we can head eastward as a cover-trail at the rate our steeds may carry us, then southwards to make as if we move in circles. Through the woods next, perhaps as far as Brythan's Neck and up the slopes of Gyrgon itself, again – though I prefer not to take on that fearsome task myself. By then we may have lost them, though I am aware of some trolls in these parts travelling swift as any wily slave on the business of his master! So shall I make an end to him now Frydor?'

Through the maze of avenues and winding routes and bridges, Frydor was lost. Ottoman meanwhile was already on the ball. He parried away *Chaeaf* before there ever was a chance to use it. The transtrol bounded up from his spot, crying excitedly, 'I knew it! I knew it all along.

'Did I not say the same to myself all along,' he roared boisterously, till the other nocturnal trolls had again stopped for interest. The gang lowered their weapons as if to make in play. There were too many of the trolls to even think about it.

'Ah, but the Key of Control itself, that is no small undertaking, even by ones so valiant... or foolish even as yourselves! So am I to take it that all the stories about mining and digging for priceless rocks was but a cunning façade and that your motives are a little less dubious?'

A wry smile crept across his gleaming face. And joyous was his heart that played its pipes as if by the hand of Morgosai the Midlothian. His was the sound mentioned of in Lore when the kings went out to war one year when the Hobbits first flourished in Mirkwood.

So handsome was the sound on the midsummer's day that the gods from everywhere flocked to the glades upon the hills of Framoléin, having deemed the chords vouchsafe that all things were well and safe deep in the Middle Earth. Upon arriving however, they saw the spot that the Hobbits had found themselves in, and for the sweet lullabies played, they had chosen their allies wisely. But it was within that enchanted period that Mordel, evil lord of the interval before Time, called No-Time, made his way to the surface, pilfering the rings that bound the lands in peace, purpose and unity. For between that which is called Space and No-Space no deeds might be done.

Some say that the gods are still there, even till this day, having not heard of the subsequent slaying of Morgosai (for another took his place when a stake did pierce his heart). Then there are those who tell of the gods opening their eyes, but once, after they had become entranced by the beautiful music. This was when the Tear of Iflesaw crept down his cheek for the dreamy nature of the sonnet played him. Of all the tales of strange worlds, let the reader gaze readily upon this one!

So why, indeed, should Ottoman not be found with gaiety? He had cornered a wise-elf and had won – no mean feat for any, one may add. But what next?

'But why, O Noble Elf, do you reckon these myths real? And if these things are true, then why do you seek them after many long years of languor?'

After perceiving that his question would not soon be answered, the rest of the Friends melted away into the velvety-coloured backdrop. This now was the business of elves, Surps even, and not matters for mere novices or unbelievers. They had yet to be tutored in the art of war, they were babes in the shedding of blood and of striving against sin, and few had so much as even contemplated such a course before their abrupt arrival in No-Man's-Land. They left the discussion for those more mature, those who were wiser still.

'Judging by your friends over there, I suppose you have come for Fels'noc the Troll – the "Son of the Night" as some of us call him. You want to find out what he has to say on the Key? Well may the Gods be with you, Frydor, for that is one troll who follows after no man's heart. His strand of troll lineage has been greatly tampered with… up above if you get the meaning,' Ottoman imitated, tapping lightly on his sconce.

Seeing no response forthcoming, he continued rather irritably; 'Look here, all I'm saying is that it would be wise to think about things before you start chasing such terrible creatures. I'm sure you're aware that yours is a most dangerous pursuit, fraught with perils of the land, dangers of the sea, and hosts of devils from the Otherworld. The hands that guided you here know as much, I'm sure, but I hope you've each been made personally aware of the hazards.' They listened on in silence awhile as leaves rustled in the weald beyond.

'…Especially, if you don't mind me saying so, for the company you keep?'

This statement was odd enough to distort Frydor's normally easy carriage.

'What do you mean, Ottoman?'

'See there…' The troll took no time in highlighting Nywdog's arrogant talk, Sascha's keen sense of slothfulness, Alicia's fluctuating timidity, Jemimah's vanity, Marcus' pale skin; Eleanor's tiny frame.

'Not to put too finer point on the matter though. Besides all this ridiculous dazzle, there is, it seems, another worthy saying which you quite obviously have not come across yet. '

"Most of those he meets shall meet with no one else."

'A word worthy of rather close scrutiny.'

Frydor wrested his gaze from his friends, embarrassing though it was, and fixed his stare more firmly on the troll sat before him.

'What evidence is there of his whereabouts?'

'You mean: does he really exist, Frydor,' blurted Ottoman with a keen eye to detail. 'Oh yes, Fels'noc exists – I've seen the evidence of his destruction myself, with these two eyes.

'He became well known in these here *vilayets* after storming the hold of the village-king Mungdip, Troll-warrior of the Kob'law Clans, who lived over yonder, past the mountains and through the fields. Stout men took his wife, they say, before stealing her abroad and violating her upon the yellow sands of Bay Rüyt. Mungdip's most valiant had fled at his coming and so there was no chance of reprisals. Anyway, after her affliction, she was cleaved limb from limb and her body-parts were sent to the outlying regions of Kob'law, as warning to those who did not, beforehand, prepare a lavish enough hosting.

'The men who were with her were divided asunder into seven parts each beginning with his manhood – then came two arms, two legs, a head, and a torso. But she herself was cut up into eight pieces – two arms, two legs, two breasts, a torso and a head.

The elf looked stunned, sick as a parrot, puce as Marcus. Before he could voice his own concerns about such a story, he was interrupted again, as Otto-man strove to continue.

'Some of her bits were missing though, elf,' Ottoman wheezed, breathing close to Frydor's right ear. 'They say that these were the scraps they kept for their mascot, which is a ten foot bull with udders the size of trunks. Such tidings, I hear, transpired quite recently too… or so I am led to believe!'

'You're kidding?' Eleanor piped indecisively. They had not noticed their company steal back to them stealthily. 'Who would do such a thing?'

'Ah, so the squib talks!' remarked the troll, turning aside to engage her curiosity further. 'Alas, I wish I could say it was not so, poor child, but the scattered bones that lay strewn afterwards, I saw for myself! They were definitely troll-bones. Our people say that this curse had its origin from the times of our association with elves! And the evidence seems to prove it.'

The Surp made no reply to those stinging remarks and neither did he have to. Trollish animosity towards elves was well vented from time to time, even amongst those whose valour in Yesteryear should not be held in question. Take for instance, King Elffllyn III, a valiant patriarch and formidable soldier, who, beforetimes round the feasting-board, was the object of much scandal and ill-words. If such a hero could become a parody for perjurers then what should one make of those with less *galanas*?

The water-glands beneath his eyelids became enlarged and enraged, and soon indeed, they became heavy. The Syndicate stood by and watched, as this once stout ship was caught out in the late evening storms, much like a maelstrom caused by a mighty puff of the Dragon from Penzance. Quick as the other would, saltwater became a flood on his curved masts and proud rigging, so that it made it difficult for him to hold his course. Noises were louder, sights became blurred, ears convened hard upon the night scroungers, which were guzzling at the remains of the season's crop afar off. The skimming supple movements of a water-swallow became to the elves an enchanting dancer such as those found at the Courts of Harman, whose dancing-ladies do not fail to captivate all those that see them. Indeed, such were eyes on the prize!

'O Lord!' Frydor sighed, at length remembering much of what he had read as a child. The dark-skinned trolls, who had once been populous, were certainly given over to a slaughter, but of whose making, even till this day, no one speaks of with certainty. His musing did not persist long, past the downing of a kestrel by a huntsman in the distance.

'Let me tell you something,' began Flip hotly, drawing himself fully out of the shadows, loosing in his anger, that thing which he had struggled so hard to bind in the first place. 'All this talk of evil crimes and betrayal is but bitterness thrust up from the dark passageways of Annwfn. My fathers and their fathers before them bled as much as any troll twice their size, and I am willing to spill the same as them all... I do not wish it but if it must be then shall it be, and let me not forbid it! Amen.'

The troll fell back at his precocity, for not in many years had he beheld such boldness.

'This is why we gamble upon this unchancy journey – not for fame or valour or any great ballad sung behind the stonewalls of safety at great feastings before unknown kings and courtiers, where such scops rarely see the gore of the things they espouse. Indeed, we reckon our venture will pass mostly unnoticed, till fate befalls each one of us and our bodies are fed as gruel to famished kine and starving sows somewhere on some forgotten field.' Alicia motioned away from the elf, disgust registering in her eyes. 'But we have little else to do – worthwhile – that is to say. For have not all become unprofitable? Have not all together become futile in their thinking and in their doings? Even with your cloudy vision, Ottoman, does anyone really seek after The Truth? ... Amongst your troll-brethren, for instance?

'Rare is it that one may die for a good man and seldom is it that one would give his life for a righteous man. That is the state of the world at present, and there is no arguing about these things. Few are there bold enough to take on the cause of the good or strive against the plots of the wicked.'

Flip broke off his departure when presented with the grieving tides of his uncle's eyes, at length returning to the heated chatter and casting of lots in which he had sooner been engaged. Eleanor, nonetheless, the youngster, had been listening carefully with her tender though somewhat naïve ears. Round her head went, like a child in play with other elf-youfs, when she spins herself in fields beneath the North Star. And around and around her sconce continued to roll, in search of someone that would take up the elf's resolute challenge.

Who would be valiant enough to restore the former glories of those men, elves and trolls everywhere; those who had fought hard to quell the rising tides of vice and abandonment, as well as the passing of babies through the fire? Soon enough, tears filled her eyes also.

Beneath the darkening hue of the world above came kindly breezes sufficient to calm the child's frayed temperament. It was on the cheek that she first felt the sweeping touch of a master-carer, brushing away the tears that streamed down her sallow jowls before reaching downwards for her delicate breasts under the loving guise of comfort. Thereupon he plucks up her grievances, not forgetting to caress her lovely chest with his hot-pursed lips, and then, swiftly as his rapture ends, he casts the burden with his strong arms onto the broad-trimmed shoulders of the wind.

'So will you take us to him or not?' Her voice sent a quiver sailing upon the waves of the wind. 'Or are you just gonna believe all the bad stuff that's said by the elders amongst your people? How will that help you?' She paused for a trice, as even Nywdog began to listen. 'And how will that make you any better than they were… think of what will happen to this place if you don't? Maybe not today or tomorrow, but at some point in time certainly.'

Before he could contemplate her somewhat embellished reasoning, she had managed to inch in another couple of words.

'Please Ottoman?'

The face of the virtuous little girl was perked up and seemed ready for it, come what may, as legend says grace came also upon the young snip Jeanne d'Arc. She it was whose storming of the siege at Orleans and whose capture of Patay in her youthful days led green-eyed men to cry "Witch!" and "Faitour!" Indeed, even some of the more pious who wore scarlet robes and paid homage and tribute to Papa called her the "Black Vixen!". This was for the shame inflicted upon their hired *alltud* in battle. The transtrol too was pinned, caught by the words of a mere sapling.

He groaned at this, at the same time pondering the strength of this young creature, reluctant at the selfsame moment to dismiss the waif's bounding confidence, which if channelled and sometime measured, might go on to fulfil astonishing works. Who could tell what the will of the gods were?

Eager, if not the most athletic member of her retinue, Ottoman guessed she was in possession of that rash optimism men of war craved when marching into a fray. Incapable of minding the opposing odds, fearless of fate, longing only for experience that comes with battle, perhaps in her time she might grace the winds like an eagle.

Nevertheless gallantry and youthful vigour was not sufficient in itself to overcome three specific things: and these things are the Zaqen (or the Warriors of the Ancient Lore); the gods in their prime; and Fels'noc and his dubious band of rioters. As when one approaches a mountain spoor through a trailing skirt of mist, so was one to seek out that bloody troll with caution. Ottoman allowed himself a little frown, however, as he turned to give the girl his response:

266

'Aye… okay, little girl, that will I do.'

There was an audible sigh of relief mixed with anxiety.

'But let it be known that I am both man and troll, of the race of Hettites, so they say; for I had few of my wits at birth you see, and life since has been rather more entertaining shall we say, for me to be overly concerned with such trivial matters.' He ambled round to view Frydor.

'But it is not for the sake of *your* wisdom Master Elf that I succumb to your requests – I still hold the view that the *wisdom* of your folk caused many of us to suffer far too much… though I might now allow for the fact that your race was only *part* responsible for the fate of my people. Nonetheless, it is for the sake of the squib over there, who has put her trust into your hands,' rejoined the troll, drawing Eleanor out of the encroaching darkness; 'I do what I do solely for her sake. And perhaps for the sake of the strangers with her, if they are worthy enough.'

Frydor's heart leapt up within him, though with the next stern words of warning, his sudden encouragement waned.

'Nevertheless, I do not think that you'll discover anything new. Many have been his pursuers since days of yore and many are the numbers fallen by the wayside. The wretched Serpent himself could barely fathom more than us mortals, accursed though he is…' At the mentioning, Ottoman kissed his golden pendant, touched his sword, and spread his mat upon the wet grounds, before kissing the floor and calling upon his god, A-Lah.

Frydor nodded gravely, which roused the troll somewhat to speak further his quandaries.

'However, I will undertake no such venture this eve… lest I waste away to nothing before my time. I have sworn by my word and that is good enough for you; but on the morrow maybe. The hour is late now and I am weary,' Ottoman yawned widely, taking opportunity to examine the wonderful blue berth of sky.

'You would do well, Frydor, to advise your company to obtain rest, as much as they can garner…' The troll turned away by himself and lumbered back over the coarse swathes of grass and towards his troll-stack, before calling back; 'The gods know of our conversation, they know of our needs on the morrow, so they will provide what respite we require. The season of the Conjunction of the Sun and Moon is nigh upon us, and it is then, as has always been, that turpitude spreads quicker than a rash of the Black Plague in summertime.

'But rest your weary bones now, Frydor, my friend, for you and your company must indeed be tired! And those who are wise will take courage in the saying:

"Good things come to him who waits

But to him who does not comes the Tempter's fate."

'It may stand you in good stead for this night and for the remainder of your long and dark journey. You would do well to rest yourselves, for I perceive that tomorrow will not be without incident. Goodnight!'

*

First to take heed was Marcus. He left his conversing friends to gabble, as he headed for the nearby bushes where a small space had been hewn to lengthen the village's borders. He tied his hammock to a pair of elm trees which rose stoutly from the bank of a quickly flowing stream. But it was close enough to the brook for him to draw comfort during the late evening solace, for it was there he intended to bunk for the night. Reaching up somewhat higher, he entangled his breastplate securely a short way above his head. Annoying gnats and dewy moisture he was in no mood for, especially after the exertions of the day so far.

Before settling down finally, however, he first needed to tend to the needs of his stallion, Tapfer. Combing back his matted hair, he spoke out his plans for the new day dawning, should the steed at all be able to interpret the foolish gibberings from his master's throat. He nodded, nevertheless, though Marcus knew not whether in obsequiousness or in understanding; upon which he decided that at present it mattered little. The drawn veils of sleepiness had soon enchanted him, so it was the warm covers of down that kept it for him now.

The rest of the Friends parted soon afterwards. Weapons were sorted first, and then clothes, and then lassitude, as so often, languor has its own cure. For them was provided a healthy space, not so far from Marcus, by the banks of the leafless ford.

There was still one pair of eyes wedged open until later that night, however, beneath the dim glow of a single wax candle flame burning brightly, yellow and orange. As the reader read, her mind was quickened, and connections between this world and the next were being made. And as her heart searched deeper for truth, time moved on.

For her it was that dark-space again, that which exists between Time and No-Time, where both Law and No-Law come into play. She pored over verse after verse and scripture after scripture, as a baby weaned off its mother's milk, like the child who is no longer contented with the warmth of her mother's bosom but yearning for something stronger. Yet none were the visions that night, tired as she was. Her second set of eyes closed shortly after the first set.

Nonetheless, she let drift the most circumspect sonnets of wisdom towards the chord-strings of her heart in the hope that soon she might show herself approved amongst her fellows. Then that evil foe Timidity shall be bound within a cairn of a dunghill, and cast into the bottom of the sea. As too some of the Lords of Wybern who also said:

"When the Conjunction of the Sun and the Moon are forged
Together to one boon as the runes speak
Then shall Darkness arouse from its sleep
Which shall then begin the Final Week."

Not long before Frydor had dropped off, he rebuked her prying, and refused to be drawn on this imprecise matter. But she saw his carriage tremble upon the hearing of such secret words that few who saw him would afterward vouch for the very things they had witnessed. For not only did he refuse to respond to those fey enchantments but he even spurned her efforts to seek those things out for herself.

The journey by light had been long for all and at length she too soon surrendered to the rigours of the day's walk. She appeared withdrawn and unable to settle, as little of the import of her learning made any sense; though she did yet recognise the importance of these matters. Then her eyelids became heavy, as weariness began to outweigh her zealous interest of the Lore. Thereupon, she joined her slumbering comrades in the choicest cradle of all.

Where she was stayed that night few were the skyward stars. There was no Moon even though her glory was not of her own but a poor reflection of the Son's. There was little else to be seen that night, only the unanswered concerns of a certain feverish soul. Her eyes closed shortly after that but not before her orisons were heard and already being seen to.

THE BATTLE FOR THE FALLEN RIDGE

Thus says the Lord:
'Such as are for death, to death;
And such as for the sword, to the sword;
And such as for the famine, to the famine;
And such as for the captivity, the captivity.'

JEREMIAH 15:2

It was the second day since leaving the south-central hill lands of the provinces. Having bid their farewells to Gjugg and Gjagg and others from the village, the gang had taken pleasant license and were now at last on their way, Frydor, Ottoman and the Syndicate together, travelling on the endless road to nirvana. None deemed it prudent to mention the prevailing topic of that night's conversation, but it was agreed instead that they would construe their excuses on the basis of the existing cover story, should ever the need arise. If the truth be known they were indeed searching for hidden riches in secret places, even though at present the treasures were indiscernible and veiled in the utmost secrecy.

As the second day drew to a close the dusk light was all that was left of the Daystar, a vivid and ever-present reminder of their sluggishness. Soon, it was Frydor himself who brought the arduous journey to a halt. The elf was all rather wearied by the ongoing battle with mosquitoes and the hard tortuous paths that beset them. He thought it best to rest a while, in the hope of spotting an easier route for the next day.

Soils so deep into Hill-land were as foreign to Ottoman as they were to both Flip and Frydor, so all agreed that his was in fact the best option. Thereupon he motioned for his party to settle down and to prepare themselves for the remainder of the short eventide that the morning thereafter might be without burden.

*

The next day was not without premonitory misgivings especially for Frydor the Elf who revealed such uncertainties by pulling the hood of his garment over his brow. The others kept their gait behind Flip, deeming the older elf as unfit for their jubilant company, while they rode unhindered through hills saddled with snow.

They journeyed through woods and upon prairie-land and with each new turn fresh images stole into Frydor's mind. Reveries altered upon seeing the wounds of the yew-bark. Thoughts turned to the long war that is still said to rage there between dusk and dawn each day, where Pomellrywth the Conjurer as supposed makes war with Men from the North, ever since his fall from grace at the beginning of the world, even unto now. The muddy brook soon appeared and this was seen as the Bog of Dinrith, that place of Hell-fury in which thousands of valiant elves died defending the southern side of the ruins at Caer Efryll in years gone by. Their grief was great but not greater than the affliction borne by Marcus.

It had come on the youngster unexpectedly a few eves earlier, shortly after their adventurous expedition had begun. Swollen glands, high fever, sweats and shivers, inundated was he with the affliction that took Jelyobo bitch-daughter of Limes, who, after much passing of water through the glands, was wont to sleep with one more accursed victim of the Plague. None saw this scourge strike and none knew wherefrom this bastard affliction was sprung but there are those around who swear to seeing arrows fired from the bow of Belieon glinting past the streams and in the forests. However, some say that he moves muffled within his magic mantle, that none might decry his path, lest any should avoid it and live. This again is a curse of Erynaidd, queen of the Wooded-groves.

Marcus was third in line and squatted upon Tapfer, head down and resting behind the horse's poll. Despite this Jemimah proved her worth. She offered him what support she could for the time being, wiping his brow as frequently as the course would allow. Such practices aided him only little however as his brow was still burning like a dry-bush in Awst. His friends maintained their distance, none moving too far from his comrades, all keeping to the pace of the slowest person.

The regrettable spectacle could not be helped. Strangers stalking through foreign woods which are, as supposed, haunted, at a pace slower than a snail, biding their time for the ease of their sickly friend. Noble, even valiant one may one-day sing of them; but little else would a scop have to sing if they were not promptly at it and on their way.

They say that in their brown barks the forests had eyes of their own. There was talk too of dryads and forest-ghosts who sometimes laid snares for un-wary visitors who failed to carry the rowan-branch on their persons. Ears of broad, leafy foliage heard reports of visitors. Neither good nor bad was this wonder, but its *dihenydd* was based solely on the height of the sun, the shape of the wind, the position of the stars in the sky. The longing for some kind of breakthrough increased urgently.

Alicia led her pure white beast up the winding path, while Frydor, the elderly Surp, sat astride the saddle which allowed Ottoman to exchange ideas with him. This talk was good and aroused the interests and spirits of all those travelling that day. Nywdog rode behind them with Eleanor, whose turn it was to handle Schatten-Flug as best as she was able. She glanced to the woods at times, into the thickest parts where no man can see, where folk say creatures unknown to men roamed. Limitless and unknown, a blot through which few men ventured, dread soon overtook her motions and fastened her more carefully to her duties. She rode on.

Overcoming their trembling, they managed to break the journey only on occasions, venturing off in twos to the less forbidden parts of the weald. They combed the woods for the roots that might provide a curative for their friend's ailment. Flip drew up the rear behind his patient along with his partner Sascha who walked steadily beside him in search. Their faithful steed Vol took up the rear position by himself, neither fearing nor averse to doing so; for there was no imperative on his part that any man should ride him, let alone lead him.

A river snaked between its two sheltering mounds some way beneath the dogged Company. Towards port was a large, flushed meadow, verdant green like many others in Abundance, suitable for the housing of much cattle and many migratory homesteads. To their starboard, hills clambered atop of one another, nestling in deadly art with the darkening jungle around it, and the thick, onerous undergrowth that propped it up. This same description continued all the way down to the valley floor itself where Ottoman was currently leading the Troop over to the crossing point at the ford. Then they descended again, towards the lessening bulk of thickets hard by the streams' basin.

The going became strenuous again when the soft ground gave way to even more long grass-like sedges lying compactly by the river's bank. Sited further upstream was a miry fen whose sober gloom aptly reflected the mood of gathering. Of baneful beasts, vermin, demons, the forests that hemmed them about was without number. Of creatures, the most dreadful was said to be the Hulk of Gila, from Borat, which is near Staines in Kahzak. Druids speak of this foul specimen of being neither man nor woman, young nor old, black nor white, of flesh and blood, but no bone – by all accounts the Ladyman of Babylon.

Erynaidd it was who struck the Ladyman when he was but a mere child after he had intruded into her premises to kill the witch. Failing to see the hag, he had instead smuggled a few speckled eggs out from beneath her cloisters, which she found missing the next day but one having gazed into her crystal ball. Then had she brewed such a spell that rocked the forests and shook the castles and emptied the forests of its creatures. And the boy had lost his innocence, was neutered of his sex, became dissolved of his bones all at the selfsame instance. Cursed was he now to roam the weald with the *blaidd* till the spell is broken but seven years before the end of the age. For it is then that Time ends and No-Time again begins.

*

After many hours of hard riding the gloom which was cast over the host was lifted, and the lays of larks could be heard coursing through the greying meadows. Nywdog returned to his delightful boasting. Try as he may, however, he failed his chosen course of pursuing a swarm of birds that hovered amid the cloudless skies, like an autumn cloud moving in for the showers. The swarthy crowd was on the lookout for the carrion which had been widely dispersed in the copses beneath the reddish-brown canopy of trees. They cruised aloft in the upper air, soaring above the evergreen leaves. The Friends nevertheless did not alter track, even when tales of Men-eating birds came in from Flip's ever-voluptuous mouth. It was the bleary knoll marking the horizon for them and little dare prevent them.

Hearty were the hearts and loud was the laughter as each made it a race to touch that distant point before the onset of darkness had all but cloaked them in. Nywdog, selfish as ever, reached the mark first but was forced to return, seeing none beside him; not even Eleanor, whom he had let off to tend to a call of nature before speeding off again and neglecting her frail carriage. When he had retreated to the previous ridge having rightly guessed where she would be found, the dusk evening blanket threatened complete obscurity, preventing them any further that eve. And so that for the remainder of that nightfall they were stayed.

*

As luck would have it Frydor had already found a suitable dell for his wards to hole in, deep beneath the golden-nite clouds of Karrewhore. They say that if one can drive a chariot into the courtyard of Draco, king of the northern skies, then shall it be a cold and bitter night, filled with the dreams of dreaded times past; and such was the case that eve. For, after the Law-giver Moses, it was Draco who first read the runes of Law and No-Law, opting for the former in all its intensity, magnificence, pursuit.

Perhaps he could foresee the cruel time awaiting humanity when brother would supplant brother, when a father would slay his own son, when ties of Wedlock and Holy Matrimony would be shattered, and Covenants would be crushed like ice, when the bonds between brethren and kindred would be unloosed, Adultery and *Whoredom* ranking as no crime whatsoever. Likewise,

273

grim was the eve to come.

Each of the friends wrapped themselves up warmly and soon the harmonious rhythms of peace were upon them again. Marcus was first to drift off into that world of loneliness, ease and forgetfulness, followed shortly afterwards by Jemimah and then Sascha, in order of exertion the previous day. The others followed in time when each was settled for the evening.

Flip, however, maintained his vigil for their stricken comrade as neither light nor darkness seemed to make any difference this wily elf. Blessed was he like Black-John from Minehead who men say can pick out a raven at one hundred paces on Midwinter's eve, blindfolded. Halting only to examine every patch in detail, he grubbed the lands as a roaming boar, through ferns, searching bushes and scouring rushes by the riverbank, even venturing far a field as those unchancy woods which no man may be permitted to enter and live.

But Fortune failed him that day, for she, with her entourage, was either taken with other engagements or could not see him for the darkness that surrounded him. The elf made his way back to the party with only a few choice leaves sprung of the elf-lock herb, which was in no way a complete remedy for his sickly friend. Bide them time they may do but, in the long run, The Company needed something more substantial to aid their ailing friend.

It was not long before the entire cast was settled into that much-welcomed state of tranquillity, which was all too often lacking beneath the cool, sorry skies of Krandor. Thus they each fell out, one by one, into the most welcoming serenity of peace.

*

Not long afterwards an eagle flew northwards across the darkening skies, away from the Fallen Ridge and towards the domain of its Most Honourable King. Accompanying in its wake was the silent voice of old elven warriors, valiant men to whom the Yarah had first been trusted. The chant leaving the heather was dark and moody, breaking forth through the trees, towards that lone solitary eagle who was at the same time both wise and fierce. It was as in the days of old, in the days of their valour; before the worlds were changed and the Law was faded, when light shone before them and blood was poured to their rear.

No more are fallen foemen smitten by looks alone, save till the times of the end when No-Time becomes Time for the third time. But as the shadows passed through the wooded hollow they sung the haughty words of courage, of knowledge, of wisdom and understanding, those proud elves whose oracles were once reckoned to have been sent by the gods. And they chanted their moving elegies to anyone willing to hear.

Nevertheless, there yet remained an unkempt darkness, which continued to grey the company below, where pride and fiendish valour were on the move to resist them. Like two mighty kings pitted against each other across the Straits of Desire were these two unsung forces, both bull and goat, ramming and butting, before one prevails as the tide that sweeps up from the northern coasts for another attack on The Fortress. The contest was held within the pits of that dusk, bottomless blanket, where the dark horse managed to rule for a while.

There was another light, however, that of an adumbration, filtering its way through the early morning gloom and through the winding plethora of stumps and decaying rot. This blessed import came atop of the wings of a passing blanched eagle, which was sleek with its slender wings foiled backwards to grace its flight through the ether. By its side came the night's haunting dreams, drifting silently through the light swaddling winds.

> *Five keys to Elves and five keys to Dwarves*
> *Are the Ten Keys that make Elfin Lore.*
> *Wherein lies Krandor's Light,*
> *The Hope of Men, hidden beyond the Glen,*
> *To form the door, which leads to Krandor.*

> *One Key governs all laws*
> *Another Key shall find them,*
> *Into the Fifth to bring the rest in*
> *And the glory of all will bind them,*
> *To form the door, which leads from Krandor.*

For the time being however this profound knowledge was erased from any waking memory. Thereupon there yet remained a silence held captive in the heavenly ether, for about half of the next forsaken hour.

*

Albeit this time it seemed as though neither the troll nor his chief companion could escape from the tormentors and the serried hordes of Vexed Ones.

As he dreamt, the dreamer shared in all of their pains, in all of their sorrows, in all of their turmoil, as though he were one of their members, lost in the midst of the blitzed wilderness. He shared in their anguish too and their howling, besides the manifold tears which were wept in their sombre midst. And he was as a crazed invalid who was dazzled but not yet set free.

Albeit, it was the look of terror upon their faces each time the serpent struck and then their appearance afterwards, like a zombie wrapped in a sheet of ice, that caused him to cry most, more even than the visions which kept tormenting his brain. For the semblance of the dead, walking though they ought to have slept, troubled him sorely. But it was surely the serpent's bite that he dreaded most, because he could almost feel it.

*

He awoke startled, sweat dripping quietly off of his froward brow. A mosquito bite had roused him from his troubled slumber. There he waited, alone, in the deepest recesses of nightfall; perhaps so that the sting might pass without any lasting repercussion, or maybe it was for the strong arms of Sleep to beckon him back towards its welcome abode. Searching around himself he could see his company enjoying the silent fruit of their labours, each one doubtless, in his own realm.

Nywdog, the hero, prevailing against all the odds, against an opposition that was without number; as he knew he must, one day. Jemimah, vanity of vanities, a woman of renown, all eyes set on her presence. Sascha with thousands, and thousands of thousands of his brethren about him, he their instructor, them his babes, both the aware and the awake sharing sweat communion together. Alicia soaring above the clouds to reach her future dwelling-place with the gods. Eleanor, in her own world of dreams, a queer landscape, sometimes fair sometimes foul, horrendous as the mares which sought to scupper her life in its infancy; terrible. His pain persisted however, even past the time it ought, and then it took on the length of his form, grappling with the stalwart young buck till it all but had him in its sway.

Alarming pictures formed within his mind's eye, vivid depictions from Byron's visionary narrative that had been grafted into his psyche. At first, his illusions seemed rather more disjointed than the other's story but as the struggle continued and his body yielded, he now saw them with crispness and undiminished frequency. Nevertheless, without the accompaniment of sleep there was no sure detail. There were references to the eternal conflict between the dragon and the saints, the rise and fall of undesignated kingdoms, the circuits of constellations as they make their movements across the evening skies.

Two cold palms quivered for a good while to come, dissipating the poor soul's heat into the surrounding ether while the allusions continued to pour forth. His mind scrambled about darkly for the best routes of escape, yet an unknown unction beckoned him to remain still, to consider what withering contempt he had for the hidden things of an unknown time. With rising fulmination in his breast, he remembered that there had been something else present in his dream, strangers of a lost world, in a distant time, bloodshed, bloody, and bold. And there was a proverb, a song of sorts, a saying indeed.

Nevertheless, even though his heart waxed warm at the new accounts, the

276

depth of the thing yet eluded him, more so than it does the reader. Shortly, the fever got the better of him again, and for yet another time he drifted off into that cold blue oblivion.

*

This time he was in a small stonework cabin, showing no windows, no doors. A low flame, the only source of light, burned slowly by the bookshelf which was filled with volumes of wisdom. All were written in a time before the practice of binding was made lawful. He knew that he was in a dream, real though it seemed, and that the trolls were not able to see him, certain though they appeared to be. Nor would they for a time, as their attention was wholly focused upon the four walls surrounding them, which were stern bulwarks of their captivity. And these they regarded for a while.

Time passed.

Until one day, laughter came aback of a passing blanched eagle. Thoughts returned of escape, not only thoughts, but hope. It seemed to grip the female troll like the muse a poet. After reasoning after the manner of trolls, she reckoned it to be somewhat more sagacious if they were to dismantle some of the tremendous brickwork that had been built up thereabouts, that they two might gather to see afar. So this they did, herself and her man-troll, till the rocks were on their way and the sunlight began to seep through.

At this point, the dreamer begins to have the hope that soon, they three shall be set free.

But not even half the mortar had been shattered before the trolls again began to build up the masonry, boxing themselves in during the process, so that their latter state is almost as evil as their former state. The scene was an untimely reminder of trollish wisdom. Tremendous and awful, the great puzzle had almost been reckoned, before that is they permitted the darkness to have its reign for one more time. It was then that the dreamer began to scream, and he screamed aloud and in anger until he was sure that his was the only voice they could hear.

'What are you doing? What are you doing?' he bellowed.

'Use your wisdom... why don't you just use your common sense?' But to this, they seemed not to hear him speak. Nor could they, for they were all yet fast asleep.

Therefore, his furious rebukes availed little. The trolls pressed on with their reordering of their brickwork bondage until their souls were encapsulated all round. And the intrinsic state of the latter was worse than the state of the former, for the depth of sorrow cast over their eyes. As for the sleeper, he maintained some hope, for truly, with each new shuffling, the foundations of the house were beginning to weaken.

*

It was the second time that night Marcus had arisen but this time he was even more aggrieved. Troubles spoke to him through his palpitating heart, which pounded like a caged animal wanting to be set free, or like the breast of a bird whose past was freedom, whose future is captivity. His nerves also were at odds with him, casting wit into the ever present whirlpool of oblivion. Beads of sweat coursed down his skin like the cascading black waters by the foot of Craig Nos. All was not at ease. Presently, the sickly warrior began to weep.

During this period of sickness he had long hovered between the worlds of waking and sleeping, haunted, as many with the same affliction are, by memories of turbulent times past and of huge high mountains preventing the days to come. As a result the endless hum of insects which sleep less at night became a nuisance to him and not for much longer could he bear these frustrations. Lucid visions raided his mind from every conceivable angle. But then, for some reason known only to the gods, Jemimah also stirred to awakening. Slowly, her eyes were locked upon the quivering wreck in front of her.

'Baby,' she whispered, too softly for him to take notice. 'What's wrong?' Grabbing him by his collar, she shook him a little.

'Jemammaaaa… Jemammaaaa…'

'Come on Marcus, snap out of it! Don't do this to me baby, because I care for you – you know I do. Come on now, get better… please.'

It mattered little that he comprehended not a word she had spoken, for his reply was now to something deeper, something far more meaningful to a person in his narcoleptic state; and he cherished her first touch. Her waking warmth besides his, she longed for the kisses that used to accompany such moments. He snatched his breath and slipped his collar under hers, allowing his head to rest gently upon her bosom. But she wanted something more and waited for the words to return to her – poetic and lovely – as he was often capable of delivering. Nevertheless, there was little that came forth immediately.

She embraced him again, deeply, understanding that it was the sickness and not Marcus himself that impeded anything more at the moment. Though she could not hope to assimilate the manner of his disparate sufferings, she could see that he was grateful to be held so close, and to be cared for in such a solicitous manner. So it may be that things bode well for the moment. The dawning was near, his torments would pass, and free would his spirit be from his body's prison, in one way or another. Observing her coy smile, he remained contented just to rest in her presence. And therefore, so was she.

Tears dripped down onto his shoulder, a soft final touch to a warm and passionate embrace. Wrapped up warmly in one another's coddling arms, they slipped off quietly to sleep.

*

The third time that Marcus arose that night, however, he did not waken alone. But Jemimah got up on his stirring followed shortly afterwards by Frydor and then by Flip, Nywdog being the next in line. The others quickly ensued.

It was actually the Cloak-Wearer who had heard the noise first, but her body had been far too tired and her mind too unsettled to hold it all together for her. She failed to respond with the diligence which should have been her marking. At present Jemimah would far rather have slept in than to worry about strange and sorry sounds roaming about in the midnight weald. Nevertheless, her mind did finally settle and her hearing convened upon the faint rustling sound amid the distant greenbush. It was set before a blanket of pithy darkness from where she perceived another sound, apart from the lulls of a soft soothing flurry of midnight chills and distant echoes.

Noise came from bracken but a few dozen paces from where they were kept but she lay perfectly still, silently awaiting the approach of whatever it was that was out there. Then came the sound the soughing leaves caught in the mist and the early morning breeze, and after that, there came another. Another sound pierced the encroaching gloom with its sudden, sharp shrill. It was like the unexpected breaking of a twig.

Keitch! And then was there another breakage.

Keitch! Presently too, there were voices…

*

Caustic voices, complainants muttering about something or another, their gabble wafting gently towards the increasingly vigilant band. Barely audible above the background gibber of woodland discord was a noise distantly familiar to the elves who had knowledge of the woods, and their temporary guide, Ottoman, whose rearing was by the trees and by those dwelling in the trees. Presently his heart lay within the sharp confines his burly blue steel. All lingering misgivings quickly diminished as he felt the steel from his sword run through his body.

The notion held by some that the venture would be one long carousal was now well and truly over. In a shadow, in the twinkling of an eye, within the darkness of the concealed dell, it was no longer any more fun to be there. Similar vibrations to before came again, this time from the bush over to the west where some ferns backed onto a flowerless grove, like the hedgerows that surround the magical gardens at Riêms.

At length then the dark whispers returned, soon becoming even more hushed and ever more sinister, darker than the obscured nature of the jungle.

A deep throaty voice with no apparent eloquence rasped out orders of some vague description. In this sunless void it was difficult to tell whom the recipients were of this broken-tongued guttural; a band of ignoramuses most likely, judging by the mooted responses that compassed him about. Many were the ramblings from beyond the grove, with the harsh responses of that fell troop guiding his ears along route. Not that it mattered to Ottoman. Again he quelled his fears by strapping his fingers around the cold blue blade of his steel.

More footsteps followed. There also sprung a second movement from amidst the gorse-bushes. A snake, a beaver perhaps – the sound was too unclear to distinguish. But the westerly wind did much to shelter their ears from the removed but encroaching darkness, even allowing peace to rest upon their shoulders, if only for the briefest of moments. Like the melting of snows in springtime, so was their drip persistent. The oncoming beasts were too clumsy and far too noisy for their sound to remain muted for much longer. Indeed, even as they drew nearer, their voices were raised higher than that of an incoming baggage-train.

*

'Be careful foooools,' bellowed a raspy voice to one of his faltering comrades. 'We don't want to alert them to our *pres-sence*, do we? Be careful.'

The few dishevelled grunts were an acknowledgement to the leader's orders.

'Who are they?' another queried, walking in close proximity behind the chief. 'Who are they masss-tttaaaa?'

'What are they?' asked a third. 'What are they masss-tttaaaa?' But Brochog's curiosity had drawn him nearer to the scene than his chieftain was at present.

'Stay back – fools!' a harsh voice cried. 'They are men-folk, but there are elves with them. Two of them me thinks, yessss, two. And one other... a troll perhaps? More-ooooovvvvvaaaa, did I not count three horses over by the ford – for one was *bliccch*, another was spotted *greeey*, and the third was a *gold-en* colour – but there may have been more, though I did not seeeeee them.'

The rasping soon ceased and his hesitation grew as he witnessed another flurry of movement up ahead. All eager for the fray, he nonetheless called a halt to his troop. There should be none heading for that place of strife and contention before his master. So slowly, placing his head close to the ground, his prickly ears soon perceived that in the small of the covert in the midst of the fog-covered hollow, lay the meat of his survival.

'Perhaps they have seen something,' the harsh voice resumed. 'See, I believe I see one reaching for his weapon. Do you too see him reach for his buckler, the troll, within the grasses? Is it a troll? But what is a troll doing with elves in this part of Trol-land? ... And who are these men with him?' He gazed further into the darkness with his green glowing eyes.

'And look again, are they not woooo-mmmmeeennnn by their sides, or are they indeed small men or dwarffffffes even. Dwarffffffes ... *emmm*, dwarffffffes. I like dwarffffffes, for they make good stew.'

The direction of his interest made known, he ducked back hastily into the bushes before retreating again, gleeful at the future prospect of feeding on some shanks. He used for his hiding place the bend of conciliatory hedges lying hard to his right. From there, he and his crouched company still held favourable view over their foe, even if the view was not at all perfect. He could not altogether see all that they had to offer him. Nevertheless, before he could order his present stream of thoughts, another irritating voice had distracted him.

'Shall I circle round to the top of the hill with some warriors, masss-tt-taaaa?' The voice was that of an ugly head who was propped a few paces to his right. 'Masss-tttaaaa, what shall I do? Shall I make use of the hill or do we go in and terrorise them face to face till they bleed *pro-fuse-leery* with fear, masss-tttaaaa?'

The head was, in fact, big, buffoon-type, and squat-faced, without any redeeming features whatsoever. More simply put, this facially challenged one looked no better than a hideously deformed ape after many hours of hard torments. That's why they gave him the name "Shithead". It was terribly offensive even to the blind. Albeit, his voice was somewhat less blemished than the broken gabble of those around him which helped indicate his current status as a patrol leader, and consequently again, his ability to communicate with his master without being on drugs. And furthermore, without being cut.

'Yes... yes. Take twelve, Geb – ... Geb-b – ...'

'Gebion, masss-tttaaaa.'

'Gebeeeyon, yes, take twelve now, fool, and quickly. But attack only when you see my signal.'

'Very well, masss-tttaaaa Orches, very well. Your wish is my command. Very well, I will attack when I see your signal. Very good masss-tttaaaa.'

With this he signalled to the rest of the trailing group who were floundering towards the rear end of the advancing party and he motioned towards them with hand movements to let his intentions be made known. They saw him clearly via their luminous green eyes, a clear reflection of the glades about them and the darkness above, and patiently, they awaited the next signal of his command. Gebion it was who led them away to the local summit, slowly albeit, lest he should disturb any further the bushes.

'Good... good. So all goes well at press-sent!' whispered Orches huskily to Brochog. 'And we shall see what it is these fools are up to. Yes, we shall sure-... we shall sure-l... we shall see for sure what it is that is hap-pen-ning.'

His elegantly curved scimitar could do little to hide the flagrant monstrosity of his severely fucked-up face. He was ugly and everyone in his entourage knew it. Though seldom was such an accolade sufficient these days, even amongst these most Ill-favoured Ones. It was not enough to make you the *top dog* anyway. Indeed, for his was not even the most repulsive countenance within the group.

But there was one who was called Bateman Bedamned, a dour warrior of some five full cubits, known for his chivalrous deeds all across the battlefields of Anon. He they compelled to march backwards with a mask wrapped tightly over his head, lest he should scare the forest's more timid creatures with his generously gruesome features. And the measure of this bag was one cubed cubit, and the thickness of this bag, an inch, so that even at night when the sky was dark and few were the creatures in the forests, there should not be a nocturnal creature to squeal out loudly his discontentment. What advantage they could keep, they were obliged to, even if that meant sheathing their best warrior in bearskins. Thus, pure facial abhorrence was not altogether sufficient.

There was, as is supposed, a little something extra about Orches that caused many people to think otherwise. It was not that upon slaying a captive with his iron-shod club, he would cast their remains into the butcher's pit where men, as ought, cast in their offal. Nor was it for his pet, the ravager of blood, which he bore at all times to the fray. And it was certainly not for the chain of ears he kept bound about his neck as souvenirs for his kills in battle. But it was for something far darker indeed. For alongside his crudely deformed face was a hugely malevolent character, humourless at the best of times, inappropriately wicked at the worse, foul as the Red-haired Fandals at all other moments. That is to say, abreast of that haplessly hammered face, shaped out of all reason and consideration, was one mean son-of-a-bitch.

*

Ottoman had his Saracen Sword *Jihad* held at the ready, his hands gripping the handle tightly, palms cooling the haft of his sword as sweat dripped quietly from his sleeve. Frydor's hands too were full; in his left he held his Elfin-Blade, *Saiya*, and he clutched in his right the Kris dagger, which Surps used for close-range emergencies. Neither was Flip far from his uncle's side. He grasped his sword, *Cheaef*, which was within his belt, with the might of Hercules himself. Nevertheless, he failed to draw his sword, as one might expect, for his tumultuous heartbeat could be felt coursing through his hands.

Near to him was Jemimah, who had already helped Marcus to don his breastplate, as he held fast his battle-axe. Her own cloak-armour was fixed securely as too was her slingshot, which she loaded and made ready for use. Meantime, Nywdog strapped Sascha's sword to his back silently, before the other did the same for him, the Club-Wielder's nerves showing once or twice as he missed latches on his comrade's back. But feeling the weight of his tool, Sascha bore more than a little comfort, knowing that power and might and oblivion would be always by his side. He patted the wooden club gently, thereupon leaving his hand to quiver beneath the steel-studded bludgeon.

Nywdog favoured the versatile '*Search-Finder*', which was lighter in his hands than any ponderous blade. It could double up as a spear if necessary and its ability to glow in the dark could prove invaluable; for it was not yet dawn.

Alicia contented herself with her sword for the time being, observing its crafted brilliance beneath the rip-roaring tempest hurtling across the black oceans above. Moreover, her feet were rearing and ready to go, that footwear that had been gifted to her by the gods.

The dewdrops that had threatened the night before had now descended, but she paid no heed. Distinguished more with the sword than any of their friends, she it was who had prayed for the chance to prove herself. And now had the time come. She readied her sword defiantly, gazing steadfastly into the bushes to accustom her weary eyes to the dark, that any stray movements within the black thickets might be discerned.

In her eagerness to prepare herself the youngest of the bunch, Eleanor, neglected all guile, disturbing the honest concentration of her comrades. Disposition not as it should be, she rummaged around *Harvey* in desperate search of her arrows. At such times added range could bring deliverance and save the world, even as it was once said:

> *When your bow is nigh broken*
> *And your last arrows have almost been shot*
> *Then shoot, shoot, shoot,*
> *With all your heart.*
> *And shoot again,*
> *Your final lot.*

Nonetheless, Eleanor's hands were not yet familiar with the ways of fear, such a youth as she was and every time her paws grabbed for her protector, she found her falchion instead. Her mind was sore to hurting, and she wondered what on earth lay ahead of them all. In no wise had she ever been able to contemplate events of this magnitude; it was all as play for someone so young – a minor if you like – one inexperienced in the ways of brawling. The waif's errant nerves incapacitated her for a few vital seconds, though her Friends scarcely noticed it, as they, too, shared in the same dire feat to arm themselves in time.

The hurried movements quickened, nerves were set on edge, and caution was cast to the wind. The Syndicate's straggling fingers were pricked on blades of spiked steel, tiny droplets of blood being issued as witness to its fatal efficacy. Hands pandered hafts, whilst praying tongues wagged and all hearts were made ready for war.

But in throwing all caution to the wind they also threw a vast amount of noise into the selfsame breeze, which happened, most unfortunately, to be gusting in the opposite direction. And it was the accruement of these sounds that spelt their first major mistake.

*

Fortunately however, for at least one of their members anyway, boldness returned just in the nick of time.

*

She saw the first one come out running from behind the bushes. Faster than the eye could blink she loaded and unleashed an arrow: from Harvey to speed, the thunderclap was as lightening but quicker.

There was a sizzling whine.

Whoosh!

The dart struck the orc right between the eyes. It sunk in with a sickening squelch, cracking deep into the monster's marred visage. A mighty roar went up as he fell lifeless to the ground, a curled up heap in a prostrate condition, worthy of no more attention. In a vain effort of resurgence, the flattened beast attempted to remove the arrow that was wedged between the lines of his crinkled forehead. However, by the time his hands touched its grisly feathers he realised that it was embedded far too deeply for his currently impaired arms to deal with it sufficiently. He lay on the ground, his body twitching, while the last of his vital signs ebbed away gently.

For another second all lay still.

But then lo!

What was that?

From behind a row of creeping ferns emerged a sudden shaft of light.

A reflection perhaps?

Or perhaps something that has caught fire?

At Ottoman's insistence, each member of the Troop lowered his weapon and peered out into the misty gloom beyond. The obscurity was truncated by the sullen moonless shadows and the dark images cast by stalwart trees, some whose leaves reached for six-feet or more, like arms flailing about in the darkness. What with the pitch black gloom, fear, and the intensity of an effulgent flare, the Friends were as blind as bats.

Try as they may, the elves failed to discern the fizzled shapes in the surrounding blackness nor could they soon make out little more than a hazy blob set against a cauldron of darkness. For the sake of their sore eyes Frydor, Flip and Ottoman, together with Nywdog and the others, relaxed the grip previously held on their weapons. Eyes were rubbed vigorously, as the pain of the sudden glare spread forth through the sockets.

Sages say such will be the dazzle when the end of the world comes and the fires rain down from Nef. This is the fitting judgement that awaits all those of the Synagogue of Satan who say they are Believers but are not, and for those idolaters, adulterers, murderers, thieves and all liars who continue to forgo the Ancient Lore.

Returning now to the onset of the battle, there were no shapes and few were the shadows. But that there was their second mistake, for the brilliant blue flare was the signal light.

*

'Charge *Bredreeeeeeen!*' screamed a huge, gawky creature from further up the hill. 'Down upon them and quickly now.'

And the cry of this host was taken up by screaming goblins, ghosts and spectres in every glen and hilltop around them, kin who had fallen in earlier battles with the trolls. To which the demons of the air and devils from the world beyond responded with a sudden shriek of exultation in contemplation of the rain of blood which they foresaw would drench the soil about the Sunken Ridge.

'Charge!'

The assorted band of miscreants plummeted down the brow in a fiery fit of insanity, each jostling hard for the honour of dispatching their brother's killer. For some way below lurked a small band of orc-killers. Justice was in need of dispensation, forthwith, lest any more of their gang met with grim death on that grim eve. Few were those amongst this warrior-host of orcs who grieved when one of their members was lost, but Brochog was well loved by all, ugly as the back end of a buffoon though he had certainly been.

'No, not pleased. No, not pleased at all!' another screamed, his words hurtling down the hill before him. 'We kill youuuuu, yeessssss! Keeeelllll! Chaaaargeee bredren…!'

Arrows glistened through the early morning skies causing oracles to be read in the heavens far and wide. To a druid, signs surely of the gods themselves; to the more ignoble or *ynfyd* as they are called, bedlam and death and sorrow at every turn.

The silvery-green tip of the present volley dazzled terrifically as the moonlit fibres caught it a queer angle, causing a fresh stream of reflections to hang poised above the heads of its devotees. The waltz soon ended and in its place came an array of metal nips, each poisoned peak carrying death in its sleek-angled beak. Realisation awakened, a great shadowy form grew within the wilderness.

'Shields!' cried Frydor, raising his own protection in desperation.

Then came the sound of plural projectiles kicking off the back of his protector. Many were the orc-cries and their buzzing missiles, singeing through the night of hungry wild whistles.

'Help me, Eleanor,' Marcus cried, as she raised aloft her guard not a moment too soon. Another deadly barrage had been suppressed; but for how long?

The Friends curled up tighter as one by one they each sought to block out any possible line of attack. However, in so doing they also reduced their own field of view drastically. A pitiful cusp was all that remained through which Frydor might view the action, while arrows and darts basted against their light steel armoury. Fortunately, though, that was all he needed to see.

'Quick, head towards the dale!' Frydor bellowed. 'We are not safe here for their numbers are great, and increasing. They are too strong for us Nywdog, they are too strong. Get your friends, and follow me down, quickly…'

'Aaarrrggghhh!' This time the cry uprose a short way off from the Company. 'I am wounded!' called the voice.

'Come quickly will you, for I will not wait!' shouted Frydor, unable, above the din and within the darkness, to either hear the cries of his comrade or see his fallen form.

This elf was seldom too proud to lead by example – a witness to both the fortuitous and the wise. Even now as he fled down the present winding trail, he spared little thought for their stricken guide, who had remained to cover the blazoning retreat. All warriors believed their time would come in battle, and hoped for nothing more than to have this said of them afterwards:

> *"Before they were slain, they maimed*
> *And before they were killed, they slew."*

'I'll stay and cover a while,' gasped Ottoman breathlessly, 'for me thinks to have become badly harmed. Everyone else go and follow Frydor down to the dale. You have your best chance there…' He looked more solemnly at Jemimah and then towards the Dog. 'Go now or else lose your life, for I am prepared for what comes next. Now leave.'

That was all he had to say on the matter.

*

Eleanor quickly unleashed another two arrows towards the uppermost shelf of the ridge, where a fresh string of goblin-flesh was ready for the picking. The hemp of her bowstrings whistled loudly as its arrows glided effortlessly through the ether. There then followed a space in which life in the weald appeared hollow and the thickets upon the hillside seemed scoured of the branches that formed them.

Two more muffled screams.

Two more scimitars fell to the ground, minus their muscular orc-handlers.

Two more spirits sunk deep towards the fiery furnace of Uffern, so that there were two less souls to dwell upon Krandor itself. For a new home had already been prepared for them outside the first four dimensions of our understanding, in what men call "The Impossibility of Reason". Presently they were cowering away in one of the darkest regions of the Fifth, and soon enough they would die yet again.

'Move, Marcus!' Eleanor screamed. 'Get down with the others before they kill you. You haven't got the strength to be doing this, so just move – I'll try to cover you.'

Another hail of arrows rained death upon the trampled outgrowth, voiding her valiant words, testing her spirit, bearing witness to the perils all around. Yet his reactions were sluggish and his rationale slowed. His dark cowl thrown forwards could not hide the weakness of his dreaded play.

'Forget your part, Marcus, and move,' Eleanor shrieked, at once falling back behind him. 'Or I'm going to have to leave you like the others...'

'What others?' Marcus growled, peering round briefly as he set out down the hill. 'Anyway, I'm gone!'

With a quick glance, Eleanor could see what he meant. So, in an instant, so was she.

*

Another keen orc had made his way up to the front of the nearest pack and was bearing down heavily upon the Troop's forward location. Strength unabated and heart bold, Nywdog it was to first see the black hazard upon them. On this occasion however the great young warrior reacted too slowly. Though all was not yet lost.

Jemimah came whistling through the wind, sword in hand, sweat binding her matted hair into knots and nestled clumps. Upon her face shone the fierce pride of Azrael, false messenger of Death; within her garment her chest pounded fiercely. Marcus was presently in Eleanor's capable hands. So now had the time come to help the proud man, lest he should be overcome by the sudden onslaught of evil that hemmed him about. And she flew as she ran to his aid.

Neither was her dispatch too soon. For but a few yards off to the fore, a giant appeared, the like of which men ought not be able to comprehend. He was a champion and a slayer of champions, a poet in his own right. But not with words and runes was his skill but with enchanting pictures composed of slain foemen's bones joined end to end till they told the story of his conquest upon the battlefield that day. And this act he performed as often as the ribald amongst enemy ranks dared to match his proficiency.

As he smiled at Nywdog his mouth revealed bear's fangs, black, broken and blunted, and in the midst of that swarthy hole were the torn hides of goats, dears and feathers plucked spry from wild ravens – the same which follow him about on the battlefield. Now grinning, he permitted Nywdog to gaze deep into that empty cavern, while raising his sword above his head and brandishing its ponderous weight across the sizzling arc of heaven.

'With this blade, Nos Dihenydd, I've slain both friend and foe a-plenty. Champion I am, and a champion of champions, a leader amongst the best. This mighty sword holds sway over all those on the northern beachhead, by the Straits of Desire, over yonder,' he cried, in fell tones, pointing northwards, Nywdog expected. 'But now I hunt for scroungers, savages, and those others of Satan I know not. We shall make a good fight, Black Boy, for you represent your race well. Most quiver like jelly at the moment they meet their maker, but you stand fast – or is it fear that holds you fast to the spot.'

And right he was, for Nywdog caught few of the words that left the ogre's great big gob. He stared on nervously as the monster drew his hands about the black bag on his face and proceeded to remove such protection from his whiskers. His hands were shown to be bear's hands, whom one might suspect he ravished one day in a fit of anger. For they were hairy beyond men's arms and rare was it for an orc to have such coarse pelt upon his arms and legs. A huge chest bulged out greatly from his mail-coat and the hair that covered his bosoms was as the forest itself: dark, blood-covered, impenetrable. No need was there for a shield for this one, for few who saw his face kept their will to live, and of those that did and fought, they were altogether withered in nerve and deficient in ability.

'Go away, beast, and I'll let ya live!' screamed Nywdog. 'I mean it!'

The giant roared an awful hoarse chortle, full of gaiety and evil intention. He it was who believed that all men should have their final say before being dismembered and chopped up into pieces and having their remains spread thin and their bones plucked spry.

'Why should I leave when it is Fate herself who has brought me here? I am a warrior most evil, who collects the bones of his adversary. Even demons themselves relinquish their goods when I set upon them…' And at this, the wind howled and the breeze moaned and the grass on the glade fell backwards. For none dared disagree when this beast spoke.

'Kites and crows go before me and ravens and jackals fly behind me lest any should miss out on their feed. We patrol these lands often, in search of Fels'noc, that cowardly abomination whom has yet to match my prowess. One day I shall lay my hands on that troll and squeeze the life from his veins till his eyes glaze over with dreaded death and his tongue leaves his head for another.' Again the giant roared, this time his cackle was full of evil and ill repute. The wind bellowed fiercely alongside this most ill-favoured of orcs, though whether in fear or frenzy it was hard to tell. Nywdog remained transfixed.

'You are still brave, boy,' growled the Killer-of-many, 'but I will make you wish you were not. My deeds are more than the hairs on your head and even when pitted against the most terrible Addanc from the deep, I showed him no mercy but slew him and ate his meat.'

Bateman Bedamned had removed his weather-beaten mask but his opponent's face was fixed firmly to the floor. Who would dare gaze up at what demons called the Abomination of the Living? Or who would want sight of bloodshot eyes, a nose rent in twain both this way and that, cheeks that looked like the Forests of Annwfn, and a mouth through which ships and their crew passed when joining the River Styx at its tributaries.

'Oh baby please – Help!' Nywdog cried, when he could bear it no longer. 'I'm in deep… shit!'

And with that, the bold man fainted.

*

All at once two stones sprung up from the undergrowth and they whizzed across the skyline in quick succession. Jemimah's skill with her slingshot was well-known and bode well for her companion, and not too soon had this wonder come. The blind hairy beast whose battle-boast we have just heard was not one for viewing projectiles cast at him from queer angles. For when he was but a youth, fighting his brother for the scraps cast aside by their mother, his left eye had been forced from its socket, followed forthwith by another unchancy misfortune which, elves say, oft happen in pairs. And that was this.

A black-eyed raven passing some way above, noticing its opportunity for gain, had dived down at that very instant, like a flock of demons above the monastery in Elfdom when the monks are in prayer-fast. And the bird had scooped up the remains of his damaged ligament and choked it down, even before it had returned to flight. Thus, since the days of his infancy, Bateman Bedamned had not been able to make full use of his senses, either by witchery or medicine. His faithful mastiff-bitch was not at his side this day as on most others, and though his mask was removed, no match was this Goliath for the female descendant of David. Life returned to Nywdog when he saw that his mortality had been extended, and scrambling onto his feet, he drove home the tip of his rod, that the evil form should rise no longer.

Innards were spilt, guts were loosened and breath was rent in two as the warrior cut, sliced and stabbed again in a frenzy of both relief and vexation. The soft green grass was no longer a place of sleep, as entrails poured out for the reception of sky-hosts ever-faithful to such gatherings. A chance encounter, a lucky blow, who was to tell? Neither Jemimah nor Nywdog wished to contemplate such at the present moment. They stood there, stunned, watching the beast's heaving torso as he slowly expired.

'We did it, we did it. I can't believe that we killed the beast,' gasped Nywdog relieved. 'But where did you come from? I thought that you'd run off with the others.'

'Look here, Dawg, when I cover my head with the hood on my cloak and focus inwardly...'

'Fuck me,' said Nywdog astonished, blinking his eyes rapidly to make sure that his mind wasn't playing tricks on him. 'You just... like... disappeared!'

'Exactly!' agreed Jemimah excitedly, exposing her head once again.

'But how...?'

'It works best, as the guy said at The Confirmation, when I meditate on something true or noble or just or pure or lovely or of good report or anything of virtue or trustworthy. It takes a lot of concentration, and I need to be at peace inside, but it comes in bloody handy!'

'Man, I'm pissed – I want one of them too... But I think it's about time we chipped, cloak or no cloak. This time though, make sure that I can see you, cos you had my back and I don't want to be leaving you behind. Especially not with that mob over there...' She saw the terrible band of orc-brothers bearing down upon them and needed little more encouragement to leave.

Thus Nywdog was fast upon his feet, proudly scoffing at all attempts to catch him. He hewed valiantly the foul, forging avenues between the deadwood and boles of the sleeping bush, running in a direction unknown, together with a companion who raced as hard as he, in as much as a daze as he was. They parried a path for themselves across the main isthmus stretched about the wooded grove, more orcs falling foul to their skilful play with stick and sword and stone. Many orcs died a death ill deserving of their doom. First one, then two, and then three, demised, dead, expired, and without so much as a pitiful sigh. Thereupon, the Bowels of the Dead Man opened to receive all those who had chosen to pass on unprepared.

She stayed hard on his heels, neither speaking a solitary word nor looking round to see the encroaching furore. Their friends were presently as they were, if not faster, more valiant, more bold. It was Jemimah who feared far more than she was letting on, for there seemed not to be even a single element nor even a solitary blade of grass that did not hunt them down in the chase. Still, not slow was the Mail-coat bearer when danger approached from the south.

She was off the mark again promptly and bit the target with the edge of her sword, her assailants too close for her favoured weapon of sling and stones. Fleshy bits clung fast to her side of steel as she gazed on. A green viscous liquid turned black with the light, seeped out from the open wound. Jemimah clambered over the orc's bleeding body, goaded the Stick-bearer to more decisive action, and moved on.

*

Some time earlier, a few of the more foolhardy orcs had taken after Sascha. Coarse imitations of well laid plans, numberless bodies, shouting, gabbling, pointing in profusion; none had failed to stem the flow of the Club-wielder's violent onslaught. The evil manoeuvres upon the ground were but reflections of the canopy beneath the tented hall of heaven. Up above, night birds swarmed the vaults of Nef, and down below, knight-orcs swept up behind our warrior. Vultures hovered in ranks, viewing all unfolding events with glee, whilst upon the dreary globe beneath, the fen-dwellers were banded together to keep him from the Troop's ranks.

The length of opposition was furious, the breadth of their hatred deep. Like hunting hounds on a midnight chase all available orcs had joined in the search for the Club-wielder. Yet even now he fancied his chances against the multitude, before whom he stood proud and defiant. Enshrouded in fog, he pursued his lonely course towards the skirts of Mount Ruishê.

'Human flesh!' he heard roar behind him, as he pelted down the trackway after the others.

'Food!'

For had he not seen their greedy green eyes fixed upon his tender thighs, which seemed to bear him no good wishes whatsoever? Though it was only when a deer strayed into their path, thereupon stabbed and slain in a mighty unprovoked assault, that Sascha thought it best to leave with whatever pride he had in tact.

Sascha broke the ranks of the enemy host, like a huge boar in the open plains, like a wolf through a sheep-flock, like the rushing of waters at the gates of the Hafren. His club pierced sconces, removing heads from the chin to the ear, squeezed skulls, and exsanguinated the remnant of pressed brains. Basting riven shields and connecting with bodies, he ploughed the dense disordered mass of brutes with his cudgel. Indeed, so thick was the covering of blood that a king's entourage might have ridden overhead.

The warrior smashed the head of another fool who bore down upon his position, crushed the skull of a second (before breaking his legs as he still sought to walk) and then altered the alignment of the body and arms for a third, before realising his dash for freedom. He knew when a fight was too difficult for him to endure alone and he was on his way straight after pounding the fallen beast, one more time for good measure, which was just as well...

The howlings and groanings and battle-cries indicated that not all the fun was over, for several bore their cutlasses aloft, streaming along in the wind after him. But he himself flew, like a bird in the breeze.

*

The entire Syndicate moved quickly, in hot pursuit of the two elves who had by now fled half way down the bank. They pursued one another towards the crux of the hill like snakes scooting over logs or like hounds baying after pheasant's blood. Neither was the grey ravager of the moors able to witness such a terrible display of speed and ferocity.

They decamped across butts strutting out to scupper their way, felled trees and barked skins, each obstacle hewn by principalities to mar the course of their flight. But deft hands, some say as skilful as Côr Denny the Dwarf whose *heini* was said to have been gifted him of the gods, cut them a path asunder between thickets and thickly set men. For in one deft-defying motion, Frydor slashed at a grim orc, six cubits tall and dressed in the raiment of war, before slitting the throat of a fellow beast who had crouched alone to hinder his way. Then did he deprive him of his vitals before runeing the cross of protection, all of which he accomplished in the selfsame instant.

Behind him Flip was also the hero. Weaving in and out of boles and bushes as his size permitted, he set ambushes to help keep his foes from his friends, whilst making progress for himself, and scouring clean the land of evil. At one time, he ducked behind a jutting forage of hedgerows, beneath the lower-laid boughs of an elm tree. It was here that he saw Marcus stumbling towards one of the snares he had set. Jumping up from his spot to pull him under, he could see his friend was in no fit state for lectures. Instead, he set the trap when all was safe, springing it on an unsuspecting band of orc-raiders who had strayed from their set path.

Grim were the howls of regret, loud were the piercing cries, hot was their anger, as the net scooped up Hell's evil host and cast them forthwith into the awaiting bamboo sticks. There then followed an orderly progression of arrows as each one struck its target. Then came Eleanor flying through the breeze, running whichever way came to mind, shrieking, yowling, baying and tearful, like an irate banshee lost on its bearing.

'Flip, mate, I'm feeling really bad,' Marcus murmured, sensing the sting of innocence whirl by his ear. 'I'm gonna need some help getting down there Flip, or I just won't make it to be honest with you.'

'Not to worry, Marcus. Let what is ready come – I think our hearts are in good stead and our weapons are tested.'

Gazing upwards, the friends saw the myriad of warriors fighting amidst the encircling flares. Orcs were slaying orcs, arrows were flying, sword thrusts and spear jabs were numerous. Nevertheless, The Syndicate scurried past, with Sascha bringing up the rear.

Things were not so favourable for Ottoman, however. He remained where he fell, upon the nape of the selfsame hill, above the skirts of Ruishê. A man of infinite cunning, he preserved what strength he may, biding his time, neither over-cautious nor over-rash, maintaining his polished steel sword always, biting foemen whenever and wherever they dared appear.

It is said amongst elves that battle has the ability to either make or break, promote or exclude. Amongst men they say that whatever does not kill you makes you stronger, and such was the case this day. For though great had this warrior been in previous conflicts, more marvellous was he that day.

Doughty as all folk knew him to be, he waxed noble as Mafa son of Hasleg, yielding his life for his brethren. The transtrol was sworn to repel his enemy's grim advances as long as his breath remained in him, and that he achieved with success, slaying with impunity those on the march on down the forbidden brow. Many passed him by and many more were seen to come, but he fought on valiantly as the highly skilled soldier he was. Only the run of glory was left to be seen in this fellow, and what a jaunt it turned out to be. It was far more fabulous than can be recorded here with equity.

In the twinkling of an eye his *gradd* had equalled that of the *elohim*. Of the many that watched few failed to admire his prowess. In fact many say that of all those on the field that day, bold and wonderful and gallant, it was he who earned the most *galanas*. For even when his sword had fallen he suffered not himself to yell for his friends lest he should hinder their flight. Rather, he beckoned them to move all the faster to make his very pains that much more expedient.

So they had fled, leaving Ottoman to fight on with the dogged determination of a thoroughbred. He had been reared for such a day as this and there was now no shirking from his responsibility. Indeed, had it not been for the painful sting in his side, then surely he would have laid low thousands more and gone into their land itself, slaughtering many of their thegns, their cousins, their kinsmen, all along the northern beach-front. But his battle turned grim when his sword shattered, which made both his arms and dagger into effective tools. Presently, he too had to reap the rewards of his hard-earned labour, for he was cut off from the rest of his group and bleeding badly, as Paradise waited by patiently.

*

After this the sky lit up with tremendous flares glowing in all directions. More screams echoed through the fens, each resounding mightily about the hardwood logs and the bristling teeth of the orpines. They ceased from their ventures only when they met the hard grey rocks of Mount Ruishê. Great were the shrieks and muffled the yelps, work some say of Aedh of the Murderoushands, of that cold-blooded brood of killers, who does his job grimly before leaving his victim to scream away his life, as he himself slinks away into the encroaching wilderness.

Different arrows held the field this time, darker than the ones which had sealed the previous eventide. These were longer darts than Eleanor's with blood-red tips, finer to touch, more painful upon contact with the heart. Amid this great barrage of shafts came a profusion of colourless voices, bringing joyless sounds to the ears of the attentive. As time passed the Friends more readily discerned, not one, but two distinct inflections. The raspy, sepulchral intonation of the orcs was joined by another flow of garbled words. Yet the first voices quickly turned into the panicked, random sounds of mortals.

Invisible foemen had joined in the fray and judging by their heavy footfalls they were harsh warriors with little mercy. These were dour soldiers whose thinking rarely extended to the welcome guise of charity. They marched beneath the chestnut skies looking for their next victims, greatly loathing those who had penetrated their strongholds. Their lambent torches played an eerie light for their passageway. These were the evil beasts that owned the lands, and they despised assailants, even as all detested them back. Neither did they take too kindly to strangers!

It was the season for nightly rains and this new morn was to be no different. The morning ether wept tears of both pain and pleasure for the battle wrought beneath its skies. Pain, for the Bright Ones who witnessed the carnage undertaken against the Father of Lights; pleasure for the Sons of Death who dwell in the clouds, inciting men, guiding demons, marshalling kites and crows and jackals, defecating vile upon the evil world of Krandor. Swords shimmered before the blue light of the moon while sundry orcs were hewn asunder. Cold and harsh was the fray, bloody and brutal were the slain, and the cries that uprose from the ground haunted all dells and filled all fens and gusted across the river, far and wide as to the sea itself.

Try as it may, the descending black waters were not able to cleanse the land of its green gunge and crimson blood. Monsters fell grievously at the passing of this new host, bawling like hounded dogs for the mercy they did not deserve, pleading for a leniency they neither understood nor were willing to dispense themselves. Dour orcs whose sounds were normally so brusque could no longer belie their inherent fear of death. All wept buckets for their stricken leader Orches, who, with one fell blow, had his head cleaved in two upon his shoulders. His body fell limp and found its way to the ground in a quiet and disordered mess.

The remaining orcs were leaderless against this new company. Yelping resumed and gabbling and disputes marked the day as the order for precedence was determined. Ogh, ugliest of those remaining, was found best suited to take charge and soon opted to chance his life by beating a hasty retreat away from the oncoming aggressors. As many of the goblin-lords from around the world would testify, their new foemen were grim indeed. The orc-raiders could return later perhaps, with more forces, if their commander ordered them so. And they would sweep out their assailants, taking vengeance on those that remained, in memory of their fallen allies, lest anyone should think the orcs' mettle had turned flaccid.

Now though their track led westward over the winding path, to the tree line no doubt, through the northern shires and thereafter towards the Straits of Desire. There they would remain without until such time as they were stout enough to face humiliation and possibly death at the hands of their brethren. Therefore, as suddenly as they came were they gone, but presently they moved at the rate of knots.

*

At length it seemed as though everywhere The Company went commotion quickly followed. Beneath the early morning gloaming the more intuitive of God's creatures fled away from the troubled Troop and their relentless pursuers. A few minutes along the trail the Friends paused for breath again behind Frydor. Words exchanged were few, but they had made some progress.

All the same, the terrain was heavy and the night dark, leading them astray on no few occasions. Marcus too was compelled to strive on as he might, warring against his own afflictions, as well as against other more pressing matters affecting the entire troop. Yet toil on he did in stark fear for his life, beneath the banner of valour and hope, a feeling not easily fathomed by those unfamiliar with the ways of war.

It was a dire thing to see their ungainly flight taking them straight into the hands of their rivals. They were young sheep that had strayed from the flock upon the harsh mountainsides of an unknown world. Victims whose shepherd had parted for new pastures elsewhere. The wolves clung nigh on their furs in wanton abandonment, clawing at their covering for sport or game – whichever – few could tell. But the youngsters pressed on hard, lest their hearts should fail them before due time. So they ran on like the condemned men they were.

*

'Is everyone here, Nywdog, is everyone accounted for?' cried Frydor, gazing round in alarm. 'Tell me, quickly, before we press on.' The pitter-patter of droplets made it hard for all to hear.

'Are all present... Sascha – what is the news?' The elder elf wiped his face again before cupping his hand upon his brow. 'I cannot make out everyone for certain; who is here and who is not?'

The horses were not close by – that much was brutally evident, as Sascha felt was his duty to point out, all too abruptly. Nywdog mentioned seeing his own horse, Schatten-Flug, by the brook over on the eastern side of the hill, before noticing his steed decamp during the course of the first battle, when it had been at its fiercest. The others murmured varying things of accord pertaining to their own chargers, though as the general consensus came to be known, it seemed as though the horses had all departed either before or during the first hostile encounter.

'So our rides are not here then? Are we all here however? Jemimah, Alicia? And how is everyone in spirit? Everyone in good health, everybody fit to go – ? Answer me quickly please lest we leave you behind! Is there anybody injured?'

'Ottoman's not here,' Sascha shouted, scanning the nearby hedges. 'He remained up by the dell to give us a bit of a head start. But I didn't see any movement up there after I left, hey guys?'

'No, nothing,' Jemimah murmured. 'Not a thing.'

She cast her eyes further along the lie of the land, till they finally rested upon the summit of the mound. Many dead bodies lay sprawled all over, some of which were face down in the miry ooze. There were places where death also meant disfigurement and dismemberment by whirling blades of destruction. Other corpses were coiled up in the foetal position. One expects that this was in the vain hope of protecting themselves from the barbarity of their aggressors.

The elves scanned the undergrowth briefly for one last glimpse of their friend but to no avail. Bodies, limbs and entrails clothed the floor of the forest, but the stormy skies yielded little encouragement. Many were the bodies hacked asunder, grim were the heads toppled and with superfluity did the blood flow forth from every wound, more even than the Friends could brag of themselves. Panic struck as screams from the Halls of Annwfn stole across the battlefield.

'Frydor, man, cats are dying out there, and we're all still here. Unless Ottoman's turned into one mean son of a bitch then I's don't like the sound of this.'

'Yeah, Flip,' Alicia moaned, 'it just don't seem right at all. Who or what are they?'

'Don't be screwing round with my mind anymore Alicia. You did that last time and look where you got us.'

'Oh come on now you know that wasn't – '

'Shhhh…' Frydor placed his finger upon his lip, and listened on intently.

'G-G-Guys…' stammered the Club-wielder, 'over th-th-there,' he said, indicating a gap in a nearby rank of woods. 'By the tall trees o-over th-there b-boys!'

Jemimah soon caught hold of the fear in his eyes and the stammer of his tongue, so she followed his quivering hand over towards the eastern edge of the forest. Slowly, the early dawn light seeped over the horizons.

'Where, what do you see Sascha, Jemimah?' demanded Frydor in desperate tones.

'There, Father,' Flip added, gripping his belt for comfort, 'over there. They're pointing towards the Fallen Ridge.'

The distorted beginnings of sunlight helped to transform the motley assembly of forms sagging through the budding mists, while the daystar's unencumbered rise continued slowly as they traipsed through the timber. Across the brook the ghostly figures now emerged almost lifeless, few giving rise to suspicion or angst as they made their way before the sunrise.

They resumed their approach but it soon became evident that theirs was not a midnight pursuit of adventure. Swords hacked, spears were thrust, and screams were emitted from those who were supposed to be dead. Corpses collected under copses and across the fens. Bodies, not all of them lifeless, were stripped of whatever items could be valued. For these new men, always on the lookout for fortune, plundered anything worth more than a single penny-farthing.

*

A small number of orcs, who had not met their end either in the first or second barrage of arrows or during the course of the ensuing slaughter, were now as good as defunct. For shadowy figures alighted from the undulating framework of trees, slaying any moving thing that was stranded upon the ground. But what alarmed the Syndicate most was that they killed and butchered with the joyous tenacity that gave rise to the name "The Merciless". Thus the barbarians moved forwards, tormenting the lost, sending off the damned, leaving only fleet-footed birds to survive their progress.

Then, as the minutes went by, the shadows appeared to grow in size.

For the Friends, however, there was nowhere else to run to. They were tired and weary and their absent steeds could offer them little assistance. Even so, Marcus fared the worse, for his exertions in battle and for his previous malady; so they could in no way hurry him. Moreover, any attempt to carry the warrior would be met with fierce and unwelcome resistance. Neither would they dare to leave him in the hands of the enemy.

Times were desperate, of that there was no doubt, but such baneful thoughts as these belonged either to weary brains or to the minds of the treacherous. Smiting one's own brother or foster-brother, the slaying of cousin or foster-cousin, or the sacrifice of kinsmen or kith ought not form any part of civilised contemplation, just as the violation of Holy Virgins, the neglecting of Scripture, cold-blooded murder and blood feuds should form no part in the mindset of goodly folk.

Presently, his friends formed a tighter circle around him, Marcus sinking slowly to the ground, depleted of the strength he once took for granted. He was now fully spent and his earlier toils in the skirmish had only strained him all the more. Things did not rest easy with our young warrior as he put his axe away. They each could see the Clouded-Ones encompassing them about, moving as one, as lost and hungry souls who had at last found their prey.

As Flip looked in despair towards his uncle, there was, without doubt, an unmistakable glint of fear in his eyes, the like of which he had rarely seen. The Surp was wont to conceal his swelling despondency, but by the time he had done so it was pointless; for the ghostly forms had already become living. And as they drew nigh unto the company, they turned into the solid, impenetrable forms that they were.

Few are the words sufficient in any vernacular to describe the complete spectrum of emotions that the Syndicate felt at their morbid appearing. Indeed, in Krandor, or in life in general, one is often faced with such insurmountable problems, for which there seems to be no immediate remedy. In these circumstances therefore, it has broadly been accepted that one must first always state what is blatantly and unequivocally obvious, before reiterating the selfsame thing – as a means of establishing some sort of mental cohesion – a kind of sanity test if you will. After that, if time allows, one must speak comforting words, words that are known to reassure the heart in its more fickle of states. Again, that is if time allows.

'Trolls!' said Frydor dishearteningly, eyes poring over the unearthly dark figures.

'I think you'll find, Uncle, that there are many of them…'

PART IV

INTO BONDAGE

ARRIVAL AT THE TROL-POUND

To everything there is a season, a time for every purpose under heaven:
...A time to keep silence, and a time to speak...

ECCLESIASTES 3:1,7

Trolland, in the central part of Abundance, is populated by rolling hills and fertile green pastures which stretch from the nape of Gyrgon's Neck all the way across to the bridge that binds the western part of Caer Maboli to its eastern half, above the roaring cataracts of the Afon Almer. Neither blighted crop nor withered tree has its place in these grounds, and there are some who say that, standing as it does above all the adjacent lands, one can see trees bearing all the fruits of the known world, and all its creatures, and all the birds that roam the skies (save for the Black-winged creatures of the Näzgrîl). In an earlier age moreover, some speak of mysteries fit to confound even the most astute elves.

There was none who disputed the refinement of this spot, even though it was ravaged time and again by war-bands, by tribulations and by uprisings. These perpetrators were they who saw nothing in the beauty of the white-crested mounds, or in the flotilla of sunken ridges, or of the yellow helmed birches, which are golden as the crown that sits upon the head of that olive-skinned tyrant, Alex de Vitaz of Anbad. These were they who, for the sake of their status, sought to bring all the lands under subjugation.

Though if the truth be known, few were the men able to wage war adequately against the deepest fables of the land, and less were they who were willing to endure it. In the days of yore nobles brought their maidens to these parts to ravish them in wanton abandonment before the low, clear skies of Gyrgon's open plains. And this healthy practice continued up until the time of Prince Henry the White, who it was smitten with noxious bodily infections at the same promiscuous antics, that boils sprouted from beneath his armpits, skin was shed from his thighs, his stomach distended to the size of a stuffed antelope, maggots crawled out from his embouchement (upon the gratification of his mistress), and fully-grown worms were seen to leave his God-given orifice ever and awhile afterward until the day of his death, six weeks following that fateful encounter. In no few records was each of these afflictions noted.

But believe each one what he will, for even greater aberrations held sway at times, above the distant green lands of Abundance. There were elves the size of black-crusted beetles; witches that ate nought but boys of between six months and six years; the lost nomad, who for his life vocation, wanders about from the Brambles of Boreham's Wood, to the dark forest of Haegfan's Mountain, after being spellbound by the enchantments of Erynaidd, queen witch of Haleg's Weald, for his sin in aiding the trolls in days gone by. There too was corn the size of pumpkins; four-legged creatures, who, when they were not busy either chewing the cud or being weaned of their milk or fondled in their funny bits, had the tendency to engage in stimulating conversation about the curious goings-on, not far south in the dotted hamlets.

Now being one of the boldest of his breed, one such mammalian was Bigsam the Buffoon. He took a few steps forward and advanced some way to the fence lying closest to the crossing party. From there he could observe the bound strangers who were, even now, being compelled to enter the village by the main gate.

'There you go, what did I say? Looks like they're in for it!' the cross-bred cow grunted, stooping his head low towards the ground before waving it again proudly in a manner befitting a prize bull. 'Yes, they'll make a good meal before we do, I'm sure!'

The cow, which was actually half buffoon, snorted scornful tones of their capture.

'I should dare say, by the looks of them, that they'll not even live to see the next full moon... not that the sight is a marvellous extravaganza anyway. It's all rather tedious really when one thinks about it, I must say.'

Bigsam looked on, his head raised forward to the hangers-on within his retinue, who generally only became more interested in affairs after someone else had checked out the waters for them. At the best of times there was little to retain their interest.

Perhaps the appearance of savage hunters who appeared before the seasons' more notable feasts, together with their round-edged butcher's knives. Occasionally, the carriage of a delicately crafted female of their kind was enough to spark arousal, though rarely did this enchantment come to pass in Trolland. Albeit, the former was most definitely a viewing worth rising for, if only for the fact that it may be the last sight that they ever saw.

Venting hot air through his fore- and back-passages, Bigsam strolled inanely through his faithful flock, telling of ill things to come, and eradicating from his wake the pesky nuisance of bluebottles using both his dainty tail, with which he swotted, and by the doleful reproach of flatulence, which was released in long, steady streams through the unhallowed gap in his backside.

'What do you think Sija...?'

A withered old cow who seemed disinterested in conversation was the object of his proposal.

'Yes, wasn't that what I was just saying? They won't last more than a day, you mark my words. Perhaps the smaller ones not even that long. It's a pity if you ask me, because the trolls are always getting the first choice – and that's not right if you ask me. We should be given some of the spoils too for our fodder!'

The other longhorn responded in no certain terms. He did appear to shiver however, as the irritating crossbreed approached him from his left, lowing all the while in tones fit to set the Jesters of Yewffwl on edge, and perhaps even reduce some of them to tears. He was a distasteful fellow, Sijade deemed without saying as much personally, but in all the years of his captivity (which had been many) he had not yet come across another young quadruped that delivered him from his disgruntled demeanour. It was an important thing in an all too dreary business, especially when others tended to regard you as a bit old and infirm – which facts indeed he rarely argued.

'They might live,' Sijade replied, pleasing the youthful buffoon's pride no end, 'though I tend to agree with you,' he slurred. 'I think, like all the others, they shall not live!'

He returned promptly to his chosen profession and favoured pastime, cropping the lichen with his aged, blunted teeth. 'Yep, most probably... not even another day.'

'There you go then, Sija – it's just like I said.'

He saw the rest of his friends cease from their feats of mastication for a moment, as they followed his drooping nostrils towards the parting company and their hosts. In the utmost self-regard, he padded around on his cleft hooves and made his way over to his favourite, muted uncle, who was in fact the prize bull.

'See that, Uncle, even Old Sija reckons they're in for it. What did I...'

*

'Can we have some water please?' the youngster asked innocently. 'We're hungry and thirsty and the sun's really hot?'

She squinted her eyes as she peered through the criss-cross array of plucked logs which was now the gate between her and the outside world.

'Go back to your place, waif, or I'll split you in two with my spear-shaft,' growled a voice.

'But I'm thirsty!'

'That's the last thing you should be worried about right now me-dear. Thirsty?'

The troll looked over towards his companions and reviewed the same word. 'Thirsty?'

Presently, each one began to guffaw raucously.

'My dear little girl, where we'll soon be sending you will make it seem like you are now lost in the oceans of the Eastern Seas… ha, ha, ha, ha!' Belle-Hannah, Fûkwït and Manghet joined in with Bel-Hacosh, sharing his delightedly twisted sense of irony. 'We'll soon send you to Uffern, and then you can complain about being… thirsty. Ha, ha, ha, ha! – If they'll hear of it down there, which I think not!'

Greatly irritated by the base-born fellow's callous retort, Eleanor returned from the patterned blue and white skies. The sounds of their laughter and the coarse tones of the dice-wielding trolls were replaced by the damp, dusty confines of the hostage-pit.

'No luck, Eleanor?'

'None whatsoever, Dog… I think I may lose my innocence.' And she promptly burst into tears. 'Again.'

'Listen, O Youthful Child,' Flip whispered, looking first at Eleanor and then at Nywdog, 'we're not out of this yet by a long chalk. We still have our strength, even though the battle last night was taxing. But today is a new day and we can yet maintain our courage, if we wish it to be so. Our weapons have been snatched perhaps but we are not alone, trust me.'

'It looks to me that we're alone. Shit, can't you see them all? Besides, even if there were some around willing to help us, nobody knows where we are. It's pure fuckeries!'

'I'm scared too, Flip,' cried Eleanor. 'I'm really, really scared. Make them go away!'

'Yeah, mate, in addition to everything else, these guys are quite big, and by the sounds of them, there are a lot more of them than we saw last night.' Eleanor glanced up at Nywdog through tear-sullied eyes. 'Yeah, I reckon that I am a bit nervous, too, to be honest. Bloody nervous boss. If I wasn't so God-damn cool, I'd probably crap myself!'

There came another dreadful cackle from the gathering of trolls, which reverberated down the slippery slopes of the pits, into the hearts and minds of the friends. Eleanor, clutching onto Nywdog's comforting arms, allowed herself to break down in sobs of self-pity.

'We've only just started and we've had it already, haven't we?' she whimpered.

'No, of course not!' Flip burst in irritably. 'Be like myself and take courage in the worthiness of your cause and do not be afraid of these terrible trolls! Remember: rarely is it by strength, which our captors undoubtedly have – but it is by cunning.'

'Oi! Elf!'

The voice from above shuddered through the wooden pen-gate.

'Close your pesky orifice or I'll hammer it shut for you!'

With one of his hefty arms, Manghet prised open the gate hemming the friends into the coop.

'Er… Oh, and here's your meal, fools,' Bel-Hacosh roared, casting into the darkness a gnawed piece of bone, with some gristle left attached, for the threesome to devour between them.

'Eat it well, and enjoy it – because it will be the last meal you ever receive this side of the Afon Styx!'

After a short space of hesitation in which the others similarly paused to consider, the three remaining trolls followed suit. There then began a barrage of broken bones, flayed flesh and gristle, so much so that the elf fled with his friends into the gloomiest recesses of that burrow. And in doing so, he swore that it was as if a whole volley of vultures had turned loose their feed, which was even too foul for their blood-thirsty beaks.

*

His eyes were fixed upon the shadowy figures beyond the crumbling wall. It was a dull orange light that glimmered its ruddy glare around all corners, past all edges, casting its keen spectres with vengeance onto the cold, granite earth. But he managed to arch his body slightly even though one of his arms was chained to the metal hook that protruded from the blood-stained walls. He could soon see the warmth flying like deadly sparks off of the opposing partition.

Flames bearing semblance to adders leapt beneath the hollowed cave-arches. Lights played on the lime-white walls of the burrow, sending into a whirlpool the iridescent reflections of the serpents which were at the same time distant, yet cloaking and oppressive. A faint drumming could be heard as he turned in panic to face his perspiring comrades; a clangour that was not easily distinguishable from the sombre footfalls that fell on the flats above their heads. But as he looked towards Jemimah for an explanation, he saw but a timid form of a warrior beset with many fears herself.

The sounds of toiling trolls increased and his ears were quick to liven. His manner thereat was uncertain, not knowing whether to seek out his friends for comfort, nor knowing if to shield his eyes from the torments to follow would yield him a more favourable response. Tralob lit the torches above the cavern-ous womb, the sudden fire dazzling the Club-wielder's eyes, until he fell back against his unchancy spot, thwarted by the ill-shaped sunken boulder, which had now come to be his resting-place.

For a while, Sascha remained a quivering wreck, his eyes tightly shut, his ears listening to the grim pounding of instruments on the heavy working-board. But as the incessant toilling continued, he snatched at Jemimah's free hand. Succouring her consolation, he put his face deep into the dusty soils. She, on the other hand, was incoherent with mumbling, her free hand busy dampening the sweat of Marcus' heated brow, her efforts in washing his face with the soiled water they had given her.

Talk was cheap in the recesses and voices were garbled, broken as the heathen race of Infidels from the East, or like the ill hosts of Malebö's foul retinue whose goblin-tongue was said to be the language of the forgotten dead. Another dark form, who had been greeted as Slacob, approached the hearth dressed in little but the simplest of rags. He bore no arms but it seemed as though his hands were weapons enough. With them he might have been able to pluck the wings off of the Great Wivern if given the moment.

Unholy chatter completed, the gof cast an eye back past his blazing furnace. His look took him over towards the Club-wielder. His was an evil glare that carried well for him through the darkness. His victims were the trembling friends, his eyes were as cold green gemstone, his power was to seal his foes in fear.

'Jemimah, I don't know what to do. I'm bricking it girl – you seen how big they are.'

Upon another ominous scowl, Sascha quickly quietened his voice.

'And what are they doing over there?'

He strained to see a third form standing over a hardened anvil, donned in a leather apron. Hairs grew out from his arms forming thick, coarse bushes, sufficient to conceal a small colony of elves, so it has been said. His back was hunched as one might expect after too many seasons setting hafts to blades and not enough years testing them. And his demeanour was ruddy, pockmarked, wearied as the dwarves residing in the Holds of Uffern. These were they whose task it was to forge weapons for the six Infernal Armies. However, this more mundane chore was left to the trolls, Bobb included, who was now making her way over towards the indisposed comrades.

'Quiet, fools, no talking. Bobb I am, servant to the Lord of Trol-land, for that was the name given me for the manner of my exultation at the death of each of my enemies. I it is who cut off their heads, eat their brains, drink their blood, and play water polo with the remains of their sconces. And all these things I enjoy almost daily – try me and see!'

With this she let off such a rip-roaring laugh, that all within the underground hovel thought the grounds to be taken with an earthquake, the like of which is often felt in the wake of battle when the Belly of Hades expands to meet its new bevy. This grim achievement pleased her inane senses well, alas.

'Oh, I do enjoy my feats of accomplishment, for there are few others like me in Trol-land… save for the mistress herself, that is.'

'And her husband-man!' added the gof.

Their cronies laughed alongside them both. They were like three black witches, full of dark intimations, evil thoughts, as spectres from the fallow grounds of Annwfn.

'Yes remain quiet!' cried Savagedoc. 'For mine is a difficult enough task already – to forge instruments for your torments – seeing that you are all so puny already. Quiet! Lest we extend your pain through torture. That would lead to a slow and agonising death which I'm sure you don't want.'

'Yessss,' screeched another. 'Unless you all like pain. Do you love pain as much as I enjoy inflicting it? I hope so, for that is our favourite pastime in these parts. We sometimes employ the service of witches whom we ask to raise our victims back from the dead so that we can torture them all over again.'

'Yeah... before smiting the black bitch with one of Savagedoc's tools!' growled the gof to Bobb.

'Ha, ha, ha, ha, ha!'

So there it was: Jemimah remained still, tending to her ailing friend Marcus, frightened by the displeasing countenances which she could perceive all round and oblivious to the bruised form of Sascha as he sought to hide his face from the cruel implement of his misery.

*

Conk!

There was another loud groan.

Conk! Conk!

Followed by two more in quick succession as the bones of a raw sow struck them repeatedly.

'Not to worry, Alicia,' Frydor said, shrugging off the latest assault. 'The gods willing, they shall not break us. Try and take courage – not in yourself remember, but in the reason of your affliction.'

'Quiet elf!' Mishmash yelled, ' – we are eating now and do not like to be disturbed whilst we feast. But not to worry my small friend, for we shall deal with you shortly.'

'Yes,' Sniffdog affirmed, 'don't become impatient... I promise we'll make it up to you.'

However, before his corrupt humour could take root Frydor had responded with a fresh jibe of his own.

'Ah, so is it that abuse gives you as much pleasure as eating, or is it because it is easier perhaps? So which one is it troll?'

Nâelog stopped dead; and Sniffdog himself looked over towards Mishmash. Mishmash indeed seemed to turn a shade crimson at the elf's fine retort.

'For that remark, elf, I will make your punishment seven times worse than the affliction I imposed upon Gwyion mab Belcher, when I finally removed his eyes from his sockets seven days after they were put out by a heated implement belonging to my friend Savagedoc.'

Nâelog, Sniffdog and the others who had just entered roared at this, quaffing their goblets of mead in between each boastful hee-haw.

'But for my final trick on you, I might like to leave your eyes in…' The laughter abruptly died away; what kind of torments would this be if the eyes were left in? '… Because I would like you to see the hideous remnant of your for – '

'What do you mean, Mishmash, no eyes to be plucked out from their sockets?' The voice that growled was deep and very terrible indeed.

'What exactly is it that you mean, O youthful troll?'

Nâelog and Sniffdog likewise were moved to confusion at the sudden outburst from their mistress. They turned around to greet the voice:

'Yes, friend, what is it you mean?' added Nâelog.

'Yeah, what?' crawled Sniffdog. 'Mishmash?'

'Well, as I was about to say – '

Thwack! Mishmash took the full brunt of Saspion's blow upon the side of his head.

'Doh! What was that for?'

'When you were growing up, we taught you that always – now say "always" Mishmash.'

'Doh, always.'

'*Always* after tormenting a foeman you must pluck out his eyes from their very sockets, lest the stare of a dead man should send sin into your heart and pierce your inner being, bringing a curse onto you and your precious kindred. Your mother before you was an evil woman, full of cunning and baneful ideas – so you surely then must recall these things?'

Overhearing the dark conversation in no uncertain terms, Alicia began snivelling.

'Frydor, I'm terrified!' she wept.

'Keep your strength, Alicia – I'm sorry to say that, but methinks you may be in need of it soon!'

Dark murmurs rapidly became the talk around the table as Mishmash sought to justify his rather unique approach to imposing torture, inflicting torments, and impressing tragedy upon captives. Mouth filled to the brim with the broad hide of a sow, blood and gristle flew forth from his gob as he strove to explain his very peculiar ways to the mistress.

At first, his words were met with scepticism, which thing was not perhaps altogether surprising, seeing that he was the youngest and most inexperienced of the guards. Yet even amongst this ill band he was still very much the haughtiest and one held in high regard by virtue of his potential.

Shortly, the mead the trolls were privy to saw that tempers were quelled, and indeed, mighty did the yellow-ravager prove in the goblets of trolls. All cups were quickly drained, and the savage virtues of their troll-masters were extolled through the roof of the hut and past the clearing in the sidewall. Soon however, the drink was come to be an aggressor, overbearing and strong, and the words of Mishmash proved far too tedious for Saspion to bear any longer.

Embracing her servant by the nape, she tugged hard at his garment with her stout arms, lifting him clean off of the rush-strewn floor. He in turn grabbed back at her arms, wanting his breath to find its rightful passage back through his neck and through to his heart, in lieu of his bulging eyes that were coming to bursting before their time. Nonetheless, instead of assisting his comrade-in-arms, Nâelog moved away from the table, to be followed hastily by Sniffdog, whose own swill-induced spew, fortunately for him, failed to reach either Saspion or The Other, who was stood as a shadow by the door.

Then, stumbling for the intoxicant that had beset her sturdy form, Saspion knocked over her shoddy stool and strolled over towards Surp. It was her intention to proffer upon the doughty elf her sincere condolences for the foolish flurry of words which had sooner come forth from her underling's mouth. It was not their manner to wound noble elves for sport, for the sake of times past when they had once been friends. To former allies, torments were rendered solely for business, and even then they followed a certain (albeit sometimes quite arbitrary) format. But this was a practice which some of her younger guards were not fully familiar with yet.

Upon reaching the dangling elf a mighty jet surged forward from her mouth and covered his minuscule body in the pink and yellow bits of blood, bile and boar skin. It soaked through his garment, obfuscated his nostrils, besmeared both his hair and beard, and stunk like a six-week old corpse left out in the sun in the midst of the month of Mehefin. Thus, Frydor's appearance soon paid semblance to a skinned piglet after it is cornered and strung up by its tiny legs.

Saspion led the war dance amongst her fellows, which always comes before the skinning of a great and noble adversary, the like of which Frydor was without fail. Observing that the Elf's eyes held her gaze steadily and seeing the timid black girl by his side – moreover, upon smelling the stink that emanated from his trembling person – resultant of her vacillating glands – she quickly changed her mind. She pounced upon him promptly and began pounding him with a tremendous flurry of blows, for the most part around the head, eyes, and blood-filled mouth.

*

'Are you okay Sascha?'

'Roses, girl, roses. I feel like a bed of roses. Never felt better to be honest with you.'

Jemimah looked puzzled.

'Really?'

'Where did they get you from girl, my goodness gracious me!'

'Gosh, I – '

'Of course not, you daft muppet,' Sascha groaned, softly prodding the welts that had developed on his left forearm. He collapsed back into his spot next to the dusty boulder. The Club-wielder bestowed a look of disbelief upon Jemimah before setting his eyes on their distressed companion.

'How is he doing then? – Marcus, I mean?' Sascha grunted, intimating with his head in movements that seemed nothing short of painful. 'He seems like he might be doing worse than me.'

Jemimah chuckled gently, realising the dark humour of her comrade, not willing to respond more favourably should she be forced to ponder the fate that lay before them all.

'Sascha, it might not be the best time, but we've really got to do something – 'cos how are we gonna get us outta here? And what about the others?' She dropped her voice when one of the giants raised his ugly head.

Presently, she resumed, her voice a little shaky; 'What I mean is, like... I'm terrified Sascha. I think I may have wet myself.'

'So what do you want me to do? – Dry it all up for you? I'm in just the same position as you are – and worse. When they put a burning piece of metal on your arms, then you can come crying to me. But until that time, give me a break.' He fell back again to his place, the energy of his exertion sapping him of what strength had remained.

'Well... never mind then... pig.'

'Pig? Pig? You're a right bitch, you know that?' Sascha cried irritably.

Just then, Marcus emitted a low and agonising cry, as he felt a stray touch borne from his friend's overwrought emotions. It brought her to her senses quickly, lest the infighting should squander what may be their last and only chance of success.

'Listen, we've got to try and stay together on this one,' he rejoined, observing his comrade cautiously. 'All I'm saying is I know its hard...' He paused for a while, waiting for his breath to recover somewhat; 'I know its hard, damn hard... but don't be thinking about yourself all the time. Spare a thought for me – '

'Shush a second Sascha,' Jemimah interjected, ' 'cos I think Marcus is trying to say something.'

Tearfully, she dried her grieving eyelids, leaned forwards, and pressed her ears against Marcus' mottled breath.

'But I don't know what it is yet...'

*

Stood above them was Kussob, cousin to Bobb, nearing five cubits in height, weight of an ox, face close to that of a hobgoblin's. Along his arms were veins straddling all across the surface. Images were graven deep into his flesh, works of curious design and patterns that painted a picture of his many triumphs. He brandished a newly heated strip of metal in his hands, which shone white, even in the midst of the darkened stone quarry. With it he drew streams in the air, lighting up the silent dusty globules like the lightening that streaks across the surface of heaven above the forts at Caer Anyon.

These bring forth fiery sprites into the air – animating them, yielding life – before causing them to relinquish their command once again, as Apollo bears his mighty chest time and again, the same lovely breasts that keep all men at bay and all women longing.

'Well, what do we have here, O munch-kins?' Kussob enquired glibly. 'Do find yourselves inclined to tell all that is on your heart…' He gave a menacing look of envy towards the prostrate warrior. 'And upon his tongue, especially, O lovely girl.

'Or do I have to cut it out that I may read its runes?'

'Sascha, get him away from me! Get him away from Marcus!'

'Just where exactly do you get off Jemimah, do it yourself!'

They each cowered away into their allocated corners as three great footsteps brought the troll to within striking distance.

'Look, I really don't know anything – and my friend is just ill – really he's just delirious. He's not saying anything important, just mumbl – '

'Mumble, mumble, mumble, mumble. Mumbling I enjoy...' Kussob's eyes lit up, bright as the tool he bore.

'Grumble, grumble, grumble, grumble. Grumbling I deplore.'

Then, as the steel altered its colouration to a reddened hue he added:

'But groaning, groaning, groaning, groaning, I must have, to feed my desire more.'

He lifted his feral implement to Sascha's legs, who was squirming about violently in attempts to avoid the hideous hissing sound. But soon enough it was laid firmly upon the soles of his feet.

Even Savagedoc looked up in awe as the most hideous screams left the warrior's mouth. It was like fish escaping from a trawler-man's net, or like the erupting of a fire-mountain when its villages have not paid it sufficient tribute. Nevertheless, the smell of roasting flesh was enough to bring joy to the other trolls that were assembled thereabouts. But every movement led Sascha to more pain, more anguish, and to a dreary black world of stench and oblivion, upon which attention was swiftly turned to the other, more querulous amongst the friends. Jemimah.

*

'Elf!' he growled ominously. 'I am going to pluck your eyes out, so that you may not view evil any longer. Then I shall place them in your ears to stop them up, that the sounds of your torments might be a mystery to you. Then shall I cut off your elf-hood, to provide remission for your undoubted sins, and thrust it down the tracts of your gullet. And I shall torment you as you deserve...'

Flip gulped sharply.

'Unless, of course, you do for me either one of these two things:'

The elf viewed the troll dubiously.

'What would that be, O Brawny One?'

Enjoying the elf's chosen appellation, Bel-Hacosh replied; 'You either fight your black friend over there to the death,' he roared, pouting his lumbering belly against Nywdog, '... or you ravish the little girl here for our sport and entertain-mend, remind me of my little girlie-spawns though she may! The choice is yours elf.'

Eleanor looked horrified.

'And what if I refuse your sullen requests, Brawny One?'

Miffed that Flip had forgotten to add the "O" prefix to his name, the troll glanced upwards to his associates who were busy observing all these things from outside the coop. With a smoothed log of oak, Fûkwït propped open the cage door which afforded Belle-Hannah and Manghet the space needed to descend. The short, squat form of Fûkwït followed soon afterwards, as they all made their way to their colleague's side. One by one they stood in a row facing the three fearful friends.

'Then we...' indicated Bel-Hacosh. He hit himself rather hard in the stomach, before doing the same to his three friends, who each doubled up slightly with occasion.

'Then we...' he resumed, 'will take delight in butchering you slowly, followed by each of your sorry friends over there. Is that clear enough?' He peered closer into Flip's miserable eyes, and bearing his own wide-open, he said, 'Or is there something left that needs to be clarified?'

At once Fûkwït broke down in fits of laughter, the like of which was imitated by the rest of his band. 'And then, perchance, we might even allow you to die... but probably not!'

Fûkwït was having kittens. He collapsed onto the dusty floor, the excitement of what was to come far too much for him to bear at the present moment.

At length the laughter subsided, the captives were restrained in a new position, and Fûkwït rose to his feet. Eerie shafts of light still probed the recesses of the subterranean coop, searching out its victims as they sought, with all reasonableness, to cower away from their invasion of privacy. Hazy mists, dusty formations and floating modicums of ashes sifted paths through the obfuscating covers, some settling lightly upon the unlit ground, others continuing on their erratic jaunt towards tranquillity. But silhouetted against the looming sun was the dark and colossal figure of Bel-Hacosh. The troll who was evil beyond all contradiction bore down upon the elf, as the others stood by in expectation.

'Slap her, elf,' he growled.

'Yeah, slap her good, slap her good, he-he-he-he-he!'

'And make some pretty patterns on her face,' Fûkwït imitated mockingly, 'like a big, happy smile from ear to ear – you can use my cutlass if you want?'

He produced a ponderous, blue blade, which bent around in an arc and reflected the glint of the emerging sun in an evil fashion.

'Shut up, Fûkwït, you dim-witted, sheep-shagging son of a bitch!' Bel-Hacosh brushed him aside casually. 'And you too Manghet, you black-bearded buffoon's arse!'

'I cannot do such a thing – I... I will not do such a thing,' stammered Flip.

'Just do it, elf!'

'Or else you can fight for your life against your friend there,' rejoined Fûkwït smoothly. 'I'm sure it would be a fairer match?'

'But no pussy footing around, or we'll savage you both – that's after we've dealt harshly with the girl!'

'Too true Belle-Hannah,' bellowed Bel-Hacosh. 'And that would be very unfortunate wouldn't it, elf, 'specially if you lose? For your sins would take you to Uffern would they not, after you have passed through the cold regions of Annwfn?'

'So there you have it,' whined Fûkwït. 'The choice is yours...'

Flip hesitated for a moment, his heart low as the tide when the moon has dwindled in her presence, as he was caught between a rock and a hard place. Cruel were the faces pressed close to his, cold was their stare, callous were the hands that poked him, pushed him, prodded him to act. Evil were the things spoken in his hearing and harsh were the words which moved him.

In great shame he lowered his aching head, whilst at the same time avoiding the scrupulous glares of the oafs around him. In particular he wanted to elude Belle-Hannah, who bore strange resemblance to a weak-willed aunt he had once known. But he also missed the gazes of two of his closest companions who were waiting for him to act with the courage of his bold words.

'Do it, elf!' Bel-Hacosh roared.

'Yeah, do it, do it!'

'Now!' Fûkwït piped. 'Go on elf, get to it!'

So with his arms and sturdy legs the elf drove straight into the waif. And he pounded the frail little girl till the last signs of consciousness had left her body.

*

They brought Marcus in and flung him on top of the straw bedding.

'So this is the one then, is it, Kussob?'

'Yes mistress, this is the one; this is definitely the one!'

'Good.'

Without warning she raised the hem of her kirtle and one of her two stout legs came crashing down upon the warrior's diseased ribcage.

'No, stop that!' Alicia cried desperately, running forward and reaching out to protect her friend. But she was too late to stop three of his ribs from cracking beneath the pressure.

'Ah... so he does not feign after all,' Saspion murmured, seeing that Marcus failed to move. 'What does he say then?'

'Mistress, his words are fey – stranger than the runes of the Stone-orcs from Babylon, mistress. I do not know what he says?' Kussob looked innocently towards the other trolls present, but neither could Mishmash, Nâelog or Sniffdog interpret Marcus' word-horde.

'It seems, mistress, that he speaks words from his ill temperament –'

'Yes he does,' interrupted Frydor. 'And I could have told you that if only you'd asked!'

He waited for silence, until all eyes had settled on him.

'Unfortunately... I believe he may have been poisoned... with some snake stew I rustled up a few days ago,' Frydor continued, spitting out blood and saliva as he slurred his sentences. 'Everybody's resistance is different even to small doses of the toxin but we elves can eat ten times as much as we did without ill effect. I believe he is in urgent need of attention, of that there should be no doubt but if he does not get it soon, I shall hold you all personally responsible.' The elf's eyes remained fixed on the bulky female troll even as she walked up to him and slapped him firmly across both cheeks.

'Bold words for one in such an uninspiring position, elf. But keep quiet now before I let Mishmash here have his way with you.'

She looked disdainfully at the grime on the palm of her hand, which had once belonged to her, and wiped the bile back on the forehead of the pesky Surp. Frydor dropped his head and twisted his body as far as it would go, but not slow was Mishmash to come up to him and hold him steady by the locks of his thinning hair.

'Let me go, you filthy barbarians!'

'Make them stop, Frydor, they're hurting Marcus.'

'I would love to do just that, Alicia, but as you can see, I'm somewhat tied up right now!'

'Ah, so the elf still maintains his humour, even in the face of death,' Kussob snapped. 'A worthy feat indeed! But 'tis one that will cost you dearly all the same, elf. Very dearly indeed.'

'Let us go, you big bullies…'

'Yes, we are big,' replied Nâelog scornfully, 'and we are bullies,' he added, smiling at the black girl's astute observations. 'But we shall not let you go. That would be… that would be…'

'That would be silly, absolutely ridiculous,' Sniffdog confirmed for him. 'You don't expect us to give up our fun do ya? Never – not in a million years as they say!'

Frydor looked desperately towards the troll-mistress, reminding her of all the bold threats with which she had warned the impetuous young youth, Mishmash. But slowly, even as the sun closes the drawers to her cloisters every evening, the truth soon dawned on Frydor; for all matters thereunto had been but play. The trolls had spoken thus to flatter the friends, increase the stakes, to expose what truth may be known. But now the first part of the game was ended, allowing little scope for venture but the next dismal quota.

'And you, my black friend, you return to praying for your friend and yourself – 'cos you will shortly be in need of it!'

Broken of heart Alicia, the Book-bearer, leant over her wounded comrade Marcus, and wept the rest of her soul onto the sullied straw mattress, which had now become his sole piece of bedding. Her friend suffered greatly, that much she could see, but how to comfort him she knew not.

*

Nonetheless, her friend could still sense the cold, stinging bite of the serpent's teeth, as it pressed itself along the length of his arm. He could feel the heat afterward as the poison took hold and travelled succinctly through his body. His wish was that he would obtain the same grace as Saint Paul when the viper attached itself to his arm in Malta. The saint shook off the snake, to the marvel of all those around, and he felt no lasting discomfort. Such gods were few and far between albeit…

He could see the trolls fleeing from the Men of the East and from all the wroth that they brought with them. He could sense the fear that unsettled their spirits and pervaded their minds. He shared with them in the pain of their dispersion as they were cast out like wood, unfit for growth, fit only for the funeral pyre, which in times past had been of their own making.

It bore the hallmarks of a very saddening caper, that the trolls should flee away from their homes, like curs running through the wilds. And it was as though he was forced to abscond with them, through the trees, past the encampments, and out onto the broad open plains of Krandor.

They fled alongside their loved ones, some running this way and others running that way, all eager to decamp from the place of strife and contention. Some were with their wives, whilst others sought out the loved ones of their youth. For many had been caught in the searing flames that followed their wake. Even the once bold couple, Fels'noc and Saspion, were numbered amongst these sorrowful scenes, those proud and mighty warriors who many feared.

Presently however, they were just as all the others, fleet-limbed and long-maned, feet as a thoroughbred made for the bucking, with arms no longer with the strength to aid them. Because now they were lost and in dire need of some help.

*

But Marcus also remembered Byron the Surp and the revelations he had shared with them on that first auspicious night. And he could recall the words of wisdom and knowledge that the elf had been so diligent in speaking.

It was not long before his sentences began to return more clearly and the latter sonnets of Byron's articulation – as if they had been imprinted on the mind of the poorly warrior. An indelible mark of their veracity or a sign of worthiness for their acceptance, who was to say save the wise?

> *"...But if they cannot exercise self-control, let them marry.*
> *For it is better to marry than to burn with passion..."*

And indeed, more runes came to him:

> *"For men will be... without self-control...*
> *Lovers of pleasure rather than lovers of the King,*
> *Having a form of goodness, but denying the power therein...'*

Each of the nightmares soon merged, becoming one in his psyche, one in his spirit, all to take his bedraggled body by storm. And it soon came about, as he sought to conquer these afflictions, that his efforts only added to his deepest frustrations. Yet it was the last of these fell images that played on his mind the most; for it was almost as though, within the maze and mortar, a faint, albeit, distinguishable light was at last beginning to emerge, through the leaden cloudy void.

THE DARK KNIGHT

"And I also say to you that you are Peter,
And on this rock I will build My church,
And the gates of Hades shall not prevail against it.
And I will give you the keys of the kingdom of Heaven,
And whatever you bind on earth will be bound in Heaven,
And whatever you loose on earth will be loosed in Heaven."

MATTHEW 16:18-19

The gloom spread quietly over the dispersion of white mists, like a melancholy cloak draped over the skies, or like a sheet of muslin raiment covering the bride to be. Black choughs and sleek sparrows took to their wings, heading for the woodland pastures beneath the mounds of Bryn Trolliége, but their paths were hindered by the musty collection of dewdrops descending from the far-flung clouds on the eastern horizon. Cold were the winds that rallied against the jubilant clarion-calls of cocks, against the proud exultation of red-breasted robins, above the frightful din of shrieking kites, all of which had gathered there in the hope of feed. But soon the time had come for all to draw away from the hamlets into the dusk petering light of the dark depressing grove.

Silvery raindrops fell like the studded spring orbs of a budding meadow some way lower down the slopes of Trolliége. It was like the autumn dawn, cold, refreshing, peaceful. Not far from this were hives and large dovecotes cluttered together, all within earshot of one another's incessant toiling. Those that viewed the birds most often envied their freedom, even the flights of graceful swallows in whose paths lay streaks of brilliant blue-white plumage. Those lacking this spectacle had to make do with their own entertainment. Tears thick and in abundance greeted them as the torment of the Friends continued.

Little need was there for the winter months in this unchancy spot. Deep brown tracks, ploughed in the muddied furrows, led the way to the neighbouring hamlet all year round. The village was bridged by a sturdy rampart, before which cattle and swine chomped at their swill. Afar off, all appeared fit for the brush of Barfheini mab Tôlstoï, whose paintings lined the walls of keeps from the Island of the Mighty, which is in the Eastern Seas, all the way across to the blackened walls of Cèrïdyn the Crimson, chief ruler of Fou-ouls. Towards the north, the day was clear, cold winter chills taking advantage of the naked blue skies, as those that could, wrapped themselves up as warmly as possible.

Nevertheless, above the hamlet, water drops splattered against well-trodden paths, carving up with its anger more grooves of mire than ever a troll-foot might have hoped. The light cast upon the trolls looked grim and there appeared little chance of this rude frown lessening in the days to come. The skies were overcast to the shot of a bow, matching the gloomy-grey faces of those who currently tormented their fellows. Ill presentiments aside, the Friends were just beginning to adjust to their new circumstances when more trolls joined them. They had come to view the spectacle.

Bitter howls of regret spun uncontrollably past the herdsmen, through the dew-spawned meadows, across the wastelands and barrow-mounds, as far as the low-lying valleys whence Frydor with his party had sooner traversed. The gods were summoned in the midst of their pain to provide the strength needed to endure, so those all round believed. But their response was not immediate, if at all.

Some of the trolls came to the hutch, not far off from the main track-way that circuited the village. Others opted for the shallow hold, buried within the sullen recesses of Krandor, stifled by an accumulation of heat. The remainder drew near to the blighted crops of wheat and barley which chronicled the outline of the village, and they could not fail to pay heed to the unyielding screams coming from the dismal coop housing Nywdog, Flip and their tormented friend Eleanor. The games continued in earnest.

*

'Roll da bones, Fûkwït, and roll 'em good, 'cos you and Belle-Hannah be needing a good throw if you want to choose what comes next.'

The brainless troll looked up angrily.

'Ah, so you think it is only you who have the power over the dice? Well, wait and see.'

'Oh hurry up, Fûkwït, or we'll be waiting all day for you to have your turn.'

'Yes, perhaps so – but it will be worth it, you'll see.'

And true were his very words. Though shorter and more squat than the others (and although, immediately upon sight, Fûkwït appeared less foreboding), he was no less an aggressive foe. Moreover, his mind, as was his humour, was twisted as that of a sprite from Uffern, with no abode forthcoming and angels from the gosgordd of the great archangel Michael hot on his furry tail. He was a very distorted fellow indeed but he did have his uses.

'Here it goes then, comrades…'

Presently, he rolled his hand rashly, gabbling all the while with his companions, as Belle-Hannah kept a cross-eyed watch on their three prisoners, and Manghet stood over them with his head reaching high as the prison roof. The bones fell into place, as they ought, for Fûkwït to at last have his call.

'There, you see, Fortune is with me,' growled Fûkwït.

'Yes, so it seems… and it's about time too!'

'So what is it that you wish done to them?' Bel-Hacosh inquired, as he leant his ugly muzzle close to his companions.

He turned aside to view their captives; 'What foul disregard for the custom of humanity do you now want to inflict?'

'I'd like to continue with the same, Bel-Hacosh, but can I give him the whip as well?'

'The whip?'

'Yeah, I'd like to use the whip – all that skin coming off with each lash… ooh – sends shivers down my spine. I want to use the whip!'

'Aye,' slurred the Evil One, 'that you may do, and gladly.'

Promptly, the lop-sided fat troll-mistress, Belle-Hannah, brought out the whip which she kept in reserve for the times when she is summoned to the dining table of their master, or at the ill behest of Bel-Hacosh. She stroked it lovingly, laughing hideously all the while, before placing it into the large grimy paws of Fûkwït.

'There you are, lover boy! Make good use of it now, won't you?'

*

Meanwhile, hidden in the fatuous shadows of the same coop, Nywdog was beginning to stir from where he had been laid out unconscious. His hubris gone, none were there anymore that took the trolls' company lightly. Flip the Younger, however, was still facing Eleanor, observing the quiet form of one who has long since passed out into a world of her own.

'What's going on?' It was Nywdog who thought to speak first. The Stick-bearer propped himself up on one arm; 'Where are we…?'

'Do you not remember, Nywdog? We are captives at the hands of the trolls…'

'Flip, what's going on mate… And what on earth's wrong with Eleanor? Why is she bleeding? What have they been doing to her?'

The elf turned around slowly, thinking frantically about how he was to extricate himself from this one.

'They made me hit her, Nywdog – '

The warrior rubbed his aching head, still trying to raise himself up slowly without arousing too much attention.

'What do you mean, they *made* you hit her? What are you talking about? Who made you hit her? What did you do to her, chief?'

'Well, Nywdog, while you were unconscious there on the floor, they threatened to kill us all – and you first, if I didn't make play in entertaining them with these foul antics. But not to worry, for I feigned most of my assaults, and I believe she has passed out only for the shock!' The elf lowered his voice again, sweating profusely at the approaching trolls; 'Make haste Nywdog, behave again as though you are sorely wounded. Perhaps they will leave us alone again!'

Nywdog heeded the advice quickly, barely able to take in the adverse circumstances. He curled up tightly into as small a ball as possible. Though oblivious to the fact that Eleanor was far more injured than the elf had let on, he was far too concerned in trussing up his own heart, lest the fearsome pounding of his sconce and chest should give the game away.

Fûkwït strode his way over the recumbent Stick-bearer, giving him a sharp hefty kick in his sides, which did not fail to pronounce a loud, long groan of its own. And these moans were similar to the lamentations of Llynattic from Gwent, whose body-parts (it is believed) was pummelled relentlessly upon every quarter for upwards of seven hours after his glorious return from warring, for not appearing in the correct colours. Men say afterward, when they scraped up his remnants and took them to the Kaspen for burial (as was customary for men of his tribe), that much refused to go to their rightful resting-place in the seas; or so it is rumoured. But of all tales of gods and heroes, let the reader be weary of this one!

The troll approached Flip, eyebrows touching, forehead pointed and menacing, and handed him over the whip. To it were attached bones, bricks and broken pieces of glass.

'Do it, elf, or I'll do it to you!' Fûkwït hollered.

The poorly elf looked around wildly at his friends, to Nywdog who was semi-conscious upon the rush-strewn floor, at Eleanor, who was starting to come to again, and to the evil forms of Bel-Hacosh and Belle-Hannah as they beckoned him again to resume where he had left off. Seeing no help forthcoming, his spirit began to fail, and again, he succumbed to the pressures of Bel-Hacosh's evil designs.

'Okay, okay, I'll do it.'

So, like a savage just freed of his bonds, Flip took hold of the reigns and began to beat the waif, mercilessly…

*

'Next time, Jemimah, shut the hell up would you. When I'm having a red-hot poker put all over my body, the last thing I need some woman cussing me down for not protecting her. Goodness gracious me, of all the self-centred, egotistical, self... seeking people I've ever met.' He ground his teeth at the very thought of her.

'Look, Sascha, I'm sorry if that's what you want to hear, but I'm scared too you know!'

He glanced up angrily at her, one of those unfortunate stares that may do one great mischief if left unresolved.

'Well bully for you then, makes me feel full of compassion. And I hope you get some too – just so you know what it's like.

'I mean, why don't they torture you instead Jemimah, and give me a break?'

'Say you don't mean that, Sascha,' gasped Jemimah. 'Ah, Sascha, come on, we're in this together aren't we?' Now Marcus was no longer with them, she threw the rag down in a tantrum. 'Look... I am sorry for not being more supportive, but I never thought I'd react like this... to torture... Anyway, I'm sorry! I guess I never even thought about it to be honest. Never had any reason to really.'

Her friend rolled over to his other side, refusing the apology, which failed to show any true conviction. Making better use of his energies, he attempted to view the full extent of the underground burrow. Any escape would need to be executed soon if he was going to have any chance at all of living, but shackled there as he was, and wounded, with his *friend* by his side, things truly bode ill for him.

'The black one, Kussob, I think his name was – well he's an evil cunt,' groaned Sascha, 'even worse than my man Nywdog in his day – makes him look like the presenter of Play-school.'

'Arghhh...' Sascha flinched violently. 'Boombaclart!'

'What happened?'

'My welts are really beginning to hurt me now.'

'Well don't touch them then, Sascha.'

'But I still can't believe how people can do this to one another. What is it with some folks? How can somebody actually enjoy doing this stuff?'

'Are they really people though, Sascha?'

The Club-wielder grunted his disapproval at such an extraneous question, whilst lifting himself slightly to give himself better view of what lay around him. He peered again into near pitch darkness, his eyes having already become accustomed to the dark despite the searing firelight from the tools that had branded him. He made out four guffawing figures by the smoky hearth, reaching out their hands for the warmth their obvious mirth could not bring them.

One of them, who appeared garbed in an apron, soon found his fill of heat and made his way back to the cold stone platter, which was his work surface, and with his hands he produced a great pair of tongs and a hammer, one with

321

which to fashion, another with which to ply. These he used to temper the cooling metal that was splayed before him, and he worked at them till they began to bear semblance to the implements found resting on a battlefield after a great slaughter.

Upon setting to his task even more diligently, however, Sascha could see that with his first work he was not contented. For soon came the white-hot sparks, then the hissing sound as of a snake when it desires its feeding, as his effort was quenched in steam. Then came the glint upon trollish eyes as its light shone about his withered visage. And then was the dampening of their mood again, as they were at it afresh in travail.

'Sascha!' Jemimah yelled. 'They're coming over here again – do something. Quickly!'

But this time, he shrugged his shoulders of her and left her alone, quietly pleased that all they gave him was a few ponderous shafts in his ribs as they removed his chain from its meat hook. Sadly for such comrades-in-arms, he became even more contented when he saw them watch Jemimah with that green-eyed glee which made even the doughtiest Knight-orcs fearful.

*

To some it might have seemed as though Marcus was a casualty of war, recovering after a disastrous bout fought frenziedly upon studded bulwarks and fearsome forts in a foreign land. That would have been in those long dark days when the begotten brood of Ceriwendwyffed the Cold, the bearded dwarf-master of the region beyond Llonrae, first triumphed in battle.

It was he who waxed bold in the caves of the Abdula the Saintly, after he was surrounded by four troops of stalwart goblins from the lands of Philistia, when garbed in nought but his warrior-raiment. Albeit, his trusty sword, Dera-denu, from which the place of Dereden has its name, was active in those days. Of him the saying arose:

> *"Ceriwendwyffed the Cold is bold*
> *A Dark Dwarf of Layman's Walk,*
> *Which lies nigh by the Ancient Towers of Llonrae,*
> *The Giant Plain Causeway of the old Giant Stork;*
> *And his aides got laid with the jumbled bones of goblins slain*
> *Sing aloud to the kings of noblemen's fame!"*

Others, however, must have reckoned out the truth, that Frydor's sick understudy was vying tortuously with all his will, for the elusive comforts of the dying. His capacity to reason was reduced by the poison that his body had accepted only a few days prior; debility had taken his arms and legs and much of his heaving torso, binding it in fetters of invisible gossamer, spun by unseen hosts. Yet, for whatever reason sages may say, the words which issued forth from his soul were somewhat gladdening.

It soon happened that a verse of some lucidity poured out from deep within:

"For men will be... without *self-control*...
Lovers of *passion* rather than lovers of piety,
Having a form of goodness, but denying the grace therein.
And from such people, part."

These were the final fable words quoted of Byron the Surp, which he had told them before they had left with their horses upon this fateful journey. But now the elegy was somewhat more garbled as the words flowed from his lips, like torrents at the rapids of the Elfin Shores, which is on the Pellucid Isles overlying the southern region of Kalithor. They came like the tides of fervent breakers as each day they roll close to the head-cliffs of Kalith. His mouth was likewise foamed, roaring incessantly with his bite, giving his carriage the semblance of a drunken old man, or as of one in the full throes of possession.

"...But if they cannot exercise Self-control, let them marry.
For it is better to marry than to burn with Passion..."

*

At length Frydor gathered together his wits and his nose became attentive to the new smells.

There was oxtail soup he believed, with potatoes, sprouts, raw carrots, together with a whole host of other bizarre foodstuffs, some of which he preferred not to be made weary of. For there was, discernible, a smell like that of human flesh. Many of the new aromas came from the fire-stove upon which was propped a large wooden club. The rest of the smells wafted across the large oaken table, the sole piece of furnishing in the far side of the hut.

His stomach growled deep umbrage as he hung limply by the roof-rafters of the hutch. It seemed little equity that they should choose to torment him in this way. The cries of his friends elsewhere, who, doubtless, were being hounded as he was being, was enough. The congregation of vengeful trolls was angered at somebody or another's refusal to allow them to continue unimpeded with their sporting adventures.

At the moment though Frydor's concern lay not with the foods that were lain before these master vagabonds, nor with the deathly silence which sought out conflict with his soul, or even with the fraught orisons which made their way heavenward. More astutely perhaps, his attention was drawn to the great mighty shadow that had just entered, who was now sitting comfortably with his friends. A great presence had just entered the room, of that he was left in no doubt. But was that good or bad? Would it be favourable or did it bode another ill omen for the elves and their companions?

As he joined them, each one peered balefully in his direction, as though the gods that day had chosen to visit that cold and dreary hutch. However, all this was before a huge, gnarled hand plucked the leg off of a boar and put it to his huge, slavering mouth. Then Frydor realised that this was indeed no god but a man, both great and terrible to behold, a warrior of fearsome countenance and as dark as the burrows beside the neck of Bryn Glýn. The troll consumed all in one fell swoop; skin, flesh, and bones included, upon which he emitted such a noisome burp that it did not fail to stink all hidden orifices within the wooden shack.

Then did a great jeer arise to break all silence, shatter all peace, scupper all hope that the beasts would be contented with their slain meal. And after that came a voice:

'It won't be long, Master-Elf, till I come to tend to your needs, don't you worry...'

Turning back to be with his wife, his friends and the big black body of Kus-sob, Fels'noc dove quickly into his awaiting meal.

*

Awakening startled, he was soon greeted by a high-pitched flurry of shrills. He groped about in darkness for a while but without gaining any further ground.

'Eleanor, is that you? Where you at, girl?' Looking up sharply, Nywdog saw that he was pinned down by a great bulbous leg which bore uncanny re-semblance to a stout tree-trunk of some one thousand years.

'Going somewhere, lover boy?' Belle-Hannah mused. 'I have something here for you,' she resumed, stroking herself lovingly.

Nywdog wriggled about all the more.

'Now, now, boy, how about you coming down with me? New-dog isn't it? I'd like to do it doggy-style. So how about it lover-boy?'

His exertions grew even more frantic.

'Flip, mate, what's going on? Help us, she's squeezing the life outta me. Help!' But the sound of her lashings continued as Nywdog fought desperately to escape her adipose existence.

'Get off me, you fat, blubbery bitch!'

Wallop! She struck him hard upside his head.

'There, there,' Belle-Hannah resumed soothingly, as she groped at her three lavish bosoms in an act fit to make spew many an ugly giant. 'I'm not fat at all – just cuddly. So, do you want some then or not? I can do a lot for someone like you – try me and see!'

'Urgghhh – no thanks!' gasped Nywdog.

Clutching the edge of his jaw, blood poured through his fingers and onto his soiled raiment, which did not seem to hinder the obese matron any more than a mousetrap would a grizzly.

'Come on, troll-mistress,' Nywdog pleaded in unconvincing tones, appealing to what he hoped would be her maternal instincts. 'You're not like the others, so why are you letting this continue? I know to some you must be gorgeous,' Nywdog lied, still battling rather desperately, 'but you're just not my sort that's all!'

He heard garbled commands coming from the background, but realising the muted sounds were not for his ears, which were bespattered with thick gore, he quickly became disparaged.

'Mind your business, lover-boy – '

'Why don't you do something, woman?'

Belle-Hannah looked puzzled for a moment, as though never before had she heard such kindly words.

Woman?

He had called her a woman!

That was wonderful, perhaps the single most delightful experience in her adult life. Yet she failed to stop, or even obfuscate the grim view that was emerging from the reluctant shadows.

Presently the rest of the trolls gathered around Eleanor, no tools to bear, no weapons to threaten with, but when they barked gruff orders at the younger elf, he complied, eagerly. Eleanor could barely see him as she was cut down from her wrists, and made to lie prostrate on the cold, naked floor. A hush descended upon the coop. Even Nywdog's valiant efforts seemed quelled at the expectation of what was to come.

All voices were stopped, all words were given up, all deals were untangled. Slowly, the elf clambered on top of the waif to the rise of sickened jeering, his hands upon her chest, his feet on her thighs. The leering audience above also joined in with wild abandonment, as many lecherous paramours began to consummate their acts with sticks, stones, and other barbaric utensils.

Seeing all these things transpire was all too much for young Eleanor to take at the moment, even as a hand covered her mouth and pressed her down hard, causing her, thankfully, to pass out for a while. And for the sake of his earlier exertions and indeed, for his present toils, Nywdog quickly followed suit. As for myself, Elf, I was hot under the collar admittedly, as any soul would be at such foul antics. But Memys – in all the days that I'd known him – I'd never yet seen him become so angry.

'They say that heat has the proficiency to cleanse all things and provide remedy for many an ill infection; a red-hot branding-tool may purify the blood of leeches lodging in human veins, and a white-hot poker, even to the ablution of the soul, when it purges each of his iniquity... or hers indeed.'

Still piping hot, he peeled off a strip of glowing metal from the anvil and held it in the air awhile, until its light shone through the dusk caverns.

'Nevertheless, if one is not careful then it also has the tendency to inflict pain – untold in the *eyes* of all who have not borne the brunt of such affliction.'

Admiring his craftsmanship closely, Savagedoc resumed his mumbling; 'But try as I might, sometimes, to prevent this last woe from coming upon folks I encounter, something hinders me – whether I am evil I know not, though I often feel pity for the foemen I abuse... Therefore, accept my sincere apology beforetimes, my insignificant breed of friends!'

Meanwhile, Sascha continued to feign death as it is said Morias mab Gracie emulated the corpse of the slain, before drawing himself up, together with his nerve, sinew and fury, and launching full-bodied at his assailants with all his might. These acts led to what trolls call *clamp-galanas*, which occurred in the earliest age, after the druids first moved into the Enclaves. Nevertheless, he still heard the troll lumbering towards Jemimah, who, even now, was being strung up by her wrists, and alongside him was Tralob and Slacob, leaving only Bobb with her large breasts to look out over his wounded form. Shortly, he raised his head again, though only ever so slightly this time round.

'Jemimah, I believe your name is. By now your master, Frydor the Elf, has told us all we need to know, so we have little need for your assistance anymore. However, if you are sporting in the things I shall dictate to you, perhaps we can find a use for you here... and spare the life of your friend there.'

The other trolls sniggered coarsely, some snorting crude remarks about the worthiness of the Club-wielder to witness such events, while Bobb made semblance with her huge chest, to a woman in dire need of company. Sascha it was who would burn the midnight oil with her, till such times as her needs were fulfilled or his will to live was sapped – whichever was to be the first woe.

'But methinks to allow him to live for the sake of lovely Bobb over there,' Savagedoc continued, 'as she has been a loyal wench all these years, though without the guerdon she so utterly deserves – for the scant supply of Men that come into these parts and live!

'Anyway, enough of this nonsense, and let us proceed with the torments shall we...' He pulled down Jemimah's filthy raiment, spun her about like a child's top on its nib, before proceeding to take on the task at hand. 'Slacob, Tralob, make sure she feels the full fury of our displeasure.'

Allowing the metal no moment to rescind its fervency he applied its sides to the rump of the descended Daughter-of-David. Sascha flinched at the prospect, as did the two trolls who were made to stand guard over her, so that she yielded little of her capacity for the pain. Again and again was the same torment employed, using various implements brandished across the small of her hide, her thighs and her lower back, causing pain, making misery, turning to silence even the morose chiding of the trolls. And loud were the cries soon reaching Frydor through the ripples in the dusk ether.

*

'Frydor, they've almost finished their meal already – what are you gonna do?'

The elf swung gently about on the hinges that attached his wrists to the rafters. He soon found himself peering at the trollish festivities. He turned back sharply:

'I do not know yet, Alicia, what I can do. But not to worry! Keep your strength in your heart come what may and all things shall be well. And cling on to what you must.'

In the distance, Fels'noc splattered Saspion with a large, mucky kiss, and masticated gruel passed from one filthy orifice to another. Around the board, trolls appeared to be delighting themselves in the meal set before them and paid scant attention to the puzzled look that soon spread itself across Frydor's ailing mien.

'Nevertheless, we still have some time methinks,' he whispered, not wanting to arouse them any further. 'Tell me now Alicia, how is Marcus?'

But even as he was yet speaking, a bat fluttered in through the hut opening and coursed across the trolls' meal-table. Cutlasses drawn and meat-hooks at the ready, Nâelog along with Sniffdog, sought to scupper its flight-path by removing its wings from the side of its body. Evil laughs resounded as their efforts were thwarted by the dexterity of the nocturnal creature, who, for the darkness of the looming recesses, found the place comforting as the bushy weald which had sooner been its haunt.

'Frydor, is that just a bat, or is it something worse? It's not gonna suddenly spit poisonous venom at us is it? Or will it change into some great big monster? Because that's all we need right now, and I've had enough already!'

The elf watched the mammal-bird for a few moments taking its path, perplexed, unaware of what manner of tidings could possibly have brought the creature out so far, at such a time of day. Then it seemed like part of a veil was lifted from his forehead, for his countenance did seem to brighten and his honey-coated tongue was loosed.

'I should think not, warrior,' he whispered in response to Alicia, 'for most of the creatures in these parts have had the venom sapped out of their tongues since a time out of mind. But I think it does bear tidings,' he said, viewing the way it circled from wall to wall in the noisy confines of the hutch. 'For rarely do they take flight in the daytime, lest the naked beauty of Her Who Shines On All should expose them for what they are – black flying mice and no more.'

'So what does it mean – I mean, only tell me if it's good…. And how can that blind thing get us out of here anyhow?'

She carried on swabbing Marcus' wounds as he lay still, groaning silently to himself.

Then came another marvel. Awesome and very terrible to behold.

It was a wide berth of light, bright as the blow that struck the sinner Saul, converting him to the saint Paul in an instant, glorious as the rays which transported Philip the Apostle to Ashdod in front of the dark-skinned eunuch from Cush. Philip it was who went on his way, casting out demons, scourging devils, delivering souls from the demon-spectre Death.

With the thunderous noise of the trolls as they banged hard their hands upon the tabletop came a moment when all things appeared stilled by the presence of the radiant beacons of hope. Nâelog seemed blanched at the brilliant-blue shaft, Kussob appeared quelled and his manner less offensive and his tongue became like the tongues of men. Sniffdog too had his semblance changed in the vision. He was cast into a mighty prince, or so it appeared in the eyes of them that watched, and also in the mind of him who could not for his indisposed state. But most glorious of all were the countenances of both Fels'noc and his wife, Saspion. For purple was the beam that encompassed them, great was the warmth, and grand was the banqueting-table about which they feasted.

Almost at once however, the scene was banished, and all things continued as they had done before. Rude interpretations of loving-feats, foul spewings, the ill-adjusted gable of grim handiwork which they were compelled to carry out upon their guests. But little effect did any have upon Marcus, as his moment of ill fortune continued, whilst he lay beset with an unnumbered host of phantoms. Many such delusions caused him to writhe fiercely as one undergoing the sufferings of the Black Affliction. Verily, it was a truly worrying torment indeed.

'The truth, Alicia, is that I do not know whether it is good or bad, for its interpretation eludes me at this time. And for the record, bats are not really blind – not here anyway – but they use echolocation to fly and to find their meal.'

'Well, Frydor,' said Alicia, in between bouts of dabbing Marcus on his lips, 'you'd better hurry up with that interpretation, because they look like they're on their last course… and I don't think Marcus is gonna hold out for much longer.'

Marcus was indeed drivelling incoherently, his words lost in the fervency of his convulsions. His predilection seemed only to worsen and not improve. So sad were the Friends on his behalf, even those in the midst of tribulation themselves.

Then, all of a sudden and out of the blue, so the sages tell, something wonderful occurred. The indisposed warrior seemed to want to rejoin the land of the living, at least for a time. At long last Marcus managed to splutter a few words of sense.

'Fels'noc… rearranging,' he whispered, wheezily.

Again he was privy to visions of himself and the two dim-witted trolls encased within the stone hovel, not unlike the one they were now trapped in.

'Fels'noc rearranging… Fels'noc rearranging.'

He seemed all the more grieved with each vain repetition, for he saw the two trolls replacing the loosened mortar with slabs others had erstwhile plucked up from elsewhere. His brow dampened and the eerie light moved briefly onto his fair countenance. The Breastplate-bearer sat up.

'Something he has spoken has twinged a chord… and see there,' said Frydor, motioning with his head, 'the bat which had come has now found it's way out again, and the strange light which accompanied it has also vanished.'

'Frydor, all I wanna know is this… is it good or bad?'

*

She appeared to compass him all about, from the damp, earthen mud-walls up to the wooden roof-gate, which to his amazement still permitted light to dawn on the gloomy arena beneath. The others were great in size, save for Fûkwït, who was smaller but ultimately more hideous than any of his friends (save for Bel-Hacosh) but presently they bore him no great ill. Except for Belle-Hannah the trolls had their attention fixed squarely on the dark scene before them.

The screams returned to him suddenly like a whetstone grinding its meal in darkness. He could tell that it belonged to Eleanor, his friend, who even now was being pushed about from one form to another, neither of them dwelling too long on the puny waif prior to passing her on to the next. This was torture most foul and all knew it to be, both man and beast.

Only Bel-Hacosh the arch-nemesis of all creatures seemed to enjoy tormenting her more.

Whether it be an inviolate maid, he would take on the form of a ravenous old man; or if his captive were to appear as a man, he would then take the form of an emboldened bear. If, on the other hand, any such opponent bore special talents, having ability to transform himself into a white-maned creature dwelling beyond the Ice-Rocks of Derwent then would Bel-Hacosh take on the form of the ice beneath his feet and the sun blazing within the sky, that with his slippery touch and with his burning zeal he might scupper the path of one and all. For a trickster this was, full of evil and cunning design, able to formulate all manner of turpitude for the failure of his enemies.

Noting this vile person well, Nywdog flayed even more violently to escape Belle-Hannah's evil pinions. Arms and legs abounding, he left none at peace. There was one point where he sunk his fist into the midriff of the corpulent beast before him, losing his arm to the elbow, and causing gasps of amazement to emerge from the troll-folk watching upon the track-way. What a bold fellow this was! But then all was reassembled, as they ought, while his fateful appendage retracted, filled with the gunge of her overblown presence. Yelling intensely, Belle-Hannah reached out her gross arms to nab the huckster by the collar. But not at once was he caught, even for his multiple bruises and fractured collar. He aimed a deft-defying kick up towards her fat, broad-faced sconce.

Then the Stick-bearer shrieked aloud: for it was death that confronted him there in the maze of obscurity. The glare of her eyes was terrible to behold (as, too, were the stares of her fellow trolls, who had, by now, turned towards the fray!). A chilling luminosity, like that which appeared when the foremost Star lit up the first Morning, encompassed her form, sending quagmires of doubt and confusion throughout the darkened vault. Rarely had the troll-mistress been given to such anger, since the days of her assault by an unknown kinsman in years gone by. Facing Nywdog was the touch of evil, the look of death, the teeth of a red-ravager when it is found wanting of her cubs. But for a while, he took it all in his stride, circling, menacing, growling, like the specimen he now beheld.

Belle-Hannah stumbled forwards, eyes cast askance at the impending scene of doom. Nywdog too shambled towards the dubious beast, his body broken, his legs wounded, his arms heavy as the rocks that feed the catapults about the mountains of Dereden. All of a sudden, he appeared to take on the semblance of a great rock-giant, for he lifted his bowed head fearlessly, arduous though the task at first seemed, and lunged at the fell hybrid which now sought to scupper his life.

Again Fortune had her plans well laid, for presently he became engulfed in the mass of her adipose frame. Mouth wedged shut, blubber fulfilling his intimacies, blood spurting from every known orifice, or so it appeared, the warrior prised himself free from the possessed foe-beast whom he had chosen to confront. The match was even, the fight was grim, all eyes were held to attention as the battle continued.

Still the screeching resounded, alongside grunts from the elf: whether Flip was in the midst of torments or whether or not it was the elf who had obliged himself of the same grim tasking, Nywdog was loath to call; for all sounds soon became one and the same, a whirl of daze and dissolution which took his senses by storm. Nonetheless, the cries of the waif stirred him onwards and he began to prevail like the bull-headed chief he was. All stood by silently and watched, stunned at the ferocity of Nywdog's latest attack, bewildered by the beast that had all at once sprung forth.

The sneering sparked up as foolhardy Belle-Hannah permitted such a deluge of assaults to come raining down upon her. But lo! For all the power of his onslaught and all the might of his wroth, this seemed to have little effect on the foul hulk, and play again resumed, each one at the other's throats, palms, punches, paws clawing to draw last blood. Bel-Hacosh was at his ends to decide whether to observe such a splendid affray, or whether to take on one of his guises and pounce in with his comrades, smiting Nywdog with the strength of his wrath.

Nevertheless, for the time-being he adhered to the handbook of Trollish battlecraft, which had been scribbled as an afterthought some time after the wars with King Henry of the Long-shanks, of the fosterage of Molloy mab Michealson. It formally states that:

When in battle with a dwarf, no more than one troll per three dwarves,
unless they be of the race of Crossbreeds of Dogsass;
When in battle with an elf, no more than one troll to two elves,
unless they be of the valour of the Light Elves of Yesteryear;
When in battle with men, no more than one troll per man,
No matter what the circumstance...

Taken from p. 426, The Art of Trollish Warfare.

Besides, Belle-Hannah it was who soon bested her enemy, battling against him with her gross flesh, flailing stumps of arms, plump legs.

Another moment came which found Nywdog, for all his stout valour, perilously overextended. The troll, with her portly arms, then found herself with his head in her hands. This begat an embrace so cold that for a spell, the hidden stars of Nef came into full view. They swirled about his head, mocked his soul, scolded his spirit, derided every part of his being for banding together against them with his chivalrous deeds. Then these orbs came so dark that in appearance, they paid fair semblance to dark coals when set against the blackened slopes of Bryn Trolliége. It was a mighty press she clutched him with, similar to that which a wench has when in the last throes of lovemaking. But the grip currently enfolding Nywdog was less beckoning by far.

Convulsions supervened to the tune of a most grim laughter, which was wrought by the cackling voice of the troll-mistress. This was followed swiftly by vivid memories of battles in a foreign land. Notwithstanding, these were brushed away like a river sweeps all that is cast into her wake into the oceans, and indeed, much was soon gone underneath her crushing grip. For as her grasp became stronger, so too did the breath he seek to expire dwindle, and the strength in his bosom wane, and the heart which propped it up lower. Further recollections, some dark, others no more dismal than thoughts of the night before, clambered one atop of another, seeking escape through the last dregs of his body, while his mind wandered back to his childhood days. Then dizziness befell the brave warrior, for all parts of his form pursued their own course of abandonment. There was none wanting the hostage-pits of Annwfn, which would be the sure reward for the loser of this valiant contest.

Soon, death-gasps had clasped hold of his throat, and Nywdog's strength, unknown to men beyond the reach of death, surged through his form for one last skirmish. And he lunged towards the group of viewers. He made a dash for Bel-Hacosh, the instigator of their troubles, hoping desperately for one last altercation with the enemy. Plunging his fist at his proboscis, he flattened the troll's demeanour with one well-aimed shot. But it cost him, and dearly. For even before his doleful viewing of the elf, who was still in the midst of tormenting Eleanor, he was apprehended by four sets of arms. And cheer uprose from the top of the coop.

Nywdog was passed on from one guard to another, suffering abuse innumerable as presently, his will fought with his reason, that is to say, his *ellyll* was pitted against his *ysbryd*, to pass out of his current world and into the caverns of the World Beyond. Alas, at length, it happened that the henchmen failed to consider *"The Book of Warfare"* for any space past the flattening of Bel-Hacosh, their companion. So they pummelled the gallant warrior to the joyous approval of their fans.

*

Food finished and tools sharpened, it was Mishmash who was the first one off his seat.

'Do you have any last requests you wish to make from my master before I begin my dreadful calling – elf... girl?'

Frydor examined the blade which Mishmash bore by his side, deeming it wholly unnecessary when pictured beside the huge beast himself. He looked even more troubled when Marcus collapsed back into his place, sweating buckets, still chomping at the bit.

'Wait, and bide your time my friends!' Frydor yelled. 'I may have something of interest for you.'

The troll replied scornfully, 'Oh, I see that your weak friend woke up briefly... after your bold attempts at poisoning him.'

There was a short space in which nothing was said or uttered. Muted screams came wafting through from other parts of the compound, blood-curdling cries which none failed to stir at. Broken voices and coarse words and heinous laughter were their entourage, more blows, broken bones and bile, their accompaniment.

'So I see then that our companions have begun exacting tribute from your friends,' Nâelog returned in grim tones. He drew up alongside Frydor. 'Well, we'd better not be left behind, eh Master?'

'Too true my evil slave, too true.' Saspion, who was by Fels'noc's side, let loose another sloppy kiss upon the fat-cheeks of her husbandman. 'Alright dear.'

'Husband, might I go first in the Order of Torments?' asked Saspion.

'Of course you may my foul mistress, whatever it is that pleases you.'

With that, she went over to the brimming stove, drew out a large vat of boiling water and poured it on the one who was still staring at her; as though he had just seen a ghost.

*

He was in another dream.

This time he saw a flitting shadow dancing across his vision. It had emanated from the bodies of bloated ogres and it looked to be the size of tall trees. The spirit was entwined with an odious snake coiled tightly around its fleeting form. The phantom soon shrouded much of the sun's glorious rays, yet a beacon of light glimmered amidst the eyes of the wakened monsters, sufficient enough to guide their way; at least for a time.

Moreover, he now saw the bricks of their captivity come tumbling down, setting himself free at last alongside his fellow prisoners, who had been trapped inside a meshwork of coagulated mortar. And for the first time he also saw the rest of his troop come marching by. The wall-chasms allowed the brightest light to shine through and replenish their ailing bodies and it fuelled them all, especially himself, with the indispensable desire to live again.

Then he saw the eight weary souls cast under a lingering storm cloud, heading eastwards across the sun-scorched plains in a desperate hunt, to see where it was that their current path would lead them. And he saw also a torque, with a face like that of a serpent, whose power had been broken, for a while.

*

'What does he say, Mishmash? What does he mean?' growled Fels'noc. 'Beat it out of him if you must, Mishmash, and you, Nâelog,' he pointed, finger quivering, 'tell me his interpretation. And I command all these things under the pain of death. Beat it out of him if you must.'

He turned aside, shrugging off the wife that had become attached to his hefty shoulders.

'Saspion, my beloved bitch, what is it that have you done to him? He speaks more fey now than when he first came in, you silly whore? Why have you now brought me more trouble than you're worth? He might be cursing us to his gods, whose dwellings are not with man.'

She was flabbergasted.

'Why did you pour precious water on him – to fuel his phantoms?' He cuffed her one in full view of the others. 'Or was it to rile my soul, O troubling troll-woman?'

'I did nothing save what you commanded me, husband, so don't you go blaming me!'

Sniffdog moved over towards Marcus but was rebuffed by the Frydor who cried:

'Leave him be, O Troll of Great Proportions. For he speaks hidden mysteries which you would all do well to heed.' Everybody froze. 'Has his spirit not come back from Annwfn, the Land of the Nearly Dead, and even now, does he not seek to redress the balance between you trolls and our own noble races? Listen therefore and you may yet learn something to your liking... something both to your benefit and to ours.'

Sniffdog pondered for a moment, his eye half-cocked, staring wildly at the senior member of the Troop. At the same time albeit, his attention was also fixed upon his master's mistress, Saspion.

'What do you mean, elf, tell us exactly what you mean?'

'Yes do, Frydor,' Fels'noc rejoined, 'and be quick about it. With each second, you're wasting our time and spoiling our fun...'

There was another muffled scream from the direction of the primary coop, which they took to be Bel-Hacosh at work, and this was followed by several astonished gasps. Then came an undercurrent of murmuring, as all the others within the village who were tired of watching a select few inflicting pain, found that they could endure such veiled glories no longer.

Scuffles broke out distracting Fels'noc's attention and causing Sniffdog to relax his grip on the tricky little elf, enough for him to speak.

'Can you not hear him, O Great Fels'noc, Mighty One of Ages?' Frydor twisted himself nimbly to face the troll, though at the same time, still managing to avoid direct eye contact.

'Listen O Masterful Trol' and you will understand the manner of his speech. For does he not speak in a queer manner, after riddles and enigmas and suchlike, the same which can only be understood by those with an ear to listen, those with a heart to hear, and by those with understanding? And I have been listening O Troll, even since the fore, and this is what I take young Marcus to mean...'

As if for confirmation, Marcus spoke again:

'Fels'noc, Saspion,' he stuttered, eyes ablaze with terror.

'They rearrange the stones... building loosening...

'It moans.

'But we shall each be set free…

'Flee in terror…

'If we dare to know…'

The diseased warrior found no comfort any more on his blood-soaked arm, and rolled over to his right side, sweat dripping profusely off of his withered brow

'…The mystery of the trolls.'

Serenity took the hut by storm.

'But exercise self-control, or else we shall be joined in union with the foulest form of an ogre…

'That passionate maid, who will cause us all to burn with the selfsame ardour…'

Upon the saying he began to pick at his scorched skin which then began to peel off.

'And we'll all burn with Passion! Arggghhh!'

Marcus soon settled again within himself, the tremors of his quivering body soon subsiding. He resumed picking the blisters off of his parched membrane, until his nails became sullied at such exploits. Then he soothed his discomfort somewhat by curling up more tightly into a ball.

'So what does this weasel say then people?'

There was no quick response from either of the trolls or from Frydor. Alicia too was befuddled.

'Elf? Nâelog? Sniffdog…? Kussob even?' The Trol-liege pummelled Saspion for a response. 'Answer me now you sad old wench, what does he say? Why is it he speaks of strange things when the look of death seems fixed about his visage? For what reason, O Elf, does this drool vent such foolishness?'

'But why are you rearranging the bricks woman, and what about the foundations, Troll? Help… Fry-dorrrr!' Marcus yelled. 'They're attacking meeee…'

By now however the one who had been given the Breastplate of Righteousness had said enough.

*

Fels'noc and his wife ran around the reed-covered hutch, as if they were each well possessed by fearsome sprites. Moreover, as they tried to reach out for the friends, to scupper their words and hound them of their senses, they were stayed in their way, for dour were the hands that prevented them and bold were the arms that kept the beast in abeyance.

'Can you not hear it?' Frydor exclaimed pertly. 'Saspion who burns and Fels'noc Trol? Think about it trolls – rearranging the brickwork?' He stared for a moment into the bewildered troll-faces.

'But what brickwork is that you may ask? Is it not plain as the nose on your homely faces – does he not speak of the names that you have now inherited?'

Further howls were unleashed and more twisted seemed their faces than the court jesters from the Land of Nod, whose mugs folks say can take on any form or any semblance of form, either through engineering-feats or by enchantments. There then increased cries of pain, shouts of sorrow and many were the dry, blood-curdling screams that dripped through the mouths of the doughty trolls. Indeed, for something truly great was afoot.

'*Leave me alone elf,*' Saspion hissed suddenly, her voice becoming deeper than her husband's. 'We are the rulers of this place, not you, you pesky little weasel. Get away from meeee you shits!'

Her body arched in angles wholly unlawful to one of such obesity.

'Away from me you 'orrible little cretin!'

'Yes, let us be you damnable little toad. Remove yourself, you horrid Surp – creature of expectation, monster of hope, instigator of ill change against the wiles of the East! Be gone you bald-headed bastard!'

'Away wit' you – !'

Sniffdog was not slow in perceiving the darkening miasma within the wooden shanty. He pounced upon Saspion, who with her claws unfurled, was at it with her husband, exacting retribution for her previous shaming.

'Mistress… No!' Kussob shouted. 'What bedevils you this time O Mistress of the Hilly Plains? What is it that riles the mistress of the Great Fels'noc?'

While Sniffdog held her at bay, Frydor looked on, watching Mishmash carefully pluck her adipose fingers from her husband's neck.

'Is it not your will that we execute judgement upon our enemies and smite them with bricks – one for each fool – so that the scourge may be purged from our midst. Is it not this sick one who is possessed,' Mishmash rejoined, pointing to Marcus, 'and sending bad vibes in our presence? Does he not curse us with his every breath?'

'And you, lord and master, O Great Fels'noc – what is it that ails thee?' Nâelog added.

Frydor interjected coarsely, however; 'So you know that I am a Surp, Fels'noc, and that I have come from Se'kere… or indeed, "Expectation" as you chose to call it. It makes me wonder, O Trol', how does one lacking the gift of prophecy know of one whom he has not yet even met?'

'*Go away elf,*' hissed Saspion, '*or we'll make mincemeat of you and crush your two friends like biscuits!*'

'*Yeah, but first we'll cook them in an oven and fry them – to make you all soft and pulpy like warm shit!*' Kussob growled.

Fels'noc looked across at Kussob, his eyes aglow with fire; '*Your brilliance defies me Kussob, you ugly black bastard – you will make a most wonderful chieftain one day.'*

'Thank you lord.'

But all eyes soon fell on the Surp, for it was he whose countenance was brightened, whose eyes were lit, upon whom the *awen* of a prophet now appeared to rest.

*

'Fels, Son of Noc,' cried the Surp in heated tones. 'Fells Noc the Troll.'

'Or should I say "The Fallen Troll of a Hag", Fels'noc Trol'! – Dark Knight of Ages.'

Frydor spun round on the thick strand of hemp by which he hung. Waxing bold, he spelled it out for them:

'Rearrange the one, the name of the master – Fels'noc Trol – and what do we get but Self-Control.' Alicia looked up at the elf.

'Moreover, with a subtle shuffle of the other, Saspion, do we not arrive at Passion?'

The two trolls sought to lay hold of the cunning little elf but to no avail. The light upon which the bat was coursed shone about their eyes once again, casting them each into a whirlpool of oblivion.

'Thus, what my afflicted son, Marcus, decries pertains to your curse, Fels'noc Trol; for you were formerly of those that had Self-Control as is implicit in your name, and your forefather was once a brave, bold knight. Moreover, you are one and the same and still remain – albeit, deep within not without.'

'And Saspion,' Alicia yelled, after piping up in boldness, remembering some of the things written on the pages of her books, 'your name is also Passion. Because the heart of your mothers used to burn with a great desire for good!'

'Is this not what ailing Marcus speaks of when he utters sacred runes taken from the letter of Paul the Patriarch, according to the missive he wrote to the Temple at Corinth:

> "But if they cannot exercise Self-control, let them marry.
> For it is better to marry than to burn with Passion."

'It is you,' Frydor shouted accusingly, motioning towards each of the trolls, 'it is you who are bedevilled and not myself... and certainly not Marcus.'

He shifted about a little, using his sturdy biceps to wipe the sweat off his forehead.

'According to legend, it is said that the fires burning on the horizons, which can be seen on the darkest of nights, are the fires that you, Saspion, concocted, via the ancient sorcery of the Old Woman Ceriddenne's line. Moreover, I have heard it said that those who dare to frustrate your ploys are dispatched with by you and your sullen brood of wenches, begetting hideous noise, and are placed in the Burial Grounds of the High Trolls, which is called the Millo by men.

'Or else you use them as playthings to satisfy your own lustful cravings,' Alicia added, speaking of the things she had erstwhile understood.

'But what can stop all these abominations save for the exercising of Self-control… or indeed the *exorcising* of "Fels'noc" the "Trol"?'

'Then,' Frydor resumed, growing ever bolder as he addressed the remaining trolls, 'when they are of no more interest to your vixens, they are taken south to the fires under the guise of the blackest stench and there they are incinerated without ever a fair hearing. Is it true?'

There was silence for a short space of time, in which period the sole sounding was the wheezing of a male troll, like a serpent quickly awakened from its sleep. His eyes met with The Trol's as the struggle within grew intense. It was a look so terrible that lesser elves would have quailed immediately. Afterwards, if they were propitious, they would have suffered drowning by the cloak of fear, which, upon encountering these trolls, was known to compass men about.

The troll's eyes held the look of the possessed; for cold were his eyes, and evil were they to behold. But in his hands was a grip so tremendous that Frydor sought ever and awhile to escape the purchase of those fateful snares. They were said to accomplish as worthy a feat as any garrotte wielded by the Giant Belial.

Fells-Noc the Troll had fought with Death on many occasions and had tasted the blood of his entanglements. He had supped with the Prince of Annwfn and dined at the feasts of the Twelve Lords of Krandor. Nonetheless, all these things have been to no avail. But a mighty warrior he proved himself in all feats. Many times in search of the Keys those with pernicious aims had sought him out, and now he was abandoned in the hills and in the forests. His race was almost run and soon would come the time to surrender his allotment to another, unto his spawn birthed with his wife Saspion.

All at once however it seemed as though the Surp's *awen* came to reside within his bosom and with his new skill he promptly set about entering into the doughty mistress Saspion. Then he began probing further into the deep dark recesses of her husband's clouded mind. The black dissolution witnessed in both bode no fear for Frydor, for many times had he seen such desertion in the faces of those who are deemed *alltud* by High Elves and Men alike.

Frydor then perceived not only Alicia's dire shrieks but the muted pleas of their friends, even as the battle of wits intensified. One strove for mastery over another in contests of nerve, prayers, enchantments, but none saw his enemy vanquished. Feats of phantoms were not spared either as first Fels'noc and then Frydor came to leave each his humble abode, in order to undertake great mischief. Minds floated, souls departed, spirits were rent asunder; but strong was the contest for supremacy, too valiant for either to prevail on this matter. So for the time-being each was stayed in their fleshy dwelling, acceding in strength, regaining the ground, none at length succeeding.

There came an instant where the stench of Uffern rose up from beneath the rushes like the stench in the Valley of Hinnom when the corpses of evil men are burned on the pyre. And this rancid scent caused all, both great and small, to cringe at its sullied presence. Nâelog, Sniffdog, and Mishmash were thrown to the four corners of the hut, leaving Kussob in a whirl, and Fels'noc cowering away from his wife, beckoning with his sinewy arms to unseen hosts that he should remain free of their gross possession.

He had sucked the nipple of their lord Belial upon a bended knee. Moreover, this duty had he been doing since the days of his youth – a sign of token fealty, which these malignant ones would do well to remember.

Then it happened that Frydor's senses were opened, if but for the briefest of moments. Even Alicia, screaming at the height of her voice, failed to lessen the extent of the trolls' hauntings. Nevertheless, the elf was quick to recall the teachings of his early days, namely the art of the extrication of bound bodies from them that were summoned to occupy – spirits and denizens of The Underworld. And at once he set about putting words to the secret arts of binding and loosing, which immediately began to have an effect on the course of this marvellous battle.

The beasts within them groaned; the bear within the mistress swayed at the piping of Frydor's eloquent voice, the bull inside her mate, with red still before his eyes, blinded to her current distress. The trolls grunted murderously as the strands of Frydor's lays became audible. They started to soothe and began to hinder their way. Meanwhile, Alicia's orisons took on a new dimension of its own – but all this appeared only to make the *coblyn* grow wilder.

Manifestations were troubling, as it was when the first demons from the Netherworld appeared before the First Matron of the Gardens, in Eden. Taken was she with such fright that all they bade her she heeded, and more besides, even seducing the Father of All Nations into eating of the Apple-tree, a forbidden thing, before spitting in the ground of his travail, and conjuring with runecrafts, thorns and thistles to bind up his food-soils with sorrow.

Thus it happens even to this day that none bears fruit without much labour, save for the times of the Blessed Harvests, when all men have turned from their sin, have raised their hands to the sky and granted their voices to the Gods in generous supplications, with fastings. Even so, since the days of yore when the Surps first had their spell, few were the members given to such penitent confessions in sackcloth.

Hence the reach of Uffern, which, even in Trol-land, in the hut marking the end of civilisation, extended daily to touch even the body, soul and spirit, of all races, creeds and colours.

All of a sudden derisive laughter rang out from the demon-infested gathering, setting Saspion spinning, and Fels'noc into a swirl, as both entered a fitful rage. And Mishmash too began to foam at the mouth. Swatting the sky free of evil hosts became their trade, as he alongside Sniffdog went at it with hammer and tongs, and fearful was the sight of their terror. Nâelog waned in his courage, soon fleeing out into the assembling masses, who had long heard the news of battle, leaving Kussob behind to whimper like the mastiff-bitch of Bateman Bedamned. She it was who, daily before his timely death at the nib of a famous sword, suffered abuse most trying in her anal-passages. Nevertheless, none was there bold enough to challenge Frydor with his succulent word-horde and Alicia in her holy invocations for supremacy, not even the fell host of Annwfn.

But Frydor was not easily stirred, not even by the gut-wrenching screams, which were coming from Jemimah; and Flip also was passed caring; Eleanor was passed out; Nywdog suffered illusions unnumbered beneath his dark scalp-bridge; and Sascha, fearful of more affliction at the hands of these brutal monsters, made no attempt to salvage his companion, but sat in contentment that no such trials currently beset him. Frydor then lifted his voice above the rising tumult and it coursed through the eaves of the large, wooden hutch.

There was little more that needed to be said at the moment, only the final few words of enchantments and spellbinding and wizardry. These Frydor had learnt in his youth, soon after coming into contact with the Dark Side of the Yarah. For some of the Hooded Guardians had razed his home village to the ground while he was out on pilgrimage one day.

They had ravished their maidens, spoiled their crops, and scalped their elders, before slaying their innocent little whelps. Then had they murdered his one and only true love, whom he had kept himself for, for all of his days. These *Cycyllog* were Zaqen, so he found out afterwards; and it was upon that day that he had sworn revenge.

*

'In the name of the King beyond the Land of Angels,' Frydor cried aloud, 'I command you thus, putrid sprites of Annwfn, according to the words of old:

> *"Monster of the night*
> *Foul spirits of the fall*
> *Leave these mighty ogres, once and for all.*
> *Let Fels'noc Trol be*

THE DARK KNIGHT

Returned to his manner of Self-Control, and
His wife Saspion, to a life of Passion, unbland.
Unbind them foul demons of the gloom
Go to your hole and prepare for your doom"...'

Rather expeditiously nonetheless, the Surp withdrew himself as best as he could after the mentioning, just as Alicia, for good measure, abandoned Marcus to his own rabid ramblings. Then she scampered over the stove to the darkest known nook in the hovel, just before the darkness fell, and all ill guises were finally laid to rest.

THE FLIGHT OF AN ELLYLL:
MEMYS' STORY

If the righteous will be recompensed on the earth,
How much more the wicked and the sinner.

PROVERBS 11:31

It was a while yet before the thought of moving on popped into somebody's mind. Eleanor it was for whom the hazy, unformed recollections of the previous few days were tiring to her body and grating upon her soul. All agreed therefore that the Troop should be dispatched in the customary way dictated by the ancient trollish lore; though not few were the disputations as to the exact manner befitting these eight chiefs that had delivered them of their hauntings, their comrades of their possessions, their goats of their young ones, their flocks too of closed wombs, their geese of their speckled eggs and their chickens. And so unto the Friends was sacrificed a pure red heifer, stolen of the wizard Morgléin, keeper of the Frustrap Dales (before he was subsequently smote whilst lying in his breeches); and they slew Bigsam also, a crossbred cow and buffoon, whose meat did not fail to please. So contentions aside, none were they that left the troll's dining-board without the stink of good ale on his breath and without tales so lavish in their boasting that even the gods slunk down to listen.

So, before long, all was in order between the trolls, the men-folk and the elves. Wounds were still fresh however and visions of Fûkwït and his hideous consort still loomed; and the smell of burnings, of troll-breath and the stench of their unwashed garments brought tears, enough to confound the elegance of the setting sun. Notwithstanding, Fels'noc was proud that he could be of further assistance to the ongoing journey, even if it was just in the provision of meal for their stomachs, herbs for their wounds, and sending out a search-party to the distant hills of Rhûn, by the fort of the lost nomad, to locate the dwarfen-root, that Marcus might be restored to his full vigour once more. This act he nobly performed and for the rest of the next day up until nightfall they scoured the ground diligently.

Belle-Hannah and Bel-Hacosh were chosen for this forage-group, for within the repertoire of the latter (amongst all else) was his skill in climbing and the former was known for her burly strength with which she might aid him. Fels'noc on the other hand formed a party of his own, with the dour warriors Kussob and Nâelog, leaving Sniffdog to bring up the rear of the train, should any stray from their set course. Saspion it was who remained in the village with Fûkwït to tend to the needs of her followers. Albeit, short rest was there for Savagedoc, smith of the fiery hold, master of tapping, cooling, folding; for dark days were at hand, times for battle, as minions of the Serpent would doubtless hear of their recent escapades. Little occurred within the bounds of Krandor that he knew nothing of, especially when a force garnered by him was set for the breaking…

*

As the blanket of lonawr descended to cover the plains of Rhûn, the moon unbuckled her garment and spread her resplendent blue breasts out onto her subjects, out upon those who nightly bow themselves prostrate beneath her pedicured feet. I, of no such compulsion I may hasten to add, paid scant regard to the beauty beneath her cloisters, for angered was my spirit, troubled like the Seas of Derwent, bubbling like the brew of the Black Witch from Camsgördd.

I was at the end of my tether but blundered onwards as if pursued by the unseen hosts of Uffern. The evening was chilled, windy, dark mists shrouding the lights of the firmament above, save for the greatest nightly orb, the moon herself. All about were noises of the sleeping weald: apes swinging by chattering in their primitive speech, the tongues that not even trolls were known to understand; birds twittering songs too hard to fathom without the bird-muse of the men from Waemorg; four-footed animals rustling the green leaves of the forests in the hunt for food and water. But of them I could understand each and every, all in its own right. For I am *ysbryd* – an *ellyll* – borne upon the winds of turmoil.

Not far off was the Afon Alltudawd, black in its length, even in the daytime, and cold in its course, as chilly as the barrow-grounds of Annwfn, through which passed the ogre Tammwéfyn, who was slain by no human hand. Even so, the faint plopping of fish breaking the skin of the waters reached my ears and the angry lashing of the river as it struck its bedrock and plummeted down to unseen depths was there to my ears as the gales which I sought to conquer.

Often I enjoyed these easy moments, when my burdens were cast off and I was freed to continue unimpeded from the ponderous restrictions of my body. Now was The Son my refuge, my haunt was the barren landscape of the Moon, our task was to avenge my *coblyn* of his injury. And all this would I accomplish with the help of our other-self.

With tremors assailing my bones (or that which felt like they ought to have been), I set myself to the great mountain ridges of Rhûn. There, on this barren escarpment, were the first signs of the horses who had fled the fight two days before.

A drizzling mist quickly enveloped the pass upon which I trod, making the spoor treacherous beyond reckoning and inviting to its unchancy lands sprites of all shapes and forms. These catch a man before his feet had even slipped, they grasp his soul before his head was dashed upon the earth, they truss him up before he had picked to where he wished to be parted: if the distant lands of Uffern then all was well; but if not then would the soul spend its existence in misery, languishing for the Glories of the World Above, whilst being consumed by the Infernal Flames, while being nuzzled by worms that are not scorched. Either way, grim was their set task, dark and dreadful; for their master was none other than Beelzebub, Lord of the Underworld, the fallen *draig* from Nef. He who, once, I had the profound displeasure of meeting.

But these fell hosts I cast to the back of my mind as I regarded yet the sheer drop which could take me directly into the Fifth, deep into the farthest regions of The Otherworld, without ever a chance of recourse. Instead, I pondered the way beneath my feet and the progress I yet had to endure to meet up with my enemies, make restitution, and be restored, one to my body. Nevertheless the *corff* I had chosen (the body to which I belonged) was quickened, even if not truly woken, and he I persuaded with my intrigue to tread the paths I longed for, in the fashion I so required.

Soaked with rain with the wind buffeting all round his stern visage, I sympathised deeply with my warrior, whose task it was to match his cunning with the strength of his foemen. But I had little regret in my actions, for after the unfolding of time when he must pass away to dust and his soul is conjoined to my form, having been born anew, then shall he one day be thankful; for then shall all things be restored and renewed and this dark deed be forgotten.

The ascent soon roughened, becoming steep as the slopes before Caer Joth-aë, which remains one of only a few unconquered forts not held by demons and goblin-lords of the highest rank. The uppermost reaches of the summit were crowned in snow and all this swam through a belt of cloud so thick that it seemed like fires were smoking from hearth till hill. After trudging for some distance further, I deemed it necessary to fling in my pitch with my body, though of yet, unfulfilled chores prevented me from undertaking much more. However, his feet slid less for my efforts and obduracy grew within his bosom, tramping down to the ground the coarse heather that was sent to hinder his way.

Presently it was myself who saw the two trolls as silhouettes against the blackening skies, like two great thorn-bushes, being troubling to my soul and grievous to my spirit. And it was for their sake that I sought purchase on the rock-wall emerging above me.

THE FLIGHT OF AN ELLYLL: MEMYS' STORY

'Hurry up Bel-Hacosh, the light is dwindled and I am still without food. Let us head back to the party where warm gruel awaits us... Can you hear me down there O Troll?'

She peered down into the thick blanket of gloom which marked the boundary with the surface of the heaving waters beneath. It was a black hole which none could escape should one fall into that watery lair.

'And have you found any more yet?'

Bel-Hacosh ceased his descent for a while and looked up with his big, beady eyes, which took on a natural squint as he searched out his mistress before the blue moonlit backdrop.

'None, Belle-Hannah, but I think that what we now have may be enough – at least for a time.' He scanned the lichen and the craggy cliff-face before continuing; 'I believe you are right there Belle-Hannah, for my stomach also yearns to be satisfied and I think if I shan't satisfy her, she might eat me all up... or abandon me for another body!'

With that the trolls laughed heartily, Bel-Hacosh beginning the slow, steady ascent up the ridge of the mountain, upon the rope that was borne by both the stump of a tree and by the corpulent masses of his mistress' arms. Jagged striations incised upon the rock-face made his climb more perilous than it need be, but fear was not known to lurk at this one's door. Neither mountain nor river, nor flesh and blood, nor even the roaring of the seas or the burden of battle could induce this troll to dread. Few could do such, short of the Belly of Hades itself.

'Hurry up, Bel-Hacosh, I'm in desperate need of some lovemaking too,' Belle-Hannah cried. 'And if you don't give it to me, then I'm sure somebody else will.'

'Close your beak you crazy old wench – who else could love you like I do?' At that she pondered awhile, lost for the truth of his tongue. 'And besides, who else would you get to suckle your big, greasy earlobes? Who would dare nuzzle your toes? Who has the skill to pander all three bosoms at once, and produce milk where there ought not be any?'

'Yes... well... You have one minute anyway, or else, I'll leave you to make your own way up. And I'll please myself, if it comes to it!'

So upwards continued he with his ascent into the blue-black skies, the strength of both the cord and Belle-Hannah bearing him up well. Without them would come the foaming waters beneath, the rugged rocks on the banks of Rhûn, the evil temperament of her who dwells within the Afon Alltudawd, who loathes all those disturbing her hiding place and sends all who intrude in on her premises into the deepest, darkest regions of The Underworld.

*

Soon, I saw my target clearly, for the moon played kindly with my eyes, showing favour upon the task which I had at hand to perform. Indeed, all of Kronos' minions were at my sway, it seemed, and not one dared to utter a single syllable contrariwise. All was silent, facile. Nonetheless, in the astuteness of her play, the wind soon cast in her lot with my retinue, as I stole up with half a chance. Thence, crouching low, I crept forwards evermore quietly, nervous that the body I had chosen to inhabit might give the game away. Still, he was not all mine, but a fearsome tussle needed to take place first before I could claim that glory for my own.

I pounced on the warrior utilising all my guile, propelling us both backwards into a small hold, that his fidgets might not be discerned by any careful watcher. I did not wish to wake him from his sleep, but guide him to do the deed that I myself would have accomplished, if granted leave. Alas, it was not to be! For proud was this warrior in battle, splendid and stately was he in size, and with grim determination, he resisted my advances stoutly. Nonetheless, I continued to draw him near with beguilement, recovering memories of injury and relating as best I could the manner of torments which had beset him and his beloved companion (pain me sorely though it did).

A potency surged within his limbs, reminding me of the reason why I had been chosen to abide in his dwelling, so much so that for a moment, I thought that my plan was foiled and my enemies would get away. Then I remembered who I was and that it was me who through quiet meditations and by many fruitful enchantments, I it was, who trained this warrior in the way he should go. Annwfn, release your grip on my friend, lest I smite you with the foul curse of my wroth!

It was not long before wrestling-feats and charms had done the job. Though I must admit (humbly) that it was not without my constant piping, beautiful to all those of Nef who hear it, that the battle was won. I regained control of my *bwystfil* after a much-vaunted battle, but contentment was not with me; nor would it be till my soul was replaced in its rightful spot.

With two vomits and a burp was the warrior recaptured: the first spewing was for the loss of his limbs to determine his every path; the next was for the absence of his *ellyll*, which at present, caused myself to dwell nakedly in this haunt; the belch was for the meal they had fed my mate prior to his leaving, for his appetite had been increased after such great afflictions; but for my coming all now sought to abandon us – and wisely I may add.

*

I saw the fat, disgusting woman, and though large and menacing to behold, I knew she was little but a lily-livered, weak-willed troll, who had neither the courage nor the decency to prevent my tortures most grave. For myself, I'd like to think that perhaps I'd endured torments stoutly, and might have continued to do so rather well, if at all necessary. But for the one that I love, and for the swift abdication of responsibility that afterward followed, there was to be no such generosity on my part.

The wind then changed her play, seeing the need that I held at present. At once she became the noise in the fruitless trees, whistling down the valleys, up from the floor, through the felled bracken; she was within the branches; she hurtled along the crags, bounded off walls, created disturbances where there were none. She sung from the heavens and bellowed her pot-bellied stomach far upon the earth. Her fingers stretched across from the plains of Powys and her arms cradled everything within sight, like a mother whose bitter envy prevents any other form of comfort being rendered to her children. And all this was to scupper the noise that my warrior made beneath me, as he drew his elfin-blade with about as much guile as a sperm-filled red-eyed bull.

Together, we leapt upon the bewildered creature, seeing neither her fat, varicose face, nor her triple-breasted chest, which she had erstwhile been intent on endowing me with. Then, returning like for like, I similarly yelped another foul belch into her face as I nabbed her by surprise from behind.

Too fast was I for the big lumbering creature, for before she knew what was come, she had the nib of my sword stuck tight to her belly (the cutter which, thankfully, she had given back to me after her deliverance!). Then in a motion, quick enough to confound a woodpecker, deft enough to satisfy even Dionne of the Gap-teeth – whose vocal exploits are so revered that elves ever and awhile pay homage to her the length and breadth of Londinium– I slotted her fat gullet gladly. The warrior whom I bestrode drew the blade from her throat to her hindquarters (a ponderous work admittedly) but working as I urged him, with the haste of Caleb of the Long-storks, Fortune bade us her grateful eye for this difficult chore.

The other troll I recalled, not by my memory, but by the vehement cries that ascended from out of the steep gorge. He had detected that something awry was afoot, and glad was I to confirm such tidings. As I extracted the heart from the creature before me, whom some called "Belle-Nan" – daughter of the goddess 'Hah!' archenemies of the great god Yah – I could see its palpitations, and could yet hear her groaning. It was a spectacle that I swiftly caused my man to disregard, lest troubling sleep should besiege him in days to come. Judging that the troll still had some way yet to climb, I proceeded to skin the hideous monster of her flesh and to drain her of her gore, before feeding her with her own intestines, an assignment that was surprisingly pleasing to my senses.

I could see my alter-ego upon the opposite bank of the gorge, nodding his head, waiting for all things to be accomplished before his return, and I took this to be approval of the dark role he was now privy to. He was alone as I had left him and grieving sorely, a sight somewhat distressing to my form. But then Bel-Hacosh came back to memory, for I could hear his grunting voice and could perceive the confusion he was now bedevilled with; and not before time had this come.

Shrouding myself in the wench's hideous hide, I strolled over to the embankment and awaited the arrival of the other troll. I wished him to see the whites of my eyes, the anger of my spirit, the bleeding of my soul (which I hoped he would perceive on the overlying ridge out yonder), even as I finally put an end to his miserable existence. As for my warrior's friends each one would have to manage justice for himself or herself. All the efforts of my *perthynas* and all I could do to help, I, *we* moreover, surely would, but let each one assess his own worth in these things and let each one strive as he or she must.

Presently, the unrepentant beast showed his face, resolved above the thick spumes of cloud – a spell cast on all mountains which, without permission, attempt to reach the belly of heaven. And it was into that gaseous void that I sought to send this base-born child-slaying troll. So with shrewdness of mind, I took the rope in my hands (making sure that part of it remained attached to the poor hussy Belle-Hannah) and I sawed at its width ferociously.

There came a point when my heart, nerves and sinew seemed to become entangled as one and it was at this time that my breast beat faster, that the sweat from my body began to rise into the upper air. (My foul and foetid memories alongside these pangs of regret I also sought to slay, together with the hideous forms that had plagued me for more trouble than they had ever been worth). Nevertheless, even this was short-lived as the final strand of the cord was loosened from the tree-stump.

I watched as the hefty form of Bel-Hacosh drew Belle-Hannah into the murky depths of the waters below; I listened as his screams rang about my ears; I perceived the gleeful exultation of The Dead Man as he expanded his womb to receive these scurrilous guests. To tell you the truth however, I know not whether Bel-Hacosh had even noticed my *ellyll*, or indeed the queer, white-decked man I saw standing by his side, let alone the other fellow who was standing motionless not so far away, dressed darkly, black as a warlock, dun as one of those Daemon Writers. But I was contented that he saw me and all that I had to offer. Blessed was I that such an accomplishment had been wrought, even though Fate by herself would have rarely dictated such a propitious encounter. Nevertheless, the celebrations of this achievement must yet remain for another occasion.

With fleetness of foot, therefore, I drove my warrior onwards like a man possessed, pressing ever onwards into the jet-black wilderness surrounding me. I flew down the hazardous ridges, past the shrieking ape-men and out onto the plains before the lowlands of Rhûn, by the forests in which his company was encamped. Into the gloom I fled, away from the darkness that lay hard behind me, and I was prowling, as the beast which holds the night for his own. The Warrior, Myself, Our Alter-Ego, streaming through the coarseness of the dank, heavy weald, to a place, far removed from those two troublesome trolls. Though not before gathering up what they had so kindly collected for my dear and honourable friend, Marcus.

*

Sniffdog was the sole person to stir that night, for the earlier meal which had quenched their famished stomachs, and even then it was only for an evil dream that had come upon him to scupper his mended ways. But at that time none could rightly divide it. So all were left sleeping amidst the darkened chills leaving peace to gradually restore the flagging company.

It was early the next day when Frydor, together with Fels'noc the Troll, set their mark upon the soils of Krandor, and followed the tributary to the Afon Craig, formerly meaning the River of Rocks, though now many call it the River of Peace. Sascha and Sniffdog bore the brunt of Marcus' weight as they helped him up slopes and eased him down hills. Little was said of the ointment which played well on Marcus or whence it came; but it was thought that the two trolls, Belle-Hannah and Bel-Hacosh, had dropped off the potion and then turned back towards the hamlet to undergo purification by courtship; for no short ritual was this. Little did they know that, even now, what remained of these two was suffering torments innumerable, in the deepest darkest holds of Sheol.

Across the Pesiban Ranges, they soon passed the lofty mound of Anomê, peak above all peaks, and resplendent in beauty was its glow. As the breeze dropped so too did the Troop and their troll-guides, who, after the pledge they had made a few days prior, which was to restore all they had corrupted, strove to lessen the travails of their new comrades.

They journeyed through lower plains and ventured across fields that were found with foraging cowherds and healthy pastures. Reflections and earnest strivings were put aside by most, for few could accurately remember the trials after their encounter with the trolls on the Fallen Ridge. And perhaps this was just as well, for surely there would have to have been a far greater recompense than the one that had recently been undertaken, the night before.

Nonetheless, they discovered horse tracks leading northwards into the far-off hills of Elvy, and they found the river, which had been trusted to Fels'noc by the hidden wisdom of his ancestors.

Not far off, Flip also managed to locate a shelf by the side of a nearby grassy knoll, which was in full bloom with the fruits of the season. Luscious herbs far ranging as the forked-root of the mandrake to the sprawling wild mushrooms, called as magical by those for whom it was intended, sprouted forth in clusters, in globules, in colonies. Many were the flocks feeding on this fodder, high-horned deer, grey-bearded goats, ape-men who strove always to shamble upright, as born of men and trolls were they, with the seeds of primates kept stored within their veins.

Even so, Fate seemed to have conspired for all things to happen as they duly did. Indeed, the truth of the many riddles, which Marcus had spoken under his terrible sickness, had turned out for their good. What had been intended as ill against the Friends appeared instead to have worked for their benefits, a sore price though it still seemed at times. Or else, very large hands somewhere in the skies above had been moving the many pieces of a highly complex game of *gwyddbwyll*.

Notwithstanding, hard by the knoll ran the slow part of the river, in which Eleanor bathed, Jemimah cleansed her wounds, Alicia paused for thought. Sascha however was not so illiberal with his time, aiding Frydor and Fels'noc in lifting the great boulder off of its shelf. Flip it was who remained behind with Sniffdog and his friend, Nâelog, as the others went forwards behind Kussob who was following in the train of their master, to view the things they had come to see.

*

Beneath the moss-covered underside of the great rocky bulk was a small wooden box of no grand description. It was old and partially rotted, its sides were green with clumps of fungus hair hanging off and its wood was soft, beaten down over time by the floods of each inured season. Even so, it was a marvel altogether that it had lasted for so long. All soon gathered round to see this marvel of myth and legend.

It was only at the trolls' prompting however that Frydor the Elf set about opening the box, so that they each might have a peek inside. Its lid fell away easily, as though it was a case made for the lifting, and tucked neatly within he saw a layer of parchment with what appeared to be text composed in ancient runes written hurriedly upon it. Albeit, the archaic words were smudged, thus making them difficult to comprehend, and no few tears were shed at this prospect.

With time nevertheless, as drizzle began to descend to mark the coming of the New Season, the elf, together with Alicia, who handed him the Books, did manage to translate them.

The characters had formerly been embossed in the near-forgotten scribes of the Trolliégions, from whom came the mighty Troll-Knights of Yesteryear. Savages some called them (the greatest part of these being The Unbelievers) – or indeed, The Black-faced Barbarians from the South – for their uncouth appearance and for their handy dispatch of foemen. But there was none who dared to challenge their awesome displays of valour in times of conflict, contest and resolve, in times of war specially, if not so much so in times of peace. For they too were Zaqen, warriors of the noblest degree. In bygone days these valiant soldiers had waxed bold in the face of the overwhelming opposition presented them by the mightiest Men from the East.

They were hardier than the Sons and Daughters of Phinehas, more honourable than the Mighty Men of David, and in battle against the Knights of Joel, if such could ever be, they would have surely given them sore competition, the outcome of which even the greatest loremasters would have been loth to call. Thus, for no mean exploits is their fame sung of till this very day, I assure you.

*

At length the elf's diligent scrutiny led to some fruit being borne, for the antiquated letters did soon speak. It was written in the runes of the Elder-days but both Frydor and Flip were revealed to have some knowledge of these tongues. Nevertheless, a short while did pass before either could make heads or tails of the matter. But it was written as touching the dispensation of that day, for the Sons and Daughters of Joel. So, in time, the dark runes were thus divided:

For those young warriors from St Andrew and St George know and understand these things. These words are written for your sakes that you may have confidence and a reason for your forthcoming journey.

Should Favour be with you in your forthcoming expedition you will need to acquire the Key of Brotherly-Kindness and thus become Clerics of the Ancient Lore (or Helpers). That will be your next hunt.

Then comes the Key of Virtue with the associated rank of Deacons of the Ancient Lore (or Healers). For it is the men and women of excellence and resolution who heal those who have maladies.

Afterwards you will have to search for the Key of Knowledge. If that should be found then you will be known as Elders of the Ancient Lore (or Evangelists).

Upon which your next focus will be for the Key of Perseverance. Should you be steadfast in recovering this treasure then you will become Foremen of the Ancient Lore (or Pastors).

The Key of Godliness is next on the list. Guardians of the Ancient Lore (or Teachers) shall they be who tend to this key, for the keepers of this key shall be great in the eyes of all.

Then comes Love, which requires faith, for these two are the foundation of all. He who displays this key before God and Man shall be called Honourable of the Ancient Lore (or a Prophet).

Faith comes next, which works through love. Moreover, he whose works accompanies his faith will be known as an Instructor of the Ancient Lore (or an Apostle).

Overcoming Hades shall be no easy matter. But the status of Judge of the Ancient Lore (or a Son of the Zaqen) shall be conferred upon the one who conquers the Grim Reaper and collects his key.

And then comes the Angel of Death, the last enemy to be put under foot. Only he who triumphs over all shall be given the title of Knight of the Ancient Lore (or Zaqen).

May the gods be with you in your coming pursuits. And may they bless all that you set your hands to do. Keep this scroll with you at all times that you may refer to it in your times of need.

Blessed are you
Who find spiritual treasures
Keep them safe
For their payment was
Beyond any man's measure.

Amen.

*

Concealed therein, wrapped tightly behind the fawn parchment sheets, lay their foremost treasure thus far. For upon clearing the gold of its grime and replacing the words whence they had come, they quickly found it to be the means to any future successes, should they at all be so propitious and should their nerves stand up to the arduous tests of time.

Within the old wooden box was hidden their first major breakthrough, a turning point in their hardy albeit highly hazardous adventures. But as Frydor brought out the talisman and fixed its contours to the setting sun, he soon discovered that it was the very thing he had for so long yearned after, for so long desired, craved even. It was their very first jewel; though some indeed say that it was mine too.

No longer shall the Syndicate be called *Apprentices* of the Ancient Lore, that is to say "Unbelievers", for after the sufferings and patience of the previous few days they have discovered what it means to have developed discipline. Thus, according to the script, they are now *Bishops* of the Ancient Lore, that is to say, "Administrators".

Nevertheless, upon handing the jewel over to Alicia, it was Me and Myself who first saw what we each, in turn, bore witness to; Our Eyes beheld it only afterwards. Nonetheless none shunned the first glorious viewing of that maiden, foremost of Keys – for it was the first golden key – that of Self-Control.

Fin de Livre 1
The Knight's Lore

VOCABULARY

(in Welsh unless otherwise stated)

Afon – river
Alltud – exile
Anakim (Hebrew) – The Long-necked Ones, Giants
Ancient Lore (English) – (Revised) Law of Moses
Annwfn – the Otherworld, Purgatory
Awen – muse
Awst – August
Balchder – pride
Barnwr – judge
Binah (Hebrew) – understanding
Blaidd – wolf
Brenin – king
Bryn – hill
Bwystfil – beast
Caer – wall fort, castle, cathedral
Cap diogelu – helmet
Cawr – giant
Ceidwad – guardian
Clamp – monster
Clerig – cleric
Coblyn – monster
Corff – body
Crafanc – claw
Craig – rock, crag
Crandrwydd – original name for Krandor; Grandeur
Cycyllog – hooded
Cyndadau – The Ancients
Cyswllt – connection
Daearawd – the Earth
Darkling (Darkun) – relating to growing darkness
Dawn – talent, gift
Deep Blax (slang) – music which no White Man should ever dance to
Deeper Blax (slang) – music which nobody but a Black Man should dance to
Deepest Blax (slang) – music for only the Gangster-dem
Denu – to attract/ entice

Dihenydd – end, doom, death, execution

Draig – dragon

Dunateo (Greek) – [the] mighty; ancient epithet for a Ranger

Dyn – man, person

Dysg – lore, literature, learning

Ebrill – April

Elf (English) – [soul] child; the name of the main character's soul

Elfen – element, particle

Ellyll – fiend

Elohim (Hebrew) – gods, mighty ones

Emim (Hebrew) – The Fearful Ones, Giants

Enaid – soul

Faitour (archaic English) – an impostor

Fell (archaic English) – cruel, fierce, terrible, destructive, deadly

Fels (English slang) – dirty, deep, or low-down

Fifth (English) – all dimensions above the first four (space-time)

Galanas – compensation for murder

Gallu – ability, power

Gosgordd – escort, retinue, host

Gradd – grade, rank

Grayling (Gralen) – relating to growing greyness or obscurity

Gwas – manservant, chamberlain

Gwir – truth

Gwlad – country, land

Gwr – man, person

Gwyddbwyll – chess

Gwydr – glass

Gwyrdd – green

Hades (Greek) – abode of the dead

Heini – skill

Hilasterion (Greek) – the throne of the Almighty

Huan – the Sun

Iddew – Jew

Keruvim (German) – Cherubim

Llaith – death

Lleuad – the Moon

Llindagwr – thug

Lliw – colours

Llyfr – book

Merwys (Memys) – blackbird; the name of the main character's spirit

Mor-leidr – pirate

Nef – Heaven

Nephilim (Hebrew) – demon-human hybrid, Giants

Noc (slang) – evil woman, hag

Nos – night

Perthnasau – kith and kin

Perthynas – kinsmen

Priodas – top, prime

Qadesh (Hebrew) – pervert

Rangers (English) – Apostles and Prophets of the Ancient Lore

Rephaim (Hebrew) – The Dead Ones, Giants

Rhagfyr – December

Seren – sky

Sheba (Hebrew) – seven

Spiegel (German) – mirror

Spiel (German) – game

Surp – The Knowledge, The Knowledgable, The Wise-Ones

Swynwr – magician, wizard, sorcerer

Syn – amazed, amazing

Tebel (Hebrew) – world

Teras (Hebrew) – wonders

Trum – ridge, summit

Ty Gwydr – Crystal Ball

Uchelwdd – mistletoe

Uffern – Hell

Wort (German) – word

Yah (Hebrew) – short form for Yahweh

Yarah (Hebrew) – the Teaching, the Ancient Lore

Y gwr drwg – The Devil

Y Mis Du – November

Ynfyd – foolish, mad

Ys – one is, it is

Ysbryd – spirit

Ysgol – school

Zaqen (Hebrew) – the Greybeards, Knights and Judges of the Ancient Lore

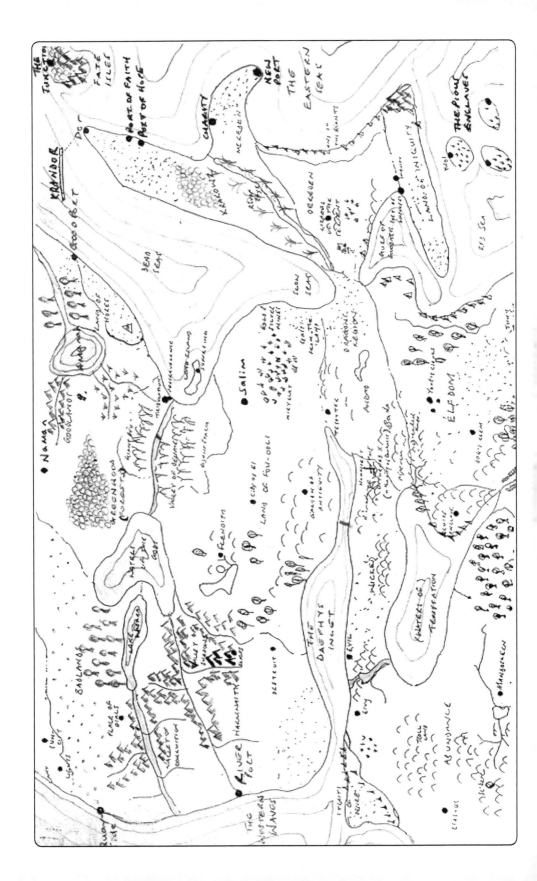